A THRONE
OF
FROST
AND
FLAME

Copyright © 2025 by Victoria K. Taylor
This book is a work of fiction. Names, characters, places, and incidents are the product of the author's imagination or are used fictitiously. Any resemblance to actual events, locales, or persons, living or dead, is entirely coincidental.
All rights reserved.
No part of this publication may be reproduced, distributed, or transmitted in any form or by any means, including photocopying, recording, or other electronic or mechanical methods, without the prior written permission of the publisher.

Book Cover by KD Guthauser at Story Wrappers Designs
Editing by Noah Sky and Jennifer Murgia

ISBN 979-8-9897885-7-6 (Paperback)
ISBN 979-8-9897885-6-9 (eBook)
ISBN 979-8-9897885-8-3 (Hardcover)

First Edition: March 2025
Snowshoe Press

BOOKS BY VICTORIA K. TAYLOR

THE FATE OF ASHES SERIES
A Crown of Star and Ash
The Lady of Fire and Light
A Throne of Frost and Flame

To Cody,
Who encourages me to fight my own dragons and who always believes I can win.

A THRONE OF FROST AND FLAME

THE FATE OF ASHES BOOK 2
VICTORIA K. TAYLOR

AUTHOR'S NOTE

Welcome back to the world of Krigor!

Just a quick note before we dive in: This story closely follows both Book 1, *A Crown of Star and Ash,* as well as the novella, *The Lady of Fire and Light.* If you have not read *The Lady of Fire and Light,* I highly suggest stopping and going to check it out now or else risk missing a lot of key points and details in this story! I recommend reading the novella after *A Crown of Star and Ash* and before *A Throne of Frost and Flame!*

For any and all CW/TW's for this book as well as any of my others, please check out my website!

I hope you enjoy your return to *the Fate of Ashes* world!

Love,

Victoria

CHAPTER 1

The black stain of death soaked her fingertips.

Deya moved her hands underneath the table, studying the pall that covered all ten of her fingers from tip to cuticle. From afar, it appeared as though she had simply dipped her nails into an inkwell. But only she could see the slight iridescent glimmer when she tilted it to the light. Like a shimmer of a threat. A promise of demise.

"The closest attack happened just last week," Aris said to Caelum. The Pillar Legion general sat across from her at the mahogany table within the Nodarian council room. His long limbs draped over the chair arms, legs extended out over the black marble floors. "Praiton wiped out a small outpost we had just east of Nodaria."

Caelum's jaw clenched, his hands raking through his white hair. Beside him, a diminutive female with a tight dark bun pressed her already too-thin lips together. Her robes glistened with the shimmering stars of the uniform of the Nodarian Prime Minister as she shifted in her seat.

"Do we have a plan for retaliation?" Caelum asked, his voice short.

The female's purple eyes widened. "*Retaliation?*" Helene Sidra echoed, horror evident in her tone. "Nodaria has barely recovered from our collapse, in case you've forgotten . . . *my lord,*" she added, as if remembering herself.

Shaking the small vial of dark red nail varnish she had borrowed from Val, Deya glanced up from the streak of paint she had laid over the first fingernail just in time to see the familiar vein in Caelum's forehead flex.

"No, *Minister*, I haven't forgotten," Caelum grit out, his tone just as caustic as Helene's. "Unlike you, I was actually *there*."

Helene's eyes narrowed at the new High King of Nodaria. Caelum's spine was rigid against the high-backed chair, his fingers wrapped tightly around the Shadow Sword he had taken from the Praiton general. The Prime Minister's gaze darted towards the black sword, and her mouth got even tighter.

Deya was not much of a fan of the sword, either. No matter how many times she saw it on his hip, she couldn't get the image of it skewering into him out of her mind.

Deya smoothed another line of paint and moved on to the next finger.

Caelum's near-death experience was barely a month ago, but already the Celestial Kingdom was getting back onto unsteady feet . . . Starting with the implementation of the Prime Minister of Reconstruction.

Caelum turned back to Aris, shutting out Helene completely. "If we do not retaliate, we will appear weak."

Saros gave a dry chuckle from across the table. "The Legion just succeeded in taking back Nodaria, Caelum," he said. "This is the strongest we've appeared in years."

To Saros's left, Val sat quietly. Her chin was in her hand, soft amber eyes trained out the window. The starry night sky of Nodaria was dazzling, even from their position within Atlas Keep. Deya's Manielian friend jiggled her leg underneath the table, her gaze unfocused.

"With all due respect, *Your Majesty*," Helene piped up, her small figure shaking with barely suppressed frustration. "Nodaria is still rebuilding. Our people were *slaughtered*. Those who survived have been in hiding for over fifty years. There is a scar on this kingdom which we must heal before—"

Caelum let out a derisive snort. "We do not have *time* to heal, Prime Minister," he spat. "This is *war*. There will be time for that nonsense after restoring the realm. Unless you have no problem watching High King Ulf crumble, like my father?"

Helene's face blanched. She let out a splutter of indignation.

"How . . . How *dare*—"

Aris cleared his throat, silencing the outburst Deya could see coming from ten leagues away.

"Excuse us, Prime Minister," he said, inclining his head to her. "I understand your reservations about having Nodaria being active within the war—"

Helene scoffed. "We have no business being at the center of this skirmish when we have just regained our way of life, *General*," she snapped. "Perhaps you and your cohorts would do best to take your business elsewhere."

With one final stroke, Deya finished her last nail. The blackness was now gone, replaced with a garish red that reminded her of blood. While it clashed with the paleness of her skin, Deya didn't care.

No one had seen the stain; no one could question what it was. No one could be scared of it. Of her.

Deya let out a small breath.

Aris bent his head diplomatically at Helene and glanced back at Caelum. "Perhaps we should resume this conversation a little later." The general's voice was still as smooth as butter. Helene's distaste had not fazed him in the slightest. Forever cool and unflappable, the general of the Pillar Legion stood, his gold armor glinting in the candlelight. The rest of the table followed suit.

Helene gathered her thick robes in hand and swept from the room, her gaze lingering on Deya. Her eyes narrowed—a sharp stab of mistrust—

before she was gone with a swish of her starry cloak.

"Rayner," Aris called over his shoulder. The Sea Fae, who had been sitting beside Deya with the same bored expression as hers, looked up from the small figurine he had been carving with a short dagger.

"General?"

"If you are ready, the ship is waiting for you," Aris told him. Rayner nodded and made to rise, but Deya reached out, her newly red fingers grasping his wrist.

"You're leaving?" she said, her grip tightening on his blue-gray skin.

Rayner smiled down at her. "I have some Legion business to attend to. But I'll be back."

"What Legion business?" Deya asked, but Rayner shook his head.

"Can't say, but don't worry. I'll be back to check on you all soon." His electric-blue eyes roamed over Deya's head to rest on the Manielian female, who now sat, alone, at the table. She had not looked away from the window, had not so much as glanced up as Saros and Aris left the room.

"Keep an eye on her, will you?" Rayner said to Deya softly.

Deya shot a worried glance back at her friend before giving Rayner a grim nod.

Val had been like this ever since they had reclaimed Nodaria. Deya hardly saw her these days. She appeared for the weekly council meetings before drifting back into the black hallways of Atlas Keep like a fiery ghost. No matter how many times Deya had tried to get her to talk, Val would only smile at her with a far-away look in her eyes and assure her that she was fine.

Rayner gave her hand a reassuring squeeze before shouldering his bow and quiver and hurrying out after Aris.

Caelum paused for the smallest fraction of a second on his way out of the room. His violet eyes fell on her, but their cold, hardened look did not change. Without a word, he turned and followed behind Rayner, passing the large portrait of his father, the late High King Castor, as he went.

It was like watching Castor's white-haired shadow pass by. During all the weeks sitting in the same chair at these council meetings, Deya had stared at Castor. She was always struck by how handsome he was . . . and just how much he looked like Caelum. Aside from the long, midnight-black hair, they could've been twins.

Brilliant purple eyes shone out of the frame as he sat on his throne, wearing a rich purple brocade jacket. Between the Star Scepter in his hand and the silver chain of a gray pendant around his neck, his regalness was unmatched. Whereas his son refused to even take off his worn leather armor.

Deya stood, the bottle of varnish still clutched in her fist, and moved towards her friend. She laid a gentle hand on Val's shoulder, making her jump.

"Oh! Deya . . ." Whipping around, Val took in the empty room and blinked. "Is the meeting over?"

"It just ended," Deya replied. She did not know what was troubling her poor friend. For weeks now, those amber eyes had seemed haunted. She found herself missing Val's spark, her familiar firecracker personality. Now she seemed muted, subdued like everything else under the Nodarian night sky.

Deya held out the small bottle to her. "Thank you for the nail varnish," she said, beaming brightly, hoping it would snap her out of whatever trance she was in. "It was just what I was looking for."

"Oh." Val glanced at Deya's hands and gave her a small smile. "It looks great on you."

Deya held her breath as Val looked at her fingers. She hoped it wasn't only because her friend was too preoccupied that she didn't notice anything astray.

Val rose from her chair, stretching as she glanced out the window.

"Are you sure you're all right, Val?" Deya asked gently. As a healer, you would think her bedside manner would be good enough to get anyone to confide in her. But Val remained stubbornly impervious to her prodding.

Even now, Val turned and gave Deya a stiff smile. "Of course, why wouldn't I be?" Her pretty, golden face was inscrutable as she looked at Deya with vacant eyes.

The last few weeks had been bedlam within Nodaria. Emergency council meetings scrapped together with distantly related relatives of deceased former councilmen, the constant retaliations from Praiton against the Pillar Legion in response to their retaking the Celestial Throne.

Tensions were high—Caelum's especially. The realm was not yet used to a new High King on the Celestial Throne. And, quite frankly, neither was she.

Yet it was Val who seemed to have stalled in it all. And Deya could only watch as her friend spun her wheels in the chaos.

They walked out of the council chambers and into the vast, cavernous hallways of Atlas Keep's east wing. The rounded halls were made up of black marble, the stars embedded in the floors and ceilings giving everything a slight incandescent glow.

Life at Atlas Keep had taken some getting used to. Once the remnants of the battle had been cleared away and the large castle restored, Deya didn't know if she'd ever get used to the way glittering trails of shooting stars would rocket across the ceilings, or the ever-moving orrery that revolved over their heads as they crossed into the large antechamber leading to the great hall.

She was definitely having a hard time adjusting to the ever-present darkness. Nothing but moonlight for weeks and weeks had her feeling permanently discombobulated, her body constantly struggling to figure out what time of day it was. While the rest of the Nodarians seemed thrilled to have this essential aspect of their kingdom restored, Deya missed the sun more than she wanted to admit.

When they reached the end of the wing, Val waved a hand over her shoulder.

"Well, see you at dinner, Deya." Before Deya could even open her mouth to stop her, she hurried off.

"Val, wait—" Deya made to go after her, but Val had already

disappeared around the bend of the corridor. Deya slowed to a stop, the words dying on her tongue. It hadn't been too long ago that she herself wore her grief like a shroud. To see it now on her friend made a lump rise in her throat.

Deya sighed, and, suddenly, a hand shot out from behind a large stone statue and seized her wrist. Deya yelped as she was yanked behind the statue, but was stifled by a set of familiar lips crashing into hers.

All the fight that had coursed through her veins at the fear of being attacked drained from her body. Her red-nailed hands wound themselves around the white-haired male who had grabbed her. A moan escaped her—something she couldn't seem to ever hold back when Caelum was kissing her—and she felt him smirk against her mouth.

"What took you so long?" he murmured, his lips brushing against hers with every word.

A molten warmth was spreading throughout her body, filling her veins, as his mouth moved to her jaw, grazing down the soft recess of her neck. "V-Val," she stuttered, her brain struggling to form a coherent thought.

Caelum hummed against her throat. Hands gripped her waist, and his hard body pushed her back against the stone wall of the statue's alcove they were encased behind.

"And who is this?" Deya asked breathily, jerking her chin up towards the statue of the fae male holding a spyglass sheltering them from sight. Caelum's hands squeezed parts of her that made her knees weak.

"Pyxis, the twelfth High King of Nodaria," Caelum mumbled, his teeth scraping the tip of her pointed ear. Deya stifled a whimper as she braced against the smooth stone of Pyxis's back in an effort to remain standing. "Now, why am I giving you a history lesson when the present is so much more interesting?"

Gods, she was pathetic. It had been weeks of this. Caelum pulling her into dark corners, kissing her when no one was looking, sneaking into her chambers at night when everyone was asleep. But during the day, he barely looked at her. And while it was true he had many responsibilities now as High King, and couldn't very well go about kissing her in front of the council, he could, at the very least, *acknowledge* her.

She didn't know what it was that made Caelum pull back from her in the days following that final battle. And while he had grown softer with her since that day she woke in Nodaria's infirmary, he only displayed it in private.

She felt like a dirty secret, something to be hidden and ashamed of. And she had to be stronger than this.

Deya pushed against Caelum's chest, desperate to separate his lips from her body. If he kept kissing her like this, she would never be able to resist.

"You could've done this earlier, you know," she said, her breathing still heavy.

Caelum raised an eyebrow. "You want an audience for the things I wish to do to you?"

Heat began to pool in her again. Gods, why did he have to *look* at her like that?

Caelum's white hair was disheveled, the single braid on the side of his head the only nod to his Bridanian heritage had doubled. Now, several loose, untied braids hung from the tied-back hair gathered at the crown of his head. He refused to dress the part of royalty, still stubbornly walking around in his black leather armor. A soldier instead of a king.

At that moment, his purple eyes were hooded and devouring her greedily, his hands already reaching to pull her back against him. But she sucked in a breath and held him steadily away from her.

"*No,*" Deya said, locking her elbows so there was now a good foot of distance between them. "But you could have at least said hi."

His eyes narrowed. "I said hi."

"You did not."

He then did a doubletake, noticing her blood red fingertips pressed against his chest. He quirked an eyebrow. "What's this?"

"It's nothing," she said quickly. "Just wanted to try something new, that's all."

At that moment, the thought of what *else* she had felt in the days since the blackness on her fingers appeared scratched at the back of her mind.

She had to lie. She *had* to. No matter how much Caelum kissed her, protected her, and ravished her, she was still scared that he did not *trust* her. What would he think if he saw the shadows creeping up her fingers? Would he think she was evil? Would he abandon her as easily as those she once thought were friends? Even with all they had been through together, Deya could not shake these thoughts.

The memory of Praiton—her former life—flashed through her mind, and small wings of anxiety took flight in her chest.

"You know how it is when that old bat Sidra is there," Caelum said, leaning back, no longer trying to fight against her. He crossed his arms—his signature defensive stance. "She and the council are already fighting me at every turn. Do you really expect me to parade this around the Keep? What would they think of me then?"

Deya crossed her own arms, and they stared each other down. Her irritation at the word "this" to describe what was strongly beginning to feel like a relationship lit a spark of fury in her. Especially since Caelum never cared to define it.

"Perhaps that you have a heart?" Deya asked, her voice waspish.

Lately, every interaction between them crashed into a stalemate, both refusing to back down. While Caelum's previous hostility for her had long since boiled over into passion, she found his mulishness as irksome as ever.

Caelum glared at her. "I don't need them in my business."

But Deya scoffed and shook her head, making to push past him, but Caelum grabbed her arm again.

"Deya, come on." He whipped her back into him, and Deya breathed in his scent—a winter breeze through a forest—and she felt herself yield just a little. *Pathetic.*

"I don't understand you, Caelum," she whispered, trying hard not to look at him. If she did, her resolve would leave her. "You never want people to see the best side of you."

Her hands tightened on the fabric of his black tunic. She wanted to sink into his arms again, but *dammit*, she couldn't let this stand.

"Deya . . ." he murmured reaching out and cupping her cheek. She melted like wax against his touch and stumbled backwards into Pyxis's back. Caelum pressed into her, and his lips brushed hers again. "I don't need others to see the best in me. All I need is you."

Val punched the wooden post so hard that blood splattered from her knuckles. She zeroed in on the combat dummy: a large wooden figure with several poles of heavy oak jutting in different directions. And, when she looked at it, all she saw were a pair of familiar amber eyes and a crooked, evil sneer.

Letting out a roar of anger, steam flowed from her mouth, and then she struck. *Left jab, right jab, up, down, bam!*

Her final punch burst a flaming hole straight through the head of the dummy—right where she imagined her brother's face to be. The fire spread from the hole, the wood cracking and crumbling, but it was weak. Her flame low and sputtering, barely singeing the wooden surface. Val swore, still panting, and kicked the charred wood aside.

This was the third dummy she had destroyed this week, and yet her fire remained weaker than ever. No matter how many times she tried, the white-hot Augusta fire eluded her, her flames orange and slow. She could not explain the sudden change—it was as if something was choking her power . . . smothering her very heart.

Breathing hard, Val shook the blood off her bruised knuckles. The dim flames overtaking the dummy sputtered against the permanent darkness of Nodaria's night sky, filling her vision. With each flicker of flame, Val's mind tried to drag her back.

A heavy brass star falling from the ceiling, crushing her leg. Rayner finding her in the wreckage, watching Deya and Caelum face the Praiton general . . . and then a wall of flames. Seeing her friends be brutalized through the blaze, screaming their names . . . helpless.

And then the words . . . the words that had haunted her for months now. *There was enough left of them to bury.*

The dull light of her flames blurred her vision as those words washed over her again like a scalding wave. It hadn't been the first time she had stared through a wall of fire. She remembered her sisters screaming her name. How she didn't know then that it would be the last time she would ever see her friends.

Because of *them.*

Life had moved on so quickly. So cruelly. Thirty years have passed since they had walked this earth, and all was fine. But now, all that was missing was them. And now time only stood still for her.

The wood cracked and Val flinched, choking on a sob that bubbled up out of nowhere.

"*Dammit all,*" Val whispered, and with a yell of fury, she kicked the dummy with all her might. Her foot blasted the wooden mass into smithereens, blowing it clear across the field she was standing in. She was breathing hard, tears burning in her eyes, flaming splinters and charred wood raining down around her.

Was that what it was like for her sisters? Watching through an inferno while she was hauled off . . . not able to do anything, to act . . .

With a jerk of her head, she shoved the thought down and stamped on it—hard. For years, she had repressed the day she was captured. Hadn't wanted to remember what it felt like to have her brothers humiliating her, torturing her, stabbing her . . . Didn't want to hear the sound of Lucia, Katia, and Atria screaming her name with a desperation that broke her heart again and again.

But since the Battle for Nodaria, she was finally left alone with her thoughts, and the memories threatened to sneak into her mind at every turn. They had crept into her head like black frost, suffocating her flames. The only time it was silent was on nights like this. Standing in the quiet, grassy field of Nodaria's training grounds, fire raining down around her, and her fists aching with a pain loud enough to drown out even her most horrible memories.

The only thing that kept it at bay.

Ripping loose a piece of fabric from the healing kit she had on hand, Val wound a thin strip of cotton around her knuckles. Blossoms of blood soaked through the thin muslin, but she kept winding it, tighter and tighter until all feeling left her hands. If only she could do the same with her heart.

Leaving the dummy still flaming in the clearing, she turned and made her way back towards Atlas Keep.

A month had passed since she had come to this kingdom, yet she felt like it had been mere days. Time passed strangely here, the sun never rising, the sky never changing. The moon waxed and waned, yet it was always an endless, dark day.

As she walked back through the Keep, she did not know what time it was, nor how long she had been outside training. The halls seemed to be deserted, black marble accented with real, moving stars, dazzling her with a distracting display in her peripheral.

She wanted to scream for the sun, yearning to feel its warmth on her face. She had been raised in a desert, after all. Sometimes, she felt more lizard than fae. But here, she felt like a fire poppy, wilting under the lack of light and heat.

Val did not want to go back to her chamber. The modest solar she had been given was comfortable and beautiful, but she hated being in it. It made her feel like a bird in a gilded cage.

So, she returned to where she spent most of her time since coming here: poring over old tomes in the late High King Castor's study, researching Deya's power.

While her friend had seemed to become more at ease with the deadly force that lurked inside her, Val found focusing on Deya's problems much easier than focusing on her own.

She pulled open the door to the study, still covered in sweat and soot from the dummy, then froze. Aris was sitting behind Castor's desk, a pile of old, dusty books stacked in front of him. He looked up, surprise creasing his handsome face as she walked into the room. Immediately, she wanted to turn and run.

"Valeria," he said, startled. "What are you doing here at this time?"

It took everything in her to school her features, to control the racing in her heart and the flush that always began when she was near the general. Even now, decades after the one and only time they had shared more than just a suggestive look, her body reacted to him. As if it were pure instinct.

"What time even is it?" Val mumbled. She forced herself to pull up a chair at the long table by the fire, which she had taken up residence at for the last few weeks. "It's getting hard to tell."

Aris let out a wry chuckle. "Yes, Nodaria certainly has a way of making time feel irrelevant."

Val perched on her chair, the collection of books she had been going through still opened in front of her. Peering over at Aris's desk, she jerked her chin at him.

"What have you been working on, General?"

Aris sighed. "Contingency plans." His tan, calloused hands rummaged through the papers in front of him. "Caelum isn't the only one who wants retaliation for Praiton's attacks on our camps. With the raids on our caravans and the wildfires spreading through Maniel, supplies are getting scarce."

Val hummed in agreement. Maniel had been burning for weeks now—a side effect of too much magic building within the kingdom. While not unusual, the intensity and size of the fires limited the Legion's movements greatly. It also meant food and supplies were getting much harder to come by.

Val watched the general out of the corner of her eye, too afraid to look at him fully. This scene was much too familiar to her, like something straight out of her memories. She could still smell the dust on the books in Aris's office at Light's Tower, could still see how his thin cotton tunic had molded to every muscle of his body.

She sucked in a breath and mentally slapped herself.

"Caelum seems to be the *only* one in this kingdom who wants retaliation," Val said. "It's not very popular here, is it?"

"No, it really isn't." Aris sighed again, then gave her that crooked grin that made her clench the desk a little too hard. "But I am surprised you were even listening at all in the council meetings. You've seemed . . . distracted, lately."

Her spine stiffened, and she looked away.

"I'm fine."

"Valeria . . ."

But she shook her head, determined to beat back the feeling that was beginning to flare at Aris's question. Her body felt more alive and alert in this male's presence than it had in weeks. Every nerve ending was alight, sensitive to his every movement.

"General, please," Val insisted, speaking down at the wooden tabletop in front of her instead of at the male who made her skin tingle like a live flame. "I'm fine."

But Aris ignored her. She felt him rise and move across the room. His closeness made her heart race, made her bloodied fingers whiten as they clenched the wood of the table.

"Valeria," Aris murmured, sitting down in the chair opposite hers. "Look at me."

No. She couldn't. Looking at him never did her any good. It was like looking directly into the sun, like gazing at a treasure that would destroy her to touch.

But she couldn't help it. Slowly, she dragged her eyes up to meet his. Hazel irises like a peridot stone looked back at her. Concern was etched on his handsome face, and for a moment, Val couldn't help but sweep every inch of him with her eyes. Perfectly sculpted cheekbones, the supine curve of his nose, the chisel of his jaw . . . It was rare that they were ever this alone, this close to each other. And it scared her.

"What's been going on with you? As your general . . . please."

Val snorted. "You can't pull rank on me for personal matters, *General*. It's an abuse of power."

Aris smirked. "Ah, so there *is* a personal matter."

"I assure you, it's none of your concern."

"Your wellbeing is *always* of my concern, Valeria."

Val blinked and then sighed. A part of her wanted to tell Aris. Other than her failing magic, Aris was the only one who knew what weighed on her. He had been there, after all. Had seen what her sisters saw, had watched as she had been humiliated by her own family.

They had never discussed it. And Val couldn't, now. To speak about it would be to give it life, to make it grow. She *wouldn't* think about it.

But, as he looked at her, she felt her throat tighten and the irritating burn began to flare in her eyes again.

"I don't want to talk about it," she whispered, her voice thick. "I *can't*."

Aris looked troubled, as if he wanted to reach out to her. Whether it was out of respect, or fear of history repeating itself, he didn't.

Instead, he leaned closer to her, so close that she resisted the urge to shut her eyes, to breathe him in like a warm breeze. She shivered as his breath caressed her cheek.

"You are stronger than you give yourself credit for, Valeria," he murmured in her ear. "When will you believe that?"

When I know it is the truth.

But she did not say it. She couldn't speak through the lump now lodged in her throat. Closing her eyes, she fought the tears down, and, with a deep breath, she smothered them. For a moment, the air around them seemed to crackle, gravity pressing down around them.

Val remembered what it was like to have those lips touch her. And with that thought, she turned her head away from the general.

Aris's lips did not linger by her ear. He cleared his throat and withdrew, and Val heard him sit down and ruffle through the papers she had sitting on the desk, as if looking for a way to clear the tension.

"What have you been working on?" he asked.

Glad for the distraction, Val turned back to the table. "Looking for answers to Deya's power."

Aris hummed thoughtfully, picking up a thick tome that looked like it was bound in animal skin. Its title was written in an ancient fae language Val could not decipher.

"Any luck?"

"Not even the slightest," Val grumbled. "Whatever Deya's power is, it seems unique."

Aris gave a dry snort. "Of course. Why wouldn't it be." His long fingers flipped a page in the book he was holding and only now that he was so close to her could Val see a pall over the general's features. His face was tired, dark shadows lining his eyes, and a faint trace of stubble accented his defined jaw. She had seen this look on him before.

Aris was worried.

"I know Deya's power concerns Caelum," he said, flicking through another page, though he wasn't looking at it. "I know he wants to protect her. It's why he's pushing so hard to defend our current advantage."

It was Val's turn to give a wry laugh. "You wouldn't be able to tell that from watching them," she said. "He barely talks to her these days."

Which was a far cry from where they had started. Val could still remember the shouting matches and arguments the two had when all four of them had first escaped Ironbalt together. She couldn't decide whether the distant coldness he exhibited towards her now was any better.

Suddenly, a stab of guilt pierced her heart. She had been so consumed by her own problems lately that she hadn't even bothered to *ask* her friend what was going on with her and Caelum. She had known that they acted on their attraction to each other weeks ago, but had it progressed? Or had Caelum put the brakes on things permanently?

Aris smirked. "I have a feeling they don't do much talking these days, if you know what I mean."

Val felt her face grow hot and she recoiled slightly. "Ugh, what are you talking about?" she cried, even though she had a pretty clear idea of what he was implying.

His lips quirked into a lopsided grin. "I see them sneaking around the Keep fairly often. In fact, I just saw them stumbling up to Caelum's room before I came in here."

She let out an exaggerated shudder and Aris laughed.

"Gods, I really didn't need that image in my mind," Val moaned. "Why even bother hiding it?"

Shrugging, Aris leaned back in his chair, the smile on his face making him look even more devastatingly handsome compared to his normal, cool indifference.

"You know Caelum," he said. "Probably thinks caring about anything short of bloodshed is a weakness."

Val did know Caelum. And she wondered if it was her imagination or not, but as Aris said this, a shadow passed over his face. As if he, too, considered it a weakness.

Suddenly, something drifted by her peripheral. Looking around, Val noticed curious white flurries falling from the ceiling.

"What the—" she began, and her breath came out in a cold puff of mist. Aris looked up too, and suddenly the whole office was filled with swirling flecks of what appeared to be snow.

"Is that . . . ?" Val spluttered, holding a hand up to catch a falling flurry in her palm.

Snowflakes were piling on Aris's shoulders as they began to shake with laughter. And then it dawned on her.

"Is . . . Is Caelum's room above this study?" she asked.

Aris chuckled, shaking the book he was holding free of falling frost. "It would appear so."

"Then . . . does that mean that they're . . ."

A blush enveloped Val's entire body as snow fell freely, an obvious sign that an untrained Frost Magic Wielder was having a hard time controlling certain faculties the floor above.

"Oh, for the love of the Mother!" Val jumped to her feet, attempting to protect the loose pages and open books on the table. Laughing, Aris rose to his feet to help.

"Perhaps we should find someplace a little less exposed to the elements to do our research," Aris said, smiling at her as he reached over almost absentmindedly to brush a pile of snow off her shoulder. The mere touch of his fingers sent a ripple of flame through her, a straight shot of desire so hot that she could have sworn it burned the rest of the snow off her.

They froze, looking at each other, frost still flurrying around them. Yet there was nothing cold about the way their gazes locked, and for a second, it was as though a large, hot hand was squeezing all the air from the room. Being here, being so close to him . . . she couldn't take it.

This was stupid. She should have run the minute she saw him.

"I should go," Val choked out through the ever-dissipating oxygen.

"Valeria—"

But Val did not wait to hear him out. Grabbing whatever books she could carry, she turned and fled the room.

CHAPTER 2

Sweat dripped into Caelum's eyes and his whole body screamed in exhaustion as he slammed a rock the size of a small house into the ground. It exploded into a fine mist of dust and rubble. Saros only nodded.

"More," he said simply. The Nodarian captain, whom Caelum had grudgingly accepted as his advisor, lounged on a wooden chair in the training courtyard, his chin in his hand, looking bored. Caelum resisted the urge to pick up the captain's chair with his Gravity Magic and slam *that* into the fucking ground too.

"What do you mean *more?*" he snapped, whirling to face his annoying older cousin.

"You are still using your magic like a child," Saros said, picking absently at some dirt underneath his fingernails. "You need to use it like a *warrior*. Consider how controlling the gravity around you will make you stronger. Think of what you can use, how it will benefit you. Stop thinking like a child simply making something float."

Caelum seethed. All this time, he had thought his training growing up had been satisfactory—especially when he got older, and his power had reached its full potential. But after his near-death encounter with Morlais, Saros and that dickhead general had decided that he needed more.

And after only a month of training with Saros, it pissed him off to no end to find that they were right.

Caelum *had* been trained like a child. He was taught how to use the basics of his magic—how to lift objects up and down—but never how to use those skills to his advantage in battle. This wasn't even accounting for his newly acquired—and barely controlled—Frost Magic. He knew he had been young, but the thought of all the time wasted while he was rotting in a cell in Ironbalt made him dizzy with fury.

"You are a High King, Caelum," Saros said, rising easily from his chair and walking towards him. "You must learn to use your magic like one."

Throughout the last few weeks, Saros had pushed Caelum to his limit with his Gravity Magic. Caelum had only seemed to grow stronger by the day, but his frustration was not his lack of power, but rather his lack of strategy when using it.

Saros and Caelum had sparred until Caelum's fingers had bled, trickling down onto that damned sword which seemed to hum with power every time he used it. It always seemed . . . hungry. As if it thirsted for something. He tried to ignore it, to fight against it—just like every other damned thing in his life.

Saros drew out his own blade—a sleek, silver Star Sword Caelum recognized as the ones given out to the top Nodarian officials during his father's reign.

"Show me the stop and reflect again," he commanded.

Caelum ground his teeth, then lunged for the captain. Saros caught his sword, and the two parried and thrust across the courtyard until Saros swung his sword in a large arc. Caelum saw the opening and pulled his Celestial Magic out of his core. He stopped Saros's blade an inch from his head, then, with a grunt, thrust his hand outward. Saros flew across the courtyard in a shower of frost and crashed into a heap on the other side.

"You could've held back a little," Saros grumbled, struggling to catch his breath as he stood, brushing ice from his chest, and glaring up at him.

Caelum sneered, panting. "Got a little carried away."

From across the courtyard, he could see Deya, training with the Master of Arms. Her delicate, lithe figure—much more suitable for a dancer than a warrior—went through the familiar exercises Caelum had learned as a child. He smiled a bit watching her, taking in how her thick chestnut hair spilled out of her braid and pooled around the slender curve of the nape of her neck. The thin black marks of her prophecy peeped over her collar, crawling down her spine, illuminated by the ever-present moonlight.

The sight of the markings made his stomach clench. The words of both of their prophecies still lingered in his mind, sometimes spinning endlessly. *The downfall of all.*

What it all meant . . . what it will all *mean* . . . It still sent a shot of anxiety through him every time he thought about it. The only person he had told about Deya's prophecy was the general. It was difficult to tell if Aris felt the same concern; he'd simply nodded when Caelum told him, as stoic as ever. He looked as if he were filing away the information for later, then said, "I'd be careful telling anyone else this information. I know how you feel about her, Caelum. And if I can see it, so can someone else. I'd be cautious if I were you."

The cryptic warning had made a chill fill his veins, followed quickly by a molten flush of embarrassment. Had he been so obvious? Aris had only seen him with Deya in the infirmary, sitting beside her bed, waiting for her to wake. He had kept his public affections for her minimal. But still, the general had guessed.

Aris's warning rang in his head, twisting with the already existing panic within him. He had never cared for someone, never loved someone—had never expected he ever would. But suddenly, Deya was everywhere. He could always *feel* her—like a tether looping his heart to hers. It was too much. Too soon. And Aris was right. If he could see it, so could others.

No, he couldn't allow anyone else to have that advantage against him. Particularly within his own council, which was as hostile as any battlefield. So, he had retreated. Kept her at bay. And while sneaking around with her wasn't always convenient, it meant he could still hold her. Be near her.

Keep her safe.

Keep *himself* safe.

He watched her now, the way her hips moved as she walked across the courtyard towards them. The way she would smile slightly when she caught him looking her way. He could not stay away from her, and yet he could not seem to fight his baser instincts of keeping her away. At least, far enough for him to clear his head. To get his bearings as the new king who was constantly under scrutiny, as a Hesperos who everybody doubted . . . As someone who could possibly even have room in his cold, black heart for someone like her who bore a prophecy as heavy as his own.

At that moment, a heavy sword hilt whacked him, hard, on the side of the head. Caelum swore and spun around.

"You're not focusing," Saros snapped, brushing dust off his black breeches. "Pay attention, or I'll make you do that ten more times until you are."

Caelum fought the urge to strangle the male where he stood when a voice whispered in his ear, "Demoralizing, isn't it?"

He caught the scent of roses and bergamot, felt her before he saw her. It was like the tug of the strongest Gravity Magic he had ever felt, spinning his head, pulling him towards her like a ridiculous magnet. While it was difficult to ignore around others, he knew it was necessary. She was a weakness he could not afford.

"Shut up," he growled at Deya, but she just smirked.

"Let's go one more time," Saros said, rolling his neck. "And then it's Deya's turn to train."

Deya's face went white, but she didn't say anything. Her newly painted nails dug slightly into the hilt of her borrowed sword, and she looked as if she were steeling herself for what was to come.

Caelum and Saros squared off again, and it took all of Caelum's effort to focus on each swing of the captain's blade while Deya was near him.

Gods, she was so fucking *distracting*. He could *feel* every damned movement, smell her scent on the air, even when he held his breath. How the hells was he supposed to concentrate on *anything* with her around?

Saros countered his wild swing and, this time, it was Caelum who was blasted across the clearing, landing with a hard *thud* on his back. At the sound of Saros's chuckle, he knew it was pay-back for how hard he had thrown him. Grinding his teeth, he leapt to his feet, magic coursing in his veins, pounding angrily in his ears as he stormed back towards his cousin.

"*Again,*" he snarled, but the infuriating male smirked at him.

"No, it's Deya's turn. You'll have your chance at redemption tomorrow, *Your Majesty*."

Caelum's fingers twitched, his desire to use some of the more deadly techniques Saros had shown him flashed through his mind. But then Deya walked past him, barely brushing him with her hips as she went, and everything whooshed out of his mind.

Deya got into position in front of the large bush of night-blooming jasmine they had been using to experiment on. Not that it had gone very well. Deya had done nothing for the last few weeks but make a few flowers wilt. It was almost as if her Decay Magic had weakened since the battle with Morlais, and her Healing Magic was still dormant since it had saved Caelum last month.

Deya shifted herself, feet shoulder width apart and held out her hands. She no longer wore the faerivaine chain around her neck—though Caelum missed it regardless. He had given it to her, after all.

Caelum and Saros watched as Deya drew in a deep breath. She closed her eyes, and her fingers began to curl. As if she were drawing life itself out of the flowers, the petals began to wither. It wasn't an out-of-control blast anymore, rather a tempered demolition. Slow and methodical,

Deya drained the petals of color and life before Caelum saw her flinch. Suddenly, she pulled back, pulling her hands back against herself, cutting off the magic all together.

"What is it?" Saros asked, but Deya was blinking and shaking her head, her hands clutched to her chest.

"Deya," Caelum began. There was an edge to his voice as he advanced towards her. "What's wrong?"

Deya flinched at the bite to his tone but shook her head roughly. "Please, Caelum, I don't want to hear it right now—"

His already short temper flared. It had been dancing on the edge of eruption much more than usual lately. Between Helene Sidra and her infuriating penchant to argue with him on *every* damn decision he tried to make and every other aspect of filling his father's enormous shoes as High King of Nodaria, Caelum was teetering on the edge of losing his fucking mind. And when Deya shoved him away like that, he nearly lost it.

Seizing her upper arm, he dragged her away from Saros. Deya yelped as his grip tightened.

"Caelum, get *off*—"

"What is wrong with you?" Caelum snarled.

Deya ripped her arm free of him and crossed them tightly, glaring. "Nothing! I just . . . I just can't do this."

Caelum's jaw flexed. "You have been dodging this for weeks now. *Why will you not use your magic?*"

"I . . ." Deya stuttered, but she dribbled off. Instead, she tightened her arms across her chest and looked away from him.

And in that second, Caelum saw it clearly on her face. "You're still scared of it," he said stiffly.

Deya just shifted, not looking at him.

Caelum let out a frustrated grunt, his hands rubbing across his face. "Deya," he said, his voice just short of a bite. "We do not have *time* for your fear. You realize that the longer you do not control that magic, the longer it controls *you.*"

Deya bit her lip, but still she said nothing. Caelum wanted to shake her. He did not remember much of Deya's battle against Morlais, but what he did know was that she had controlled it, if only briefly. It was important that she mastered it, that she *bested* it. She was their best hope in this war.

But when she did not say anything, when she merely looked down at the ground, something else drifted, unbidden into his mind. Something that haunted him as much as his past.

The balance of one, the downfall of all.

"Fine," Caelum spat, thrusting Deya away from him suddenly, desperate to rid himself of that grim reminder. "Continue to be weak, then."

Deya stared at him, dumbstruck, before her face set like stone. Whirling away, she stormed through the moonlit training grounds, kicking open the gate and disappearing from sight.

How dare he, Deya thought, blowing like an angry storm through the Keep's immense grounds. *How dare he call me weak.*

In fact, it was exhausting work making herself *look* weak. Trying to reel in the magic that felt like it had the strength of a thousand mountain trolls thundering inside of her. Even then, as she marched out of Atlas Keep's gates towards Arctos, she could still feel it flowing in her veins.

But she couldn't use it. What if the shadows creeping up her hands got worse? What if it reached a point where she could no longer hide it? What if Caelum saw, and that look of disgust and fear she had seen flicker across his face a moment ago was how he permanently looked at her? But far more concerning than that were the voices. Even in the calm, tempered state of their training, Deya couldn't help but notice them when she used her magic. The way shadows seemed to shimmer in her mind, filling her head like noxious smoke, before she shook it away.

Deya walked farther away from Atlas Keep, through the grass, along the thick turret of trees that lined the perimeter of Arctos. Although the sky was pitch black, there were still lights from all directions. Starlight filled the lanterns lining the main bridge, the moon and stars so bright, they could almost be mistaken for sunlight.

When she had first arrived here, the landscape was barren and rocky. However, when Caelum plunged the kingdom back into nightfall, over time the greenery began to come back. Bursting with solely nocturnal plants, Nodaria's landscape was now lush and rich, the grass such a dark green it was almost blue, the strange, beautiful night blooms bursting from black trees and shrubs. And all of it was covered in starlight.

What Caelum hadn't mentioned when they first arrived here was that starlight was *alive*, living balls of Celestial light. They bobbed and flitted along like glowing bugs, bouncing into her eyes and attaching to her clothes. She batted them away as she walked, not in the mood for the eager balls of light.

Nodaria was as beautiful as Oswallt had told her. Yet, there was so much *wrong* that she couldn't appreciate being there properly.

She and Caelum felt so right one minute, and then so wrong the next. Then there was this power. . . this dangerous, terrifying, mysterious power. Even with the return of her Healing Magic that day—strong enough to bring Caelum back from the brink of death—she still could barely sense it underneath all the destructive magic heaving inside of her core.

Val was barely speaking, Rayner was gone . . . and slowly, Praiton was destroying every outpost the Pillar Legion had. They were picking them apart bit by bit.

Yet here she was, sitting comfortably in Nodaria while a war raged outside the border. She didn't blame Helene for fighting to keep Nodaria out of it. Right now, it felt like the kingdom was the only safe place besides Bridah in all of Krigor.

And it was as Deya thought this, she felt something seize her ankle. Deya froze for half a second, just in time to see something thick, black, and hairy slither around her leg.

Then, she was yanked off her feet.

She hit the ground, her scream not even leaving her mouth before she was pulled, feet first, backwards into the dark forest.

The impact of her body hitting the ground knocked the wind clean out of her. She shouted but couldn't catch her breath as whatever held her tore through the forest of trees. Deya gasped and spluttered, her hands reaching up to protect her face as brambles, rocks, and dirt ambushed her from all sides. Her fingers scrabbled to hold on to something—*anything*—but every time she managed to grab a sapling or branch, she was ripped away by monstrous strength.

Desperately, Deya's other foot kicked and flailed, trying to smash whatever was wrapped around her ankle when, suddenly, she was flung like a bug flicked by a horse's tail. She came careening down, crashing onto the hard Earth.

She lay there for a moment, her lungs struggling to breathe, her body aching and screaming in pain, when she heard a dry, rattling breath. Scuffling sounds moved nearer, the rustling of leaves making all the hair on the back of her neck stand on end.

Move! she chastised herself, but her body hurt too much. All she could do was lift her head slightly, just enough to see what was breathing like that . . .

Four thick, black, claw-tipped legs stalked towards her. They were many-jointed, like that of a spider's, and covered in long black hairs.

But the legs weren't what gripped Deya's body with icy terror. Attached to the round, bulbous spinneret was what looked like a male's torso—and atop that, the most terrifying head she had ever seen. Like someone had thrown a black sack over the face, the head was a shapeless bulb. Four gleaming red eyes looked at her over a pincer-like mouth. And then, it spoke.

"*Your kind is weak*," it hissed. Its voice was a rasping whisper, unlike any sound she had ever heard. "*How am I to get a good meal out of you?*"

Deya's body finally began to move. She dragged herself backwards as the *thing* crept closer. Now that she was up, the moonlight caught on its body, and she could see shadows undulating like smoke from its enormous back. She had seen this once before. From the Shadow Sword that Caelum now wielded . . . it had smoked just like that when Morlais had held it.

This must be a shadow creature.

Unlike the nyraxi, which Deya had encountered many months ago, this monster was different. It was . . . intelligent, cunning. Its red eyes roamed over her as its long, taloned limbs reached out as if to touch her. Deya recoiled, her stomach heaving.

"*Enough*, magror!" a voice cried.

Breathing hard, heart pounding wildly, Deya looked up to see who was there to save her. But her stomach sank at the group of unfamiliar males walking into view. There were only three of them, but each wore a hood colored green and white. And the insignia on their broach . . .

"You . . . you're the Silver Daggers," she whispered, still struggling to move, but managing to pull herself to her feet. Her limbs felt heavy . . . sluggish. Something was wrong. Something more than just having the wind knocked out of her.

The male closest to her laughed. "Look, the demon girl knows who we are. I'm flattered," he murmured, his hand reaching towards the broach of the silver dagger pierced through a set of scales. "Now hold still before the magror's poison sets in, and you start to fall apart."

Poison.

Deya's vision was beginning to get fuzzy as she took another step backwards from the group. The Silver Daggers were an infamous Praiton institution. Worse than that, they were an assassin's guild. They were often called the Dagger of the King, but as Deya's eyes struggled to keep the magror in view, she knew that they were now using much worse than mere daggers.

The males closed in, the magror creeping around her, still hissing. Its large hairy legs were elongated and unnatural as it prowled in a circle.

"What do you want with me?" Deya asked. It was a stupid question—she knew what they wanted. But she had to stall. She had no sword, nothing within reach. Could she risk using her magic? How in the Mother's name did they manage to sneak into Nodaria without being noticed?

"We're gonna bring your pretty little self to Lord Decius, of course," the male at the center said. "But it won't matter if you're missing a few parts, I'm sure." He leered at her, and Deya felt her legs begin to tingle. The poison had seeped in through her ankle when the magror had grabbed her. Her left foot was now completely numb, and it was slowly spreading up her legs. But she could still run if she had to. Without her magic, she knew she was outmatched in this fight.

But as Deya's knees bent, ready to sprint in the opposite direction, the male to her right laughed.

"Uh uh, not so fast, demon girl," he sang.

Deya had just pushed forward and stumbled a few steps on heavy feet before the magror's limbs shot forward again. They seized her by the leg, but this time, Deya was prepared. Unlike the time with the nyraxi, when Deya was helpless and trembling, only surviving because Caelum had found her in time, things had changed. She was *not* that girl anymore.

The magror's jerk of her leg was all she needed. As she fell to the ground, bottom first, her hand shot towards her boot. She grabbed for the knife she kept tucked there and, with a flash of silver, the magror's taloned hand went spinning off into the distance. It let out a roar of pain, black blood splattering her. It smelled like death, but she held her breath as she hurled the knife across the clearing. It sank into one of the assassins' chests, who keeled over like a felled tree.

The Silver Dagger members converged on her. Their leader withdrew two serrated blades, while the other fled towards the magror, which was still howling in pain. Deya lunged for the fallen assassin's dropped sword but had to roll as the leader attempted to stab her. All she was able to grab hold of was the knife she had thrown. Yanking it free of the other male's chest, she swiped across her body, slashing a clean cut across her attacker's throat. The male froze, spluttering, before collapsing beside his fallen comrade.

Shaking, mostly numb from the waist down, Deya struggled to rise and catch her breath. Before she could wonder what had happened to the third male, thick tendrils seized her wrists.

"*No!*" Deya screamed, but the air was knocked from her lungs a second time as the magror slammed her to the ground, pinning her with two of its remaining three limbs.

"*You . . . will . . . pay,*" the magror wheezed.

Deya could see its black blood dripping onto the forest floor, could feel her wrists start to tingle as whatever poison those hairs secreted sank through her bare skin.

She had no choice. She was about to be paralyzed and then probably spun into this creature's web for dinner. There was only one way she could survive this.

With the last remaining feeling Deya had in her hands, she wrapped her fingers around the rope-like legs of the magror. Then, she ripped the door off her power.

Like a monster finally escaping its prison, the magic exploded out of her. The magror gave an unnatural screech, attempting to yank its arms free of her hold, but she held tight, held for dear life. Her fingers were trembling, the poison battling with her magic, fate deciding which would win first. Deya let out a scream, closing her eyes as her magic spread up the creature she was holding.

It started slowly. Black shadows began to swirl in her vision, creeping through her mind like hushed, hurried whispers. Then, like a dark wave, they bombarded her on all sides. It was all Deya could do to hold on to the magror and push through the suffocating darkness pressing into her mind.

One minute, she held its legs—the next, it was ash and dust.

Deya's arms thumped to the ground, the feeling trickling from her whole body. But even though her body stilled, the power coursing through her veins did not. Screams filled her mind, swirling with the shadows her power had filled it with.

No, no, no!

Deya struggled against it, thrashed under its terrifyingly oppressive weight, but it was like trying to lift her head while being held underwater. Gasping for breath, her mind and body screaming in panic under the whispered shrieks in her mind, she fought her way out of the dark shroud that had fallen over her. Slowly, her vision began to clear.

A flash of silver caught her eye. The third assassin had been hiding behind the magror, and as the last of its body floated into the wind, he advanced with a furious roar.

The scream she attempted was lost, her hands paralyzed, her legs useless—her life over. Suddenly, a sword burst through the chest of the assassin. He stood for a moment, staggering in surprise as he looked down at the bloodied blade protruding from his chest. And then he fell to the ground.

And, through the swirling shadows still filling her vision, Deya saw who stood behind him.

Skinny and dirty, it took her a second to recognize the face underneath all the blood and bruising that surrounded his once tanned Ganiean features. But when he opened his mouth, there was no mistaking it.

"Bloody hell, Dey. How'd you get yourself out of this one?"

"Luc?" she breathed in bewilderment, right before her head hit the ground and her vision turned white.

CHAPTER 3

Deya couldn't move a thing. All she could do was listen to the sounds of faint cursing and mumbling as someone attempted to remove chains. And then she felt something warm begin to pulse against her chest.

Her eyes snapped open.

Deya gasped and made to sit up, and an explosion of fear and shadow burst from her. The dark surge of her power rushed up and as her hands touched the grass underneath her, she felt the delicate blades turn to ash under her touch. Yelping, panic still clenching her tight around her throat, she thrashed in fear, unsure of what was happening before bloody and dirty hands pushed her back down.

"Hey, *hey*. It's okay. You're okay. Stay still, Dey," a familiar voice murmured. "If the poison reaches your heart, I doubt I could bring you back. Only you could do something like that."

Deya's breath sawed out of her as memories of where she was and what happened to her came flooding back. Panting, she felt the magic in her simmer and fade as her breathing slowed. Her vision cleared with each labored breath, and she was finally able to see the outline of Luc as he moved over her in the darkness. His Healing Magic pulsed with a warm yellow light as it worked to remove the poison from her body.

"You've come a long way, eh?" Luc smiled grimly at her as his hands passed over her paralyzed form. "I never would've thought you could have taken on a group of Silver Dagger assassins and . . . whatever that creature was. What's gotten into you?"

When it felt like her mouth could move again, Deya stuttered hoarsely, "Luc . . . h-how . . . wh-what . . ."

She couldn't think what to ask first. Fighting between relief at being safe, confusion as to what he was doing there, and anger at the memory of the last time she had seen him, Deya struggled to look at him properly.

Luc was skinnier than she had ever seen him. Emaciated. He was badly beaten, and Deya could see the remnants of what looked like faerivaine shackles lying a few feet away. So that was what he had been struggling with earlier.

"It's a long story," Luc said, shooting her a small smile. Gradually, feeling began coming back to Deya's limbs. First, she flexed her fingers, then her arms could lift, then she could sit up.

"Your Healing Magic . . . what happened to it?" Luc asked, glancing up at her as he moved towards her legs.

Deya shook her head. "It's a long story," she mumbled.

Finally, she was able to move, and the first thing she did was cast an anxious look down at the patch of dead grass below her, before scooting away from him as if to hide the evidence of what she had done. Anxiety pulsed in her chest at the memory of the terrifying blackness that had momentarily suffocated her. At the loss of control. The fear . . .

With a shuddering breath, she tore her gaze from the dead grass, and back towards the thin, frail male crouched before her. Luc sat on his knees in the dirt, looking down at the ground, his expression remorseful. Deya regarded him warily.

His eyes darted up to look at her. "Hey, Dey," he said, weakly. "Long time no see, eh?"

She narrowed her eyes, not feeling particularly warm towards him, even if he had just saved her life. "What are you doing here, Luc?" she asked, her voice cold. "What's happened to you?"

Luc sighed and shrugged. His clothes were torn and tattered, and he bore the distinct look of someone who had travelled a long way in a short amount of time.

"Clarita turned on me," he said, his voice barely a whisper. "Just like she did to you. But I managed to escape before they sent me to Ironbalt. I followed the Silver Daggers out of Praiton. Stowed away with them on their cart." He nodded back behind him to where Deya could see an old, rickety covered cart and a horse a few yards away.

"Why would they send you to Ironbalt?" Deya demanded. "What was your crime?"

Luc's eyes were wide, haunted. He stared at the ground and shook his head, and Deya saw his fear, his pain . . . It was a mirror image of her own when she had first fled Ironbalt.

"Clarita promoted me." He gave a rueful shrug, as if embarrassed to even admit it. "She asked me to work on a special project with her. Help her make potions and things for the troops. But while I was working for them, I heard things. Plans Decius was making . . . orders he issued. I heard him send the Silver Daggers after you. And I . . . I tried to talk to Clarita. To reason with her." He glanced up at her, shame in his eyes. "I thought she would be understanding. Turns out, I was a fool. The next day, I was hauled off to the dungeons. So, before they could send me off, Ramona helped sneak me out of my cell, out of Stonehall. I stowed away in their cart, hoping to find you."

Deya's stomach clenched at the familiar story, yet she steeled her heart. "So, Ramona helped you," she said, her bitterness heavy in every word. "Must be a real friend."

Luc had the grace to look ashamed. "I . . . I'm sorry, Deya. Truly.

Back then . . . when you were imprisoned . . . I swear to you, I did not tell Clarita what you said . . . what we overheard . . . but somehow it got back to her." He rubbed a frazzled hand through his long hair. "You know how it is in there. The damned walls have ears. When Clarita found out, she threatened me. Said I was just as guilty as you were. She cut me a deal. Say nothing and she'll forget I was even there. But because of that, you . . ."

Fury bubbled in her veins at the mention of Clarita Killoran colluding with the one person she had thought was her friend. She knew the end of this story, of course. Luc had said nothing, and Deya took the fall.

"So, you sold me out to save yourself," she spat. "And yet you came looking for me? For what? Do you think I'll protect you after what you did? Do you think I'll *forgive*—"

"No," Luc cut in, shaking his head, angry tears welling in his dark eyes. "No, of course not, Deya. I deserve all your ire, all your hate. I *deserve* it. But I didn't come for your protection. I came to warn you."

Deya stilled. "*Warn* me?" she echoed. Glancing around at the bodies surrounding them and what was left of the magror, she scoffed. "Your warning could have come a bit sooner."

But Luc was shaking his head. "No, the Silver Daggers are only the beginning." He stared at her, his bloodied face deathly serious. "They will not stop until they get you. They want you back, desperately. I don't know why, but they won't stop until they have you, Dey. But there's more. They're searching for something . . . something dark and dangerous."

The familiar words thundered in her ears and her blood ran cold. Months ago, Oswallt had told her the same thing right before he died.

Getting to her feet, Deya flexed her fingers and toes. They were still a bit tingly, but otherwise sound. Then she froze. Peeking out from the chipped red nail polish, was the shadow staining her fingers. It had spread now, further than her cuticles, almost halfway to the joint at the tip of her finger. Heart pounding, a cold frost of fear coating her chest, Deya took a deep breath and balled her hands into fists.

"Come on," she said. "Let's get back. Then you can tell us about what you intend to warn us about."

"Us?" Luc echoed. But Deya did not answer. She decided Luc's punishment would be to introduce him to the High King of the Celestial Throne.

"*Deya!*" Luc shrieked from somewhere up by the starry ceiling. "Deya! Tell him to put me down!"

Caelum had her shoulders in his hands, holding her out in front of him while those glowing violet eyes scanned her body for any injuries. "What were you thinking?" he demanded, his hands roughly spinning her in a circle in front of him. "You could've been *killed*, Deya! What happened?"

"I'm *fine*," she placated, allowing him to rotate her like the orrery above the throne room. "I was ambushed by Praiton assassins . . . and they had a shadow creature with them."

They were back in the council room, the darkness outside making the stars on the ceiling look even brighter in the large round room. Saros and Val sat around the table beside Aris, both looking wide-eyed up at the thin male hanging upside down from the ceiling.

At the mention of shadow creatures, Aris's gaze darted up from where he was sitting in front of the fire. "Another one? Do you know what kind—"

"It was something called a magror," Deya said. She shivered and her hands rubbed her body, remembering the way it felt when it was as useless as a wax doll. "It was worse than the nyraxi," she told Caelum. "It . . . it *spoke*. It could *think*."

"*Deya!*" Luc screamed again, but both Deya and Caelum ignored him.

Caelum rubbed at his jaw, processing what Deya had just told him.

"It is troublesome," Aris murmured from across the room. "Shadow creatures were never seen in this realm until the start of the war. It worries me to see Praiton employing ones as powerful as a magror. Not to mention enlisting an assassin's guild to track down Deya."

"Now, how did *this* come to find you?" Caelum growled, jerking his chin upwards at Luc, whose face was beginning to turn a mottled purple. She had already told Caelum who Luc was. And, needless to say, he was not happy with their new houseguest.

Sighing, Deya told the story of killing the two assassins, then the magror—though she was careful not to tell them how—and then how Luc had come to her rescue when the poison had taken hold of her.

"He said he came to warn me," she said, glancing up at Caelum. "That he had overheard pertinent information from Decius, and that is why they targeted him."

Caelum nodded. Then he drew his sword. The shadow blade shone, iridescent in the starlight as he held it, point up, towards the ceiling.

"Right," he said, holding up his hand. "Tell us what it is you want to tell us, runt. Then I can decide how I'm going to skewer you."

"Caelum—" Deya began, but Caelum's fingers curled. Luc dropped a full ten inches from the ceiling, coming closer to the point of Caelum's sword.

"*Deya!*" Luc shrieked again, his voice reaching a pitch that could break glass.

"I'm losing my patience," Caelum said, his voice a deadly calm. "Tell us what it is you came to tell us."

"Okay, *okay!*" Luc cried. His hands grappled at the air, as if looking for something to hold onto. "The night I was imprisoned, I was leaving the infirmary. Night duty," he added, looking at Deya—still upside down. "And I heard part of the head council having a meeting. Decius, Clarita, a few other Praiton officials. They were discussing . . . you."

"Me?" Deya echoed, and Luc nodded.

"It was hard to hear. There were a lot of voices, and I could only hear bits and pieces. But they were talking about how they wanted to bring you back and . . . and something called the Heart of the Mother."

Deya, Caelum, and Aris all looked at each other.

"The Heart . . .?" Caelum began.

Aris stared off into space, his long fingers rubbing his shadowed jaw. "I've never heard of that." He glanced backwards at Saros and Val. "Have either of you?"

Both captains shook their heads. There was a beat of silence, and then Caelum let out a breath.

"Right, is that all?" he asked, looking up at Luc.

"Y-yes, I mean . . . I guess," Luc stuttered.

Caelum nodded. "Thanks for letting us know." Then he snapped his fingers. With a scream, Luc fell from the air. Deya moved forward, knocking the sword aside so Luc fell with a crash against the hard marble floor.

"Knock it off, Caelum," she admonished him. Caelum grunted, glaring down at the Praitonian male on the floor as if he were a stain he wanted cleaned. "We're not killing him."

"Are you serious?" Caelum snarled, rounding on her. "This *runt* sold you out. He *bartered* your life for his own pathetic skin. He is not worth the rags on his back."

Luc shrank down into the floor, but he stared up at Deya, and she looked back.

"He's right, Dey," he whispered. "I wasn't the friend you deserved. I *do* deserve to die for that. Let him kill me."

Caelum shrugged. "Good enough for me—"

But Deya shot him a withering look, and the High King of Nodaria grumbled before sheathing his sword.

She gazed down at the male who she once considered her best friend. The male she had confided in, laughed with . . . trusted. The sight of him brought a lump rising in her throat. The memories of the time when she thought she could have a life within that castle. When she thought she had finally found a friend.

She didn't forgive him—not yet—but, if he was to be believed, he had risked death to come here. To warn her. It wasn't enough to make up for what he had done, but it was a start.

"We will not kill you, Luc," Deya said, finally. "You may stay here . . . on a trial basis."

Luc let out a small breath, just as Caelum growled, "Like hell he is."

Deya turned to him, arms crossed. "If I ask to let him stay in the servant's quarters under close supervision, *Your Majesty*, will that be sufficient for you?"

Deya saw Aris smirk out of the corner of her eye, and Saros chuckled across the room.

Caelum stared down at Deya, those purple eyes just as intimidating now as they were when they had first met. There was not a flicker of softness in them at that moment, but when he spoke, Deya could sense a tinge of concern in his words.

"Are you sure about this?"

She nodded.

"I don't trust him," he whispered to her.

Deya gave him a sad smile. "Neither do I," she whispered back.

Caelum stared at her for a moment, then turned to Luc who was getting to his feet, brushing off his dirty, tattered clothes.

"This is my warning to you, runt," Caelum said, his eyes flashing as he advanced towards him. "You give me one reason and I promise you—" Caelum raised his hand again and Luc suddenly gasped, his hand flying to his throat, choking and spluttering for breath.

"Caelum!" Deya cried, but the High King held out a hand as he tightened his hold on the gravity surrounding Luc's windpipe.

"*One wrong move*," he growled in Luc's ear, then he dropped his hand. Luc collapsed back onto the ground, gasping for breath, rubbing his throat.

Aris rose from his chair, the general's height impressive, even compared to Caelum.

"Saros, can you please escort our guest to the lower chambers," Aris said, looking over his shoulder at the Nodarian captain. "There is something I must discuss with Valeria, Caelum, and Deya."

Saros inclined his head, rising from his chair and taking Luc by the arm. Only Deya could see how tightly he gripped it.

"I'll talk to you later," Deya said to Luc, who nodded, eyes still wide.

When Luc and Saros left the room, Aris turned to Caelum, his handsome face troubled.

"Caelum," he began. "I think you know what I'm about to say."

Caelum's arms were crossed. He leaned back against the wall underneath Castor's portrait and didn't speak. Deya glanced between the two of them.

"What?"

The general sighed. He moved towards her as if he were approaching a timid animal. Deya immediately backed away, a sense of foreboding creeping through her.

"Deya," he said carefully. "I'm afraid it's no longer safe for you here."

Deya's gaze whipped towards Caelum, who was still staring down at the floor, his jaw grinding together.

"You don't intend to . . . *send me away*, do you?" she cried disbelievingly.

"Deya, we have no choice." Aris reached out a hand, placating her. "We must take Luc's warning seriously. If Praiton gets hold of you . . ."

"Where do you intend to send me if Nodaria is not safe?" Deya demanded. "Light's Tower?"

The general's gaze shifted back towards Caelum, whose hand was rubbing a tense rhythm against his chin. "No, they'd expect you there, and Light's Tower is not as insulated."

"Then where?"

There was a long pause during which Aris and Caelum looked at each other, almost as if they were having a conversation the rest of them couldn't hear.

"We have no other choice, Caelum," Aris said softly. "You heard him. They will keep coming for her unless we put her somewhere they cannot reach."

"I know," Caelum growled.

"*Where?*" Her patience was beginning to wear thin. She was staring at Aris, but it was Val who answered.

"Bridah," she whispered. Deya had almost forgotten she was in the room. They all turned to look at her. Val was sitting at the head of the long rectangular table, her red hair illuminated by the fire behind her. She looked at Aris, her gaze boring into him. "You want to send her to Bridah, don't you?"

"*What?*" Deya cried, whirling back around to glare, not at Aris, but at Caelum. "You are *not* sending me to Bridah like I'm some . . ."

"Some *what?*" Caelum snarled. "Some liability? I do not have the resources to protect you, nor do I have the patience to deal with the backlash I will face when Helene Sidra and her ilk learn that you are a Praiton magnet."

Deya recoiled from him, temper flaring, but Aris stepped in. "Deya, this is for your safety, as well as Nodaria's," he said gently. "Caelum is right. Nodaria is not equipped to protect you. Bridah, however . . ."

Deya shook her head, crossing her arms, balling up her stained fingers in frustration. She was sick of feeling like a helpless piece of glass that had to be protected. Hadn't she proven that she could protect herself? Hadn't she just fought off three assassins *and* a horrific monster? Yet, Caelum had the nerve to call her a liability.

The only thing stopping her from flying completely off the handle was the look on Caelum's face. His words may have been acidic, but she could tell by the furrow in his brow, the way his hands wouldn't stop rubbing at his face and neck, that he was more concerned about her well-being than he was Nodaria. She knew he put on a show for the others, but she could see as clear as day that Praiton's attack had him rattled.

Deya felt herself deflate. If Caelum was this worried, perhaps she shouldn't be so petulant.

Taking a deep, steadying breath, Deya turned to the Pillar Legion's general. "What about Bridah?" she asked. "Would I not be endangering them, then?"

"Bridah is well protected," he said. "There is a reason Praiton has tried and failed to breach it for decades now."

Deya nodded slowly, thinking. She glanced over at Caelum. In that moment, the coldness in his eyes were gone. The only thing left was a quiet fear.

And with that, Deya sighed. "Alright," she capitulated. "If you truly think I will not endanger Bridah, put me wherever."

Aris nodded, his shoulders sagging with the breath of relief he let out. "I'll contact Kindra and arrange it. Valeria," he said, glancing back at Val. "I need you to return to Light's Tower, to your regiment—"

"*No.*" The word came out of Val's mouth with so much force that all three of them stopped to stare at her. She had half risen from her chair, her face flushed. Her expression was frozen, as if her outburst had surprised even her. "I'm not going back to Light's Tower, General. I *won't.*"

Aris's spine stiffened, and Deya looked at Val. The panic in her eyes at the thought of going back to Light's Tower was evident, but why?

The general's jaw flexed, the only flicker of emotion Deya could see on his face. Aris was always like a cool breeze, as smooth and strong as steel. He regarded Val the same way he did everything: with a calculated calm that left Deya feeling unsettled. He opened his mouth, but Deya felt herself speaking before she could stop.

"Val could come with me," she said. Val's eyes darted to meet hers and relief flooded her face. "I'll need someone to watch out for me. I don't expect the *High King of Nodaria* will be able to." She shot Caelum a scowl, but he did not look up from his feet to meet it.

Aris looked at Deya, those bewitching hazel irises dangerous in the firelight, before nodding. "We will discuss this further, Valeria," he said finally.

With a gesture at Val, he motioned for her to follow him. He and Val left the room together, leaving only Deya and Caelum standing there in the empty chamber.

After a long pause, Deya turned to him. "A liability, huh?"

Caelum let out a gusty breath. "Deya..."

But she waved him off. It didn't matter anymore. Turning away from him, she tucked her hands under her arms as she stared up at the portrait of Castor hanging above them. It had been commissioned before he had died, according to Caelum, but had never been properly displayed. Now, Deya couldn't help feeling like his familiar purple eyes watched her, as they had through countless council meetings.

Hands slipped around her waist from behind, and she felt Caelum's chin on her shoulder. "Please, Deya," he murmured into her neck. "They almost took you today. Your being here is a risk. Just... please."

Irritation that he couldn't admit what was truly worrying him rushed through her. She was tired of the confusion, tired of wondering if he was putting up an act or still harboring the same resentment for her as when they first met. But with the way he looked at her, she had a distinct feeling that it wasn't the latter.

And with a sigh, Deya relinquished.

"Valeria."

Val was storming down the hall, heart beating hard, determined not to look at the Pillar Legion's general who was striding after her, an unusually dark expression on his face. The panic that had overtaken her when Aris had commanded her back to Light's Tower had been uncontrollable. The perfectly cultivated calm that had settled over her like a hardened shell during her four-mile run around the Keep had cracked like cheap glass at the mere mention of Light's Tower.

And as she flew through the hall, the intrusive thoughts beat tiny, flaming fists into her mind.

Light's Tower. Without them. Alone with no distractions.

Val snarled and mentally shoved the thoughts aside.

No, no, no. Shut up.

"*Valeria.*" A strong, calloused hand clasped around her wrist and, before she knew it, she was being whipped back around by the general.

The moment Val looked at him, she suddenly felt it. The aches in her body, the tenderness of her cracked and bleeding knuckles . . . the exhaustion of what it was taking her to fight off all those tiny, horrible thoughts.

Light's Tower. Without them.

"Valeria, what has gotten into you?" Aris demanded. His grip bit into her wrist, and Val's breaths began to come out in short gasps as she stared at his fingers wrapped around the bruised, golden skin of her wrist.

She had reached a point several weeks ago where her grief had frosted over. Where she had been numb. Empty. Bereft. Where the memories of her sisters did not pierce her like a sharp arrow, but rather scraped against her like a million dull blades. Over and over again, the memories had overwhelmed her until she had no choice but to shut it all out or risk succumbing to endless, agonizing sadness that threatened to swallow her whole.

But now, everything in her was still and contained. Even with her weakened flames, there was nothing she couldn't handle, nothing she couldn't fight through. And yet, standing there in front of the general, the molten panic and burning grief whirled through her like a fiery tornado.

Aris's face loomed in her view as she felt his hand brush her cheek, pulling her back out of the dark hole she was careening down.

"*Breathe,*" Aris whispered earnestly, guiding her back against the wall, his hold still firm on her shoulders and face. "What's going on with you? Why do you not wish to return to your unit, to reform the Fireflies—"

And at that word, it was as if something splintered within her.

"The Fireflies are *dead*, General!" Val exploded. Aris started, looking down at her, his face stricken. Val was panting, tears beginning to pool in her eyes. Her whole body felt like it was cracking into pieces and the only thing holding it up was the pressure of his touch.

Understanding dawned on his handsome face and his expression crumpled. "Valeria," he murmured. His hand slackened on hers and Val ripped her wrist free, but she didn't push him off. She was afraid that if she did, she would crumble to the floor.

On the surface, she appeared fine, but inside, she was crying their names. A silent, desperate scream. A scream they would never answer. That's what grief was, she supposed. A painful, silent scream.

It would creep up on her. Every time she successfully stuffed it away, it would flow back, a hot blast of heat, an endless wave of sorrow. A grief that threatened to drown her. The realization that they were really, truly gone. That they would never greet her at Light's Tower, never welcome her home. Never say hello again.

She would never see them again.

In that moment, she felt her own life like a betrayal, her own heartbeat like an echo of guilt. How could she still live while they were gone? How was she expected to keep going on without them? How . . .

"Please, General," she murmured, looking down at her feet, struggling to hold in the tears that wanted to fall. "I understand I should not have challenged you like that, but I'm needed here. Let me stay here with everyone. Or at least go with Deya. Please."

"Valeria." Suddenly, his body was gone from hers, and the tears that she had been holding back began to fall. She had not cried since her first night back at Light's Tower. Since everything had changed. She held it all back, pushed it all away. But in this moment, standing in front of Aris, it broke loose.

Her tears splattered on the black marble between their feet, and the sight of it made her choke angrily on a sob bubbling up. And then his hands were on her face, pulling her gaze to him. Their eyes met; those hazel eyes that never seemed to hold anything other than questions were now filled with a mournful sympathy that hurt her deeper than any sword.

"I know it is not much comfort," he murmured, his thumb reaching up to catch the hot tears falling from her eyes. "But I know exactly how you feel."

Val drew in a short trembling breath, urging the tears to stop as she looked up at the general. He was right. It wasn't much comfort. She knew he blamed himself for the fall of Ganiea, but whose loss weighed on Aris? Because for the first time in the long years she had known the general, pain soaked his features. The mask had slid down, just a little, and while it wasn't comforting to know Aris may be as broken as she was, it filled the cracks in her heart to know she was not alone.

With a sigh, Aris withdrew his hands from her face and moved away. She hated how she instantly wished to have him touch her again, how cold she felt without him.

"Go with Deya," Aris said, his brow furrowed, his eyes downcast, as if he didn't know how to look at her after that. "Protect her, look out for her. We can discuss you returning to your unit at a later date."

His tone was businesslike. She took the hint.

"Yes, General."

CHAPTER 4

Deya did not have many things to pack in preparation for Bridah. She gathered her meager possessions the following day and dressed in furs and a thick woolen tunic. After braiding her hair back into its usual plait, Deya paused to stare at her stained hands. The shadow was even darker in the new day. The memory of the voices that had filled her mind after her encounter with the magror sent a ripple of fear down her spine as she slid the gloves over her blackened hands. Perhaps it was a good thing to be sent to Bridah, after all. No one would question her for wearing gloves there.

All that was left was to wait for Caelum to be done with one of his many meetings, to transport them via portal to the Frost Kingdom.

In the meantime, Deya found herself heading down towards the lower floors of the Keep to see Luc. She had lain awake all night, thinking about the return of her old friend. During her time in prison, she had spent many restless days thinking about what she would say if she were ever to see him again. The image of him sitting silently in Clarita's office, his eyes downcast while Clarita sentenced her to her doom was still so fresh in her mind. A moment she would never forget. To hear his confession that Clarita had bargained with him. That he had taken it . . .

A part of her agreed with Caelum. Betrayal of that magnitude did not deserve forgiveness. Despite it all, a stupid part of her wanted to believe her friend, to accept him back, mistakes and all. But Deya wouldn't allow that part to win—she *couldn't*. How many times could she let her kindness be taken advantage of? How long must she force herself to swallow the very compassion that had doomed her?

Sometimes she believed Caelum was right. Love and compassion were merely a weakness. One she should shake.

The instant she thought it, she immediately turned sour. Caelum's view of those things was the precise reason they were in the position they were in now. In other words, a complete stalemate.

When she approached the guards stationed outside of Luc's room—placed there specially by Caelum—and entered, she found Luc; still skinny and bruised, but looking much more like his old self again. He had already eaten a few large meals and looked less peaky than when she had seen him the other night. Saros had given him fresh clothes, and he didn't even seem to mind the small servant's quarters he had been put in.

He looked up from his tray of food and smiled at her—that same crooked smile which had pushed her through so many hard days at the infirmary. The same smile which had made her old life easier, made her feel like she was welcomed. Wanted. Liked.

"Hey, Dey."

Deya sighed. "Hello, Luc."

And in that moment, she knew she did not have it in her heart to be as ruthless as Caelum.

"So, you and the High King," Luc said, grinning over the tray of food as she settled on the small stool across from him.

Deya froze, her cheeks flushing. "What makes you say that?"

Shrugging, a familiar glint entered his eye. "He's awfully protective over you for someone who seems to hate everyone."

Deya picked at her leather breeches and tried to control the burn in her cheeks. She didn't trust Luc with her business, after all. "We've just been through a lot together since Ironbalt," she said. A twinge of irritation scratched at her chest at having to keep up this ridiculous pretense that she and Caelum meant nothing to each other, but she pushed it aside. She couldn't dwell on that now, no matter how much he seemed to be trying to make her believe it.

"Right," Luc hummed, sounding like he didn't believe her at all. "Either way, he can be kind of an ass to you sometimes, can't he?"

She didn't respond, instead picking at the loose thread like it was the only thing she could see. Because of course, Caelum *was* an ass to her. But it was only in front of others. Though, in some ways, that was worse.

"He's not an ass to me," she mumbled finally, and Luc gave a sarcastic snort in return.

"I thought you'd finally grown a backbone, Dey," he said, chuckling. "Don't let me down now."

She glared at him, the familiar words hitting her like a slap in the face. And just like that, she was right back where she was nearly a year ago, standing in the stone halls of Praiton's castle, the smell of burned flesh and her own timidity filling the air. Had nothing really changed after everything?

Deya blinked and tried to shake off the sting of his words while Luc took another bite of toast.

Her old friend seemed out of place in the Celestial Kingdom. Her mind couldn't wrap around having him there, sitting in Atlas Keep, the forever moonlight pouring in through the window and framing his dark, unruly hair and deep brown skin. She couldn't help remembering the snide things he used to say about the collapse of Nodaria, the flippant way he regarded Praiton's misdeeds.

"Luc," she said. He looked up at her as he took a bite of his toast. "Why did you come to warn me, if you believe in Praiton's cause in the war?" she asked. She was afraid of the answer, afraid it was going to affirm her worst thoughts about her ex-friend. And, maybe, she happened to be a little afraid that it would *disprove* her thoughts about him instead.

Luc lowered his toast, his brow furrowed. "My mind has been changing for a while now," he admitted softly. "It started when they imprisoned you." He rubbed at his hands, and only then did Deya notice the bruising along his wrists—obvious signs that he had been shackled for several days. She felt her blackened fingers find the scars around her own wrists.

"I suppose I trusted our kingdom because it was the easiest choice to make," Luc admitted. "I didn't want to be at odds. I liked my position in the castle, in the infirmary. I didn't want to be . . . outcasted. But when I saw how they turned on you, the fear that it would happen to me one day was hard to ignore. And when it finally *did* . . . **I knew I owed you an apology. Owed you** *something.*"

Deya nodded, digesting this. She knew Luc had always only wanted to fit in. Clarita had given him special treatment. He'd loved being part of a group, of an exclusive club. Luc had always wanted to be accepted. Selfishly, Deya wanted to hate him for being spineless and self-serving, chasing Clarita's validation, but with a stab she realized that she had always wanted the same thing.

"What about the others?" she asked softly. "Ramona, Bertram, Kynwyll . . . did they ever talk about me after I had been imprisoned?"

Luc's face fell. His silence told her all she needed to know. They had probably laughed at her, whispered to each other that she had deserved it, that it was her fault . . . cackled with Clarita over her demise. And Luc . . . did Luc laugh with them?

"You hurt me," she said after a moment. Her voice cracked and blood rushed to her cheeks. Drawing in a deep breath, she held it, willing the tears she felt brewing to stay back. "You hurt me so bad, Luc. I thought . . . I trusted you. I thought you were my friend."

Luc stared at her, his hand still clenching the limp piece of bread.

"I know I did," he said softly. "I'm sorry, Deya. I'm so sorry."

And in that moment, the wound in her heart—the one that still ached and bled when she thought about Praiton, about everything she had thought she had, and everything she had lost—healed a little. In that second, the pain lessened.

Embarrassment washing over her, Deya rose and looked down at her old friend.

"Where are they sending you?" he asked.

Deya simply smiled. "Where they can't get me."

She wasn't going to tell Luc. Not yet. And while she hadn't completely forgiven him, she hadn't dismissed the idea that maybe, one day, she could.

Luc chuckled. "Fair enough." He looked up at her, and his wide brown eyes were filled with concern. "Be careful, Dey. Decius meant business when he said he would stop at nothing."

Deya shot him another tight smile and a nod, before leaving the room.

Caelum and Aris were waiting for her in Castor's study. Caelum looked tense, still wearing his usual all black tunic and leather breeches. He was running a hand on the onyx hilt of the Shadow Sword like a nervous tic.

"Where's Val?" she asked Aris, her gaze sweeping the study, looking for a glimpse of red hair.

The general gave her a tight smile, those green-gold eyes evasive as he replied, "She will be by later today. Right now, it's only you and Caelum."

"You're coming with me?" She turned to the white-haired male who was pulling a thick black cloak off the chair closest to him.

"Only for the day," he said, not meeting her eyes. "I can't stay, obviously."

She had known Caelum wouldn't be able to stay with her, but the thought of him leaving her all alone in a kingdom few had ever seen before sent a shiver of fear reverberating through her. The Frost Kingdom was so remote, so reclusive, she had no idea what waited for her on the other side of that portal.

She turned to Caelum. "How are we getting there?" she asked. "I thought you can only portal to places you've been before."

Caelum glanced at Aris, his expression cagey. "I can portal someplace new if there's something there I can channel . . . something I can sense."

Deya tilted her head. "Like what?"

But Caelum grunted, turning away from her, and Deya could see the slightest tinge of color beginning to creep up his collar. Deya stared at him curiously but decided to drop it when Caelum made no move to answer her.

"Be sure to get an audience with Ulf," Aris said to Caelum. "He is the oldest surviving High King in the realm. It's very possible he may know what this Heart of the Mother is."

Caelum nodded at the general, before turning towards the far wall of the room and taking a deep breath. He raised his hands and pulled apart the air between them, tore the very fabric of the universe. A large, spiraling portal of purple light came spinning into view, sucking all the air out of the room and bathing them all in a luminescent glow.

"Goodbye, Deya," Aris said. "Be safe. I will send Val to you later today."

Deya nodded, and she walked into Caelum's waiting embrace. Together, they both stepped through the portal.

Caelum felt the familiar sensation of being squeezed through a very tight hole. The only other feeling he had in the suffocating darkness of the portal was the warmth of Deya pressed against his side.

It was harder to navigate them through the portal this time. Portaling to a place he'd never been before was risky—especially doing so with Deya at his side. But all he could do was concentrate on the object that Aris had sent via owl to Bridah the day before. An object that seemed to pull him towards it like the way the moon draws the waves. And, even with all the effort it took him, he still could not shake off the nerves that gripped him. This was his first journey to the Frost Kingdom. His first experience with what could be considered his other family. The very thought was enough to set off his deepest and most repressed anxieties.

When the portal spat them back out, they almost collided, headfirst, with Kindra. The willowy, white-haired female stood in the center of a large entry hall, watching as he and Deya stumbled into the room. Caelum's boots slipped slightly under the slick icy floor, and he grabbed for Deya, clinging to her for balance. Everything in his body ached, as if he had fought his way through the portal using his muscles instead of his magic. Bridah was a far journey—he expected it to take a toll on him, but this . . .

Gasping slightly through the newfound pain, Caelum struggled to right himself. The sudden cold clung instantly to his bones, even through his thick traveling cloak. And as they both regained their balance, Caelum released Deya as if she were made of hot steel and took half a step away from her. He didn't miss the hurt, angry look she threw his way, but he couldn't waste his time feeling guilty. As much as he liked having her against him, he had to put some distance between them now that Kindra was there.

"Welcome to Bridah, nephew," Kindra said in her unusual, thick accent, giving them both a small smile, which was more of a smirk.

Straightening, Caelum suppressed a wince at his sore muscles and cleared his throat. "Kindra."

He still did not know how to address his aunt, even after several weeks of knowing about her existence. But Kindra's smirk only grew wider at his awkwardness, and, coughing slightly, Caelum looked around. The floors were made of a smooth glass—almost ice—and the tall, rounded walls were built with thick, frosted wood. They curved upwards, making Caelum feel like he was inside the hull of a very large, icy ship.

Turning to Deya, Kindra extended a cool hand. "You must be Deya. I did not have the chance to meet you on my last visit to Nodaria."

Deya took her hand, giving her a small smile.

Caelum hadn't had much time with his mother's sister when they first met in the infirmary, all those weeks ago. When he had woken after the battle with Morlais, Kindra had been unable to stay. As the head of the military in Bridah, Kindra, like him, was too important to be away from the kingdom for long. But she had stayed long enough to tell him a bit about his mother.

The clawing curiosity about Asti only intensified as he stood in front of her older sister. His eyes swept every inch of her, as if looking for details he could recognize in himself. Her blue eyes were the same shape as his own—the same wide curve to them, the same downturned corners. And when she smiled, there was something familiar that he couldn't quite put into words.

"Come," Kindra said, gesturing behind her, down the long hallway. "Father is looking forward to meeting you both."

Caelum's chest tightened. When he didn't move, warm fingers closed over his, jolting him from his panic. He felt a soft voice in his ear.

"It'll be okay. Come on."

They followed Kindra down the corridor, both craning their necks to look around. Fangdor Castle was unlike anything Caelum had ever seen before. Its corridors were long and narrow, the ceilings vaulted into a high V above their heads. Each beam of wood was carved with intricate markings filled with frost, icicles dangling below them.

Their feet padded over cushioned rugs, the slick glass floor underneath showing their reflections in the spaces between. It was only as he took in the multitude of lanterns lining the halls that Caelum realized there were barely any windows. As they walked, Caelum caught slats of light peeking in through the wooden roof, but otherwise the fortress was insulated. Sealed.

"Fangdor is designed to keep the heat in as best as it can," Kindra called from over her shoulder. "While we Bridanians have a higher cold tolerance than most fae, we still feel it eventually."

"Good to know," Deya mumbled, her breath coming out in puffs of mist as she rubbed her arms underneath her cloak. Caelum bit back the desire to rub them for her—he couldn't touch her. Not in front of people. It was the worst kind of torture, to look at her and *not* touch her. But he grit his teeth and looked away.

Kindra led them to a large, circular wood-paneled room. Benches lined the rounded walls, as if it were an auditorium, all circling a small fire at the center. Shields with the Bridanian crest hung from the walls, banners fluttered from the rafters, and at the front of the ring of benches was a large wooden throne.

Castor had always liked his throne as regal as he was. The High King's seat in Nodaria was a polished bronze and gold, with every constellation and planet carved into the sides by artisans from across the kingdom. Caelum hated sitting on it. It made him feel even more like a fraud than he already did.

Ulf's throne, however, was made of the same frosted wood as the rest of Fangdor. Carvings in the Bridanian language decorated the arms and legs—markings that were jagged lines and slashes, not too dissimilar to the lettering branded onto his own skin.

The seat itself was massive, towering several feet in height, the back of the chair intricately carved with patterns and details that stretched up the icy wall. It was so tall it almost looked like a giant's chair. And what was more, the chair was empty.

"Oh, *Faor*," Kindra grumbled, twisting back and forth to survey the empty throne room. "He's never where he says he'll be." She continued mumbling in a strange language, letters and words stumbling from harsh sounds to rolling purrs.

Caelum had never heard Bridah's native tongue before and he couldn't help but feel like it was a secret he wasn't meant to hear. So few outsiders had stood where he and Deya were now. How many had been here besides them? How often had his father come here? How did Castor come to spend enough time with Kindra and her sisters to end up siring an illegitimate offspring with one?

All these questions swirled like snow in Caelum's head, and he was about to open his mouth to ask Kindra when the large wooden doors exploded open.

A burst of frost and snow whooshed into the room, blowing Caelum and Deya back with the force of a fierce storm. Stumbling, Caelum held his arm over his eyes while Deya's hands grabbed hold of him, attempting to stay upright.

"*Kyandra!*" a deep voice boomed. "*Er vár gestr, minn feílan!*"

Kindra heaved an aggravated sigh, squinting into the cold wind as she replied to the ice storm in the same, melodic language it had spoken in, sounding exasperated.

Through the billowing wind of frost and snow, a large figure loomed into view. Broad shoulders muscled into the room, so wide they barely fit through the rounded wooden doorway. A hulking male with snowy white hair and beard lumbered his way through the throne room. Long, light blue robes crunchy with frost swept across the glass floor, fluttering around the ankles of feet the size of small boats. Each footfall made the ground creak, the ice crunch, and the walls shake as the male approached them.

The High King of the Frost Throne stopped in front of them, and they both had to crane their necks to look up at him. Twinkling blue eyes gazed back at them from the clouds of fluffy white hair surrounding his face. His ruddy skin was painted with the Bridanian markings, like Kindra's, and creased with the faintest of wrinkles—something only the old fae possessed. The bright blue eyes pierced through both of them, before crinkling into a smile.

"*Heil og sal,* my friends," Ulf said in a deep voice, with an accent so thick that even the words said in the common tongue sounded foreign. "Welcome to the Frost Kingdom!" He spread his large arms wide, nearly knocking a shield from the wall with a dustpan-sized hand.

"Th-thank you," Deya stuttered from beside him, and Ulf beamed at her, reaching out to grasp both of her small, gloved hands in his enormous ones.

"You must be Deya. *Smafugl, heil og sal!*" He shook her hand jovially, pumping her thin arm up and down while Deya stared at him, her mouth gaping like a fish. She obviously was not sure what to make of the male before her, who was supposedly the most powerful High King alive. Caelum, too, couldn't help but ogle this giant, who was nothing at all like he pictured.

"It . . . It's very nice to meet you, my lord," Deya said, dipping into an awkward half-curtsy when he finally released her hand.

Ulf waved her words away, shaking his enormous white head. "Please, please, none of this *lord*. It is Ulf. Only Ulf, *Smafugl*."

Deya blinked at him 'Small . . . fugel?" she stuttered.

"*Smafugl*," Kindra said, rolling her eyes at the High King. "Father likes to give people names in Brynorsk, our native tongue," she explained. "He is calling you Little Bird."

But the High King had now turned his piercing blue eyes towards Caelum. And the look on his face made Caelum's cold, black heart clench in his chest. Tears lined the icy irises, and the High King's large hands pressed against his chest as he stared at Caelum as if he were looking at a painting he found breathtaking.

Hesitantly, he reached out and grasped Caelum by the cheeks. He would've recoiled from any other attempting to do this to him, but when Ulf's large, cool hands cupped his face from chin to scalp, he found himself still. It was a sensation Caelum had rarely felt in his long life, being held by a parent.

"My Asti," Ulf whispered, his thick fingers clenching tight Caelum's face. "Oh, my Asti. *Kyandra* was right. My Asti is in your *Lostjarna*. I see her as clear as the day."

Caelum stared back up at the giant of a male and said nothing. No words would come, nothing seemed to be able to push past the irritating lump that rose in his throat.

This was his mother's father. His *grandfather*.

"Los . . . yarna?" Deya repeated, glancing towards Kindra, but Kindra did not look away from her father, who was still staring at Caelum like something missing finally returned.

"Lost Star," she whispered. "He called him the Lost Star."

Ulf let out a long, shaky breath, the power of which nearly blew Caelum back a few inches—before releasing his face. He clapped him on both shoulders, and his knees buckled.

"Ah, but I also see Castor in you too," he said, patting Caelum on the shoulders, causing him to double over with each impact. "That *bjastarør* was my dear friend, yet if he were not dead right now, I'd probably freeze him to death." He gave a booming laugh and gestured for Caelum and Deya to sit.

They perched awkwardly on one of the rough wooden benches, and, ignoring his throne altogether, Ulf collapsed down onto the bench in front of them. It splintered under his weight, one of the legs giving way, but Ulf did not so much as bat an eye.

"Thank you for taking her in, Ulf," Caelum said, glancing sideways at Deya, who was still watching the large male with wide gray eyes. "I know Bridah's safety has always been our primary concern."

Ulf waved a large hand. "It is no trouble. The dirty Praiton bastards cannot reach us here. Though I love when they try." He let out another bark of a laugh, and waved at Kindra, patting the dilapidated seat next to him. "*Minn Feílan*, did you not tell that golden general that it would be okay?"

"Of course, I did, Father," Kindra said, sitting on the bench beside him, careful to avoid the collapsed leg. "And please, speak the common tongue. We have guests, for Flykra's sake."

"Ah, forgive me," Ulf said, chuckling and patting Kindra on the leg. "We are not used to having guests."

"It is remarkable," Caelum said, looking at them both, "that Bridah has managed to maintain fluency of their native tongue. Only the very old speak Nadarak in Nodaria."

"It is because of our way of life," Kindra said, flicking a piece of frost from her pale skin. "The common tongue does not reach us often since no outsiders come in. So, throughout the centuries Brynorsk has remained our primary language."

"Fascinating," Deya murmured. She was studying the two in front of them like an interesting patient she was supposed to be assessing. Caelum stepped on her foot, jolting her out of her reverie.

"Anyway," Caelum said brusquely. "The reason we are here is because Praiton not only seeks Deya, but something else. Something called the Heart of the Mother. Have you heard of it?"

Ulf's bushy white eyebrows crinkled together. "The Mother? We know nothing of the Mother Goddess. Flykra is our deity, Bridah's heart and soul. She is who we answer to."

Caelum sighed and Deya caught his eye. The disappointment on her face was evident. They had hoped that, as the oldest High King in the realm, he would have answers for them. But Caelum was quickly realizing that Bridah and its inhabitants were not at all what he had bargained for.

"I am sorry to disappoint," Ulf said, noticing their troubled faces. "While we may not worship the Mother, Fangdor has many libraries in its halls. You are welcome to whatever we have. *Fao sem er mitt er fitt*, what's mine is yours, my friends."

Caelum nodded, giving Ulf what he thought was a grim smile.

The High King chuckled. "*Lostjarna,* are you always this serious? This is Castor in you, without question. My Asti was as bright as a fresh snowfall. Always smiling and laughing. She loved life, my Asti."

Kindra was quiet, her eyes downcast. The Bridanian war paint on her face looked smudged and blurry as she rubbed at her eyes.

Before he had found out about Asti, Caelum had not thought of his mother much. He had wondered who she had been, how she and Castor had met, but never about *who* she was. He had assumed Castor had met her in a whore house on a faraway shore, or perhaps in one of the free kingdoms in the realm. That she was faceless, and nameless. Never someone to meet, to *know*. He had never expected to be sitting in front of the High King of Bridah one day, watching him mourn his daughter. He never expected to see the loss of his mother weigh on somebody other than him.

"My mother . . ." Caelum began, looking between Ulf and Kindra. "What happened to her? How did she and my father . . ."

Ulf's blue eyes grew sad. "These questions haunt us all, *Lostjarna*," he said. "For none of us know the answers. Your other grandfather, Altair, was a good friend of mine. Castor grew up with Kindra, Hedda, and Asti. This was at a time when Bridah was much more open, not quite as guarded. We hold our secrets like shields, because there are now those who would cut into them. In those days, it was different. Altair would send Castor here; I would send the girls there. I hate to say that neither I nor Altair kept as close of an eye on the *bajorn*, our children, as we should have."

Kindra smirked. "No, you definitely did not," she said. "The trouble we used to get up to . . ." She shook her head, her gaze distant.

Caelum couldn't imagine his father as a child. Castor had always been larger than life itself, bigger than even the moon and planets. To think of him as a young adolescent running through Bridah—a black haired anomaly in the icy sea of white, an antithesis to Caelum's own upbringing—was a strange thought, indeed.

"When Castor became High King, he was betrothed to Nova almost immediately," Ulf continued. "It was his duty to carry on the power of the bloodline. Nova was his second cousin, and he cared for her; I know this, and he never complained. But I do not know if he ever loved her."

"He didn't," Kindra said suddenly. Deya and Caelum turned to look at her. Her arms were crossed, her eyes still fixed on the ground. But there was a steeliness in her gaze, a familiar scowl on her face. "He still came around to see us. Castor was devoted to Nodaria, duty-bound. But there was always a part of him which couldn't let go of the freeness of his youth. Asti always secretly coveted him. She was much younger, much less experienced. Yet she pined for him for years. I never realized Castor returned her feelings. I was blind." Her blue eyes sparkled with unshed tears which only seemed to make her angrier. "I failed as an older sister. I know that now."

Ulf reached for Kindra's hand, and she allowed him to take it, her jaw grinding together, just like Caelum's did.

"You did not fail. The hour of our doom is set, and none may escape it. It was Asti's time to go to Flykra, *Minn Feilan*." And when Deya opened her mouth to ask, Ulf smiled and answered her unspoken question. "My Little Wolf," he said, with a chuckle. He tightened his large grip on Kindra's hand for a moment, before rising to his feet. "Kindra will show you to your rooms, *Smafugl*," he told Deya, giving her a warm smile. "Please, make yourself comfortable. *Lostjarna*," he said, turning to Caelum. "Please come by often. You are a blessing from our goddess, a piece of my heart returned to its home. Your presence is most welcome, just like your father's was."

Caelum stared into the kind blue eyes, crow's feet crinkling around them. In that moment, he wondered how much of his mother remained in the two people across from him. He wondered what kind of mother she would've been, how she would've cared for him if given the chance. The lack of answers made him want to break something, the frustration of wondering how Castor had kept such an enormous secret for so long . . .

Anger at his father bubbled up inside of him. He was sick of not knowing, of stumbling through the discovery of his parentage blind, inheriting the burdens without any of the blessings.

And as he nodded his acknowledgment to Ulf, he made a promise to himself. He would find out what happened to his mother. And he would make it right.

<hr />

"Your main lodging will be through here," Kindra told Deya as she led her and Caelum through the wooden halls of Fangdor. "You have a suite to yourself. I was sure to ask for more wood for your fire, to keep you warm."

"Thank you," Deya said, already feeling the shiver of cold beginning to grip her in an unyielding hold. It was all she could do to steady the embarrassing chatter of her teeth. Especially since none of the others around her seemed remotely fazed by the frigid temperature.

When Kindra held open the door for them, Caelum followed her like a white shadow, Deya stepping after him. She saw the room before her and let out an audible gasp. The walls were made up of intricately carved wooden poles reaching towards the tall ceiling. Furs covered every surface from the large wooden bed to the stone floors, a fire crackling merrily in the hearth.

The first windows she had seen in the whole castle gleamed from above. Skylights arched along the vaulted ceilings of the room, and cool, dim sunlight shone down on them. Deya resisted the urge to run into it and spread her arms out. She knew it was probably not warm at all, but it was the most light she had seen in weeks.

"I will let you settle," Kindra said, still standing in the doorway. Her beautiful, angular face twisted into a small smirk as she watched Deya spin around the room. "Dinner will be held in several hours—if you wish to stay, Caelum." And with that, the princess of the Frost Kingdom left the room.

Deya turned towards the large wooden bed and dusted her fingers over the thick blue quilt set on top of it. It was soft and warm, and she wanted nothing more than to heap all the furs and blankets on top of herself and huddle by the small fire. All the furniture was made of the same worn, frosted wood. It was cozy and warm but felt like nowhere Deya had ever been before.

She felt Caelum's eyes on her, following her around the room. The way Caelum had shoved her away from him the minute he saw Kindra had set her blood ablaze. Luc's words were still echoing in her ears, reminding her of everything she had thought she'd overcome.

I thought you'd finally grown a backbone, Dey.

Walking across the stone floors, Deya approached the lancet window at the far end of the room. Frost curled up the thick pane, spreading in a crystalline pattern, blurring her first look out into Bridah. It was blankets and blankets of snow, as far as the eye could see. Smaller, wooden houses, like boats flipped upside down, were gathered in a tiny village surrounding the castle. White-haired children played in the snow, the sound of laughter floating towards her through the pane. The sun hung above them, a weak strain of warm light, making the snow glow slightly.

A hand brushed her back, and Deya felt Caelum come to stand beside her. His purple eyes looked out the window, taking in the children, the outskirts of Frostheim. He had been quiet the whole time, and Deya knew he was processing their meeting with Ulf. Seeing Caelum embraced like a child had been unusual. Seeing him tolerate it was even *more* unusual.

"Are you okay?" Deya asked softly, looking up at him.

He was still staring out the window, his hand braced against the glass, but his eyes were unseeing. With a jerk of his head, he nodded.

"I'm sorry we couldn't find out more about your mother," she said. "But I have nothing but time here. I'll see what I can find."

Still, he did not speak. His breath fogged the glass in front of him, and Deya could see the tension in his jaw. But just like that, he let out a sigh and turned to face her. His hands snaked around her waist, drawing her into him. But when his lips touched her neck, Deya pushed him away.

"No."

He paused and withdrew, his eyebrow arching. "No?"

She took a deep breath but held steady. Once again, they were back in the same position—Deya's gloved hands against his chest, holding him at a distance. A safe enough distance for her to think, to remember that she *did* have a backbone. That she had the strength to put her foot down, to say what she wanted.

"You pushed me away again."

Annoyance flashed across Caelum's face. "This again? Kindra was there. I wasn't—"

But Deya held out a hand again to silence him. "I don't care who was there. You can't keep doing this to me. It's not fair."

Gods, the look he gave her could have turned her to stone. She felt herself waver when he did not respond, but she pushed on. Reaching out, Deya ran her gloved hand down his chest, dragging her fingers lower, reaching towards his belt. Caelum's stomach tightened under her touch, and that electrifying crackle of energy began to hum between them again.

"I want you to admit it," she breathed, her other hand coming to grip him around the waist, her fingers tightening against him. "This is not just some prophecy. This is not just a side effect of magic. I want you to admit to me, right now, what this is between you and me."

Caelum's breathing was uneven, but his hands remained stiff at his sides. His eyes closed as she lifted on her toes, her lips grazing his jaw as she whispered in his ear.

"*Say it.* Tell me that this is real to you, too, Caelum. *Say it.*"

He took in a deep, shuddering breath, his fists flexing as he turned away from her. But he remained as still as stone. Deya let out an exasperated laugh.

"Fine," she said. Her hands dropped from his body, and she took a step back. "Until you admit it, you are not permitted to touch me."

Caelum swiveled his head, his eyes opened, and the purple gaze sliced through her. Before she could blink, he was upon her, turning her so he was at her back, pinning her in place against the cold glass of the window. Deya gasped, her breath misting the pane.

"Oh?" Caelum breathed in her ear, his hands gathering her clothing in fists from behind. His touch burned a trail down her stomach, teasing lower like she had done to him. "And who is going to enforce this rule of yours?"

"M-me," Deya stuttered, and Caelum gave a dry chuckle.

"And you believe that? Deya, I have spent the last few weeks learning every inch of you. How you fight . . . how you breathe . . . how you come . . ."

A shiver rolled up Deya's spine as his teeth grazed her ear, and her hand slid down the window a little further.

"But you're going to tell me that you can resist?"

"Y-yes," she whispered, but it came out shaky. She wanted him more than she could express, more than she could hide. The cold in the room was beginning to dissipate with the heat radiating from them both, beads of condensation beginning to roll down the glass. But she couldn't let him win. He was too much of a stubborn bastard, too used to getting his own way through sheer force of will. She *had* to hold strong.

The laugh he let out nearly made her give. "Fine," he said smoothly. "Have it your way."

And then he was gone. His hands, his body, his heat, it was all gone in an instant, leaving her pressed against the frosted glass, panting and shaking. The inadvertent mewl of protest that left her made Caelum smirk, and she shot him a loathsome glare.

"We shall see who cracks first," he said.

Deya huffed, straightening her clothes, the flush across her face and body still hot from his touch. "Don't count on it," she snapped, but Caelum only laughed.

"I'll be back with Val," he said, and, with a burst of wind and purple light, Caelum stepped through the portal, vanishing from the room.

Flustered and annoyed, Deya turned back towards the fire but paused when something caught her eye. Sitting on the bedside table, as if it had been there all along, was a familiar hairbrush. *Her* hairbrush.

Deya picked it up, slowly turning it over in her hands. She had not remembered packing it—couldn't even remember seeing it in the last few days. How did it get here?

Suddenly, Caelum's words from earlier floated into her mind. *If there's something there that I can channel . . . something I can sense.*

Deya let out a dry laugh, putting the brush back down, thinking how funny it was that, despite all his denials, it was *her* that Caelum could sense halfway across the realm . . . even if he refused to admit it.

CHAPTER 5

When Deya awoke the next morning on her first official day in the Frost Kingdom, it was to find a small, sprite-like female with the same ice-white hair and bright blue eyes as Kindra throwing back the hanging blinds from the lancet window.

Deya bolted out of bed, startled awake by the sound of metal scraping on metal.

"I'm sorry to scare you, Miss Deya," the female said, her pale hands raised, blue eyes wide. "But I was instructed to wake you."

Panting, Deya pressed a hand to her chest. Her heart was hammering. Since Ironbalt, Deya's nerves were constantly on edge. She was quick to spook, to jump and flinch. While it was an irksome side effect of her last year, it did benefit her in some instances.

"That's alright," Deya said, pulling herself out of bed. The floor was freezing beneath her toes. "Who . . . who are you?"

"Karyna, miss." The small girl was bustling about the room, pulling her bed clothes back into place, chucking another log onto the fire. "I am your lady's maid, placed here by the High King to assist you in anything you may need."

Deya watched, mystified, as Karyna finished tidying the room, before hurrying to the large, wooden wardrobe she had not yet looked inside. But when Karyna threw it open, a collection of thick, woolen dresses with fur trim greeted her. All were in varying shades of blues and greens with delicate patterns stitched onto the hems and sleeves.

Deya walked towards them in a trance, her blackened fingers reaching towards the garments, not even thinking that Karyna may see them.

"Where did these come from?" she murmured, pulling on the sleeve of one of the frocks. It was made of rough-spun blue wool. Simple, yet beautiful, with a corseted vest and a fur cloak.

"Lady Kindra sent them before your arrival," Karyna replied, her thick accent less melodic than Kindra's, harsher on the vowels. "She said that outsiders tend to under-dress here."

The constant shiver trembled up her spine as her cold toes shifted against the icy floor. Kindra definitely wasn't wrong. Already, she yearned to be back under the heap of animal furs on her bed.

"Would you like to wear that one?" she asked, a small smile tugging at the corners of her mouth.

Deya nodded eagerly, and Karyna laughed, moving to help her out of her night things. It was strange to be waited on like this. Karyna's hands were small and nimble, yet cold as ice as she helped lace up her new dress and pull out warm, fur lined boots.

"How long have you worked at Fangdor?" Deya asked as Karyna tightened the laces on the shoes.

"Since I was small, miss."

"Do you like it?" Deya asked. "Does Ulf treat you well?"

"Oh, yes!" Karyna cried, so obviously taken aback that she nearly forgot to finish lacing her boots. "Our High King is kind and generous. Me and my siblings were brought to Fangdor very young, and trained in all matters of the castle. He considers us family. He even carried my little brother to the castle infirmary himself when he fell ill last moon cycle. King Ulf is a great king."

Deya smiled at Karyna, watching as her white-blonde head bobbed as she finished lacing her boots. The female couldn't be much younger than she was when she first started working at Stonehall, and yet her energy was brighter. Happier. She wasn't bowed by stress or fear. Karyna was well taken care of . . . content and free.

"Miss Val asked me to wake you. She told me to tell you to . . . um—" Karyna turned scarlet as she mumbled, "hurry your ass to the library."

Deya let out a snort of laughter. Karyna, still blushing, wilted at Deya's reassuring laugh before giggling, too. It was a relief to hear Val speak like that. It felt like ages since she had given Deya a bossy command like that.

Karyna led her towards the library, down long wooden halls drifting with snowflakes and dim sunlight. Fangdor was bustling with people this morning. Servants, priestesses—even everyday citizens—walked past them, speaking in the same lilting, song-like language that Ulf and Kindra had. Brynorsk was a strange but beautiful language, so different from anything Deya had ever heard.

The ancient languages of each kingdom were so rare that Deya had only heard one other before. Nadarak.

At the thought, the prophecy on her back seemed to tingle.

Nadarak had seemed more chant than song, yet there were some similarities between the two . . . almost as if they were sister languages.

When Deya entered the library, it was to find Val, already nose deep in books, her ruby red hair bundled on top of her head in a messy bun.

"Took you long enough," Val grumbled, puffing a strand of red hair from her face.

Deya smirked. "Well, good morning to you, too."

Fangdor's library looked more like a large cathedral. Skylights like the ones in Deya's room cast cool daylight down onto the rows of rectangular wooden tables gathered in the center. Arches of carved wood spiked against the vaulted ceiling, carvings depicting snowflakes, creatures, and Brynorsk letters in intricate patterns crawling upwards towards the wooden beams. A fire crackled in the hearth, but Val was still bundled up to her neck with furs and cloaks. She huffed gusts of cold air as she flipped the page of a large book.

"It's bloody freezing in here," she mumbled as Deya sat down in front of her. "I can barely feel my fingers."

Deya took in the mass of books surrounding Val, including the growing discard pile behind her. It was far more than she should have been able to cover in such a short span of time.

"How long have you been in here?" Deya asked, moving to peer at the teetering stack of books behind her. As she got closer, she saw the dark shadows under Val's eyes, which furiously scanned the page in front of her.

"Since dawn," Val replied, a slight croak to her voice. "It wasn't like I could go outside to train in this hellacious weather. I had to do something."

Sitting down next to her, Deya peered at her cautiously. "Did you sleep well at least?"

"Like a fish on a block of ice," Val mumbled. Deya took in the slightly sunken nature of her gold cheeks, the permanently bruised and cracked knuckles on her hands. The Nodarian Master of Arms had mentioned to Caelum that Val trained nonstop. That she would often destroy the training dummies from how hard she would hit them. Not to mention the miles Deya often saw her running around and around the training ring every day.

For a moment, Deya felt ashamed that, during her distraction with Caelum and his ever-frustrating mind games, she hadn't realized that her friend had been clearly trying to distract herself.

"Val," she began hesitantly.

Val glanced up at her and Deya was relieved to see that, for the first time in a while, Val's amber eyes were bright and alert.

"Yes?"

Deya paused. She was going to ask her if she was all right but wondered if Val might be sick of people asking her that. For the moment, Val was present with her and looking more alive than she had in weeks.

Shaking her head, Deya shot her a tight smile. "Never mind."

Val seemed to know what she was going to ask and gave her a grateful smile in return.

"What have you been researching?" Deya asked, determined to steer the conversation away from Val's mental health.

Val slapped the thick leather tome shut with an irritated huff. "I was attempting to find any mention of the Mother Goddess *at all*, but there's nothing but Flykra, Flykra, Flykra," she grumbled.

Deya chuckled. "Well, it *is* the Frost Kingdom."

"Yes, but Flykra is one of *five* goddesses," she said. "*Six*, if you count the Mother. It's remarkable to me that the Bridanians have avoided all mention of any of them."

"That is by design," a voice said from behind them. Kindra strode into the room—closely followed by Karyna carrying a tray of hot tea. The furs draped across the Frost Princess's shoulders exacerbated her willowy frame as she smirked at them—a smirk that looked so much like Caelum's it made Deya do a doubletake. "Bridah remains strong if we focus our prayer on our true deity."

"You sound like Praiton," Val mumbled, dragging another book over to her.

"Perhaps," Kindra said coolly. "But unlike Praiton, we do not kill and conquer in the name of our goddess." Val fell silent, looking sheepish as she averted her eyes from the Frost Princess. Kindra's ice-cold eyes assessed her as she continued. "As Praiton topples another one of your Legion's outposts to the east, Bridah remains safe." She tilted her chin upwards in a firm defiance, her lip curling slightly. "Our people are not ignorant. They are aware of the other goddesses. They simply have no interest in them. No matter what Praiton does."

At the mention of another fallen Legion outpost, Deya's heart skipped a beat. She knew that time *was* of the essence. Even before she had been sent to Bridah, rebellion camps had been going up in flames almost weekly across the realm. If they took too long to find answers, there may be nothing of the Legion left by then.

"Do you have any information on any of them elsewhere?" Deya asked, rising to her feet with renewed vigor and grabbing for the nearest stack of books.

Leaning over her shoulder, Kindra's long, calloused fingers flicked through some of the books Val had piled on the tabletop. There was a faint dusting of snow on each of them, a permanent side effect of the Frost Kingdom's ever-present winter.

"If you cannot find them here, then we do not have them."

Deya and Val both let out groans.

"Well, I'm glad to know this has been a massive waste of time," Val said, shoving the books aside angrily.

"It is a big library," Deya said, peering around the room at the walls and walls of books piled onto shelves. "Maybe there's something hidden in here that we haven't found yet?"

"It'll take weeks to make it through all these books." Val slumped back in her chair, and judging by the fire crackling in her eyes, Deya could tell the news of another outpost attack had set her on edge, too. "We don't have *weeks*."

Karyna, who had been pouring both Val and Deya a cup of hot tea, paused, her small, delicate hands still clutching the ivory pitcher. "I do know of someone who may be able to help you," she said suddenly.

Deya, Val and Kindra's heads all whipped around to look at her.

"Who?" Val demanded.

Karyna flushed, her gaze darting away nervously under the weight of their gazes. "He is our version of what you may call a High Priest in your kingdoms. Frode has been around for almost as long as the High King. He claims to be a direct conduit to the gods."

Deya's heart skipped a beat. A direct conduit? Did that mean he could . . . *speak* to them? Could he, perhaps, speak to the Mother Goddess Herself?

But before she could react, Kindra rounded on Karyna, her eyes blazing. "Frode is a madman," she snapped, her tone sharp enough to make the small lady's maid cower in fear. "Do not go filling their heads with thoughts that that raving lunatic can help them."

Karyna immediately dropped into a curtsy, babbling hasty apologies as she took the now empty pitcher and scurried from the room, as if attempting to outrun Kindra's wrath. But the damage had been done. Both Deya and Val shot each other hopeful glances.

"But if he can speak to the gods," Val said turning towards Kindra desperately, "then what harm is there in going to see him?"

Kindra's face darkened. "Even if he *can* speak to the gods as he claims, Frode lives far from Frostheim, in a small ice cave due north from here." She rolled her eyes and scoffed slightly. "You will die attempting to get to him, without a Frost Magic wielder. It is mad to even consider it."

Regardless of Kindra's warning, Deya's mind was racing, attempting to picture a map of Bridah. It took her a moment to realize she had never seen one. To the rest of Krigor, Bridah was uncharted, unmapped. Not a thing known about its landmarks or terrain. But, judging by the harsh winter wind whipping against the thick glass of the library window, and the layers of snow blanketing the village of Frostheim, it had to be brutal.

Val glanced at Deya, her face troubled. She knew they were both thinking the same thing. Going out on their own in Bridah *was* risky. *Dangerous*. Like Kindra said, neither one of them could survive out there for long, not without a Frost Magic Wielder to accompany them.

"Maybe Caelum . . ." Val began, clearly reading Deya's thoughts.

"He can't control his Frost Magic fully," she lamented without thinking, her chin thumping onto her hand. "And besides, he'd never agree," she mumbled.

Kindra whirled around, her blue eyes flashing in an alarmingly familiar way. "My nephew does not know how to control his own magic?" she demanded, all discussion of Frode clearly flying from her mind.

Deya stuttered, afraid she had stuck her foot where it did not belong. "He, uh, is working on it still," she amended, but Kindra's expression turned more severe.

"*Working on it,*" she spat. "He is a High King! For Flykra's sake, he is the grandson of Ulf! My sister's blood! Our magic is a core part of our souls. We cannot achieve inner harmony without it—"

"Well, that just confirms it," Val mumbled under her breath. "Caelum is about as unharmonious as you can get—"

"You must bring him to me," she ordered, not hearing Val's muttered epithet, and rounding on Deya. Every inch of her tall frame extended to its fullest and most intimidating height. "I will train him. He *must* master his magic."

"I—" Deya began, but her words petered out. How could she tell Kindra that *no one*, probably not even the Mother Herself, could get Caelum Hesperos to do *anything* he did not want to do? And Deya had a strong feeling he would not want to be trained like a child by a *second* person. She knew being trained by Saros was humiliating enough for him.

But at that moment, Kindra looked so intimidating, so demanding, that she could not say no to her.

"I'll . . . try," Deya said weakly.

Kindra nodded, seemingly satisfied. She adjusted the furs on her shoulders, repositioning the weapons around her waist. "You are not to visit Frode on your own," she said. "If you are insistent on seeing a nutter who is madder than a runover hare, I will take you myself—but I am unable to leave the fortress for long. If you can wait a couple weeks when some of our warriors return from the border, perhaps I'll have some time to escort you then."

She gave them both a tight smile before turning on her heel and striding out of the library, leaving a tense silence in her wake.

Val turned towards Deya. The look on her face told her she was thinking the same thing. "We don't *have* weeks," Val whispered.

Deya nodded, her head spinning.

Praiton was destroying all their outposts. The Legion's routes had been decimated, and Light's Tower's supplies were dwindling. Deya knew the general was concerned, because *Caelum* was concerned. Every fight with Helene Sidra, every outburst at the council meetings, Deya could see it for what it was. *Fear.*

The Legion was losing, and the Silver Dagger's attack on Deya was their attempt to drive the nail into their coffin. Val was right. They didn't *have* weeks.

Taking a deep breath, Deya squared her shoulders before turning to Val. "Your magic. Would it not keep us warm long enough to get us to Frode?"

Val blinked, the gold in her skin blanching just a little at Deya's question. "You think my magic can survive that?" she asked in disbelief. "Deya, there's a reason Maniel has tried and failed to conquer Bridah for so long. My magic is no good out there . . . I could *die* out there."

Deya pursed her lips, turning back to look out the large, frosted window across the room. Snow swirled so thick outside that nothing but a blur of white could be seen through the glass. She had hoped secretly that Val's magic could be the alternative solution to finding a Frost Magic Wielder to escort them, but disappointment was quickly settling on her. Stupidly, she had forgotten about Ember Magic and its weakness to the cold. And not only would Val be of no use in the cold, but she could actually be in *danger* out there.

Turning back to Val, she said, "Is there anything you can do? Any technique to protect yourself from the cold?"

Val's amber eyes drifted towards the window too and her brow furrowed. "There is," she said softly. "It may not be of any use in this severity of cold, but it's something Manielians have to learn if we live anywhere else in the realm. I'm a bit rusty at it, but . . ."

"Can you do it?" Deya leaned closer to her friend, her gloved hands ringing together. "I'd rather go alone than put you in danger, Val. I wouldn't ask you to do that."

She didn't say anything for a moment. Her eyes hadn't left the window, as if she were weighing her options. But then, finally, she let out a breath. "Give me that atlas," she said. "We need to find the cave Kindra mentioned."

Deya blinked. "Are . . . are you sure?"

Val nodded, her face grave. And Deya knew what she was thinking. Even if Val wasn't sure, they did not have the luxury to hesitate. It was either act now or doom them to destruction.

"We will leave as soon as we can."

Deya opened her mouth as if she were about to argue. A million fears flashed through her mind. Fear for Val's safety. Fear it was too risky. Fear that there was no other choice. But then, deciding against it, she closed her mouth. With a small, resolute sigh, she nodded. "Okay."

CHAPTER 6

Deya and Val spent the next few days hidden in an empty chamber within Fangdor, mapping and plotting their journey to the High Priest, as well as readying Val to face Bridah's indomitable cold. Each morning, Deya would slip from her room before Karyna could wake her and squirrel off towards Fangdor's armory, grabbing as many supplies as she could fit under her cloak before sneaking back into her room. She'd meet Val after breakfast, and with a hasty excuse to Karyna that they were off to explore the castle, they'd slip away to the upper floors where no one would disturb them.

Deya turned a page in the large atlas book they had found within the library titled *Maps of Bridah,* her gloved hands toying absentmindedly with the petals of the white flowers nestled in a vase beside her. She peeked over at Val and saw her friend sitting in front of the low burning fire, her legs crossed, her eyes closed, and a furrowed look of concentration creasing her brow.

Val drew in a deep breath through her nose and let it out slowly.

The slightest bit of heat reached her from across the room and Deya knew what she was trying to do. Val had explained how Manielians could control the heat within them if they focused hard enough, almost as if in a meditative state.

"Being able to keep the heat concentrated within our core is the only way we can survive in severe cold," Val had explained to her. "But it takes a fuck-load of concentration," she added with an irritated grumble.

Even now, Deya could see the light beading of sweat on Val's temples as she breathed in and out with slow, rhythmic movements. The room was cold, even with the small fire burning in the grate, and Deya drew her cloak closer to her with a small shiver. As quietly as she could, she flipped a page in the atlas and saw Val's brow twitch at the sound.

"*Deya.*"

Deya winced. "Sorry!" she whispered, shrinking down into the armchair she was sitting in.

Val's eyes opened and she let out a puff of hot air that Deya could feel from across the room. "This is pointless," Val muttered, rising from the floor and dusting herself off. "It's one thing to do this while we're here. It's another to do it out *there.*"

Deya watched her pace the room, her hands still toying with the petals of the flowers beside her.

"Do you think you'll be all right out there?" she asked hesitantly, her eyes following Val's troubled movement back and forth.

"Hard to say," she mumbled. "It should be enough if I don't break concentration." She sighed and stopped her pacing. Tilting her head backwards, she spoke to the ceiling. "Ember Magic is all about your emotions. Keeping things tempered and controlled. It's not something I've ever struggled with, but it's different to take this out in the field. Danger can wreak havoc on emotions."

The thought of her own dark power crept into her mind, and she felt her heart clench in her chest. The memory of how it felt after she had used it to destroy the magror, how out of control and panicked she was.

As if a black, shadowy hand had pressed down on her and held her by the throat. Echoes of the whispered voices that had flitted through the darkness filled her ears again and, with a hasty jerk of her head, she shook them from her thoughts.

"Are you sure you're okay to go out there?" Deya asked, determined not to let herself dwell on the fear still scratching at the back of her mind. "I don't mind going alone. I'd rather—"

But Val silenced her with a pointed look. "I'm not going to send you out there alone, Deya," she said resolutely. "It'll be enough. It *has* to be enough." And with that, she sat back down on the carpet, tucked her legs underneath her, closed her eyes, and drew in another deep breath.

Deya watched apprehensively before turning her attention back to the book in her lap.

Although she knew finding a Frost Magic wielder was their best option, Deya still had not asked the most obvious person. Caelum hadn't been back to Bridah since delivering her there several days ago, and although she still had not fully dismissed the idea of asking him, even with his temperamental handle of his Frost Magic, she couldn't help but worry he would not only refuse, but stop them from going entirely.

Deya's gloved hands wrung together in her lap, and she shifted in her seat again. Caelum did not want her risking her safety, even if it was the fate of the realm on the line. And besides, she had proven she could look out for herself now. Even without her magic.

Glancing up, she made sure Val's eyes were still closed before, slowly, she took off one glove. The blackness that had previously only reached her cuticles before her encounter with the magror now brushed the skin below her nails. Fear prickled in her chest as she rotated her hand, looking down. There was no question about it. The blackness had grown. And not only had it grown, but *something* had happened when she had used her magic. A stain that ran deeper than the one on her skin.

Absentmindedly, Deya reached out and touched the silken petals of the white flower again. And as if reacting to the panic building inside her, the petals instantly turned to ash. Deya yelped, jerking her hand away from the flower and scrambling backwards, fear pounding in her temples.

"*Deya,*" Val growled again and Deya jumped, hastily shoving her hand back into her glove.

"Sorry," she mumbled, and Val huffed and closed her eyes again.

But far from being able to relax back into the silence, Deya felt like she was curling into herself. She clenched her fist, her heart beating in her throat. And all the while, whispers echoed in her head before, with a deep breath, they faded away.

"Right." Val rose from the floor so suddenly that Deya nearly dropped the book she was holding. "A few more days of this and I should be okay. I say we leave as soon as possible."

Deya blinked up at her, her heart still fluttering in her chest, but she held her breath and swallowed the panic down. "Are you sure?"

Val let out a heavy sigh, before turning towards the fire. "No," she said. "But what choice do we have?"

And as the faintest trace of ash drifted past her in the cold air of the frosty room, Deya could not help but agree that they had very little choice indeed.

Caelum sat on the ledge of the astronomy tower—someplace that had become a frequent haunt of his—and tried to steady his breathing. In the quiet, isolated moments like this, he could feel his Celestial Magic thrumming all around him. It surrounded him. Suffocated him. *Weakened* him.

In the beginning, keeping the astronomy tower's upper floor elevated as Castor had done had seemed easy, but as time went by, and the demand for his portals, power, and patience grew, it became harder and harder to carry. Eventually, he was forced to task a small number of soldiers to assist him in holding the tower aloft—a small, revolving number of Gravity

Magic users. Although it had alleviated the burden slightly, the failure made his chest ache—right next to the painful throbbing in his abdomen that occurred every time he sent out more than one portal within a day.

Caelum's head dropped back against the stone wall as he struggled to breathe. Sometimes it felt too much. Too heavy. Drawing in a deep breath, he let out a slow exhalation, feeling the anger and frustration rush out of him. He had been locked in an argument with Helene for nearly an hour at that day's council meeting.

All he had wanted was a Legion outpost in Nodaria. Someplace he could've kept an eye on and protected from Praiton's advances. A place where excess crops and supplies could go towards aiding the Legion. But, according to Helene Sidra, this was the equivalent of raising the flag to war. The small female's eyes had practically bulged from their sockets when he had requested it, her face turning purple to match her irises.

After that, it turned into a shouting match between him and the Prime Minister. It had taken every ounce of control he had not to throttle her. But, thankfully, his father's ever-watchful eyes glared down at him from above the table and he had been able to reel it back.

And then Aris stepped in.

Caelum *hated* having to defer to the Pillar Legion's general. Aris had a way of finessing the council that neither Saros nor Caelum seemed to possess. It was a smarmy aplomb which never failed to make Caelum want to hit the pompous ass when he began his damage control. And yet, he was grateful for it.

But Aris was not a permanent solution to the Celestial Kingdom's discord. The general was never in one place for more than a couple of days, constantly having to cycle between the many outposts in the realm and Light's Tower. Caelum could not keep relying on him to put out his fires.

As the weeks went by, Caelum began to think more and more that he was not cut out to be a High King. He did not have the diplomacy, the refinement, nor the patience. And every day that he stared down his father's portrait in the council room, the more his own inadequacy weighed on him.

It felt like Nodaria was slipping through his fingers. And, at the same time, so was Deya.

All he wanted was to curl up next to her in bed. To breathe in that intoxicating, infuriating smell of roses and bergamot which acted like a sedative and an aphrodisiac all at once. She had insisted he wasn't allowed to touch her until he confessed his feelings for her, but he was hoping he could wear her down.

Because, the truth was, Caelum didn't *know* what his feelings were for her. He had never felt anything like what he felt when he was around Deya. Not when he was a young adolescent, fooling around with one of the star seers, nor in any of the other females he had ever encountered.

Deya was different. She was the brightest star in his sky. He could find her with his eyes closed, with a pull of a connection he could not explain. She was an irritating mystery he was too afraid to solve.

At that moment, a cloud shifted in the sky. Caelum started, his eyes darting up. But no . . . it had to have been a trick of his imagination. Clouds didn't move like that. The only time he had ever seen something like that was bathed in the light of a blood moon, high atop the battlements of Burningtide Sanctum, right before . . .

Caelum sat up a bit straighter, spinning his legs fully over the window's ledge. He had never tried this, yet knew how it must be done. Holding his breath, Caelum pushed off from the ledge. But instead of plummeting down to the ground, he rose up, up towards the roof of the suspended tower.

His feet met the smooth black stone of the tower's rounded roof, and for a second, he took in the Nodarian night sky, completely uninhibited by window, wall, or rock. And the sight he saw made his blood run cold.

A large black mass traveled through the sky high above. It was slithering like a large snake between the clouds, a scaly tail flicking to-and-fro. He had never seen a beast this big, this intimidating. Its girth took up miles of sky, its movements casting a dim shadow on the ground even though it was hundreds of feet above the clouds. Its immense wings beat, making the enormous body rise and fall.

Caelum knew what it was. And this time, unlike Burningtide, there was no question.

A dragon.

Molten hot panic gripped his throat, a fiery fist of terror that squeezed all the air from him.

A dragon was flying southeast.

Right towards Bridah.

Scrambling from the top of the roof, the only thought in Caelum's head was of Deya. If the dragon was heading towards Bridah, he had to get there, had to warn Ulf or Kindra, had to make sure Deya was okay—

Caelum leapt from the roof and, with a grunt, ripped open the air, before falling right into the open portal.

When he tumbled into Deya's bedroom, the wild adrenaline and fear still beating in him like an enormous drum, it was to find it empty. The bed was made—not even a wrinkle on the blue quilt—the fireplace quiet and cold. And the panic that set in was like an uncontrollable frost, spreading through his veins.

It was nighttime, the blanket of snow over Bridah giving the land outside her window a quiet, peaceful feeling. She *should* be here.

The panic roared harder inside him as he took in her empty room, the image of what could only be Titus's dragon flitting through his mind again. Wild dragons were never seen so far from Maniel. No, this was a problem. An urgent one.

"Deya?" he shouted.

He ripped open the door, preparing to go tearing through Fangdor like a fucking nightmare, when he nearly collided, headfirst, with her. Books went flying out of Deya's gloved hands, and the small "Oh!" of surprise that escaped her mouth made his heart skip a beat.

Roses and bergamot filled his lungs, and for the first time in several days, his body's desire to relax had the opposite effect. It pissed him off even more.

"What are you doing here?" Deya asked breathlessly, dropping to her hands and knees to begin scooping up the pile of books on the floor.

"Where the *hell* were you?" he demanded. Deya flinched, but he was too angry to care. The panic from seeing that creature fly over Nodaria was twisting around him like a lambent flame. A flame that wanted fuel. His breath was coming out in jagged gasps as he gripped her arms tightly, the panic becoming fury as if out of instinct.

They had sent her away, separated her from him to ensure her safety. Yet here she was, wandering the halls at night as if she did not care what he had given up to protect her.

"I was just . . ." Deya began, her face flushing, but Caelum's eyes narrowed. Stooping beside her, his fingers wrapped around the spine of an enormous book that had fallen, face first, its pages splayed open. *Maps of Bridah*. Panic beat like a drum in his ears as he rounded on her.

"What is this?" he demanded, shoving the silver-embossed cover towards her.

Deya turned pink. He could feel her blood rush up her chest and to her face, felt her heart quicken with guilt as if it were his own. The bizarre connection to her could be troubling at times, but at that moment he found it very useful. But her guilt melted into anger as she squared up to him, facing his wrath.

"I was just reading," she snapped but Caelum's eyes narrowed as her gaze darted away, as though she were too afraid to look at him.

"What are you planning?" Caelum hissed. All he could think about was that dragon, about leaving her here, alone, without any way to protect her himself. It was like a cart sliding downhill, the helpless feeling of losing control to his panic that so often turned into rage. "Why would you need to know about anything outside of Fangdor's walls?"

Deya, recoiled, fear flashing on her face. "What is *with* you? You're acting like—"

His nostrils flared and Deya flinched as if steam had issued from them.

"Like *what*, exactly?"

A ripple of a memory, the phrase triggering a sense that they had been here before. Yet Deya was not the same girl she had been, the night they washed up on the shores of Elbania for the first time. Caelum had watched her grow, become surer of herself. It had pleased him to see her come into her own, but now he regretted picking a fight with *this* version of her.

"A *prick*," she spat. Her eyes glinted, and it was obvious she knew as well as he did how much that word infuriated him coming from her.

For a second, all thoughts of dragons flew from his mind. This was not what he had wanted when he had come here. He had wanted to warn her, protect her, bury himself in her— forget about the council, forget himself and his failings. Forget the fury left boiling in his blood, a fury he had wrestled back all day.

But it was not in his nature to turn away from a fight. Even knowing a High King would.

The thought ignited another spark of anger inside him as Deya wrenched the book from his grasp.

Without thinking, he moved towards her so fast that she nearly tripped trying to scramble backwards. A squeak escaped her as he grabbed her chin, the books toppling from her arms onto the bed as she gazed up at him with wide, furious gray eyes.

"*Say that again*," he growled.

Deya looked up at him, the defiance burning in her gaze. Leaning closer—so close that her scent threatened to overwhelm him—she sneered. "*Prick.*"

The word rode a wave of hot air against his mouth, and he had to resist the urge to devour her whole.

"Tell me where you were," he demanded.

Deya glared at him. "And if I don't, *my lord?* What will my punishment be then?"

Caelum's grip tightened on her, and he saw the smallest flinch of pain in her eyes. "Keep it up and you'll find out," he snarled.

Reaching up, she smacked his hand away with a hiss. In that moment, they were right back to square one.

This was what he was designed to do. He was not meant to be a king, or a lover. He was meant to fight, to scream and rage, to tear things apart with his bare hands. This was all he was meant to be.

"Do *not* leave these walls, do you understand me? The threat to you outside is *real*. If you put yourself in danger, Deya, I *swear*—"

"As touching as your concern for me is, *my lord*, I can take care of myself. If you came here just to pick a fight with me, you can go," she snapped, her gray eyes glimmering with hurt. The sight of it pricked something in Caelum's cold heart, but he shoved it back.

"I am *here* to protect you. To make sure you are not putting yourself—and thus this *realm*—in even more jeopardy," he spat.

Deya recoiled from him, and he immediately felt a twinge of regret.

"Is that all you care about?" she asked, her voice soft, the hurt obvious now. "You protect me for Krigor, and nothing else?"

Caelum stared at her, breathing hard. For a second, he remembered the panic he had felt when he saw the dragon. How his first and only thought was Deya. He knew this was a test, knew what answer she wanted from him . . . knew he could not give it to her. In the end, it would just be another thing to fail.

"Yes."

For a moment, Deya stared at him. Then she blinked. Her gray eyes shone in the firelight, a reflection of the tears she held back, before her face set. Turning away from him, she stacked the books she had dropped in a neat pile on her bedside table.

Her spine was rigid, shoulders stiff, and Caelum stood there and felt the wall come up around her. The wall he had slowly broken through, the wall that used to wrap around him, too. Now shutting him out.

"Fine." The word was so cold and sharp, it could have cut glass. "In that case, *my lord*, Kindra asked for me to relay a message to you," she said.

Caelum closed his eyes. "Stop that."

"Stop what, my lord?"

"*Calling me that.*" He couldn't bear that title coming from her. She had been the only one who hadn't referred to him as a High King. To her, he had remained Caelum.

"She insists on training you on how to use your Frost Magic, my lord," she continued, sitting on the bed, staring down at her gloved hand as if examining her fingernails.

Caelum stared at her, his chest still rising and falling with anger and regret, her words rushing over him. *This* was the damned icing on the cake.

His training with Saros had been relentless, demeaning, and embarrassing. Although the captain did not have the raw power he did, his battle skills were annoyingly exceptional. And he made it known.

Caelum had spent so much time eating dirt during training that it had not done much for his temper. And now another estranged family member was telling him he needed to be trained like a damned child?

"Absolutely fucking not."

Deya shrugged coolly, still not looking at him. "Kindra insisted."

"I have no interest in being 'trained' by anyone else."

She fixed him with a steely gaze, and he felt his face flush. "You can barely control your Frost Magic," she said, her tone biting. "Mastering this would mean strengthening Nodaria, and thus the *realm*. Obviously, that is of the utmost importance to you."

Grinding his teeth, he stared at the Praitonian girl before him, her shoulders back, her face smooth and impassive. Yet he knew her better than anyone. He could see, as clearly as the moon in the Nodarian night sky, that he had broken her heart. Again.

Caelum paced away from her, allowing himself a moment to glance out her window. There was not a shadow in the sky. No hint of a wing or a tail. He was stupid to rush here. Stupid to think that Bridah's walls would not hold after all this time. And if the book in Deya's hands was any indication, she had not a single thought for her own safety in her head. Telling her about the dragon would be foolish. The silly girl would just do something to put herself in more danger if she knew.

"Fine," he snarled finally. "Tell Kindra I will be back to speak to her in the morning."

Deya nodded and turned her back to him again. Caelum stood there, staring at her, and for a rare moment, his heart hurt. The hopeless frustration he had felt about everything in his life lately swirled around him.

Nodaria, the Celestial Throne, his parents . . . None of these things were meant for him.

And as he pulled open a portal with labored effort and looked back at Deya to see she hadn't so much as turned around, he began to feel that maybe she was not meant for him either.

When he hurtled through the portal back in Nodaria, he hit the black marble floor with a bone-aching crash. For a minute, he lay there, panting, his whole body aching. Stars which had nothing to do with Atlas Keep's ceiling and floor danced in his vision, and for a moment he felt like heaving. These damned portals were killing him.

Slowly, gasping for breath, he pulled himself up off the floor and leaned against the wall. This had never happened to his father. In all his life, Caelum had never seen Castor weakened, even once, no matter how many portals he threw into the air.

But here he was, dizzy and dying after only two.

Fury at his own weakness boiling in his blood, Caelum opened his eyes. His vision still white, he resisted the urge to steady himself against the wall, and spitefully straightened up. Then with a furious grunt, he pushed off down the halls of the Keep, the image of Deya's hurt expression flashing through the dizziness. Fighting with Deya wasn't what he had wanted, but he had done what he intended. He had made sure she was safe. But as for Bridah . . .

Caelum walked quickly down the halls, starlight whirring in his vision. He made a beeline right for the door of Castor's study, where he knew he'd find what he was looking for.

Aris stood in front of the fire, leaning across the table over a large map that was spread out in front of him; obvious markings of fallen outposts littered the parchment. His tired eyes looked up at Caelum, who was still panting, reeling from everything he had just experienced in the last hour. The looming shadow of the dragon, the fight with Deya, fear of Bridah falling, it all swirled around him.

And when the general straightened up to look at him, his mouth opening in question, Caelum could only muster a single sentence.

"We have a problem."

CHAPTER 7

Their plans were set. Deya and Val had agreed they could only spare a few more days for Val's training before they had to make a move. With the aid of the atlases in the library, they plotted a meticulous path to Frode's cave, finding small pockets of cover to take shelter in on the way.

Even with all their preparations, Deya couldn't help but feel a strong sense of foreboding. Venturing out without a Frost Magic wielder was damn near suicide. She knew this. But they had no other choice.

Caelum had been there several times over the last few days to train with Kindra, and each time he brought back news of another attack . . . another ambush of their supply caravan towards Elbania. But besides his clipped debriefs, he avoided Deya altogether.

The memory of their fight in her bedroom still sent a stab of pain and fury through her heart each time she thought of it. Caelum was always insolent and stubborn, but it had been a long time since he had been cruel.

She knew something must have happened in the Celestial Kingdom's council meeting that day to put him in such a terrible mood, but she had not gotten the chance to ask.

And now she wondered if she would die out in the tundra of Bridah without ever getting to know if he truly meant what he'd said.

Deya tightened the straps on the burlap sack she had stolen from Bridah's armory. It was stuffed full of supplies—food, blankets, kindling, firewood, and weapons overflowed from the mouth of the bag. She shoved her fist in, punching it down so she could snap it shut.

"We are completely insane for doing this, you know that, right?" Val hissed. The Manielian female was bundled in so many layers Deya could barely distinguish her face from all the furs and wool. A thick, roughspun hat was on her head, as well as gloves and a scarf wrapped so tightly around her neck that she resembled a snowman.

She looked almost comical, and Deya fought the insane urge to laugh. She knew none of this was funny and that Val was right. They *were* completely insane for doing this.

"You know we have no other choice," Deya whispered.

It was just before daybreak and Fangdor was still and quiet. Karyna was due to wake her in several hours. When the lady's maid realized she was gone, Deya knew she would sound the alarm. They didn't have much time.

"You didn't ask Caelum?" Val asked, her golden hands twining a clump of firewood to her own satchel. "Surely going with him is better than nothing?"

Deya felt the familiar pang in her heart and shook her head. "No," she murmured. "No, I didn't."

Even if she had begun to consider it before his last visit, it was entirely out of the question now. She could not depend on Caelum. That was obvious now.

They finished strapping the supplies to their backs. Deya's spine felt like it was liable to snap like a twig under the weight of all their provisions.

"Ready?" Deya asked.

Val faced the door and drew in a deep, steadying breath. Her eyes seemed to blaze with heat, and in that moment, Deya could see the shadow of the captain she sometimes forgot Val was. Even in all the layers, the Manielian female looked intimidating and determined under the dim light of Fangdor's flickering lanterns, gripping the bronze hilts of her dual swords. She let out a breath and Deya felt the tell-tale release of heat as Val focused. Then she nodded.

They looked at each other, and in that moment, a million things passed between them. Worry, fear, panic . . . trust. She knew she was safe with Val. Deya trusted her with her life.

They crept through Fangdor's quiet wooden halls. Their feet barely made a noise on the icy glass floor as they tiptoed towards the entrance of the frozen fortress.

Pausing in front of the heavy wooden door, they looked up at it, having to practically bend backwards to take it all in. It was adorned with snowflake carvings, intricate knots, crisscrossing patterns, and sharp Brynorsk letters. The door towered over their heads, reaching towards the vaulted wooden ceiling.

Val glanced over at her; her amber eyes illuminated by the lanterns in the hall. She nodded. And then they pushed open the door.

Nothing prepared them for the gust of powerful, icy wind that nearly knocked them flat on their backs. The gale burned Deya's eyes as she threw up her arm to shield her face.

"Holy Mother Goddess of Calida," Val moaned, wrenching her scarf up almost to her eyes.

Deya quickly followed suit, tugging her balaclava up over her nose, which had turned red and numb within seconds.

Their first glimpse into Bridah was nothing but a swirl of blistering wind and snow. For miles and miles, Deya could only see white, except for the blurs of wooden huts in the distance towards Frostheim, Bridah's capital city. There was no sun in the sky, not even a hint of its warm beams could be seen stretching above the white horizon. No reprieve.

"We have to head towards the northeast!" Val had to shout at Deya just to be heard over the roaring wind. "We have to get out of view of Fangdor before daylight."

Deya gave a jerky nod, and together, they sank their feet into the thick snow.

The trek out of Fangdor's grounds was made easier only by the fact the castle's servants shoveled the walkways clear of snow every day. The ground was harder and steadier under their boots as they slipped and staggered north towards the range of the Verja Fjords. But as they headed further from the castle's walls, the paths stopped, the neatly dug snow devolving into an impenetrable wall of frost.

They skittered to a halt, taking in the expanse of fresh, untouched snow. In the beginning of an early morning glow, Deya almost wanted to say it looked magical. Miles and miles of powder sparkled before them, a sheet of diamonds and white silk. But Deya saw what it really meant: no cover, nowhere to stop for Gods knew how long, and an endless, painful, frozen slog through a foot of slush.

"Great," Val spat, rubbing her gloved hands together furiously, a great exhalation of heat escaping her with each word. "The only bright side is that maybe we'll be too frozen for the ice hounds to sink their teeth into us."

Deya's teeth were chattering, her fingers long since numb as she clutched them to her chest. Beside her, Val breathed gusts of hot air into her hands, sending steam billowing out around them.

"If we hug the Verja Fjords," Deya said through the thick scarf over her mouth, "we may be able to find a little bit of shelter from the wind."

"It'll take too long to reach the Fjords to follow them," Val said. "The only chance we have is to go straight through and pray we find someplace to warm up."

Deya knew she was right. Bridah's border was surrounded by the Verja Fjords—a natural, impenetrable barrier from the rest of the world. Now, coincidentally, it might be their only hope for survival.

The first few miles were difficult. The snow was softer here, much more akin to trekking through cold, wet sand. It nearly reached Deya's bottom as she and Val dragged their feet, leaving long trails in their wake.

"Aren't you worried we'll be followed?" Val asked, glancing back after about an hour of concentrated silence.

Deya looked back to see two, deep grooves trailing behind them, all the way back towards Fangdor's walls. It was obvious, and a little frightening to think of being followed.

Fangdor and its inhabitants must be awake by now. Karyna could have already alerted Kindra, or even Ulf, to their disappearance. As large as Ulf was, Deya found herself more afraid of Kindra coming after them. The Frost Princess had already told them not to pursue Frode on their own, and Kindra did not look like she was one to be disobeyed.

"We'll just have to go faster," Deya insisted, determinedly dragging her legs a few more paces through the wall of snow. "Can't you melt the snow ahead of us to make this a bit easier?"

"Do you really think I can melt anything right now?" Val retorted, her teeth chattering behind the scarf. "It's all I can do to keep my heat contained. My internal flame is so cold I can barely feel it. We need heat and light for our magic. This place . . . well, this place is just about my worst fucking nightmare."

Deya fought back the rapidly spreading panic in her chest. If Val was unable to contain her heat, they might not stand a chance. Manielians thrived in warmth and light, some legends even saying their blood was thinned by the Mother in order to accommodate their own natural heat. Secretly, she had hoped Val would be a better source of warmth in the insurmountable frost with all the excess preparation she had done, but Deya did not foresee her own ignorance of Ember Magic. In hindsight, it was stupid of her not to realize it.

Miles of snow, untouched by any signs of life stretched before them, and still, Deya and Val trekked on. Breath misting, bodies numb, all Deya could hear was the slow, deep breathing of her friend as they struggled to keep putting one foot in front of the other.

Then, suddenly, Val stopped. She looked around warily, over the white haze of snow and frost that surrounded them. Only the absence of her even breaths alerted Deya.

"Val?"

Val did not respond. Her amber eyes were fixed on the horizon, her mouth opening, as if in question. "I thought I just saw . . ." She trailed off and her brow furrowed before she shook her head, as if to swat away the thought. "Never mind. Let's just keep moving."

Deya was too cold to ask what Val thought she saw. Yet, Val's eyes continued to scan the horizon, and the sound of her steady breaths did not return.

They stumbled on, snow and wind ambushing them on each side. Deya was so frozen she could barely feel her face, could hardly keep her eyes open against the horrific, skin-flaying chill as they plodded along through the thick snow. From the corner of her eye, Deya saw Val stumble and she reached out and seized her hand without thinking, steadying her. It was a mark of how desperate they were getting with each frozen mile that they did not let go.

They passed nothing until, through the blistering wind and furious flurry, Deya saw a glint of light.

"What is that?" she asked. Her lips were dry even underneath the fabric of her balaclava, and she was numb all the way to the bone. But as they neared the ball of flickering light, she felt a surge of hope . . . which was dashed as they got nearer.

A lone wooden post stood sentry in the middle of the white abyss, a flickering lantern swinging in the gale. Two signs hung from it, each pointing in opposite directions . . . and each entirely written in Brynorsk.

Deya swore. "Brilliant," she spat, whirling around in a circle, attempting to dig out the compass she had stashed in her pocket. "Now we don't even know where we're going! That could very well read 'danger, turn back now,' while we walk right into it and—Val?"

Deya stopped short, turning as she felt her friend's hand slip from hers. And then Val crumpled to the frosty ground.

"Val!" Deya threw herself down next to her, frantically trying to clear the layer of snow that had already descended on her. "Val! Val, wake up! Are you okay?" But Val did not move.

Deya's gloved hands scrambled for the scarf around Val's face and pulled it down, attempting to check to see if she was still breathing. But when she tore back the thick wool, it was to find Val's golden skin was almost blue.

"Shit," she breathed. She *knew* she should've stopped, should've checked in on Val the second she had paused nearly an hour ago. Whatever she had seen—or thought she'd seen—had distracted her enough to lose focus. She had let go of her heat, and now she was barely breathing.

Hands shaking with panic and cold, Deya lifted one of Val's eyelids, assessing the pupils. They were dilated. A weak pulse fluttered in Val's neck against her fingertips. Many years of healing experience told her that Val would not survive out here much longer.

"*Shit!*" Deya hissed again, her arms cradling her friend, rubbing her up and down, hoping to generate some heat. "*Shit, shit, shit!* Val, c'mon. You can't do this now! I need you!" Her voice cracked, and she felt the stab in her chest like an ice pick.

How was she supposed to carry Val to shelter? They were in the middle of nowhere, and it had taken every ounce of strength to make it this far. Val was too heavy to carry, and even if she tried, it would be slow. Would she make it in time, or would Val be dead before she even reached the fjords?

Molten panic was pounding in her chest, but she knew now was not the time for hesitation. Standing, she took a deep breath.

Seizing Val under the arms, she pulled her against her chest. She couldn't sling her across her back with the number of supplies already bound to it, so she was forced to drag Val backwards, attempting to finagle the compass out of her pocket to check the direction she was going.

Deya pulled Val as fast as she could through the thick snow, all the while praying to the Mother that her friend's heart would not stop beating.

Her Healing Magic was not what it used to be. It felt like an old friend which had changed with time and distance. She could still feel it inside her chest, but she did not know how it would act if she tried to call upon it. It was so closely threaded through the death and decay that wrapped around her core—she did not dare try to extract it. Which meant her only option was to keep Val alive at all costs.

Deya pulled Val with all her might, slipping and stumbling as she dragged her backwards through the thick snow. Finally, a looming shadow fell over her and Deya almost cried with relief. The Verja Fjords were as large and imposing as ever. Reaching so high that she could not even see the tops of them, the rocky ice walls disappeared from sight into the gush of sleet and snow. The wind immediately began to lessen the closer she got to their walls.

Deya stumbled against the ice wall, running her fingers desperately against the slippery surface, looking for a crevice big enough to fit inside. Her heart was pounding, her head spinning, and it was almost as if she could hear the tick of a clock mingling with her friend's faint heartbeat as she kicked and pounded on the thick ice.

"*Please*," Deya moaned, tears beginning to sting her eyes when, finally, her foot plunged through a sheet of ice in a shower of shards.

It took several good kicks for the ice to crack enough for Deya to force her way inside with Val and collapse onto the ground. Her whole body screamed in pain and exhaustion, her breath scraping against her chest like jagged talons.

The roaring wind from outside ceased the minute they entered the cave and Deya was allowed only a second to rest before scrambling to build a fire.

Val had stopped shivering almost half an hour ago—a sign that was beginning to make Deya sweat, despite the brutal cold. Val was still, her skin deathly blue, and barely a whisper of a pulse beat in her neck.

Deya's gloved hands shook with frigid exhaustion as she ripped kindling from their bags and struggled with the flint and rock to strike a spark. She had packed it merely as an afterthought, taking for granted the fact that Val was with her.

But she'd never anticipated this.

The rock struck the flint over and over, the pathetic spark flickering before petering out.

"Come on!" Deya practically screamed before, finally, a spark caught the kindling, and a small flame burst forth. Scrambling onto her knees, she blew on it gently, coaxing it to life, crying with relief when it began to engulf the rest of the branches.

She grabbed Val's cold, limp arm and dragged her closer to the fire as it began to grow. Lying on the ground beside her, Deya wrapped her whole body around her friend and prayed for her to live.

The fire began to slowly warm the cave, and soon even Deya's own shivering abated. Tightening her grip on Val, Deya tried to infuse as much of her own heat into her as she could. And then, she waited.

Smoke filled the cave, undulating into the air, making the icicles hanging above them glisten with condensation. The wind howled outside the cave, a reminder of the bitter conditions they had barely escaped.

Why had she not stopped to remind Val to concentrate on her magic? Why had she not listened to Kindra? Why had she been too prideful to even tell Caelum? The thought of him sent a cold stab to her heart. To think they had spent their last night shouting at each other.

Deya closed her eyes and tried not to think about the last time she had been in a cave. How, instead of being curled around Val, she had been wrapped around Caelum for the first time. And how, during that night, hope had blossomed that things would be different between them. Would be . . . right.

Suddenly, Val's body gave a violent shiver and a faint, rasping breath racked her body.

"Val!" Deya clambered over her friend, still holding tightly to her heavily layered frame. "Val! Are you okay?"

Val's amber eyes flickered. She drew in a shaky breath through blue-gray lips, her mouth opening and closing mutely.

"Where . . ." she breathed, but Deya hushed her, placing her gloved hands on her face, attempting to warm it.

"We're safe for now," she assured her, a laugh exploding out of her that almost quickly turned into a sob. "Just rest and get warm. It'll be okay, Val. It'll be okay."

Val shook violently as she looked up at Deya. "I . . . I lost concentration. I'm sorry . . . I thought I saw . . ."

"Shh," Deya said softly, rubbing her hands up and down her friend's arms. "Never mind that now. You're okay. You're okay."

Val's body continued to shake in Deya's arms, but still, she held fast. Eventually, the shivers subsided long enough for Val to reach out a hand. Stripping off a glove, she reached dangerously close towards the fire. Her fingers curled around the flames like a swaying snake, before suddenly, she thrust her hand completely into the fire.

And just like that, Deya felt her body still.

Val ripped the other glove from her hand and Deya watched, mesmerized, as she shoved both of her arms into the flames up to her elbows and let out a long, shaky sigh.

"Better?" Deya asked.

Val nodded. "Thank you," she whispered. "I don't know how you did it . . . but I know it must have been difficult to get me here." Twisting to look at her over her shoulder, Val gave her a grateful smile. "You saved me."

Deya smiled back and tightened her grip on her friend. "Did you doubt that I would?"

"No, but I won't lie and say that I didn't doubt that you *could*," she said smirking.

Laughing, Deya slumped against Val, the strength draining from her all at once. "Trust me, I didn't think I could either," she said. "But I couldn't let you die. I wouldn't." Val gave a weak chuckle and Deya shifted over her, looking down at her friend with a soft worry. "Val . . . you knew coming out here with me would kill you, even with training to contain your magic, didn't you?"

Val didn't speak. Her eyes remained fixed on the fire, her breathing still shaky and ragged. Then, finally, she breathed, "Yes."

Deya sat up on her elbows, still staring down at the angular silhouette of her friend, the tiny whisper of the word making her heart ache.

"But . . . *why?*" she whispered. "Why come out here with me? Why not say anything? Why risk—"

"Because you're my friend," Val said, and suddenly, her voice was stronger. Louder. Her fingers clenched over the flames as she shook her head. "You're my friend, and we needed to do this. I wouldn't let you come out here alone. I couldn't. Never."

A small lump rose up Deya's throat and she felt herself choke on it. Back in Praiton, she had always secretly wished for a loyal friend. Someone to rely on and trust with something as sacred as her own life. The years of disappointment that her time in Stonehall Castle had given her had made her feel like she would never be fortunate enough to find that. Someone who could be called a real friend, that she could believe in. And while so much had changed since then—while she now was able to call four people true friends—looking at Val now, she felt a wave of emotion.

Val, who had not only saved her from the pits at Ironbalt, but also trekked through an inevitable cold death for her . . . Words failed her at the overwhelming surge of gratitude and love she felt for her friend.

She didn't say anything. She couldn't. Instead, she wrapped her arms around her friend's shoulders again and squeezed her, hard.

Val turned to look back at her, a ghost of a smile on her face. Although the color was starting to come back to her cheeks, there was still a faint blue tinge frosting her features. Her nose was red, and weather-beaten, her eyebrows and hair damp with melted frost. But, at that moment, Deya did not take for granted that she was alive.

They lapsed into silence, Val still elbow-deep in the fire with Deya wrapped around her, listening to the gentle cracks and pops of the wood. She couldn't help but notice Val flinch with every flicker of the flames until she eventually closed her eyes altogether. After what Val had just said, Deya found she could no longer continue to pretend to not notice.

"Val?"

Val hummed in acknowledgement; her amber eyes now shut tight. Sitting up on her elbows, Deya peered down at her friend again, her brow knitting with worry. It wasn't too long ago that Deya herself had flinched at the sound of wood cracking. But to see Val—who was often never seen without her flaming swords—flinch at the very sight of it unnerved her.

"What's been going on with you?" she asked softly. "Truly?"

Val didn't respond, but her amber eyes opened as she shifted against her.

"It's nothing."

"Val," Deya implored. She dropped her arms from around her, sitting up to look down at Val fully. "You and I both know that's not true."

Val scoffed, her fingers tightening within the orange flames. "Honestly," she muttered. "You sound like Aris."

"Aris?" Deya asked. "What does Aris have to do with it? Wait . . . did he *do* something? Did something happen—"

Then, to Deya's alarm, Val laughed. The sound echoed off the icy walls, but the laugh was cracked . . . sad.

"No, Aris did not do anything," Val said, her laughter melting into a forlorn smile. "But sometimes you do remind me a lot of Katia."

"Katia?" she asked softly, the name tickling a memory in the back of her mind. "Wasn't that . . . ?"

Val's back was still turned to her, but Deya could see the glimmer of her eyes in the firelight. Moisture flickered in them, and a small tear ran down her nose. And then it hit her.

"Oh . . . *oh*, Val, is that what this is about?" she whispered, her hand coming to rest on Val's back. "Is it about your friends?"

Val stiffened at Deya's touch but did not shake her off. And as Deya's fingers rested on her spine, even over the layers of clothing, she could feel Val's shoulders shake.

After a heavy pause, Val whispered, "I suppose it took it awhile for it to hit me. That I'm never going to see them again." She sniffed and Deya's hand tightened on her clothing, her chest aching. "And it's all my fault, Deya . . . If I had been stronger. If I had just fought back harder when I was captured . . . But instead, I let them take me. And they had to watch me go."

A fist tightened around Deya's heart as her eyes burned with tears for Val. She had never heard Val speak of the day she was captured, but she had always wondered how someone so capable and powerful had been taken in the first place.

"What . . . what happened the day you were captured?"

Val jerked her head, the tears flowing freely down her face now. "It was . . . Gods it was so awful." She drew in a deep breath that trembled with her tears. "The Legion had gone to the border of Maniel on a surveyor mission. And we were ambushed by the Blood Riders."

Deya blinked. "Blood Riders?"

Shaking her head, Val bit her lip. "They're an elite unit . . . My brothers' unit."

Deya felt her body rise from the cave floor as she stared down at Val, her mouth opening in shock. "Your . . . *brothers*—"

"Yes, my damned brothers," Val said, sitting up, too, her hands still gripping the flames. "They were the ones who captured me. After they beat me nearly to death and banished me from Maniel and I joined the Legion, they decided they made a mistake by not killing me. And that day, they decided to make it right."

Deya stared at her, watching as her hands strangled the embers, as if trying to choke all life from them. Her tears were frozen against her golden face, and Deya felt her own cheeks burn from the wet tracks of her own.

"Your own *brothers* threw you in Ironbalt?"

Shaking her head, Val's fingers clenched into fists, making sparks shoot from the small pile of wood at her feet. "They did so much worse," she whispered, her amber eyes roaring with flames and fury. She drew in a breath that trembled, and when she spoke again, her voice shook. "They murdered my sisters."

All the air seemed to leave the cave at those words, the spark and crackle of the fire and the howling wind, the only indication that the world hadn't stilled. Deya stared, horrified at Val.

"H-how . . . how can you be sure?" she breathed.

"You heard what Aris said the night we arrived at Light's Tower," Val snarled. "*There was enough of them left to bury.*"

Deya swallowed through the lump in her throat, forcing out the horrific image the words brought to mind.

"That was my brother Leo's doing, I am sure of it," Val said through gritted teeth. "He's the only one sick enough. My eldest brother wouldn't let him cut *me* to bits, so he settled for them. The three people I cared most about in the world, and he tore them apart."

Her voice broke on the last word, burying her fist in her mouth. She sat on the cave floor, panting, steam beginning to billow from her skin. The walls of the cave glistened with moisture as the temperature increased rapidly, as if Val were about to burst into flames herself. Deya even felt a little bit of sweat begin to line the collar of all her woolen layers.

"When I was faced with them, I froze." Val spoke to the fire, her gaze far away, as if she were reliving that moment. "My brothers always thought me to be weak, and after everything I had done, every accomplishment I achieved . . . It all meant nothing when I faced them again." Reaching up, she swiped angrily at another tear rolling down her cheek. "I bowed to them again, and because of me, my sisters are dead. And now my magic is—"

Deya did not know what to say. She sat beside Val, both of them staring into the fire, lost in their own thoughts. She knew what it was like to blame yourself for the death of a friend. To think over and over about how, if she had only done something differently, that person may still be there.

An image of Oswallt floated into her mind. She could still see him as clear as day, laughing in his prison clothes, puffing out his cheeks and imitating Clarita Killoran's walk in the cell beside her. She could still hear his laugh, that rasping giggle that made her heart clench with pain.

Val angrily swiped at the tears on her face and shook her head. "Every day is just a hole. A hole that I'm falling down. I cannot see the end of it, and there is no light," she whispered. She shook her head, and a tear slipped down the bridge of her nose. "I'm sorry, I can't . . . I can't think about it . . . Let's not talk about it anymore."

Deya blinked as she watched her friend straighten her spine and raise her chin. Shining streaks of tears still ran down her face, but Deya watched Val harden herself, as if shutting out the memories, the thoughts . . . the pain. She knew that everyone dealt with grief differently—something she had been exposed to over and over both as a healer and as a survivor of war and death. She knew Val was strong—both mentally and physically. But watching her now, her amber eyes empty and resolute, Deya worried if Val was perhaps too strong for her own good.

"My mother used to have a saying," Deya said quietly, "that as children of Mav, we are equally close to life as we are death. That, even when we die, the next life is only around the corner."

Val looked at her, her amber eyes red.

"She used to tell me that when I'd ask about my father," Deya continued, her finger tracing a line in the snow. "She'd say life can take many forms, even in death, and that the ones we love will find their way back to us . . . even if it's not in the way we expect."

For a second, Val just stared at her, before turning to wipe away another tear. Then, she scooted closer to Deya and leaned her head on her shoulder.

"Thank you," she whispered to the flames.

Deya smiled and wrapped her arm around her friend. Together they sat by the crackling fire, and this time, Val did not flinch.

CHAPTER 8

When Caelum arrived in Fangdor Castle that afternoon, it was with the intention of going over training with Kindra again.

Training with the Frost Princess had been grueling and embarrassing—worse than what he endured back in Nodaria with Saros. Kindra was headstrong and powerful, and she did not have the patience for Caelum's lack of control. Frost Magic, he quickly found out, was much different from Celestial Magic. For one, it was solely linked to his emotions, which had been walking a razor-thin edge even more lately with his dealings with the Nodarian Council. And because of this, he could barely contain the powerful Frost Magic that threatened to burst from him with every surge of rage.

It had only been a few sessions, but it felt like he had now spent more than half of them frozen in a pile of snow, steaming with anger as Kindra smirked down at him and instructed him to try again. He now dreaded the very sight of Fangdor every time he threw himself through the portal into the center of it.

But, this time, when Caelum hurtled into the halls of Fangdor Castle's main hall, it was to find the entire place in an uproar. Servants and soldiers rushed past him, a few even knocking into his shoulders. He had refused to portal into Deya's room for the last few days when he had come for Kindra's training sessions. It had been hard to even look her in the eyes the few times he had caught glimpses of her.

But the minute he stumbled into the hall, a flush of panic overwhelmed him, just like it had the last night he had shown up in her room. Even though he and Aris had met with Kindra and Ulf immediately after the dragon sighting and been assured the Frost Kingdom was on high alert, fear still rippled through him. Had the dragon breached the walls after all? Had the attack started? Was he too late? But he listened for the sounds of battle and heard none—no swords clanging, no sounds of magic and fire, no roar of a dragon.

Caelum's feet began to move over the icy floors as he made to follow the wave of panicked servants that was coursing around him.

"*Kindra!*" He heard himself shout, but his own voice felt far away in his ears. Servants whirled around to look at him as he pushed past them, their eyes wide as he kept bellowing his aunt's name.

His heart was pounding a violent tattoo in his chest, his mind spinning, his magic pulsing like an artery. And all the while, he searched inside himself, digging through his own fear and dazed panic to find the thread that seemed to tie him to Deya—the thread that let him *feel* her, even when he could not see her.

But all he felt was cold.

What had happened to her? Where *was* she? Where was Val? The only reason he had felt comfortable leaving her at all was because he had left that blasted harpy to protect her. Had they both left? Had they been attacked? Was Bridah compromised? Had—

"*Lostjarna!*" The booming voice shook the rafters, causing snow to break free from the wooden walls and drift down onto Caelum. He whirled around.

Ulf strode through the hall towards him, the ever-present winter wind that seemed to follow the High King everywhere he went blowing banners and people alike from his path.

"Ulf!" Caelum cried, half-running towards the enormous male. "What's going on? Has something happened? Where—"

But Ulf held up a large hand to silence him, shaking his head. "Please, *Lostjarna,* be calm first. Steady yourself."

It took one look at Ulf for Caelum to know it wasn't a Manielian attack. In that moment, he knew, as surely as he knew the sun rose in the east, and the moon pulled the tides, that something was wrong. And it had to do with Deya.

Caelum's magic was churning within him like a boiling ocean, and he wondered how Ulf could see it. It wasn't until he caught sight of himself in a shiny Bridanian shield behind the High King that he saw his eyes glowing a violent indigo. A sure sign that he was just as unbalanced as he felt.

Taking a deep breath that did nothing to steady his nerves, he grit out the only thing he wanted to know. *"Where is she?"*

Ulf's blue eyes shone with power as he looked down on him, the calm twinkle gone from them. "We do not know," he said in his thick, melodic accent. "But we will find her."

Ulf's words shattered all his remaining calm, sending a fresh ripple of panic and fury through him. Before he could stop it, a blast of frost erupted from him, blowing the High King's blue robes back. Servants shrieked and dove for cover as the furious winter wind surging from him ripped shields and banners from the walls, sent snow cascading from where it had been resting in the rafters.

Kindra came careening into view at the disturbance.

"Caelum, be calm!" she shouted, but Caelum could not hear her over the roaring of his own magic. All he could think of was that Deya was gone. And they did not know where she was.

Ulf and Kindra were both speaking to him, but no words could penetrate his reeling mind. Then, through the fog in his brain, an image floated to the forefront. A thick, gray book with a silver cover. The words shining at him as he bent to pick it up and shove it in Deya's face. *Maps of Bridah*.

Caelum let out a furious snarl, which caused Kindra to take a step back from him. Then, without another word to either of his kin, he whirled around and made towards the heavy front door. With a growl of fury, his Celestial Magic blew the wooden door practically off its hinges, before he strode over the threshold and out into the blistering Bridanian tundra.

Even though Val still felt frozen on the inside, the time spent with Deya in the cave had revitalized her inner flame. It now felt stronger than it had when they had left that morning, though she could not say why. She supposed crying on her friend's shoulder must have helped a bit, too. Flushing at the thought, Val glanced over at Deya, who was busying herself with repacking their supplies.

It hadn't been the first time she had admitted to Deya the sadness in her heart that she tried so hard to ignore. But it had been the first time she had allowed it to crack through with tears. Embarrassment over being so weepy had begun to set in as they prepared to exit the warmth of the cave, but Deya hadn't seemed to mind. And she was grateful for that. To think, it was all because she had thought she'd seen—

Val shook the thought from her mind, anger at herself washing over. *No*. To entertain as ridiculous of a notion as that was stupid. It happened so suddenly. Just a streak of red through the blur of white snow. So quickly, she could've imagined it.

She *did* imagine it. What she thought she saw was impossible. End of story.

"Hold on," Val said, holding a hand out to stop Deya from stamping out the small fire. Deya paused and watched as Val crouched to the ground and began to dig at the icy floor, fingers scraping up layers of ice and snow until she felt rock. "Aha!" she exclaimed, extracting a handful of large, layered rocks that were buried deep underneath the snow and dirt.

"What are those for?" Deya asked, watching with a bemused expression as Val took them and tossed them right into the fire.

"Heat," Val said simply. After several minutes, the stones were removed from the flames, and Val dumped them into Deya's hands. She yelped in pain.

"Gods, Val!" she shrieked, dancing the stone back and forth between her gloved hands. "I'm not a Manielian, remember? I can't hold—*ow*! Ow!"

"Sorry," Val said, laughing, gripping her own stones in her hands, and feeling the molten warmth spread through the leather of her gloves. "But hold onto those, even if they burn. Because they won't in a second. And you'll be glad you have them."

There was nothing in the world that Val wanted less than to step back outside of that cave. But this time, when they did, they each had half a dozen burning stones shoved into every tiny crevice of clothing they could find and a reinforced hold on her breathing. And after leaving her confession of sorrow in the cave, smoldering like the embers of the fire they left behind, Val found she felt strong enough to make it to Frode.

It was nearly dark now, but the sky had not fallen into shadow. Brilliant blues and greens lit up the horizon, a banner of watercolor lights and sparkling ripples of neon yellows and purples. Dazzled by the sight, Val felt herself stop in her tracks, the wind ambushing her like a cold punch as she let out a hot breath, but she stood and stared up at the sky, her mouth sagging open.

She was faintly aware of Deya standing next to her, pulling back the fur-lined hood of her cloak to stare upwards, too.

"The Verja Auroras," Deya breathed.

They had spent days reading about Bridah—its geography and its mysteries opened to them within Fangdor's library. The Verja Auroras were said to be Flykra appearing in the sky every night. Val had originally thought this was ludicrous—a silly Bridanian folktale, perhaps—but in Val's many decades of life, she had never seen anything as breathtaking as this. So breathtaking that she could almost believe the Frost Goddess herself was coming out to greet them.

"Come on," Deya whispered, shouldering her pack, and pulling her hood and scarf back over her face. "While the stones are still warm."

That would buy them about twenty minutes at this rate. With the winter sun gone, the cold was even more intense, the wind a howl of fury. Already, Val's internal flame was flickering lower and lower as she and Deya slogged onwards, back on their pre-plotted track they had lost when Val had collapsed. The thought of how close she had come to death sent a shiver down her spine. And as they moved on, Val could not help but still scan the snowy horizon, looking for something she knew could not be there.

But, finally, through the bluster and wind, a stone structure loomed into view. Val knew what it was, but it still didn't stop her from ogling the massive pillars. Standing like lone sentries in the tundra, carved stones stood tall, lined in a circle, all sporting carvings of Flykra.

Bridah's sacred prayer circle, Flykige was even taller than the books made it seem. It seemed to glow in the light of the auroras in the sky, and when Val and Deya stepped into the circle, the wind and snow stopped. It was as if someone had dropped a glass right over them; the roar of the wind, the flurry of snow, it all stopped so abruptly that the silence felt louder than the elements did.

They glanced at each other, and Val could see the worry in Deya's gray eyes.

"I suppose this is normal magic for Flykige?" she asked, her voice small and quiet in the impenetrable silence.

Val's eyes darted around the circle. Not even a snowflake drifted in from the sky, though the ground was still heavily powdered with snow.

"I don't remember reading anything about this in all our research, do you?"

Deya shook her head, her gaze brushing up the enormous stone pillars of Flykra. There were five stone statues surrounding a stone platform frosted with snow and sporting a carving of an intricate snowflake. Val couldn't help thinking that the statues of Flykra surrounding them bore a strong resemblance to Kindra.

Flykige had been the closest landmark they could find to Frode's cave during their plotting. They were close now.

"Let's keep moving," Deya whispered.

Val couldn't help but moan inwardly. The quiet and calm in the circle was peaceful, almost bewitching. Something about these stone effigies held her in place. A tug on her sleeve jerked her out of her daze.

"C'mon, Val," Deya murmured. And, grudgingly, Val allowed her to pull her away.

The wind kicked off the minute their feet left the circle, the blistering cold more brutal than it had been before they had entered Flykige. But this time, they were determined. Val knew Frode's cave was only a few kilometers from the monument. Karyna had told them he liked to be close to the sacred spot, that the only time you could spot Frode out of his cave was performing rituals within the circle.

They left Flykige behind, the snow getting less dense the further northwest they traveled. It was as if someone had walked this path often, the snow more heavily packed, less cumbersome the further they went.

Val was shivering, the stones in her pockets only holding vestiges of their former warmth. She squeezed them in her gloved hands, as if trying to eke out the last few degrees of heat while she counted her breaths, feeling the ball of flame she kept in her heart flicker against the cold. Slowly *in, out, in, out*. If she collapsed again, they were done for. They had to keep going. They were almost there . . .

Suddenly, a cave's mouth opened before them, yawning into view through the heavy sleet. A carved-out chunk of rock with ragged edges, its opening a gaping maw so dark, they could not make out an ember of a fire or even a whisper of life. Val and Deya froze before the cave's entrance, staring at it as if it were the entrance of the Underearth.

"Should we pull sticks for who goes first?" Val muttered to Deya after a long pause.

Deya's small frame looked positively diminutive underneath all her layers, and for the first time in many weeks, Val saw the timid girl she had first met.

But Deya was anything but a coward, and as she watched the small female square her dainty shoulders, all she saw was Katia.

"I'll go first," Deya said, and Val smiled and grabbed her hand.

"Together," she said. Like she had promised Deya, she would never abandon her friends. Never again. Glancing over at Deya, she tightened her grasp on her fingers. "I will always have your back," she said to her. "You know that, right?"

Deya gave her a small smile and nodded. "I know. I have yours, too, Val."

And with a deep breath, they both stepped inside the cave. The inside was equal parts ice and rock, the glaciers glistening in the dim light of the auroras outside. Val took off her glove and, with a flick of her fingers, a small flame burst from the tips, throwing the cave into sharper relief.

Val's ears pricked, attuned to every drip of water, every rustle of wind, attempting to locate a sign of life within the glacial hole. She found Deya and she drew her back, keeping a hand tightly fisted onto her cloak.

"Stay close," Val breathed. "Keep hold of me and do not let go."

She could not draw her swords, no matter how much she wanted to. The small licks of flame lining her fingers were the only thing she felt safe enough to use to guide their way. Alerting whatever was in this cave to their presence was not the safest thing, even if Frode was harmless.

They crept further, the ice shining in the fire light, small rodents fleeing for the shadows.

"How deep is this cave?" Deya breathed in her ear after several minutes of wandering, but Val could only shake her head. The cave felt never-ending, the twists and turns unnerving even her most finely-honed tracking skills. She did not know where they were in regard to the entrance, how many left or right turns they had made. And that worried her.

"If we keep going left, we should find the center of the cave," Deya whispered, but Val wasn't so sure about that. She was beginning to feel as though they were retracing their steps, maybe even going in circles. But Val listened to Deya, and at the next fork in the cave, she went left.

And crashed headfirst into a wall of snarling ice.

Val leapt backwards, her hands reaching for her swords, but the frosted shadow let out a roar that rattled the rock of the cave, forcing Val into Deya.

"What the—" Deya gasped, but Val had finally grabbed hold of one of her swords, her flame shooting up the hilt, and the cave flooded with light.

A large, crystalline bear stood in their path, its mouth open, incisors the size of the stalactites above gleaming in the firelight. Made completely of ice, its body was translucent, crystalized patterns spiraling up its enormous back haunches, its eyes glowing a menacing, electric blue.

"Holy—" Val breathed, but the last word didn't even escape her lips before the bear lunged for them.

Val shoved Deya towards the back of the cave, before thrusting both hands outward. With a scream, a wall of flame burst from her. It was not a full Heavenly Fire, but the barrier erupted between her and the bear, catching its body at full blast. It burst into frozen shards.

Panting, Val turned towards Deya, who was rigid on the floor, staring where the bear had exploded.

"Are you okay?" Val cried, but then Deya's eyes widened, and she let out a shriek of surprise.

"*Val*, behind you!"

A frosty breeze whistled by her, blowing strands of hair into her face. Turning, Val caught sight of the bear's icy remains slithering through the air, as if caught on an errant breeze. It wove past her, twisting and turning, its frosts and flakes coalescing until the enormous bear burst from the stream again, fangs bared. And launched itself right at Deya.

"*No!*" Val shouted, but it was too late. The bear had landed right on top of Deya, pinning her to the ground with its icy feet.

Deya screamed, her hands reaching out to catch hold of the bear's fangs, which had opened, ready to bite. Val ran for her, spinning her flaming sword over her head. In an expert arc, she sliced the bear's head clean from its glacial body and it burst into swirling glass again. But this time, Val was ready.

With a furious roar, Val sent a blast of white-hot flame right at the rippling glass, which had been attempting to slither away again, disintegrating it completely. Panting, Val turned back to Deya to check to see if she was alright, when she felt a sharp, icy point touch her cheek.

"A Manielian this deep in Bridah," a thick, guttural accented voice rasped in her ear. "How peculiar . . . Why does Flykra deliver this? What does a Manielian want with Frode?"

Val froze, the hand clutching her sword still outstretched. Slowly, her eyes roved from the point of the ice-tipped spear pressed against her cheek, before following it up its rough carved hilt, towards the person who held it.

A small, hunched male quivered beside her, his torso naked of any fabric or furs, skin only covered with thick symbols and Brynorsk letters tattooed and painted across his body. His arms and legs were spindly, the white hair on his head thinning, contrasted by the long beard trailing from his chin to nearly his abdomen. But it was his eyes that caught Val. They were slathered with dark paint, a smeared mask illuminated by the irises, which burned with the same electric blue glow of the bear's.

"Wait!" Deya cried, scrambling from the floor, and rushing towards him.

Frode swung the spear towards Deya so quickly that it slashed a gash right across Val's cheek. Blood sprayed the air and Val swore, spitting in pain and rage.

"We come in peace! Kindra sent us!" Deya cried. Her hands were raised in the air, standing between her and the odd male before them. Val cradled her bleeding face and waited, holding her breath.

It was a half lie. Kindra had done no such thing, but still, Frode's glowing eyes darted between them, the shadows around them fixing on Deya. He hummed, a deep, rough rumble of intrigue as he peered at her, leaning closer. He tilted his chin up, blue eyes shining even brighter, as if attempting to look under Deya's skin. Val felt Deya recoil back against her, but she did not back away.

"*Kyandra,*" Frode mused. "Why would Kyandra send death to me?"

"We don't mean to harm you," Deya said quickly. "Only to ask you a few questions. We need answers urgently . . . to keep Bridah safe."

Frode stared at her blankly. Then, he lowered his spear, only to round on Val. "You broke my ice bear."

Val blinked. "I-I'm sorry?"

"*My ice bear,*" Frode repeated. "He just wanted to play with you."

When Val and Deya only stared at him, nonplussed, Frode let out a wheezing explosion of a giggle that shook the male's round belly and thin shoulders.

"*Come!*" he crowed, turning from them, and beckoning behind him as he walked into the cave. "*Come,* friends of *Kyandra.* Let us ask your questions where Flykra can see us."

CHAPTER 9

"I don't like this," Val whispered to Deya the minute Frode was out of earshot.

She didn't blame Val. Kindra had mentioned that Frode was mad, but something about seeing it first-hand . . . Watching the peculiar male walk away, Deya couldn't help but shiver at the way his blue eyes had burned into her. . . assessed her.

"I know," Deya murmured back absently.

"Deya!" Val hissed, snapping her fingers in her face, drawing her attention back to her. "This male is three logs short of a campfire. What can we possibly learn from him?"

"Kindra did warn us that he's a little . . ." Deya hesitated, wincing. "*Eccentric.* It'll be fine, Val. We need to do this. He's the only lead we've got."

Just then, a cold wind tickled their spines, and something nudged persistently at the back of her leg. Whirling around, hand leaping to the hilt of the sword at her hip, she stopped short from drawing it. The ice bear had reformed, but this time it was smaller, less ferocious . . . almost adorable. Now more cub than bear, it bumped against her hand with its nose, its blue eyes twinkling rather than simmering.

"Follow Bjarn!" Frode's voice echoed to them around the cavernous walls, and, exchanging a hesitant look, Deya and Val followed the shimmering crystal creature through the cave.

They found Frode standing in an enormous cavern, a large fire roaring at the center. At the apex of the ceiling was a hole, letting the light from the Verja Auroras shine down upon the High Priest of Bridah.

Frode was chanting at the fire, a bear skin headdress now atop his balding head as he threw herbs into the flames, speaking in a low, melodic chant in Brynorsk. The beam of blue-green light falling on them made her realize what he meant by asking questions where Flykra could see them.

Bjarn darted past them, running towards Frode, chasing the green sparks that burst from the fire with the herbs he threw in it.

"What is he?" Deya asked Frode, watching as the shimmering bear cub chomped its translucent mouth at the sparks, attempting to catch them.

"A Frost Sprite," Frode replied, his hands dipping into a canister of paint beside the fire, slathering it onto his fingers. "But most importantly, he is my friend." He let out another unhinged bark of laughter, revealing a toothless smile. "Yes, Flykra bore many Frost Sprites. Spirits that still exist between the ethereal plane and ours. Bjarn was a gift from Flykra to Frode, indeed." He giggled again and the sound bounced off the cave with an eerie cadence.

Val was watching Bjarn with a leery look on her face. Her arms were crossed tightly around her body, still clutching her sword, golden cheek dripping blood. Deya nudged her with her elbow, jerking her head at the sword. With a grumble and an eyeroll, Val re-sheathed it.

Deya watched as Frode began to draw sigils and runes along the cave floor. The figures circled the fire, the paint bright red . . . as if it were blood.

"What do you wish to ask Frode, friends of *Kyandra*?" Frode asked distractedly, still crawling on his hands and knees around the fire, slathering the blood-like substance across the floor.

"We . . . uh . . ." Deya found it hard to concentrate as Frode crawled like a child around their legs, even having to lift her foot to allow him to finish drawing a symbol beneath her. "I'm not sure if you're aware of the current state Krigor is in—"

"Flykra tells Frode much," the priest said, drawing a wide circle around Deya's feet. When she made to move, he seized her ankle, holding her in place. "Yes, Frode sees much of what has become of the realm. I pray to Flykra to protect our land, and She always answers."

"Are you talking about the glacier wall and the Verja Fjords?" Val asked, watching with narrow eyes as Frode scuttled to her next, tracing a blood-red circle around her boots.

"The Fjords, the glaciers . . . all Flykra's ways to protect Her children," Frode replied. "She tells Frode often how Her sisters envy Her freedom."

Val blinked. "She *tells* you? How?"

Frode looked up, and Deya flinched at the way his electric blue eyes deadened when looking at Val. "She whispers to Frode—speaks to Frode much like you do now, Manielian." He pointed a blood-stained finger up at Val, a menacing gesture that even made her take a half step back. "Flykra tells Frode how She is hunted. Hunted by *your* blood."

Val looked stricken. "Hunted by . . . by Calida?"

Frode rose from the ground, his knees now streaked with red, his fingers still dripping the paint onto the cave floor. "Yes," he said, his voice a low growl. "The Ember Goddess hunts Flykra. The blood of her blood thirsts for our end."

Val stared at Frode, and Deya could see her fingers twitch. Heat was beginning to emanate from her friend and Deya knew she had to act fast before things got out of hand.

"But this is why we came to you, Frode," Deya began, jumping slightly when the old priest's head whipped around to look at her. "We want to protect Bridah. To restore balance to the realm."

Frode let out a wheezing giggle, those ghostly eyes of his widening to glowing saucers framed by the shadowed mask he wore. "Restore balance? *You?*" He cackled loudly, the sound echoing off the craggy walls. "You are the tipping of the scale, girl. You are *Dodsbringern.*"

Deya's blood ran cold. The cave and the fire before them proved to be enough insulation from the gale outside, but the dread that seeped through her veins at Frode's words froze her anyway. She did not know what that word in Brynorsk meant, but she knew it could not be good.

"We came to ask if you know anything about the Mother Goddess," Val cut in quickly, her eyes darting towards Deya, who was still rooted to the spot, her heart pounding with fear. "Particularly . . . if you know what her *heart* is."

Frode was still staring at Deya, that same cold, curious glow in his eyes. But finally, he turned away from her and walked back towards the fire.

"The Mother does not speak to Frode often," he said, holding out his hand above the fire, the blood paint dripping from his fingers. The minute the liquid touched the flames they burned a bright blue, the blaze billowing to tantamount heights before dwindling back down. "Mav worries as well for the state of the realm. The Mother is balance, but the scales have tipped too far. They must be righted."

Val shifted in her painted circle, the impatience evident on her face. Deya couldn't help but feel the same. Frode spoke in riddles, in circles as convoluted as the caves they were in. She didn't know whether to believe him or view him as Val so evidently did: a quack.

"But her *heart*," Val pressed him. She made to move from the circle, but Frode hissed at her until she took a hesitant step back within its painted confines.

"The Mother's heart is obvious," Frode said. He reached into a pot beside the flames which looked suspiciously like it was filled with bone. "Her heart is the pillars of this world, the balance of life."

Deya and Val looked at each other, but Deya's mind was racing. She had grown up in Praiton after all, had sat at the feet of the High

Priestesses before Mother Clarita, had gone to school in the small village. She had learned just about everything having to do with Mav, the Mother Goddess. Yet "the Heart of the Mother" was not familiar to her. But when Frode said this, a spark lit in her mind.

"Her heart is her children," she whispered. She glanced up at Frode, excitement bubbling up in her. "It's her children, am I right?"

Val glanced over at her, then back to Frode, her face hopeful. But Frode just gave another wheezing giggle, as if someone had leaned down too hard on a fire bellow.

"In a sense," Frode said, giggling still. "When Mav birthed the five Pillar Goddesses, it was for the purpose of balance. Yet power tipped scales where power should not."

He shoved a fist into the jar, pulling out a handful of small, delicate bones that could have belonged to rodents. Holding one up, he held it out to them. "Arista was born first. The Goddess of the Earth, of the Harvest. She brought stability to the realm, a grounding to the Earth. A foundation. This is where life began." He tossed the bone in the fire and the flames burned a bright, vivid green before holding up two more.

"Then they came in pairs: Calida and Flykra." Both bones went into the flames one by one, bringing with it a blaze of bright teal and a roaring red. "Then Eula and Astrea." Blue, then purple flashed before their eyes, burning into Deya's retinas.

Frode held up the largest bone then, one that looked like it could possibly be fae. His eyes looked maddened in the dancing colors of the fire, and Deya's heart thrummed in her ears. "Fire balanced ice. Sea balanced sky. But what balances all? What controls what cannot be controlled?"

Deya felt her mouth move without thinking. It was as if it were engrained in her blood, burned into her skin, etched into her veins and her bones.

"Life," she whispered. "Mav is life. Mav is the balance."

Frode looked at her, the fire still roaring the same color purple as Caelum's eyes. "Not just life," he rasped, holding the bone between his thin fingers. He held it up before them. Then, with a violent *snap*, he broke the bone in two. "Mav is life," he said, throwing half the bone into the fire. It lit up the cave in a blinding flash of golden light so bright that both Deya and Val had to shield their eyes. "But She is also . . . death."

The final bone fragment hit the flames and the reaction was instantaneous. The fire let out a shriek, as if something was being burned alive. Flames billowed in all directions, and, from the center of the fire, blackness blossomed. Deya watched it grow, felt the white-hot panic spread with the familiar darkness that swallowed the brightness of the fire. The smoke turned to shadow, the flames roared jet-black . . . and then it was extinguished.

The silence that fell over them was louder than it had been in the center of Flykige. All Deya could hear was her own heartbeat, and the sound of her blackened fingers scraping into a fist beneath their gloved exterior.

Val was staring at the smoldering logs, her brow crinkling with confusion. "But *the Heart of the Mother* is something Praiton is seeking," she insisted. "It sounded like an object. An artifact of some kind. How can they be seeking her children?"

"No, no, no, no," Frode sang, shaking his head, his paint-soaked fingers rubbing red streaks down his already maddened face. "You are too literal, Manielian. You are seeking something that *represents* her children. Something as old and magical as the Mother Herself."

"But *what* is it?" Val demanded, impatience dripping off every word now. "You know! I *know* you know!"

Frode did not speak. His eyes roamed slowly towards Deya, even when he answered Val. "Maybe," he breathed, his voice so low that she could barely discern the words. "Frode could know . . . or he could not."

Val swore in frustration and made to step out of her painted circle, when a gust of cold wind blew and suddenly, Frode was right in Deya's face. His bare feet brushed the painted circle, his glowing eyes as wide as the Nodarian moon, and Deya's breath caught in her throat as his painted fingers seized her by the face in a spider-like grip. Val yelled and lunged for them, only for Frode to whip out a hand, trapping her in place with a glacial wall which sprung up from the painted circle.

"There is a darkness in you, *Dodsbringern,*" Frode breathed. His face was so close that his breath washed over her, causing her to squirm and recoil. But something held her body in place—a vise-like grip not unlike those of Frode's bony fingers. "Flykra is watching you. *They are all watching you.*"

And with that, he let Deya go. She fell to the floor, gasping as if the High Priest had attempted to suck the air from her lungs. A second later, Val ran to her, scooping her up.

"We're going," she insisted, dragging Deya onto unsteady feet.

Frode was standing in the center of the cave, the glassy eyes of the bear headdress glistening in the moonlight as he watched them go. He wheezed out another giggle. "Goodbye, friends of *Kyandra.* Thanks for coming to play with Bjarn."

The Frost Sprite gave a gentle rumble at their retreating backs as Val hurried Deya from the cave, her legs still shaking, and her heart sinking with dread in her chest.

※

Val held onto Deya long after leaving the cave, even though her legs appeared steadier. Paint from Frode's fingers still streaked her face, looking like bloody fingerprints, and every time Val looked at it, a sick feeling gripped her insides.

They did not speak as they began the long journey back through the tundra towards Fangdor, and Val couldn't think of anything to say to her.

There is a darkness in you, Frode had said to Deya. Val's feet plunged into the snow, step by step, her mind so foggy that she barely registered the freezing cold as they plowed on.

Val had done so much research on Deya's power, attempting to find something—*anything*—alluding to the source of it. The *cause* of it. But she had always come up empty. Yet, Frode seemed like he saw something in her. Something . . . ominous. What did that old kook know? What had he sensed?

For a fleeting second, a tremble of fear moved through her at holding Deya so close. An image of her reducing a Praitonian general to cinders flashed through her mind. They had always known Deya's magic was dangerous . . . possibly even dark. But it had been something they had pushed aside, maybe even refused to acknowledge. Now, though, with Frode potentially validating their worst fears . . .

Shaking off the thought, Val chastised herself for even considering it. This was *Deya,* after all. Deya, who refused to kill in cold blood, who was kind and caring. Out of all those who could've been given this power, Val was grateful it was her.

"Well, that was a colossal waste of time," Val mumbled, attempting to jar both of them out of their thoughts.

Deya's eyes were unfocused, her gaze fixed far away, as if she were also mentally still in Frode's cave. "Oh, I don't know if it was," she said softly, her breathing labored from the trek through the snow. "He did give us a direction. We know her heart has to do with the other goddesses."

"Do we really know that, though?" Val grumbled. The snow was beginning to get thicker again as they moved further back west. "That old quack may have just fed us a load of toss."

Deya didn't reply. She seemed just as determined to put one foot in front of the other, but Val could see it in the furrow of her brow and the purse of her lips. She was troubled. What Frode had said had upset her, even if she wouldn't say it. It was something she recognized easily, having been guilty of the same in the past—something Lucia used to call her out on all the time.

They pushed on in silence for another few miles, Deya lost in her thoughts, and Val thinking about her best friend. Lucia had never let her suffer in silence. Like the mother hen she was, Lucia would poke and prod until Val finally cracked and told her what was wrong. She could still remember the way Lucia looked when Val had confessed to her about the night with Aris. The way her golden eyes had appraised her, how she had listened without a sound. Without judgment.

It was as Val thought of this, that she saw it again. What she thought she had seen miles before in the roaring blizzard. What she had thought was impossible. A streak of red flashing through the falling snow.

She froze, her legs stopping all on their own. But . . . no. It *couldn't* be. She had already determined this before when it had nearly cost her her life. It was only because she had been thinking of her . . .

Deya stopped, noticing that Val had frozen in her tracks.

"Val?"

But Val was squinting through the blustering wind, her eyes desperately trying to disprove what she thought she saw again. What she *couldn't* have seen. Snowflakes rushed through the air, blowing into her eyes—and then, Val saw her.

Lucia stood several feet ahead of them, her long tawny hair streaming in the wind. Val's heart shot up through her chest, coming to rest somewhere in her throat as she took in the ghost of her best friend.

But she was more solid than a ghost—more than mist and vapor. Lucia's golden skin glowed, her red hair starkly contrasting the bleak whiteness all around them. But it was her eyes that made tears begin to bubble up her throat. Lucia's eyes looked at her with a quiet familiarity, a knowing smirk lifting the corners of her mouth in the way it always used to. She was a picture from her memory. Something golden, warm, and lost. And she was standing *right there.*

"Lucia . . ." Val breathed. Deya turned to look at her, eyes wide.

"Val, what are you saying? What . . . what is that—"

But Val wasn't listening to her. Her feet moved on their own, stumbling through the thick powder towards her friend. Lucia raised her chin, her eyebrow quirking in the way that it always did when she was impatiently waiting for something.

"*Lucia!*" Val cried, speeding up. But then, Lucia turned and began to move in the opposite direction, walking away from her.

"No . . ." Val murmured, her hand reaching out, the snow and wind buffeting her, holding her back. "No . . . wait, come back!"

"Val, what are you doing?" Suddenly, hands were grabbing at her, stopping her as she lunged after the ghostly vision of her lost friend.

"Let me go!" she cried, thrashing desperately against Deya's hold. Lucia was disappearing into the snow and sleet. Panic rushed through Val's body, making her fight harder against Deya.

"Val! *Val!* That is *not* Lucia! Don't go—"

She wasn't sure if it was the roaring of the wind in her ears or her own wild heartbeat, but Val did not hear the rest of her words. And at that moment, when Lucia looked back and jerked her head to follow her, it was as if Val's mind was wiped clean.

With an almighty shove, Val broke free of Deya's grip. Sprinting through the snow, the cold wind burning her eyes, all she could see was that red hair and those catlike golden eyes sparkling at her through the raging frost. Val ran for her sister and barreled straight into her waiting arms.

The minute her arms closed around the familiar willowy frame, it was as if the wall she had built around her pain splintered. Every memory, every thought, every feeling of anger and sadness she had bottled these last few months burst from her as she held her friend again.

She had never gotten to say goodbye to Lucia, Katia, or Atria, a fact that had haunted her through every bone-aching training session, every exhausting, never-ending run she forced herself to endure to forget it. How their last night together had been in that dark cabin in one of the Legion's warships, piled on top of each other like stones in a riverbed.

She had never gotten to say goodbye . . . never gotten to apologize for leaving them behind.

Val tightened her grip on Lucia, and tears flowed, hot and fast, down her cheeks. "I'm so sorry, Lucia," she gasped into her shoulder. "I should never have let them take me. I should've—"

But she stopped. Her grip tightened around Lucia's body, feeling Lucia's hand coming to rest on her back. Manielians always ran hot. Even when their core temperature was at their lowest, they would still feel warm to the touch. Yet, Lucia was as cold as death.

Something was clawing at the back of her mind, urging her to *listen* to it... A warning.

Val pulled away to look at her friend. Her familiar face peered back at her, her angular features wrinkling in confusion. Val's mind felt like the snowstorm around them, nothing but swirling fog and icy wind blasting through it. Her head was spinning, her thoughts cloudy, unable to hear or see anything other than the female in front of her.

"Lucia..." she began but Lucia shook her head.

"We do not have time," she said in a voice softer than a whisper, barely audible over the howling wind. But there was no mistaking Lucia's voice, the faint roll to her words characteristic of someone born into an old Manielian family still audible. "I must go. Please, come with me. Do not leave me again."

Val's heart clenched. Shaking her head, tears threatened to fall again. "No, I won't leave you again. I'm sorry. I'll come with you... I'll go wherever you need me to."

The fog filling her brain made her lightheaded as she moved to follow Lucia. The Manielian female held out a hand for Val to take, and Val weaved her gloved fingers into Lucia's cold hands.

For a moment, as they walked away, Val couldn't remember why they were out in a snowstorm, what they had been trying to do... who she had been with. It was only her and Lucia against the world again. And as she and her best friend began to walk in the direction of the fjords, Val could barely hear the sound of her name being screamed over the roaring wind.

She's not real. She's not real.

It was a small whisper in her mind—a flurry caught on a cold wind now filling her brain. But it was much too easy to ignore.

"Where are we going?" Val asked. Lucia was walking faster than her, dragging her along through the thick bed of snow. "Lucia, *talk* to me. What's going on?"

But Lucia did not respond. She did not even turn her head back to look at her as her hand tightened around Val's. The grip made Val wince, but Lucia's fingers clamped down on her. An icy, sinister claw.

"Lucia—"

But then, a streak of chestnut brown hair whirled past her. There was a flash of silver, a mottled scream, and then Val was being jerked backwards, out of Lucia's grasp. Dark liquid sprayed through the air, speckling the snow like wax from a candle as Lucia let out a terrible, unearthly screech, jerking her hand back to clutch it against her chest.

Blinking, she attempted to focus on what was in front of her. Deya stood between her and Lucia, a silver dagger clenched in a shaking hand.

"Get away from her!" Deya shouted, brandishing the dagger at Lucia.

Val's mind churned and spun like the snowflakes falling around them, even when she gave her head a little shake. Her vision blurred as Deya swam into and out of focus, yet, when she looked at Lucia, she was as clear as the sun on a summer's day.

Lucia glared at Deya, still clutching her injured hand, her golden eyes darkening as she looked at the small female. Val's eyes registered dark blue splatters on the snow and her mind sharpened.

"Deya, what are you doing?" Val fought to move past her, reaching out towards Lucia's bleeding wrist, but Deya shoved her back with a firm hand.

"Val, stay behind me. Don't go near that thing!"

"That *thing?*" Val cried. "What the hells are you talking about? She needs my help, Deya! Let me go!" But as Val tried to push past her once more, this time, Lucia moved strangely. It was as if her body was contorting with the wind. Her shoulders dropped like a marionette whose strings were cut, her head drooped, and her long tawny hair fell into her face.

And then she lunged at Deya.

Lucia slammed into Val's smaller friend, sending her hurtling into the snow. Deya let out a scream, her hand shooting up to catch Lucia's wrist as she attempted to seize Deya by the face, just as Frode had.

And at that moment, Val saw the distortion of the familiar features. Like a flicker of light, Lucia's eyes blackened, her skin paled, her hair darkened, nails sharpening into spikes. But, with another blink, she was Lucia again, screaming in pain as Deya's free hand slashed the knife across her chest, crying in surprise and agony as Deya threw her off and pinned her to the ground, both wrestling for dominance.

"Stop it!" Val screamed. "*Stop!* You're hurting her!"

Val didn't know what she was doing. All she could see was Lucia crying in pain as Deya held the knife aloft, ready to strike again. But the knife Deya held was not dripping with Lucia's crimson blood, but rather a dark blue liquid.

Val's eyes watched as the liquid coagulated on the tip of Deya's blade, beading into a delicate drop as it fell, landing with a gentle *plop* beside Deya's footprints in the snow. And as she stared at it, she realized there were only two sets of tracks littering the white powder. Hers and Deya's.

"*Val!*" Deya yelled as Lucia fought underneath her, the tip of her knife still poised over Lucia's throat, held only at bay by her clawed grip. "*Val!* Do something!"

But what could she do? Her mind fought with what she knew was real and what she actually knew, deep down, was impossible. Two of her closest friends fought to the death in front of her, and all she could do was stand there.

When Lucia knocked the knife from Deya's hand and forced her back to the ground by the throat, Val's reverie was broken by Deya's choked scream. The fire in Val's chest that would crackle merrily at the sight of Lucia was dormant. Cold. And as Lucia's face contorted monstrously again and loomed over Deya, an ember of fury lit in Val's stomach.

Lucia's clawed hand held Deya down as she leaned over and, with a loving, gentle caress, began to blow a cold, wintry wind down upon her face. The gale around them began to circle, moving like an icy cyclone, whipping snow and sleet up in its deadly grasp.

Deya's screams were swallowed by the mist as her eyes glazed, her skin paled, and her lips began to turn blue. Suddenly and without a second thought, Val threw herself at her sister, fire erupting from her hands.

Val collided with Lucia's cold body, sending her flying into the snow, struggling to pin her down by the shoulders. Out of the corner of her eye, Val could see Deya lying motionless in the snow where she left her, but she forced herself to focus on the distorted visage of her best friend struggling underneath her.

"*Sister!*" Lucia screeched but Val grit her teeth in concentration, screwing up her vision, attempting to focus through the roaring storm in her mind. Lucia looked up at her in pained confusion, her golden eyes lit by the fire crackling around Val. It was faint now, but if Val concentrated hard enough, she could see past the glimmer of magic, could see the black eyes hiding underneath that of her sister's, see the horrific truth underneath the veil.

"How dare you," Val snarled, her voice strained as she struggled to hold Lucia down. "You are *not* her! *You are not her!*" But no matter how loudly Val yelled the words, nothing could block out the look of pain on her sister's stolen face. Nothing could blot out the way it looked to have Val's hand clenched around her sister's throat. Despite everything her mind knew to be true, the sight of it made her gasp for breath and slacken her grip momentarily.

It was all the creature needed.

Lucia seized Val's hand, and sharp claws dug into her flesh. Val screamed as she was thrown backwards to the ground. Her fires extinguished the minute she hit the freezing snow, and she barely caught her breath before Lucia pinned her down and loomed over her, just as she had Deya.

But the thing on top of Val was no longer Lucia. Blue splatters of blood cascaded from the wound Deya had given it, splashing into Val's eyes, fully clearing the fog from her vision.

Lucia's hair was still auburn, her eyes still golden, but her skin had grayed, her nails and teeth now sharp spikes which shot towards Val's throat, piercing the soft flesh.

"*You are not her,*" Val gasped. Her fingers scrabbled around the claw clenched around her windpipe, the skin flashing between tanned and gray with each gasp for breath. *"How dare you pretend . . ."*

The words froze in her mouth as a trickle of cold mist issued from Lucia's gaping mouth. Val's skin began to seize, the air wrenched from her throat in a dry rasp as a chill so numbingly cold billowed down on her. And as her vision began to blur, the wind suddenly stopped.

Lucia pulled her face from Val's, the mist still emanating from her mouth as she looked around, confused. Then, a burst of purple light exploded into view. A black blade whirled through the air and another spray of blue liquid showered Val and the snow around her as the sword slashed Lucia across the back.

Lucia let out a horrific screech as she collapsed. Val struggled against the ice in her blood to sit up, her gaze following Lucia's as she whirled to face the intruder.

Caelum had emerged from a portal above them, the Shadow Sword clenched in his hand, and a murderous spark lit in those purple eyes as they moved from Val to Deya, lying immobile on the ground.

Breathing hard, he turned his attention back to Lucia.

She had righted herself, standing in front of Caelum. Her shoulders rolled like a body without bones, her head drooping towards her chest, arms limp, legs bowed. And when she looked up, Val could not deny it this time. Her eyes were as black as pitch.

"Val! *Move!*" Caelum roared, spinning his sword with one hand, preparing himself as Lucia homed in on him.

Like a puppet being thrown, Lucia sprang for Caelum, black eyes gleaming, claws extended. Her mouth opened wide, the same deadly cold mist billowing out like a cloud. But Caelum did not so much as flinch. With a snake-like movement, he thrust his hand forward.

Lucia froze, suspended in midair, hands still outstretched. She blinked, and suddenly her eyes were gold again as they darted towards Val. There was naked panic within them, and Val's breath caught as Caelum raised his sword.

In that moment, it didn't matter what Val knew to be true. Because even with everything she knew, it was impossible to see anything except the vision of her best friend, pleading for her.

"Please, sister..."

But the words were barely out of her mouth before Caelum swung.

As if in slow motion, Val watched the head of her best friend go spinning into the air, her red hair streaming, mouth still open in shock, before hitting the ground and coming to rest in the snow at her feet.

Val stared at Lucia's empty golden eyes for a moment. She blinked and, in each blink, she could see it—*hear* it—her imagination giving life to Aris's words.

There was enough left of them to bury.

Lucia's head became Katia's. Then Atria's. Then she could see all three of them lying in a dismembered pile at her feet, their blood soaking the ground...

Red blossomed in her vision. The fire in her chest gave an almighty surge. And then the pain inside of her broke loose.

Fire exploded from her, furious fire turning any tears that escaped her eyes into blistering steam. Falling to her knees, Val's screams echoed in the wind that had resumed with Lucia's death as she stared down at her friend's severed head. Pain and fury flooded her veins, fire rippled in waves, pain wrenched at her heart.

There was enough left of them to bury.

The fiery tornado consumed her, the rage eating her alive as the image of Lucia's head filled her mind until it was all she could see. Then, their bodies became the face of her elder brother... and he was laughing. Laughing as he killed them. Laughing as he cut them to bits, just like he had promised her.

"*No!*" Val screamed, scrabbling at the snow, attempting to grab hold of the tawny hair. "*No!*"

At that moment, a blast of cold blew her backwards. Her flames bowed, bent back by a sharp, cold wind. Hands seized her, stopping her from reaching for her sister's body. Val was wrenched upwards and jerked around to face the white-haired Nodarian who was as pale as the snow around them.

"*Val!* Stop! Val! Look at me!"

She could only vaguely feel Caelum holding her back as she panted with rage. Tears were falling, but she could not feel them as they blistered into steam.

Pieces. That was all that was left of her family. Pieces buried underground. Pieces covered in blood and flame. Pieces of her . . . lost forever.

"*Val.*" Arms encircled her, pulling her tightly into the male's chest. Cold flooded her body, extinguishing her flames like a deluge of ice water as gentle hands cradled her head, a low deep growl in her ear. "*Breathe.* It is not what you think. You need to calm yourself. *Breathe.*"

Caelum's voice drifted to her over the roaring of her internal flame. Her ragged gasps of anguish began to abate as she clung to Caelum. Slowly, Val felt the panic ebb. The fog filling her vision faded, and the feeling of Caelum's arms around her stilled her out of control flames.

Panting, she pulled back and gazed up at Caelum. For a moment, the malicious amber of her brother looked back at her, before she blinked, and they became the familiar purple, staring down at her with an uncharacteristic concern. "Caelum . . . what . . . was that?"

"I don't know," Caelum said, shaking his head, his hand still holding the back of her head steady, soothing fingers smoothing through her hair. "But it was an illusion, Val. Look."

He jerked his head towards the ground and Val turned to where Lucia's head rested. But it was no longer the familiar head of red hair. Instead, in its place, a pale creature with a sunken face, black hair, and equally black eyes stared back at her. She could see a row of sharp, needle-like teeth protruding from its mouth, its blue blood pooling in the snow beneath it.

She stared at it, breathing hard. She stared and stared, willing the image of her sisters' broken bodies to clear from her mind. It had been an illusion, after all. A fake. It was not real.

But when the images did not fade, unmitigated pain overwhelmed her as she looked at the beheaded beast in the snow, realization crashing over her. She had been more than fooled—she had been *made* a fool. A weak, broken fool preyed on by monsters. All because she had wanted to see her best friend one more time.

And this time, when she finally broke and Caelum tightened his grip around her, Val could not stop the tears from coming. And as she sobbed into Caelum's chest, she feared that they would never stop falling ever again.

CHAPTER 10

Caelum sat beside Deya in Fangdor's infirmary, and he couldn't stop his hands from shaking. His leg bounced uncontrollably as he held the Shadow Sword in his lap. Whenever he looked down at the iridescent blade, he could see Deya reflected in it, streaked by lingering smears of blue liquid.

Deya's skin still had a grayish tinge to it, her cheeks stained with what looked horribly like dried blood. As he watched her small lady's maid lay a hot towel across her forehead, it was all he could do to not grab her and take her back to Nodaria with him. There she would be safe . . . that is, if he never let her out of his sight again. He surely couldn't leave her here in Fangdor, where the biggest danger was herself.

"Excuse me, Your Highness," the lady's maid whispered—Karyna, he thought she'd said her name was earlier. "She *is* okay, I promise it. She just needs to warm up a bit."

Caelum gave her a short nod, his head too filled with the day's events to come up with a polite answer. He could still see that horrible creature—

its grayish-white skin like translucent paper, black hair lank and stringy—looming over Deya, breathing frosty death down onto her face.

But what was most disturbing to him was the hold it had on Val. He had never seen the Manielian female like that. It was as if she were bewitched. But Caelum knew now that her madness was not just from the monster who had entranced her, but that of her own bottomless grief.

A shiver rolled down his spine as he remembered what he had seen in that snowy clearing. As he had held Val, attempting to calm her, a searing bolt of pain had prickled the back of his mind the minute he touched her head. There had been a bright flash, and his vision went white. Then, suddenly, he was watching *himself* cutting the head off a beautiful red-haired girl with golden eyes, saw her head spin in the air . . . and then pain. Agonizing, heartbreaking pain the likes of which he hadn't felt since he had seen his own brother's head on the floor of Atlas Keep.

But as suddenly as the vision had appeared to him, it was gone, leaving him shaken, still holding onto Val as she sobbed into his chest.

Only now, in the calm after the storm did Caelum realize that, for the first time in his life, he had gone *inside* somebody's mind. He had seen, just for a second, through Val's eyes. And he now realized why she had been so inconsolable.

Suddenly, Caelum coughed, and he felt his whole body ache with the movement. Grunting in pain, he slumped back in his seat and pulled back his hand to reveal a light stain of blood creasing his palm. He whispered a soft curse and hastily wiped the blood on his breeches. He had gone too far again. Done too much. Portal after portal . . . the amount of magic it had taken for him to hold the cold at bay, to reach Deya and Val in time. Even now, the shaking in his hands and legs came from more than just the cold.

With a frustrated hiss of pain, Caelum shifted in his seat, reaching out to rearrange the hot towel on Deya's forehead. He wiped a bead of moisture from her brow, his fingers still shaking slightly as he replayed Val's memory over again.

It was not uncommon for Nodarians to have second sight in some way. Most of the star seers had a rather irritating habit of being able to read his mind at times. Io's annoying omnipotence was the cause of much grief in his childhood. He never was able to lie to the old seer and her all-seeing purple eyes.

But it was the first time *he* had ever experienced such a thing. And he found he never wanted to fucking do it again.

The door opened behind him and the sound of large footfalls crashing onto the icy floors jolted him out of his seat.

"*Lostjarna,*" Ulf said. He opened his arms wide, as if to embrace him, but Caelum bristled. Crossing his arms, he took a step back from the enormous male and gave him a stiff nod.

"Ulf," he said in a clipped tone.

Ulf lowered his arms, and his lip twitched slightly underneath his bushy beard, as if he saw something Caelum didn't. "How is she?" he asked, his piercing blue gaze moving towards Deya.

"Cold," Caelum snapped, his tone as icy as the floor underneath them.

Ulf let out a gentle hum and he raised a large hand, resting it across Deya's forehead. Drawing in a deep breath, wintry wind whistled through the infirmary as if being sucked right into the High King's large chest. Then, with a powerful *whoosh,* cold wind billowed out of his nostrils with the force of a blizzard. When Ulf removed his hand from Deya's face, her cheeks had a bit more color in them than before.

"She will thaw," he said, with a small smile at Caelum. "Though it is lucky you found her when you did, *Lostjarna*. She was almost lost to the snow."

"It was not the snow which almost took her." Anger was surging through him, a hot heady sensation burning all frost from his veins.

He had trusted Deya's safety to Bridah. Had given them this girl who infuriated him, maddened him . . . who held him in such an inescapable grip that the thought of losing her still set his blood ablaze. He did not want to admit that her death might mean his own.

"What *was* that creature, Ulf?" he asked, the edge still sharp in his voice.

Ulf sighed. "A skathi," he said. "A creature borne of blizzards and snowstorms. It feeds on those weak of mind or broken of heart, showing them what its victims truly desire."

A chill crept up his spine at Ulf's words. That *thing* had preyed on Val, had sensed her weakness. Then, a horrible image flashed through his head of the skathi choosing *him* as its victim . . . and instead of Val's friend, it was *Deya's* head which was sent flying through the air. His stomach roiled.

"Snow is a beautiful thing," Ulf said, his melodic accent thickening gruffly as he walked towards the window at the far end of the room. "It blankets everything, turning all things pure and beautiful. It holds its mysteries, and new life hides underneath. And yet its touch can harm. Its weight can kill." Ulf turned to look at him, and an uncharacteristic seriousness lurked in those ice blue irises. "All of Flykra's secrets are hidden in this snow, *Lostjarna*. Skathis are only one of the things that protect it. Especially with our friends in Maniel keeping watch on us, be sure that your Little Bird does not escape the nest again."

The ominous statement lingered in the air for a moment as Caelum stared his grandfather down.

"I cannot be here to guard her," Caelum grit out, his fists clenching. "This is the reason I sent her to you."

Ulf's calm face did not change, even as Caelum's temper rose. "I understand this."

"And yet you let her walk to her icy death," he snarled. The tell-tale cracking of ice formed under his feet from his barely controlled rage. "There is a *dragon* out there *hunting* her! How am I supposed to trust her here if you can't even watch—"

But Caelum's words died on his tongue with a single, frosty look from the High King. The older male's large form seemed to expand as he gazed down at Caelum, and for the first time since he had met him, Caelum could see how he was the most powerful High King in the realm.

"Your father had the same temper," Ulf said, his voice still dangerously even. "He learned to sheathe his tongue as he grew, but you my friend, have far to go." Ulf inclined his head. "I am very aware of the severity of our little scaly problem. I have been looking into it fully, *Lostjarna*, I assure you."

Caelum's nostrils flared, but he did not reply. His fury was pounding fists in his chest, egging him on, daring him to challenge this enormous male who was exuding power in front of him. But then something grabbed him by the wrist.

"Caelum . . ."

Whirling around, Caelum's hand reached for his sword but dropped it instantly when he saw Deya blinking up at him from the bed, her still-gloved hand wrapped around his wrist. While her color had not fully returned, there was a flush in her cheeks that had not been there before Ulf had touched her.

"What's going on?" she murmured, her voice still groggy as she attempted to sit up. "What's wrong? What happened? Where's Val—"

But before she could say another word, Caelum engulfed her in a hug so hard that he heard the air leave her lungs.

"*Ooff!* Caelum, what—" she spluttered, but Caelum only tightened his grip on her.

"You said you would behave yourself," he growled in her ear. After a moment, Deya chuckled and wrapped her arms around him, the scent of roses and bergamot filling his head, chasing away thoughts of the skathi and the feel of the cold.

Since she had gone missing, all he could think about was the last time he had held her like this . . . what he had said to her, how he had treated her. The fact he had almost lost her to the snow, like Ulf said, made a cold fist of fear clench his heart.

"I know, I'm sorry," she murmured in his ear. "But I swear, we had no other choice—"

"That is subjective," a harsh, angry voice said from behind them.

Caelum released Deya in time to throw himself out of the way as

Kindra whirled into the room. Her warrior's paint was smudged, as if she had been wearing it for hours, and there was snow covering her hair and clothing. She also looked positively murderous.

Deya recoiled from the Frost Princess, shrinking down into the bed clothing, as if she were trying to disappear entirely.

"You were too busy to take us, Kindra. I'm sorry—"

"Take you *where?*" Caelum demanded, shooting Kindra a furious glare. "Did you put this idea into her head?"

Kindra gave Caelum the same look Ulf did moments ago—a withering stare that made his toes curl in his boots. "I did not give her any such idea," Kindra snapped. "I expressly forbid them from going to see Frode—"

Ulf turned from where he had been gazing out the window at the snow. "You went to see Frode?" he asked Deya, his eyes wide with alarm. "How in Flykra's name did you make it back alive?"

"Frode?" Caelum glanced back and forth between Kindra, Deya, and the High King. "Who the hells is Frode?"

"A nutter whose opinion was not worth facing death for," Kindra snarled, turning her withering gaze to Deya this time.

Deya had the grace to look ashamed. "We were desperate, Kindra," she whispered. "We had no other leads, and time was of the essence. Frode was our best chance to find out what the Heart of the Mother is."

"And?" Kindra demanded. "Did he tell you what it was?"

All three of them stared at her expectantly. Caelum held his breath as Deya shifted in the bed, wringing her hands.

"Well . . . not exactly."

Kindra swore and turned away, ice crackling at her fingertips, just as it had on Caelum's earlier. "Well, I am glad you nearly killed yourself and your friend for that. I hope it was worth it."

"*Kyandra,*" Ulf murmured, reaching out a large hand and clasping his daughter's shoulder firmly. "Be calm, *Minn Feílan.*"

But Kindra shrugged off his grip and strode across the room, throwing herself into the chair by the fire. "Well, tell us," Kindra demanded. "Tell us what Frode had to say."

"Watch how you speak to her," Caelum snarled, turning towards his aunt. The way Deya was recoiling from Kindra and her rage was beginning to rile him again.

Kindra's ice blue eyes fixed on him, and she rose from her chair. "You'd be best to watch *your* tone, nephew," she said, her voice low and deadly as she made towards him. "You may be High King, but you do not rule this kingdom, nor do you rule me." Caelum growled and made to move towards her, but stopped short as Ulf raised a hand.

"*Enough*," Ulf roared, and the deafening volume of his voice made them all stop short. "I will hear no more of you two for now." He turned to Deya and inclined his bushy white head to her. "Please, *Smafugl*, tell us what Frode had to say."

Deya took a deep breath, her fingers still twisting in their gloves. "He did tell us that the Heart of the Mother has to be something involving all five goddesses," she said. "And that her heart is essentially that . . . Her children."

The room went silent, each of them mulling this over. Caelum sat back in his chair, his fingers drumming haphazardly on the hilt of the Shadow Sword.

Maybe it was everything happening in Nodaria, maybe it was seeing large dragons fly over the Keep, but he hadn't thought about the Heart being the goddesses. Now hearing it stated plainly, the Heart of the Mother being the Mother Goddess' children seemed almost obvious. But it still did not answer what the Heart really *was*.

"Do you know of such an object?" Kindra asked, the sneer in her voice still detectable, even if she had calmed down now. "It is not as if Praiton is seeking the actual goddesses themselves."

"No," Ulf grumbled, his large fingers stroking the fluffy bristle of the beard on his chin. "It must be something more symbolic."

"I thought the same thing," Deya said. "But Frode did not know of any such object . . . and nor do I." Caelum could hear the weight of disappointment in her voice. Her eyes darted to stare at her gloved hands twisting in her lap, and Caelum wrestled with his desire to scold her. She had risked her life for so little. The thought of losing her made a fierce, painful ache throb in his chest.

But Ulf gave Deya a reassuring smile, as if to comfort her. "It is no matter, *Smafugl*," he said kindly. "Frode has at least given us something to narrow your search."

Caelum knew Ulf was just being nice. From what Deya had told him, there was nothing about the Mother Goddess in Fangdor's library that they could find. In his opinion, what Frode had said wouldn't help narrow anything down. But he could tell by the way Deya hung her head that she was beginning to think their journey was for nothing, too.

"All the same," Kindra said, breaking the silence. "I advise you not to leave Fangdor's walls again, Deya. Especially after what Caelum saw."

Deya's head jerked around to look at him and Caelum closed his eyes. He had not wanted to tell Deya about what he saw that night he came to see her. He didn't want to worry her—or prompt her to do something reckless—especially when, as the days had gone by without incident, he had begun to doubt what he had seen more and more.

"What do you mean?" Deya asked. "What did Caelum see?"

Ulf and Kindra both looked at him expectantly. Waiting.

Caelum drew in a slow, deep breath. "While I was in the astronomy tower a few nights ago, I saw a dragon fly over the Keep. A dragon headed towards Bridah."

Deya froze, and Caelum could see what little color that had returned to her face leave it again.

"What?" she breathed.

But it was Ulf who cut in. "Please, do not let it concern you, *Smafugl*," he said. "Titus's dragon has been around for many decades now and has never been able to breach our fjords and walls. I do not think we have anything to worry about."

"Still," Kindra murmured. Caelum's aunt was reclining in her chair, her long limbs spread out across the floor, her pale fingers tracing the battleaxe at her hip. "From my limited understanding of Manielian dragons, the dragon's power depends on the bond between rider and beast. For the last several decades, that bond has not been strong enough to best our walls. However, having it so far from Maniel is something to be concerned about. And while I know that general of yours has something up his sleeve, I stand by what I said." Kindra leaned forward, her blue eyes piercing Deya with a menacing light that even Caelum could feel beside her. "It is not safe for you to leave the castle again. Am I clear?"

With a small gulp, Deya nodded.

The room fell silent again, but Caelum was still thinking about what Kindra had said about Aris having something up his sleeve.

After a beat of silence, Deya looked up at Caelum. "Where's Val?" she asked. "Is she okay?"

Caelum glanced at Ulf and the words stuck in his throat. Ulf shifted his large feet, rubbing his hands together, both he and Kindra averting their eyes.

"She's fine," Caelum said finally, but he couldn't meet Deya's gaze. "But . . . we took her back to Nodaria."

Deya sat, bolt-upright, her face white with alarm. "You sent her *back*—"

"She *asked* to go back," Kindra cut in. The female shifted in her seat, her lithe pale fingers moving from her axe, toying with the long white braid hanging from her head. "After your run in with the skathi, she didn't think she'd be able to stay here after what she saw."

Deya stared at Kindra, her mouth falling open. Caelum felt her stomach drop as if it were his own, her heart clenching at the news that Val had asked to leave. She looked at Caelum, the desperation in her eyes evident, as though asking him what it was Val could have seen to leave her behind.

Caelum watched her closely as she wrung her hands together, and a thought struck him. "Why didn't you use your powers to stop that skathi?" he asked her, a lethal softness to his voice. "You were both nearly killed by it."

"I—" Deya began, but she fell silent, her gaze darting from him to rest on the floor, as if she couldn't look at him anymore. "I didn't think . . . it all happened so fast."

He narrowed his eyes at her; all the while he could feel the rapid beat of her heart against his own, the flush of her fear . . . of her *guilt*.

Ulf clapped his large hands together, breaking the tense silence that had fallen over the room. "Now, now, enough of all that, my children, for *Vetrnaetr* is upon us soon!"

Caelum stared up at the male, nonplused as Ulf beamed beatifically down at them as if he had just bestowed upon them a great gift. Thankfully, Deya asked the question that was burning in his throat. Except she asked it much more politely than he would have.

"What is . . . *veter natter*?" she asked. Kindra snorted at her pronunciation, causing Deya to flush, but Ulf chuckled.

"Vetrnaetr is our winter solstice, our long night," he said. "Our most anticipated festival of the year." He rubbed his hands together, like a child in front of a feast, his blue eyes lighting up with his mischievous sparkle again. "It is a fortnight from today and you are all invited, of course! It has been many cycles since we have had outsiders with us for Vetrnaetr. Please come, *Lostjarna* and bring Miss Val and the golden general, as well."

While Deya smiled at Ulf and Kindra, Caelum resisted the urge to grumble. He was not exactly a fan of parties or festivals, had usually hid from them as a child. Now, with everything going on amid the war, he found he was in even less of a party mood than usual. Bridah may be its own insulated snow globe, shielded from the war, oblivious to the plight its sister kingdoms were facing, but Caelum saw nothing else.

Looking up at Ulf, he gave him a pinched version of what he thought to be a smile. "Maybe," he said.

Ulf inclined his head, a knowing twinkle in those blue eyes, and Caelum felt a twinge of annoyance. His grandfather barely knew him, yet he looked at Caelum like he knew more than Caelum did of himself. The reminder that Ulf saw his father in him—or, worse yet, his mother—made a pit appear in his stomach.

As Ulf and Kindra headed from the room, the silence and tension between Deya and Caelum seemed to grow by the second. Now the relief that Deya was okay had faded, his own fury at her leaving Fangdor was beginning to storm back into place.

"Caelum—" Deya began, but Caelum held up a hand, grinding his jaw. Since becoming High King, Caelum had been trying to keep his temper under control. However, his temper now felt as if it was always brewing, just underneath the surface.

Fear of losing Deya had held it at bay, but now . . .

"Explain," he growled, leaning back in his chair, his arms tight across his chest.

Deya blanched, stuttering slightly, a garbled explanation of Praiton raids and descending pressure of the Legion's collapse tumbling from her mouth, but Caelum silenced her with a deadly look.

"You realize," he said, his voice soft, that gently roiling rage beginning to bubble, "that we have placed you in Bridah for *your safety*."

Her cheeks were pink, but she raised her chin with a forced defiance she often used to mask her fear. "I thought it was for the *realm's* safety, my lord—"

"Do not start with that again."

"With *what?*" Deya flung the blanket off her lap, getting back onto unsteady feet. "I apologize for leaving Fangdor without permission, but it's not like you bothered to tell me about the dragon! And besides, you know we had no other choice—"

"You could have asked *me*," Caelum snapped. And as he said it, the words needled at him, as if they had pierced a nerve he did not know he had. "You asked Kindra and maybe even Ulf to accompany you, but you never thought to ask *me*."

It was not a question. It was an accusation, a statement. She had not trusted him enough to ask. Was she afraid he'd say no? Scold her? Then, the worst fear bit into him . . . that she was *scared* to ask him. Afraid of that ever-simmering temper which he had unleashed on her so many times before.

Deya hesitated. Her mouth opened then closed, as if she had bitten down on her retort. But her lack of an answer was answer enough.

Caelum let out a humorless laugh, shaking his head and turning away from her, suddenly unable to even look at her.

"Caelum," Deya began again. She grabbed his wrist, but he shook her off, taking a deep breath, attempting to steady that boil in his blood. It was his own fault. He had bitten and snapped like a caged animal all his life, especially to Deya. It was his own damned fault.

But even as he attempted to pull away from her, Deya pulled harder. She jerked him back and her gloved hands reached up to touch his face. The leather scraped his skin, and he closed his eyes at the feeling.

"I didn't mean anything by it," she murmured. "Honest."

He felt himself leaning into her, being drawn back helplessly like the tides to the moon. No matter how far they both pushed, they always seemed to end up back here.

Caelum jerked his chin away, dislodging her hand from his face. "I have to get back to Nodaria," he said stiffly. "I'll inform the others of what you have learned."

For a second, Deya looked disappointed at his dismissal, her hand recoiling back to her, as if she had touched something cold. Then she sighed.

"Please come for Vetrnaetr," she said softly. "We can talk then."

But Caelum didn't know what good talking would do them now. There was a veil between them, and he knew it was not his imagination that it was getting darker and darker by the day. Before he knew it, he feared he wouldn't be able to see her at all.

CHAPTER 11

Val stared at the dark blue walls of Atlas Keep. The never-changing night sky cast her old bedroom into shadow . . . one that never moved.

She was back in her same dark cage again, but this time it was worse. This time, it was accompanied by the guilt of leaving Deya behind.

She had promised Deya she would protect her. Had sworn to never abandon a friend again. But she had stood there and let the skathi freeze her . . . and then had left without saying goodbye or even seeing if she was okay. It had only been two days since she had fled the Frost Kingdom, but still the ghost of a cold wind constantly tickled her neck . . . a memory of a nightmare she couldn't escape.

Val had spent the whole day in the Nodarian training ring, just as she had for weeks before. She had punched the dummy until her knuckles bled, had run until she collapsed. Pushed herself until the image of her brother's face looming over her friends' mutilated bodies had been shoved from her mind. But no matter how much she broke herself, the image always returned.

But most of all, she was angry at herself for not only hiding in Nodaria, but also from everyone else within the starry Keep. She hadn't even seen Caelum since he had brought her back here—much less the general.

Val felt an unpleasant squeeze in her chest at the thought of Aris. Caelum had been out all day with the general and Saros at the Nodarian outpost they had set up outside of Arctos—much to the disgruntlement of the council. Would he tell Aris about what had happened in Bridah? Would he tell him that she'd returned?

Stretching her arms over her head, her toes curled, and the short shift dress she wore rose up with the movement. Her body still ached from that day's training. Even now, fresh from a cool bath, her skin glistened with moisture as her body mended itself from the minimal heat she had exposed it to.

You're getting weak, a voice in her head leered. It sounded an awful lot like her eldest brother.

At that moment, a brisk knock sounded at her door. Sitting upright, Val stared at it dumbly for a whole second. Who would be calling at this time of night?

Standing, she hurried to the door, and ripped it open without a second thought.

Aris stood in the doorway, his arm against the doorframe, looking harried.

"General." Her voice came out like a squeak, causing her face to flush. It had been weeks since she had seen Aris, and for a moment, Val was struck by how tired he looked. "What are you doing here?"

Aris's eyes raked across her body, as if on instinct, before they snapped back to her face. "Caelum mentioned you were back," he said. "That you left Bridah."

Val flushed, subconsciously pulling the door closer to her barely clad form. "Yeah, about that . . ." Val mumbled, averting her gaze. "Had a change of plans."

One dark eyebrow rose, and Val squirmed slightly under his gaze as it examined her, as though trying to see through her to what she wouldn't say. "Can we talk?"

"Of course." Val hastened to open the door fully, letting the exhausted general into the room before closing the door behind him.

Aris breezed past her, the gold of his armor flashing in the light of the fire lit in her hearth. For a moment, the general stared into it, before his gaze moved back to her. Val sensed his eyes drinking her in again—taking in the heaviness of her breasts and the hard outline of her nipples peeking through the thin fabric—before locking back onto her face.

"Why did you leave Bridah, Valeria? What happened? Caelum didn't say."

Val crossed her arms, shifting slightly, still not looking at him. "Nothing." She couldn't bear the thought of having to tell Aris about her cowardice . . . her weakness.

"Valeria," he began, but Val shook her head fiercely.

"Really, General. There's nothing to be concerned about. Now tell me what it is that's brought you here at this time of night."

Aris didn't move for a moment. He fixed her with his hard gaze, before finally turning away. He paced the length of the room, his hands rubbing through his short brown hair. Usually perfectly styled, it now stuck out in odd directions—something Val observed happening more frequently of late. He stopped by her bed, his hands on his hips.

"General?" she asked hesitantly. While her solar was bigger than her room in Light's Tower, it still felt much too small with Aris in there with her. "What is it?"

Aris sat down on the edge of her bed, leaning forward, his elbows on his knees, his head bowed, before he finally spoke.

"I have something I've been meaning to discuss with you," he said, speaking to the ground. "I was going to go to Bridah this week to talk to you about it, but since you're here . . ."

Val blinked, but then Aris put his head in his hands. Years ago, she never would have believed she'd see the general this exhausted. Aris had always been composed, unfazed. But over the last few months, it was hard not to notice Aris faltering. And how he only seemed comfortable letting the mask slip when he was around her . . . as if he found her safe.

Val did not speak. She held her breath and waited.

After a moment, Aris sighed and lifted his head, but when he spoke, he still looked down at the ground. "All these years, we have prepped and planned for Bridah to be breached. Every false alarm, every bloody operation, every failed mission, every death . . ." He paused and looked up at her, his last words weighing on her heart. "Has Maniel and Praiton just been toying with us? This whole time . . ." The general swore softly, and his large hands cupped his chin, rubbing at his mouth in a way that made Val's throat go dry.

"What are you talking about?"

Aris's head rose from his hands, but still he spoke to the ground. "Caelum saw a dragon fly over Atlas Keep towards Bridah last week."

Val's breath caught. Immediately, her mind flashed to Deya, fear for her friend's safety gripping her throat. "A . . . dragon. Are you sure? Was it Titus's? Are you positive—" But her mind was reeling. Seeing a dragon—even Titus's dragon—this far from Maniel was not only unheard of . . . it was *alarming.*

But Aris sighed and Val felt a strong sense of foreboding settle in her chest.

"Valeria, you know as well as I that it is only a matter of time before Titus makes a move on Bridah," he said softly. "After Burningtide, we know he and his dragon's bond have gotten stronger. And whether he moves for Deya, for the Heart, or to take down Ulf, no matter what terrain we fight on, or whose territory we are in . . . we cannot win against a dragon."

Her whole body went cold. She rubbed her arms, and Aris's eyes followed the movement. It was then that she was reminded again that she was practically naked in front of him in the thin shift dress that could barely be called fabric.

Crossing her arms hastily over her chest, she shifted her weight, fear enveloping her.

Because Aris was right. She remembered the night they had caught wind of Titus succeeding in securing a dragon, recalled it so vividly. Aris had sat on the corner of her small twin bed in Light's Tower, just as he did now. And just like then, Val felt the foreboding and fear creep along the edges of her vision, almost drowning out the heat of the nearness of the general.

It had been the Legion's greatest fear . . . A dragon burning down Bridah.

"But . . . then what do you suggest we do?" she asked. "If we cannot win, what do you propose?"

Aris did not speak for a long moment. With each second of silence, Val's feeling of foreboding compounded. No matter the obstacle, no matter the challenge, Aris always had a plan . . . even if it was completely psychotic.

"Valeria, you once told me that any Manielian can seek a dragon at Mount Cinis. Is that correct?"

Val froze. She stared at the general, attempting to find any sign that he wasn't implying what she thought he was. But the general gazed back, the cool mask back in place, unreachable once again.

"Anyone can try, *maybe*, but to even survive near Mount Cinis takes the strongest Ember Magic. And forget the heat, to survive a dragon's Trial by Fire . . ." Val shivered at the reminder. The ritual required to claim a dragon. To bow at its mercy and survive a dragon's flame—the hottest flame there was. Val shook her head, terror building in her. "The heat of the volcano alone could kill a High King—"

"But it *can* be done," Aris insisted, and Val recoiled. His tone was so steady, so insistent. This was no longer the Aris that she knew—the Aris who gave her secret, soft smiles, who once kissed her like she was air, and he was drowning.

No.

This was the general of the Pillar Legion. And he had a plan.

"What are you asking?" Val breathed.

Aris rose in one swift movement, and in that second, Val felt every inch of him. His hulking figure seemed to fill her bedroom—nothing but gold and glimmer, muscle and movement. Aris was always beautiful, but now, he was more intense than she had ever seen him.

"Valeria, the only way out of this is to fight fire with fire."

She shook her head, horror filling her, making to turn away, but Aris seized her wrist, forcing her back. "No . . . General, *are you out of your mind?*"

His grip tightened on her, and he looked pained, as if every word was costing him to say. "You can *train*. We can build up your tolerance to the heat, *prepare* you. I would not suggest this if I thought you could not do it, Valeria," he insisted, pulling her closer to him, gazing down at her with a fiery fervor that made her legs tighten. "*You* are the realm's only hope. *Our* only hope. To fight Titus—to even stand a chance—*we need a dragon.*"

But Val was staring at him, too horrified to think straight. The room was spinning, her mind whirling. Every rumor she had heard of Mount Cinis swirled through her head. How her brothers had talked about going; how Leo had cackled with the thought of burning kingdoms down; how Lorenzo had silently coveted the idea of honing something so powerful . . . and yet both had dismissed the idea as too dangerous.

If her brothers could not do it, surely there would be no hope for her. With her stifled magic and her broken heart, she could no sooner face a dragon than learn to fly by flapping her arms.

"You don't understand!" Val cried, pulling free of Aris, panicked heat beginning to flush her body. "Mount Cinis is *suicide*! No one other than a High King has tried it in *living memory!*"

"Valeria," Aris said, his voice choked as he reached for her again, seizing her by the waist this time, holding her steady. "It is the only hope the Legion has."

Val was shaking her head again, tears of abject panic beginning to well in her eyes. "No . . . *No!* I can't, General, I *refuse!* Ask any other Manielian! Ask Lycas or any of the Fireflies! I am *not* strong enough for that, General, I—"

But Aris's fingers tightened on her waist. And suddenly, she was crashing into his chest, the cool feeling of his golden armor meeting her warm body taking her breath away. One strong, tanned hand grasped her face, and Val saw, for the first time since that night in his office, a look of unbridled emotion on the general's face.

"Listen to me, Valeria," he said urgently, his lips so close she could almost feel them on her own. "I have seen what you can do. Have seen your power, watched you fight. *You* are the strongest we have. Not Lycas, not the Fireflies, not *any* other damned Manielian on our side. It is *you*. *Only* you."

Fear was pressing down on Val, robbing her of breath as she struggled to look away from Aris—as if by avoiding him, she could also deny his insane plan—but he held fast.

"You are *strong*, Valeria. When will you believe that?"

She could not look at Aris, could not see that blind belief he had in her, in her strength she was beginning to believe she no longer had. Val closed her eyes, squeezed them shut so hard she saw tiny sparks in her vision. But then, a flash of her brother's face rocketed through her mind, and she felt a fire of anger searing through her.

Val had never doubted her powers. Not within the Legion, not when going head-to-head with Caelum or any other fae, creature, or otherwise. Ever since she had left Maniel, she had *always* been the strongest Ember Magic wielder around. None could challenge her . . . none besides her own family, at least.

A flame of fear burned within her as the faces of the two people who haunted her every waking moment flashed through her mind. The only time she had ever doubted her power was when she had faced *them*. When she stood before them, she wondered then if it was all a front. Just as she knew, deep down, that Aris's cool, distant façade was just smoke and mirrors, was she the same?

A fraud of fire and flame.

Someone whose power could never compare to *theirs*.

With a great amount of effort, Val pulled away. She was trembling, her body glistening with the heat of her panic and fear . . . of her cowardice. But she pushed it away and shook her head one last time.

"I'm sorry, General," she whispered finally. "But I can't do it. Not this . . . Anything but this."

For a long moment, Aris looked at her. His hands slid from her body, and the absence of their heat made her want to scream. The intensity of his gaze—the excitement of his plan—faded from his eyes. And all that was left was disappointment.

Finally, he bowed his head and turned towards the door. When his golden armor brushed against her bare shoulder in a cold caress, Val closed her eyes, willing her heart to steady.

Aris reached the door and paused as he opened it. Turning back, their gazes locked.

"Lucia would think you could do it," he said softly. And with that, he turned and left the room, leaving Val to sink to the ground, the feeling of her own crushing weakness smothering her broken heart into embers.

Caelum watched from his knees as Kindra paced in front of him. The room was cold—so cold that his breath came out in white plumes. Frost coated his fingers and clothes, cracked underneath each of his aunt's footfalls as she walked around and around him.

"You are not trying," she said, her voice echoing around the stone of the underground training room she had taken him to. "*Balance* your emotions, nephew. *Control* them."

Caelum panted, the ice melting from him as his blood boiled. In that moment, the memory of training Deya at Light's Tower flashed through his mind . . . only this time, *he* was Deya.

The irony was not completely lost on him.

"This is bullshit," Caelum spat. He got to his feet slowly, eyes blazing, frost crackling, but Kindra only smirked.

"Because you were raised on Celestial Magic," she said. "Frost Magic is a very different beast. Our magic comes from our hearts, our emotions. Not from our resolve or our wills."

His breath was still coming out in hot clouds of mist as he watched his aunt pace in a circle. "I *am* controlling my emotions," he ground out, but even he knew it was a lie. Everything was swirling around him like the frost spinning in the air.

The furious council. The threat of a dragon now looming over their heads. How he had woken last night, soaked in sweat, shaken awake by a nightmare for the first time since he had returned to Nodaria. Only this time, it had not been memories of his slain family, but a new horror. One of him physically holding up the astronomy tower with his own two arms, trying to keep it from falling on him and the citizens of Nodaria who crouched around him.

But no. Even with all of that exploding out of him in frost and fury today, all he could feel was Deya. He had been avoiding her ever since she had returned from her illicit journey to Bridah's High Priest, yet he could still feel the anxious tremble of her heart when she thought of Val. The unsettled sadness that pressed down on her when she thought about him.

He could not explain this phenomenon—could not even begin to *describe* it to anyone. But it was getting more maddening with every second, as if being haunted by a silent ghost.

A hot, acrid boil of emotions swelled up in him, and frost splintered from his feet, exploding from the ground with spikes of ice. Kindra leapt out of the way just in time as a jagged glacier erupted where she stood.

Dusting herself off, Kindra looked down on him, a cool glint in her ice blue gaze. "Perhaps we should take a break," she said, "while you tell me what it is that is troubling you, nephew."

Caelum pulled himself to his feet and turned away, still breathing hard. Shifting his footing, he dislodged his heel from where it was stuck to the ground, embedded in the ice that had sprung, uninvited, from him. It was happening more and more lately, even when he tried with all his might to reel in the explosive feelings he had constantly simmering inside him.

They didn't know how much it took for him not to tear the whole kingdom down with his bare hands. And yet the council still viewed him as nothing more than a rabid, savage bastard who held as much right to the Celestial Throne as the damned stable boy.

And Deya . . .

Shaking his head, Caelum shook frost from his clothes. "Nothing is bothering me, Kindra."

The Frost Princess just let out a derisive laugh. "You cannot lie to me, boy. Not about this." She sat down on one of the glaciers still jutting from the floor, the cold on her skin not seeming to faze her in the slightest. "You are very much your father. And I knew him better than anyone."

Caelum stopped short. When he looked back at his aunt, it was only to find her knowing smirk on her pretty, angular face.

"Now come," she said with a brusque jerk of her chin. "Tell me what it is. It is not the dragon, is it? I thought we had exhausted all that worry in our last meeting with the general."

When Caelum didn't respond, one pale eyebrow rose in interest. "Then it is things within Nodaria? I hear that reconstruction has been challenging."

Caelum grunted, his arms tightening over his chest, but still, he did not respond. Kindra's face spread into a knowing smile.

"Ah," she murmured thoughtfully. "Then perhaps it is your Little Bird."

His spine stiffened and he snapped, "She isn't *mine*."

"No?" Kindra's smirk grew even more catlike as she assessed him from her throne of ice. "Are you sure about that?"

"Yes," Caelum snarled, whirling on his aunt, his fury surging back to boiling temperature. "She is not *mine*. I belong to no one."

The words spilled from him—a hot, outpouring of anger, as if to wash away what he really felt. The *truth*. That he was plagued with her.

Haunted by the incessant scratch of emotions against his heart. Emotions that were not his. He could not say it, though. The honest to gods' truth was that he sounded insane even *thinking* it.

Kindra regarded him warily for a moment, those ice blue eyes unblinking. It was as if she could guess something even he did not know, as if she knew exactly what he was feeling.

Finally, she rose from the glacier. "If you say so," she replied calmly. She walked towards the door, brushing past Caelum in a cool gust of frosty air. He gritted his teeth as it passed over him, as if it were a ghost breathing down his neck. "If you say nothing is the matter, then we shall resume training at the next week, after Vetrnaetr." His aunt turned back to him, and Caelum had the distinct feeling of being seen through, right to his bones. "In the meantime, try to control yourself."

And with that, she left the room, leaving Caelum standing in a field of ice and frost, feeling more lost than he ever had before. Lights danced in his vision, and he swayed where he stood, covered in frost and sweat. Steam rose from his hot body, and he felt this overwhelming urge to give into the exhaustion and sink to the ground and rest.

But, instead, he gathered the rest of his strength and—with a strangled yell of exhausted effort—threw a portal spiraling into the air. It cast the dark training room into a brilliant purple light, before Caelum launched himself headfirst into it.

When he hit the ground on the other side, he did not land on his feet. Instead, he crashed to the floor, his body limp, his muscles and bones screaming in pain.

Panting, Caelum rolled onto his back, coughing. With a shaky hand, he reached up and swiped the sweat from his face. When his hand came back, it was covered in blood again. He swore, punching the floor before struggling to rise. Frost and ice circled him on the black marble of the quiet corridor of Atlas Keep, and he said a silent prayer of thanks that no one was around to witness this. Their king, spent and exhausted from only a few portals and hours of hard training. As if it were proof that he truly did not deserve the throne they forced him upon.

Pulling himself into a sitting position, Caelum leaned back against the cool black marble of the wall and closed his eyes. His breathing sawed out of him, his chest rising and falling, and for a moment, in the still quiet of the hall, he could feel it . . . a rhythmic beating alongside his heart.

He knew it was her. Could almost feel her on the other side of his fingertips and the sensation made him want to scream. This feeling had happened with Deya before, of course. He could sense her nearness, like an animal could sense rain. Could feel her fears and her emotions as if someone whispered her thoughts into his ear. But it had only gotten stronger with time, to the point where he could no longer ignore it. Ever since he had entered Val's mind, he wondered if it was possibly a product of this newfound second sight he had developed, but he couldn't be sure.

What *was* this irritating feeling? As if something was tied to him . . . *bound* to him.

His eyes flew open, the word stirring a memory in him.

"You have mated. Your auras are different. Fused. It is a sign that you have mated, bonded by something more than just physical."

That was what Io had said to them when they had arrived at Mount Mors.

Caelum hadn't thought much about it, dismissing the concept of mates and soul bonds as folklore and legend. Childish tales told to those who wanted to believe in love within a world where war and blood triumphed over all.

It couldn't be real . . . Could it?

Before Caelum knew what he was doing, he hauled himself to his feet. Still swaying slightly, coughing through sore lungs, he staggered towards the east wing, past the great hall and up the steps leading towards the astronomy tower. He staggered with each step, his head spinning with the effort to remain standing, when he turned the corner and nearly crashed, head-first, into a soldier. The force nearly knocked him into the wall, sending him falling backwards. Swearing, he looked up fully intending to shout at the offending party, when he stopped.

A young soldier stared at him, and Caelum froze. The boy looked familiar from somewhere, but where . . . His eyes scanned him, and he could feel his gaze linger on the smear of blood on his shirt, the way he could barely stay standing. His lip curled, as if in disgust, before he hurried away without a single word. Caelum stared after him, still wondering where he had seen his face before. With a mild tingle of panic over *someone* seeing him in this state, he pushed on.

He hadn't had much time to go see the other star seers, preferring to mostly hide on his own in a secluded alcove of the tallest tower. But this time—after he had gathered what little strength he had on the way there to reach the suspended floor of the tower—he landed roughly in the entryway before veering off towards the open area where the star seers frequented, his mind still on the young soldier in the hall.

Atlas Keep's observatory was an open, rounded room. Pillars dotted the low walls leading to open windows with no glass, giving a full, unobstructed view of Nodaria below. Dainty bronze telescopes were mounted between each pillared archway, while thin, gauzy blinds of a purple material billowed in the night breeze.

The minute Caelum walked through the door, a gaggle of star seers jumped at the very sight of him. Some bowed, others blushed and ducked behind telescopes, but Caelum only had eyes for the small, elderly female sitting in the far corner. The sight of her drove all thoughts of the soldier from his mind.

Io was perched behind a spindly telescope, one purple eye trained to the sky. A gnarled hand twisted the eyepiece, focusing it quietly up towards the Heavens as he approached.

She did not even look up from the eyepiece when she spoke.

"To what do I owe this pleasure, Your Highness?"

Caelum shifted, clearing his throat. Io often left him feeling uneasy— as if she could sense all that he hid, knew all that he buried.

"I wanted to talk to you. I have some . . . questions."

Io smiled. "Of course you do," she said softly. She withdrew from the telescope, and when she turned to look up at him, Caelum saw her in full light. Io had aged significantly in the short time since he had seen her last. Her purple eyes were clouded and struggling to focus on him. There was a small tremble to each of her movements, and a hollowness to her wrinkled cheeks that had not been there before.

Io gestured for him to sit on the small stool opposite her, and Caelum sank down on it.

"Are you okay, Io?" he asked, but Io only sighed.

"Don't you worry, child. I am as fine as I can be at this age." She studied him, and Caelum noticed her gaze was slightly off center, and yet he knew she saw him fully. He briefly wondered if she could still see the blood staining his mouth or the pallor of his complexion. Hastily, he rubbed at his face. "Now tell me what brings you here today."

Caelum sighed and cast a glance backwards at the other star seers—all of whom seemed to be listening intently to their conversation. Io tutted and flicked a withered hand at them. They scattered like moths from a light.

"Something happened the other day," he began. Io did not speak, and Caelum got the distinct feeling she knew what he was going to say, but he barreled on anyway. "I went into somebody's mind. I saw what they had seen, as if it were a vision. Why am I suddenly receiving second sight after all this time?"

Io's wrinkled face remained impassive. Instead, she leaned back in her seat, her gnarled fingers tenting together as she regarded him. "When a High King passes, his power is said to filter through the bloodline to his next kin at their coronation. There is an ancient magic that lives on within the passing of each throne to new hands."

Caelum's spine stiffened. "Why have I never heard of this before?" he asked, his mind reeling from another bit of information his father had neglected to tell him.

But Io sighed. "Forgive me, child, but you were not even considered in the line of succession given . . . given your unique parentage."

A squirm of irritation needled through him, but he couldn't dispute this. He knew he was considered the end of the line when it came to who would take his father's place when he died. His hands clenched at the reminder of what he already knew: It shouldn't be him on the throne at all.

"It is something not often discussed with those outside the royal line," Io continued. "But, if I'm being frank, I am surprised that this is the only new power you have inherited thus far."

"What do you mean?"

Her fingers tapped lightly on her chin and her foggy gaze shifted to look out over Caelum's shoulder towards the sliver of moon in the clear sky. "There should be more power manifesting within you. But it's as if your father's magic has left with him . . . like there's only the ghost of it remaining." Io sighed. "I know nothing of your mother, nor what became of her, so I have no answers as to what her blood mixing with your father's might mean for the passing of the royal magic, but . . ."

Caelum's heart was thrumming in his ears—a loud staccato that drowned out all thought. He had always felt abandoned by his family—especially now, as he fought his way through the truth of his parentage, through the mysteries and lies that had died with Castor. The thought that even his father's own magic—his *inheritance*—had also possibly abandoned him felt like a slap to the face.

Blinking through the frustration beginning to cloud his vision, Caelum shook his head and said, "But this second sight . . . is this the reason why I can sense—"

But before he could even finish his thought, Io smiled. "Why you sense that girl? Why you feel her constantly? Child, we have already talked about this."

His chest was heating, irritation scratching at him at how Io always seemed to know. The old star seer leaned forward, her gnarled hand reaching out to grasp his wrist in a surprisingly tight grip.

"That girl is your mate, Caelum. I thought you had finally stopped fighting it."

"Mate bonds aren't real," Caelum grunted. He pulled his wrist free, trying to steady his breathing amidst his rapidly beating heart. "I have never heard of anyone being mated. It had always been legend, conjecture. Why can I feel her—"

"Because you are bound to her. A *soul* bond." He could see himself reflected in Io's cloudy eyes as she gazed past him—*through* him. "Legends speak of mates as rare, impossible ties. Ancient stories claim the Mother created mates only between those of different kingdoms to create harmony in the realm. You could walk past your mate and never even know it. But the minute you *act* on it—"

Caelum's face began to heat, and he remembered the way Io's eyes had alighted on him and Deya that day in Mount Mors. The morning after the first time they had—

"Once you *act* on it, the bond is established, the magic *alive*. And the closer you become, the stronger it grows."

His breathing was shallow as he attempted to process what Io had said. It felt as though he were falling from a great height, trying desperately to grab anything to stop his fall. To be *bound* to Deya . . . unable to escape the cosmic pull towards each other.

It was too much. He couldn't be bound to anyone, to *anything*.

It was a weakness he could not afford.

Io leaned forward, the dark hood on her head drifting around her face like a curtain of hair. "You cannot outrun your fate, boy," she said softly. "And that girl . . . that girl is yours."

CHAPTER 12

Life in Fangdor Castle without Val became bleak for Deya. Each day passed with a new inch of snow, the same steel gray in the sky, the same guilty weight in her heart. She wrote Val a note and begged Kindra to send it to Nodaria via raven, but was dismayed when Kindra informed her that no ravens could survive the weather over the glaciers at this time of year.

So Deya sat in her room, the note to Val begging her forgiveness and pleading with her to come back sitting, untouched, on her bedside table.

No matter how she looked at the situation, the fact remained that, in the face of danger, she had frozen at the memory of the shadows filling her head. Paralyzed by the uncontrollable black wave that had moved through her . . . She couldn't bring herself to do it. She was too afraid to deal with the skathi using her magic. Instead, she had let it attack them both. The memory of watching the skathi disappear into the snow with Val haunted her every day after.

In the end, she had been too scared to use her magic, even when it had most mattered.

After that, Deya spent day after day in the library, turning brown, brittle pages, and counting the snowflakes falling from the ceiling, landing amongst the tomes about Flykra and Bridah. But nothing about the Mother, nor anything that could point to an artifact representing all of the goddesses.

The lack of progress in her search pressed down on her, images of dragons filling her head while she flipped hopelessly through book after book. And while she found nothing that could solve the mystery of the Mother's heart, she did find out a great deal about Vetrnaetr.

In the few books that had been translated from Brynorsk into the common tongue, Deya learned that *Vetrnaetr*—the Winter Nights—were broken into two of the longest days in Bridah. During these times the sun did not set for a full day, and the moon did not rise for another. Bridanians ate, drank, danced, and even sacrificed an animal or two for the feast celebrating it. Reading on the activities distracted Deya from her real task, often catching herself lounging in an armchair by the library fire, running one blackened finger down the spine of a book about Bridanian holidays.

As Vetrnaetr came closer, Fangdor became busier with preparations. There were more servants preparing rooms for guests, more cooks bustling to and from the kitchens with fresh meat and root vegetables for roasting. Kindra and Ulf were largely absent as they readied Bridah for a celebration the size of which Deya had never seen before.

Having grown up in Praiton—an amalgamation of all the nations in Krigor— Deya had not seen a single tradition given precedence over any other. Even Praiton's own celebrations of the Mother Goddess paled in comparison to the Bridanians' fervent desire to celebrate Flykra.

From the window at the top of Fangdor's library, Deya watched as a collection of castle workers carried large wooden poles carved with Flykra's likeness into the center of the courtyard. They were hung with garland and wreaths, the snow covering everything making Bridah seem magical for the first time since her arrival.

The door behind her banged open, and Karyna came hurrying into the room carrying a stack of thick woolen dresses that looked bigger than she was.

"A little help!" Karyna choked out, stumbling over the threshold.

Deya laughed, getting up and hurrying over to the small female, who almost collapsed as Deya relieved her of the armful of gowns.

Over the last few days, Karyna had come out of her shell. Perhaps it was the hours Deya spent wallowing and begging Kindra to contact Val, but Karyna had become a steady, comforting presence at her side. The winter days made it difficult to stave off loneliness, and without Val, Deya feared getting through each day in the Frost Kingdom alone.

But Karyna never allowed that to happen. Everywhere Deya went, Karyna went. And although she wondered if it was because Kindra ordered the lady's maid to not let her out of her sight, Deya found she was thankful for the girl, mandated or not.

"What on Earth are all these for?" Deya laughed, holding up a long dark blue dress with delicate silver thread woven onto the sleeves and hem.

"You, of course," Karyna said, huffing a long piece of white hair out of her face. "I believe Lady Kindra wants to prevent you leaving the castle ever again by smothering you with fabric."

Deya snorted as she held the dress up. The embroidery was intricate, the silver thread sparkling in the light as she turned it. "Why would I need a dress this fancy, Karyna?"

The small lady's maid gave her an exasperated look. "For Vetrnaetr, of course. It *is* tonight."

Deya felt her heart clench, the smallest familiar flutter of wings taking flight in her chest. She had not heard from Caelum since he had left the night they returned from Frode—a whole fortnight past now. She wasn't sure if he was going to come back for Vetrnaetr or not. No matter how hard she tried, she could not shake the memory of the hurt in his eyes when he realized she chose to walk to her death instead of asking him for help.

Caelum never showed vulnerability, no matter how much she begged for it. Funny how the one time it appeared was because she had hurt him.

Karyna seemed to notice how her face fell at the realization. She lowered the dress she was holding, her expression turning sympathetic. "The High King will come. I'm sure of it," she said consolingly. "And I know he'll bring Miss Val, too."

Deya gave her a small smile, knowing full well that Karyna wasn't sure if Caelum would show either. "Thanks, Karyna."

The two smiled at each other, and Deya forced back the pang of loneliness she felt. Even with Karyna by her side, she couldn't completely fight the isolation which had crept into her bones like the frost on the windowpane. She had been forced out of Nodaria by Praiton, separated from the friends she had been with since escaping Ironbalt all those months ago. Sent away and locked up, just as she had been in those prison cells.

An unexpected shiver rolled up her spine at the realization that her escape from prison was almost a year ago. Where had the time gone? It felt like only yesterday when she had lost everything she used to hold dear. And while Karyna helped to ease the loneliness, she still ached for a familiar face, something to reassure her that her new life was not attempting to abandon her as well.

Deya glanced down at her blackened fingertips, which were balled together in her lap. Something had been bothering her since she had come back from Frode's. Something she could not seem to find the answer to on her own in Fangdor's library.

"Karyna," she said suddenly. The small female looked up from where she was sorting through the pile of fabric.

"Yes?"

"I saw something in my reading that I wasn't able to translate," Deya hedged. Her fingers scratched against the fabric of her skirt, the cold fear Frode had instilled in her beginning to pulsate in her chest. She could still feel his fingers on her face, his cold breath on her cheeks. "What . . . what does *dodsbringern* mean?"

Karyna froze, her face paling as she straightened to look at her. "What . . . what in Flykra have you been reading?" she stammered.

Deya's heart quickened, a molten flush spreading up her chest. "Why? What does it mean?"

Karyna shook her head, her blue eyes still wide. "Oh, but *dodsbringern* is not something to bring up now. Not before the Long Night." She lowered her voice, as if the gods themselves could hear them. "It's bad luck, you see? It is a bad omen."

"But what does it mean?" She could hardly breathe over the panic. The anxiety. The urge to grip Karyna by the shoulders and shake it out of her battled with her fear that her black hands would give her away.

"It is an evil creature. A wicked force. It means . . . *Death Bringer*," Karyna whispered, and all the air trickled out of Deya's lungs.

She slumped back against her chair, her nails digging into the palms of her hands until they left half-moon marks embedded in the skin. Curling her blackened fingers, she reached for her gloves and numbly slipped them back on.

"Anyway, enough of all that, let's get you ready for our Long Night!" Karyna said, plastering on a cheerful expression and grabbing Deya by the hands, yanking her from her armchair by the window. "*Long Night into morning make short rise of sun . . . Let us languish in moonlight and revel in fun!*"

Laughing, Karyna skipped out of the room, dragging her out of the library and back through Fangdor, Deya's hidden fingers in one hand and the beautiful blue and silver dress in the other. And even though Deya tried to smile along with her, she could not help feeling like a disease. As if just by touching this girl, she would bring to her a dark death.

As the winter sun began its descent for the next two days, Karyna dressed Deya in Bridanian finery. She unwound Deya's simple plait to shake loose her long chestnut curls before twisting a few sections into smaller braids, pulling it back in an elegant half up-do at the back of her head. As if Deya didn't feel enough unlike herself, Karyna finished her look off with subtle Bridanian markings in white paint: simple dots lining her eyebrows and a thin line down the middle of her brow.

When Deya looked at herself in the mirror, she looked almost as much of a Bridanian as Karyna, even with her dark brown hair.

By the time Deya and Karyna entered Fangdor's main hall, it was filled with talking, laughing, music, and shouting. A large fire burned in the center of the cavernous wooden hall, and plates upon plates of steaming food littered the tables surrounding it. Already, people danced around the fire, touting large tankards of ale, singing songs in Brynorsk, pounding on the tables with their fists or weapons in time to the music.

The moment Deya and Karyna crossed the threshold, a small white-haired boy came hurdling through the crowd, crashing right into Karyna's knees.

"*Niel!* Behave yourself! Where in Flykra's name did you get *that?*" Karyna admonished, pulling the boy back by his ear. The boy giggled, swinging a large battleaxe twice the length of his small body.

"Where do you think?" A large, rugged male came loping over to them, seizing Niel from behind and jerking him upwards, causing him to shriek with glee and drop the axe. "He pilfered it from me."

Deya could not help but stare at the male. He turned, flashing a smile at her with teeth as white as his hair.

Besides Ulf, this was the first Bridanian male she had clapped eyes on this close, and she felt a blush creep up her face. His white hair was shaved on either side, cropped to the skin, with the rest of the snowy white strands braided and twisted in a knot at the top of his head. Piercing blue eyes twinkled at her from under thick black face paint, a smudge of kohl striping from ear to ear, crossing over the bridge of his straight nose, dots like her own running from forehead to brow.

"This must be the outsider," he said, beaming at her and holding out his hand. "*Heil og sal,* I'm Espen."

Deya could only stare stupidly at him. Her brain seemed to float in the smoke emitting from the fire as she blinked at the large, muscular male in front of her. Only when Karyna bumped her with her hip did Deya snap back into her body.

"Deya," she stuttered finally, holding out a hand. Espen seized her extended limb, not by the hand as she expected, but by the forearm, underneath her elbow.

"Deya, these are my brothers," Karyna grumbled, scooping up the battleaxe and shoving it at Espen. "And need I remind you to keep your weapons out of reach of him? You know he already thinks he is a soldier."

Espen grinned down at his sister with the same heart-stopping smile before saying something to her in Brynorsk. Whatever he said made her roll her eyes and shove him in the shoulder.

"Karyna! Come dance with me! *Gleoja*, please!" Niel begged, yanking on Karyna's skirt with an alarming strength.

Karyna yelped, shooing his hand away, and cried, "I cannot leave Deya, Niel! You will have to wait!"

"Oh!" Deya flushed, shaking her head. "No, Karyna, go! You don't have to stay with me!"

Karyna opened her mouth to argue, but Espen held up a hand. "Yes, *systir*, it is your turn to babysit the little heathen. I'll keep Deya company," he said, slinging the large axe over his shoulder. And when both Deya and Karyna began to protest, Niel gave Karyna's hand another hard jerk, and yanked her out of sight into the crowd.

"Quite strong for a small fellow, isn't he?" Deya muttered, chuckling under her breath.

"Oh, yes," Espen said, watching with a smile as Niel and Karyna began to dance wildly around the fire, twirling in between smoke and sparks. "Niel already believes himself to be part of the Berserkers, even at cub age."

Deya blinked at him. *"Berserkers?"* she echoed. "And . . . cub?"

Espen let out a gravelly laugh, the battleaxe catching the light of the flames, illuminating the intricate Brynorsk markings lining its handle and etched into its silver blade.

"It truly is interesting to have an outsider among us. I cannot say I have encountered many of them." His melodic accent was as thick as Karyna's, and Deya had to strain over the din of the room to understand him. "Berserkers are our elite warrior group. *Kyandra* is our leader, my *hersir*. And yes, we often call our young cubs." He shrugged, watching Niel flail his arms in the middle of the floor with a fond smile on his face. "Though he is not quite a bear yet."

Deya, too, watched Niel jump and prance among the other Bridanians. People as delicate and spritely as Karyna mixed with those as burly and intimidating as Espen, all smiling and laughing. Alcohol was flowing and the beat of the animal skin drum in the corner pounded in her pulse and chest.

"How are you finding Bridah so far, Deya?" Espen asked, leaning down, having to almost shout in her ear to be heard. His proximity made goosebumps cover her arms, the hair on the back of her neck standing on end.

"Cold," she replied, and Espen laughed.

"Well, let's get you warmed up," he said. Was it her imagination, or did a mischievous glint sparkle in his blue eyes when he said that?

Against Deya's better judgment, she followed Espen towards the grog table. His large shoulders moved through the crowd, and her eyes followed them down to his tapered waist. He was burlier than Caelum—the only other male body she truly knew—and the faintest traces of black tattoos crept out from the collar of his fur cloak and the sleeves of his woolen tunic. But unlike Caelum's tattoos, these were not created with magic but rather ink and needle.

"Have you ever tried frostfire mead?" Espen asked, handing her a large mug, which Deya took with some apprehension.

"No, can't say I have," she replied, giving the frothy liquid a tentative sniff. A swirling aroma of strong and spicy fragrances filled her head, along with a hint of berries. The scent seemed to wrap its arms around her, drawing her in, encouraging her to take the first sip, and she obliged.

The cold liquid washed over her tongue, an explosion of spiced fruit and strong fermentation crashed over her taste buds, and she began coughing almost immediately.

Laughing, Espen thumped her on the back with a large hand as she choked and spluttered, the spices of the mead still clinging to the back of her throat.

"Easy there," he chuckled. "Frostfire is strong. Too many of those and I'll have to carry you up to bed."

Deya's head whipped around to look at him, mead sloshing over her cup as her cheeks flushed. But Espen was busy waving to someone in the crowd, oblivious to the fact that Deya was parsing that last proclamation for subtext.

Stop being ridiculous, she chastised herself. *He isn't propositioning you. Stop acting like an idiot.*

Attempting to steady herself, Deya turned away from Espen and took a deep swig of her drink. Her head spun as the mead sank into her veins. Lights popped in her vision, as if the drink had grown hands, picked up her brain, and begun to dance with it.

Deya felt herself closing her eyes, rocking back and forth to the beat of the drums and the chirruping of the pan pipes and lyres. Lifting heavy lids, she swayed with the music and looked around.

Everywhere she looked, Bridanians celebrated, and yet all she could see was Caelum. Searching for Caelum in a crowded room used to be easy—the only white-haired fae in a sea of color. But now, she was surrounded by white-haired fae, and *she* was the odd one out. Was this how he had felt his whole life?

Her head swiveled back and forth, eyes scanning the crowd, looking for the white-haired male with purple eyes. But he was nowhere to be seen. A sharp pang of disappointment pierced her heart, and she turned from the door, staring down hard into the now half empty depths of her mead mug.

Through the perfumed fog swirling in her brain, a small voice whispered in her ear: *Why should you feel bad about being attracted to Espen? It's not as if Caelum has claimed you. In fact, he refuses to.*

Anger surged through her and her permanently gloved fingers tightened on the mug.

"Are you all right?" Espen turned from the group of large males who had come to greet him. His hand drifted along the small of her back, and Deya looked up at him, trying to focus on those bright blue eyes through the hazy fog of the mead.

If Caelum would not claim her, why did she still search for him? Why did she still feel him, as if he was tied to her ribcage by some invisible string? She wanted to rip it from her, sever the connection which pumped agonizing yearning for the male through her body. If he did not want to acknowledge this, she would follow his lead.

Looking up at Espen, she gave him a coy smile. "I'm feeling a little dizzy," she said, using her gloved hand to fan herself. "I might need to get some air."

Espen chuckled and nodded towards her mug. "I told you frostfire mead is dangerous. You take a drink, and the drink takes you." He plucked the mug from her hand and offered her his arm. "I think, what you need, is actually a spin around the fire for Flykra." The roguish grin he gave her might have been charming if she wasn't so caught up in her own hurt.

And as she took his hand and allowed him to lead her towards the dance floor, images of Caelum flashed through her mind. How he had refused to acknowledge their feelings. His assurance that he only cared about the realm and not her. His toxic, commandeering control he attempted to exert over her, even when he swore he did not care about her.

It whirled through her mind, along with her body as Espen pulled her into the center of the circle of revelers. They all had joined hands, kicking their legs in time to the music, spinning in a group. Espen took her hands and gave her a reassuring nod.

"Just follow my lead," he murmured, the smile he gave her making her face flush. Deya nodded, her hands shaking as she placed them in his. Espen began to dance, pulling her arms back and forth, their chests meeting and parting as their legs kicked in opposite time. After a few awkward fumbles, Deya began to find her rhythm, moving against Espen, feeling his body, reveling in the heat of him as they moved faster and faster within the dancing circle.

Oh, how *wonderful* she felt. How light and free. Lights twinkled in her vision as she giggled with Espen, trying to keep up with his footwork, her brain drifting on a pink fluffy cloud made only lighter by her and Espen's frantic dancing. She couldn't remember how long it had been since she had danced like this . . . had *let go* like this.

Espen got closer and closer to her, his hands no longer holding hers, but wrapping around her waist. It felt so foreign, yet familiar. He was cold to the touch, like somebody else she wouldn't think of right now. She refused.

And as she spun and danced and twirled, her footing got more unsteady, and, before she knew it, she was stumbling, laughing into Espen's arms.

"Ah, the mead has claimed its next victim," Espen chuckled, as he adjusted his grip on her, holding her limp body up as she giggled. His whole torso pressed against hers, and even though it felt nice, she suddenly could not shake the feeling of molten anger and anxiety that began to melt the joy straight down her chest.

Espen righted her, but Deya stumbled, balancing herself with a hand on his shoulder, attempting to breathe through the sudden feeling of fury. Her breath was short, her chest tight, like something hot was pressing against it.

As if someone had given that damned string in her ribcage a furious tug, Deya whipped around to look at the door.

Caelum stood in the entrance to the hall, stock-still, and staring at her and Espen with furious, glowing purple eyes.

CHAPTER 13

Val watched Caelum pace the length of Castor's office again, his purple eyes burning holes into the black marble floor, his fingernails digging into the hilt of the Shadow Sword.

"You're giving me motion sickness," Val said dryly, glancing up from the book she had opened in front of her.

Caelum gave a furious growl before turning on his heel and beginning to stride back the opposite way.

Val sighed and flicked a page with a lazy finger. She hadn't read a single word since Caelum had entered the office and began his frenetic pacing back and forth. Val was amazed he hadn't begun to wear grooves on the floor with how many laps he had already performed.

"Just *go*," she commanded him, finally fed up with the black and white blur whirling past her again. "There is no reason for you not to. You haven't seen her in weeks. You really should go."

Caelum grunted and Val shifted in her seat, attempting to dislodge the guilt which had settled in her gut like a stone at the thought of Deya.

It had been weeks since the skathi had attacked her, and yet the image of Lucia's head landing at her feet still looped through her mind.

Val rubbed her brow, her chest tight from the memory, her throat burning with shame.

When Caelum had told her Ulf had invited her to their winter festival, the thought alone made Val faint with nerves. Just like she could not be in Light's Tower, she did not think she'd ever be able to show her face in the Frost Kingdom again.

"Why should I go?" Caelum snarled, still making his furious rounds back and forth. "She made it very clear she does not care for my help nor assistance. *Both* of you have."

Val scoffed, rolling her amber eyes, and resisting the urge to hurl a book at his head. Maybe the impact would snap him out of his dramatic tantrum. "Deya did not want to ask you because she knew you would stop us. And I'd say she was right."

Caelum finally stopped short, frost crackling at his fingertips as he whirled on her. "I understand why you went," he snapped. "You don't think I want to know why Praiton is targeting her? Do you not think I want to stop them, too? I am doing *everything* I can to stop them."

Caelum was breathing hard, and Val deflated slightly, a rare sympathy for Nodaria's High King rushing over her.

She had watched Caelum leave each council meeting looking angrier and more frustrated by the day. The male who used to snap and bite at everyone and everything had grown quiet since he had become king. His fury had turned into a quiet seething, a frustrated burn of stress and nerves. She could sense his fear, recognized the same feeling of being a fraud she herself had carried for so many years as a captain . . . a feeling she still carried, especially after her last conversation with the Legion's general.

But underneath all the political stress, Val could see something bigger bothering Caelum. She knew better than anyone what it looked like to deny your feelings for someone, even when it was staring them in the face.

Even when denying it might kill them.

"Caelum," Val said, her voice softer than before. She stood from her chair by the fire and approached him. This level of understanding for her and Caelum was new territory. The antagonism between them had long since fizzled, and Val was more embarrassed over the number of times she had sobbed on this male's shoulder.

And although she did not tell anyone what the skathi had turned into, in a strange way, she felt as though Caelum knew. Since she had arrived back in the Celestial Kingdom, when he had not been to meetings or tending to Legion business, he had often sat with her in Castor's office. It may have been in a tense silence, but she recognized his effort. Caelum tried to be there for her in the only way he knew how.

If she'd been told several months ago that she was to become friends with the acidic male, she would've laughed herself to tears. But the thought of those times was what gave her the strength to say what she really thought.

"Why deny yourself something good?" she whispered. "Don't you deserve to be happy?"

Don't you? A small voice scratched at the back of her mind, but she shoved it aside. Caelum was breathing hard, staring at the corner of the room, the mental battle raging behind those purple eyes.

And then he closed his eyes and let out a deep breath. Turning away from her, he pulled apart the air with his hands. The spiraling purple disk came spinning into view along with the familiar feeling of all the air being sucked out of the room.

Val smiled as Caelum moved towards the portal, pausing as he looked back over his shoulder at her. "Are you sure you don't want to come?"

Hesitating, she considered it for all of a second before she felt the ghost of a winter wind on her neck, remembered how her internal flame had all but extinguished . . . then the image of Deya, lying frozen and motionless in the snow.

Shaking her head, Val gave him a small smile. "Say hi to her for me," she said softly.

Caelum paused, looking at her with an intense, piercing look. And in that moment, Val realized she wasn't the only one who recognized her weakness in the other.

He gave her a stiff nod. "Tell Aris I'll send a portal for him in ten minutes."

A cold bolt of fear zipped through her, and Val's heart leapt into her throat. "Wait," she cried. "Aris is going?"

But it was too late. No sooner were the words out of her mouth than Caelum disappeared into the portal with a loud *whooshing* noise. And then everything was quiet.

Swearing, Val threw herself back into her chair and stared at the open book in front of her, her long red nails drumming an anxious rhythm on the wooden arm. She had not seen the general in over a week and the thought of facing him sent a shot of molten anxiety through her.

She couldn't say she hadn't been avoiding him. The general had remained at Atlas Keep recently, but the thought of running into him again after their heated exchange in her bedroom had sent her stomach roiling. So, like the coward she was, she fled into Arctos most days, hiding within the public libraries and the local taverns to pass the time. The last few days, she had sat at the Astral Tavern, drinking and reading more and more books about dragons.

It was bad enough that she was spending most of her evenings too drunk to read the words, but she had found she couldn't get Aris off her mind. Especially his last words to her.

Lucia would think you could do it.

Damn him, she thought angrily, shoving aside the book, nearly pushing it off Castor's desk. *What does he know about what Lucia would want?*

But no matter what she said, she knew she was just being petulant. Because, in the end, Val couldn't shake the feeling that Aris was right.

An image of Lucia seizing her by the shoulders in the middle of a fiery battle flashed through her mind.

"You are stronger than this. Braver than this."

They were the last words she had ever spoken to her. And they had been a lie.

Val was *not* stronger than she was that day. Her battle with her brothers had proved that, proved that she was not worthy of being called their captain. A sharp pain pierced her heart at the thought of Lucia, and she quickly shoved the thought of her sisters from her mind.

If she couldn't protect the three people in the world she cared for most, how was she to save a realm?

Val glanced back at the corner Caelum had disappeared into and then towards the door of the office. Would the general attempt to convince her again? Should she try to flee the office before he arrived? Or would that look too pathetic?

But before she could decide, the door swung open.

Aris strode into the study, his golden armor smudged and dirty in places. His hair was mussed, as if leagues of wind and weather had moved through it, but it was his eyes that drew her. War, it seemed, had taken its toll on the general. The last time she saw him he had seemed tired and wan. Now, there was a shadow in those hazel eyes, as if a storm brewed behind them.

He had taken only three steps into the office, toying with his large golden broadsword, before he did a doubletake.

"Valeria," he said, stopping short, his feet skittering on the carpet. "What are you . . .?"

Judging by the shock on his face, it was safe to say the general had not expected to run into her here.

"Caelum said he'd send the portal for you in ten minutes," she said in way of greeting. She got to her feet, turning to gather her books, trying to distract herself from the irritating pounding of her heart that never failed to start every time the general was in the same room as her. Aris's eyes followed her, making the back of her neck burn with his gaze. Would he press her about the dragon again?

"Are you not going to Bridah?"

"No," Val mumbled, shoving a sheaf of parchment into an opened book, and slamming it shut. "Winter festivals really aren't for me."

"Valeria." Hands reached for her wrists, but when she made to push past him, he planted them on the table, trapping her. The sudden movement put her close to him . . . *too* close. Heat burned her cheeks, and she ducked her head, avoiding his gaze.

"You're being evasive."

Val angled her chin imperiously towards the ceiling, still not meeting his eyes. "My apologies, *General*. How do you suggest I be more straightforward?"

Aris's eyes narrowed but a small smirk played on his lips. "By looking at me, *Captain.*"

With a deep breath, Val turned to look at him and her breath caught. Gods, she would never get used to being this close to him. Aris leaned closer, studying her. He never seemed as rattled by their proximity as she was.

"You never answered my question the other night," Aris said, and Val's heart skipped a beat. "Why did you leave Bridah? What happened?"

She couldn't fathom how it was possible for the general to have full, serious conversations with her without ever breaking eye contact. The intensity of his stare was beginning to make her shiver, as if her skin were pricking to attention, hungering for his gaze.

Sighing, Val said, "It's a long story, General. I will not bore you with the details." While she was relieved he had chosen not to push her on the dragon again, it still hurt to be so near to him. She attempted to pull away, but Aris's hand caught her around the waist, holding a finger up with another.

"Ah ah," he murmured, wagging the finger in her face. "I know your game, *Captain*. Do not try to evade your general's direct question. Now, tell me what happened in Bridah, and that is an order." The shadow of the familiar cocky smirk pulled at his lips, the only indication his assertion of power was not serious.

Val grumbled, attempting to twist out of his hold again, the heat in her blood increasing as if her traitorous body yearned to touch him—as if it still remembered how it felt to.

"Let's just say the cold did not agree with me," she mumbled finally. Her voice quivered as she averted her gaze. The shame of the whole thing proved to be too much. She couldn't bear to tell him how foolishly she had acted.

For a moment, Aris did not speak. She felt his eyes sweep every inch of her face with an abject acuity; a gentle flush left behind on every place his gaze lingered too long. Then, suddenly a loud *whooshing* noise and a burst of bright purple light filled the room. The portal Caelum had promised spun into position in the same corner he had left through minutes ago, yet Aris did not look away from Val to even acknowledge it.

His eyes drifted from hers, down her face, running along the curve of her lips. Val wet them without thinking and the smallest flicker of a wince passed over Aris's face.

"Your portal is here, General," she said finally, but her words came out in a breathy whisper. Gods, how did they always wind up like this? The damned magnetism between them, like flame to metal, could probably wrench them into this same position across several kingdoms.

But at Val's words, Aris blinked, and the spell was broken. His hands slipped from around her waist, and he pulled back, glancing at the portal, as if noticing it for the first time. "Why are you not going?"

Val tried to give him a brave smile, her brain able to think more clearly now that he wasn't touching her. "I just . . . can't."

Maybe it was the tremble in her voice, or perhaps it was because, as she said it, the image of Lucia walking through the snow drifted back to her like smoke from a fire, but her eyes burned with unshed tears, and she jerked her head away. But nothing was ever lost on the general.

With one last glance at the portal, Aris took Val's hand and began to pull her towards the door.

"General, where—"

But Aris did not answer her. With his hand firmly clasped around hers, he pulled her from Castor's office and out, through the Keep.

The halls of the cavernous castle were empty, the stars even twinkling fainter than usual as they strode through the corridors and out into the moonlit courtyard. Val hadn't spent much time looking around this part of the castle, preferring to keep to the training fields during her time here. Yet Aris bypassed the deserted training field and led her through the darkened garden.

Starlight sprites bounced around their feet, careening out of view, sticking to Val's sleeves and pinging off Aris's armor, but the general did not slow his stride until, finally, they were climbing a steep, grassy hill. The trickle of water reached her ears, and Val stopped as they approached the apex of the small incline.

Dark, purple-green grass, rich and lush, stretched across the steppe overlooking the running river below. The bridge towards Arctos twinkled with starlight far below them, making it feel as though they were looking out over the edge of the world. Nodaria's curious night blooming flowers blossomed from all surfaces, including from the black wrought-iron bench facing the cliff's edge, which Aris led her to.

He collapsed onto it with a sigh, his long arms draping over the chair, his legs spreading out as his head dropped back, as though bathing in the moonlight above. Val stood and watched him for a second, hesitating about whether she should join him before sinking down beside him.

"What about Vetrnaetr?" Val asked softly.

Aris shrugged, his eyes closed, looking more relaxed than she had seen him in a long time. "If you're not going, I'm not going."

Val cocked her head at him. "But . . . why?"

Opening one eye, Aris looked at her out of the corner of the one visible hazel orb, a small smile tugging at the edge of his mouth. "A general goes where he is needed, Valeria."

The familiar phrase rushed back to her like a bolt of lightning, and she felt her heart clench. Biting her lip, desperate to keep the tears she felt rushing forward at bay, she turned away from Aris and stared out over the moon garden.

For a few moments, they sat and listened to the trickle of the waterfall behind them—a stone effigy of Astrea, her hands full of stars and water, flowing down over the rocky cliffs, and tumbling into the stream below.

Aris sat forward, his elbows on his knees, his head bowed before he finally spoke.

"I wanted to apologize to you."

Val blinked. "For what?"

With a soft, humorless laugh, Aris shook his head. "For one, asking you for what I did the other night. It was too much; I know that now. But you know, me and my wild ideas."

Val could only stare at him, her heart fluttering feebly, everything in her frozen, waiting.

"But that's not all." He let out a long sigh, looking down at his hands, as if afraid to look at her. "I know I have let you down, Valeria," he said softly. "I promised you that day . . . I promised to take care of your unit."

Val froze, something sharp and cold piercing her through the heart at his words. Her hands clenched into fists, and she held her breath as he spoke.

"I'm not making excuses for that day, but we had lost half our numbers. The operation was in shambles . . ." Aris shook his head, his fingers running through his short brown hair. "And we had just lost you. Your unit . . . they weren't just inconsolable. They were determined."

Val felt a roaring in her ears. It was loud, overwhelming—like a dragon's growl.

"I was busy . . . distracted. They slipped out of camp after you before I even noticed they were gone." Aris stared down at his hands, which flexed until his golden knuckles turned white.

Val closed her eyes and bit her lip so hard she tasted blood. "Did they say anything to you?" she whispered numbly. "After I was captured? Did they say anything?"

The general didn't reply. His hazel eyes were fixed across the horizon, locked onto the large, golden moon in the sky. He let out a small sigh. "I thought Lucia was going to kill me when I called us to retreat," he said. "She had come up to me and demanded we go after you. When I told her we couldn't risk it, she . . . she said that now that you were gone, *she* was the acting captain of the regiment. And that she would lead like you. Bravely. Selflessly. And because of that, she refused to leave you behind." Aris bowed his head. "Their deaths are my fault, Valeria. I know they are. You are not the only one who mourns."

Lucia's words washed over her like a hot wave—like a lost treasure she had thought she'd never find. Even though she hadn't been there, she could picture Lucia saying this so clearly—her face bright with fury and sadness. *Bravely and selflessly.*

Tears burned their way up her throat, filling her chest and eyes before she could stop them.

But she couldn't let them out.

If she let herself feel this grief—this bottomless, endless grief in her heart, a blackness as never-ending as the Nodarian night sky—she feared the tears would never stop.

Burying her face in her hands, she struggled to breathe as Lucia's words roared over her, struggled to push down on the sobs threatening to burst. Suddenly, rough hands seized her, and she was pulled into Aris's chest. Her head laid on his shoulder, his arms tight around her, his fingers woven into her hair, just as Caelum had done that horrible day in Bridah.

For a moment, Val squeezed her eyes shut and fought the pain, and the guilt, before finally, a single tear slipped down her face.

Softly, quietly, Val cried for her sisters in Aris's arms. Cried for her loss, for her emptiness, for everything that she lacked—cried for that horrible, nightmarish day in Maniel when she was captured. When everything changed.

No matter how she looked at it, Aris was wrong. *She* was the one who had let the Fireflies down that day. In the end, their deaths were *her* fault and hers alone.

But then, like a blaze of fire through the night sky, her brother's face lit up her mind. The jeering, twist of his smile, the wheezing gasp of his laugh . . . and the image of her sisters' mutilated bodies lying in the bloody snow at her feet. The memory of the skathi's illusion made her gasp before her grief turned hot, the flame inside her burning her insides. Her tears dried under the heat of her skin.

Because it wasn't *only* her fault.

It was *them*. Always *them*. Taking everything from her, stripping her back to nothing but a weak, trembling child. And now, here she was, hiding from the Legion and the responsibilities that came with being a captain of the regiment like a coward. Refusing Aris. Refusing what only *she* could do for the realm.

Bravely and selflessly.

Lucia *had* believed in her. Had trusted her wholeheartedly. Her brothers had beaten her that day, and probably would again . . .

But, a small voice in her head whispered, *not if you had a dragon.*

Val's tears slowed and stopped. The voice curled like a flame in her ear. With a dragon, she *would* be stronger. Would become the leader Lucia believed she had been. With a dragon, they would never come for her again. With a dragon, she could put all of this behind her.

Pulling back from Aris, Val's breathing steadied. A new, cold calm was washing over her, a stillness brought about by the voice in the back of her mind.

Aris watched her wipe her eyes, the same look of gentle concern still on his face.

"Valeria, are—"

"I'll do it." The words fell out of her mouth and Aris blinked.

"Do what?"

"I will go to Mount Cinis," she said. And although her voice shook, and everything in her body was screaming at her not to, Val pulled her shoulders back and said it again. "I'll do it."

Aris stared at her for a whole moment, the silence in the moon garden deafening. Even the cicadas had stopped stridulating, the breeze dying around them.

"Are . . . are you sure?" the general breathed.

No, a voice in her head whispered. It was a different voice this time, almost childlike—soft and scared, begging her to rethink what she had already decided, but Val ignored it. If risking her life going to Mount Cinis was the Legion's only chance, she had to take it.

Bravely and selflessly.

After all, she had nothing left to lose anymore.

"If you think it's the only way . . . then, yes. I am," she said. "Besides, if I have a dragon, no one can ever best me again, right?"

For a moment, Val wondered if Aris could hear the quiver in her voice. Those peridot eyes swept over her, studying her with the intensity of a sunbeam—as if he could see right through her. But what she didn't expect was his face to fall at her words . . . as if he pitied her.

"Valeria . . ." he began, and for a moment, Val thought he was going to argue with her, but she didn't want to hear it. She had decided. She knew there was a strong possibility she may die doing this, but if it meant never having to be looked at the way Aris was looking at her now, then she'd have to face it.

Aris seemed to read the determination in her expression. He deflated, swallowing the argument she knew he was about to say. Because, in the end, Aris was the general of the Pillar Legion. And Val was only a part of his plans.

❄

"Caelum, wait!"

Deya had disentangled herself from Espen's grasp and began to fight through the crowds to reach the entryway, but Caelum had already vanished.

Deya craned her neck, looking for a glimpse of white hair, but immediately felt stupid when she realized finding him wouldn't be as easy this time. Rising onto the tips of her toes, Deya swiveled, looking over the heads of the celebrating Bridanians, but Caelum was nowhere to be seen. As if she had simply imagined him.

But she knew she hadn't. A white-hot flare of anger was still pounding in her chest, an emotion that was not hers. It mingled with her own stricken anxiety, making her heart throb as she pushed past people and out into the calm and quiet of the entry way.

"Who are you looking for?"

Deya whirled around to find Kindra watching her with sharp, ice-blue eyes. The Frost Princess was dressed in elaborate Bridanian armor. Its thick blue fabric was accented with threads of silver, like Deya's dress, but was covered with leather and furs. Her long white hair was twisted back into dozens of plaits, pulled back where an unusual headdress of what looked to be a deer skull sat atop her head. The antlers made her look even more imposing as she looked at Deya, eyebrow raised.

"Kindra, I . . ." Deya stopped short, trying to breathe over the weight of the conflicting emotions still raging in her chest.

But Kindra eyed her, as if she had heard exactly who she was calling for a second ago. With a silent jerk of her chin, she motioned towards the long, dark corridor leading back towards the stairs, before turning and walking through the doors into the hall.

Deya paused, the sounds of the party drifting towards her as the doors opened, before plunging her back into a muffled silence. With a deep breath, she hurried in the direction Kindra had indicated.

Fangdor's halls were dimly lit, and revelers stumbled past her, giggling, and singing, some of them carrying mugs of frostfire mead back towards the main hall. But Deya followed the chilly draft issuing down the corridor—cold even for Bridah's standards—her heart in her throat.

Caelum stood at the end of the long hall, staring into a portal spinning between two Bridanian shields. His jaw was rigid, his eyes blazing with power—and palpable fury.

"Are you just going to leave without saying anything?" Deya asked, stopping several feet behind him.

Caelum did not turn, but she knew he felt her approach, just like she had felt his presence before. His spine had stiffened, his shoulders growing rigid.

"Seemed like you were busy," he snapped, speaking to the portal, still not turning around. "Sorry to interrupt." Acid dripped from the sentence and his sneer was evident, even with the small amount of his face she could see. But she could feel the storm inside him, as if she had plucked a conch from the shore to listen to its hollow depths. Anger crashed against an emotion which felt horribly like hurt, and her desire to reach out and comfort him took over.

She moved forward, reaching for his arm, but Caelum whipped around, jerking his elbow free of her grip, holding out a hand to stop her from coming any closer.

"Go back to your party, *princess*," he snarled, frost crackling at his fingertips, disgust and fury creasing his features. "Glad to see you're finding ways to fill your time here. And Mother only knows what else."

Deya felt her face flush as her mouth dropped open. "How . . . How *dare*—"

Caelum scoffed, his hands balled into tight fists that shook slightly, his sneer only second in ferocity to his snarl. "How dare *I?*"

He moved on her so suddenly, Deya barely had a moment to step back. He was in her face, the irritating calm of their raging emotions settling now that their hearts were pressed together. She knew he felt the same calm within him, knew it only angered him more.

"What were you going to do?" he growled in her ear. "Were you going to let him take you back to your room? You think he can satisfy you?"

Deya's face burned, and even though being pressed against him was the only time that damned connection between them was calm, she shoved him away from her with as much force as she could muster.

"Maybe I was," she spat, glaring back at him. "It's not as if *you* have claimed me. What right do you have to be jealous over who I let share my bed?"

Caelum was breathing hard, his purple eyes still glowing. With one blink, the portal behind them closed, leaving a deafening silence within the hall.

Deya could hear his heart racing, feel her own breath rising and falling in time with his, and she wanted to scream with frustration. This connection, this *bond* that had them so entangled with each other— mind, body, breath, and blood. It all seemed so unfair that not even ancient, powerful magic such as what linked them to each other could best the stubborn rancor of Caelum Hesperos.

"You lock me up here like a princess in a bloody ice tower," Deya spat, jabbing a finger like a dagger towards him. "You leave me here with *no one*. And you don't even come to *see me*. You claim you do not care about me, Caelum, so forgive me if I'm beginning to believe you."

The High King stood before her, his arms stiff, his eyes burning with the purple light which had not faded when he had closed the portal. Frost was beginning to grow under his feet, creeping like crystallized veins towards her, but she did not care. Let him freeze her to death like a skathi, it made no difference anymore.

Spreading her arms wide in front of her, she let out a hollow laugh. "You win, Caelum," she said. "I believe you. I will not try to get you to admit what is a lie." She began to back away from him, his furious glare tracking her every movement as she backed down the hall.

"Deya—" he growled, a hint of warning in his tone, but Deya ignored him.

"You think you're so special, *my lord*," she said. She held up her chin, glaring defiantly at him, although tears were filling her eyes with every word. "But there's a whole room full of males who look just like you, and I'm not feeling very picky tonight." And with those last words, Deya turned on her heel and stormed away, swiping angry tears out of her eyes before they were able to fall.

CHAPTER 14

Caelum stood in the hall, alone, his Frost Magic crackling with his temper, his mind racing. He swayed on the spot, before turning and spitting a mouthful of blood onto the icy floor like it was venom. He was drained from the number of portals he'd had to make in such a short period of time, and that bastard general didn't even bother to show. And now, he had a sneaking suspicion that one more portal might kill him—which meant he was stuck here for the night.

The image of Deya wrapped up in that Bridanian's arms came back to mind and, with a furious roar, he punched the shield off the wall in front of him, then swore at the top of his lungs. The shield clattered to the floor, the din rebounding off the walls as Caelum paced around its dented frame, rubbing his bruised hand.

Deya's angry face floated in his vision, and the feeling of the words that had lodged in his throat as she stood in front of him pulsed in his windpipe.

What did she expect him to say? That she was *his*? That nothing—

male, female, or otherwise—had the right to touch her, except him?

He stared at the dented shield on the floor, breathing hard, his vision blurring.

He shouldn't *have* to say it. Gods, couldn't she feel it? Every time he took a breath, every time his heart beat, it was as if hers were right beside it. In tandem and torment, they were as bound together as any two separate beasts could be.

"Is that you, *Lostjarna?*" The familiar booming voice echoed through the hall. Loud thumps shook the wooden walls and Ulf appeared. He took up most of the rounded corridor, accentuated by the impressive blue robes and enormous deer headdress he had on. His kind blue eyes crinkled in concern as he took in Caelum and his bruised fist, next to the smashed shield on the floor.

He raised an eyebrow. "Did the shield offend you, somehow?"

Caelum sneered, rolling his eyes. "I'm not in the mood, old man."

Ulf chuckled and a large hand landed on Caelum's shoulder, causing him to double over. "Sometimes, you remind me much of Castor. He was just as petulant in his youth as you. I about near beat him to slush as a boy one Vetrnaetr."

Ulf's large hand began to steer him back down the corridor and Caelum's feet moved in spite of himself.

"I wish you had," Caelum muttered. In truth, he wouldn't know what he'd do to his father if he had him in front of him. Pounding him to a slush sounded promising, though.

Ulf laughed. "Aye, he impregnated my daughter and left me with an ornery, overpowered High King for a grandson with two sets of royal magic. You tell me who has more to be angry over, *Lostjarna.*"

Caelum grunted and Ulf led him back towards the well-lit, raucous great hall, which was packed almost to the rafters. Caelum had not been in this room before and was immediately overwhelmed by the size of it. The center of the hall was lowered into a rectangular pit with a fire roaring at its center. Long tables lined the lower floor, and, at the head, Kindra and several other people sat at an enormous table.

"Come, *Lostjarna*, let us celebrate the Long Night," Ulf said, smiling down on him. "All problems will be gone by the next sun."

As he and Ulf maneuvered through the crowd, Caelum's eyes darted through the party, trying to catch a glimpse of Deya. She wasn't hard to spot. Her chestnut brown hair was visible, even at a distance. She was standing at the mead table, taking a deep pull of her drink with the same Bridanian male she had been dancing with again.

Fire ignited in Caelum's blood, and he threw himself down into the chair next to Kindra, his eyes not leaving Deya. Kindra sat beside him, her back straight, her shoulders tall, the deer skull on her head casting a strange shadow down on the table as she turned to look at him.

"Good of you to join us, nephew," she said. Caelum grunted and Kindra smirked in that knowing way of hers. "What troubles you today, my lord?"

Caelum ground his teeth at her sarcasm, but his traitorous eyes followed Deya as she was pulled back onto the dance floor by the Bridanian male. His nails tapped on the wooden table, ice appearing which each thump of his fingers.

Kindra's eyes followed his gaze, and she let out a knowing, "Ah."

"*What?*" he snarled.

Kindra shrugged. "I will admit, Espen is quite the catch," she said, taking a demure sip of her drink. "He is a skilled warrior. One of my best. Quite popular with the females, too. Perhaps not the brightest, but Flykra does not always give with both hands."

Caelum ground his teeth as he watched as *Espen*—what a stupid name—wrapped his arms around Deya, dancing to the sound of the lyres in a quick, bouncy two step. Deya was smiling again, the tears he had seen in her eyes gone as she gazed up at the large male.

"Are you just going to let her dance with him?"

"Why do I care who she dances with?" he muttered, grabbing a mug from a passing mead tray.

Kindra let out a dry chuckle, her eyes mirroring his, watching as Deya wrapped her arms around Espen's neck, leaning up to say something to him, her lips brushing his ear.

"You do realize, nephew, that part of the Long Night is finding someone to spend it with," she said, but her tone was even, as if she knew too well what he was battling inside.

Caelum's fist tightened on the mug and ice splintered the wood. Mead dripped onto his lap and Kindra tutted. "I have taught you better than this," she said, taking the mug from him and licking a drop of the amber liquid from her finger. "Control your anger, Caelum. Be one with the ice, not against it."

Caelum was too angry to listen to her. Their training sessions had been helpful, yes, but so much of Frost Magic was linked to his temper and mood. Perhaps that was why Bridanians were so happy all the time. But as he watched Deya and the male get closer, laughing with their heads together, he was amazed he hadn't exploded with ice and rage.

"I do not know who you think you are fooling," Kindra said.

Caelum jerked to look at her. "What are you talking about?"

But she just smiled, a knowing, sad smirk. "If I did not know it was impossible, I would say you were more my kin than Asti's." She pounded a fist to her chest, her smile bitter. "We have a warrior's heart, me and you. We do not love, because all we know is how to fight. Love is another weakness, another thing to fear losing. And we do not have time for such liabilities."

Caelum blinked at her, her words resonating with him. He had always said his heart was cold and black, unfeeling and closed off. But when Kindra looked at him, her expression was filled with something he could not place.

"But a warrior dies alone, nephew," she said, softly. "And without love, there is nothing to fight for." And it was then he realized what it was in her eyes. Regret.

His gaze drifted back towards the dance floor just in time to see Deya with her arms around Espen's neck, a bright, almost drunk smile on her face, before he leaned down and kissed her gently on the mouth.

Everything in Caelum's body went cold. He froze in his chair, his stomach swooping, as if he had been dropped from a great height. He saw Deya hesitate—recoiling from Espen at the first brush of his lips—but then, in slow motion, Caelum watched her mouth move against his.

Kindra glanced sharply at him, no doubt seeing exactly what he was. "Caelum—" she warned, but her voice was a distant echo in the blood roaring in his ears.

Deya's eyelids fluttered open, her lips still moving against Espen's . . . and then she looked right at him. She watched him watching her as she kissed him, her hands coming to wrap around his neck, the vengeful gleam in her eye igniting a feral monster inside of him. It roared with fury as he leapt from his chair, sending it flying to the floor.

"Caelum!" Kindra cried, rising to grab hold of him, but he was moving too fast, his vision going black. All he could see was Deya and the Bridanian male, who was soon to be a red stain on the wooden floor as he stormed towards them.

Deya saw him coming and shoved Espen off her, and he was immediately taken with the crowd, buffeted out of Caelum's reach, but it was no matter.

"Caelum—" she began, but he had already seized her arm and begun to haul her from the hall, her protests and thrashing lost in the noise and bustle of the party.

"*Let me go!*" she screamed as she pounded her small fists onto his arm, pulling against his grip, even using her foot to try and kick him. "You do not get to storm over here like a bloody barbarian and yank me—What are you doing? Caelum, what—"

But Caelum merely ducked under the arm he still had hold of to lift her bodily over his shoulder, her feet leaving the floor entirely. She gasped in fury and surprise as he stormed with her back up the stairs of the empty castle, her feet swinging in his face, her head dangling down the backs of his legs.

"You are *unbelievable!*" she shrieked. Deya must be drunk because Caelum had never heard her screech like that. "You have *no right*—"

"*No right?*" Caelum snarled. He reached the door to her bedroom and kicked it open, the wood splintering under the heel of his boot. Dumping her back onto her feet, he slammed the door shut and glared down at her, the burning rage still pumping through his veins. "You want me to claim my right, Deya, is that what you want?"

Deya stuttered, her mouth opening as he moved towards her, grasping the hair at the back of her neck in a firm, yet gentle hold. The smell of her, the feel of her, the way the storm in him quieted the minute they touched . . .

A warrior dies alone, nephew.

"You are mine," he snarled, frost crackling, cold wind blowing through the room. "You are *mine* and no one else's. If I ever see someone lay a *finger* on you, I will snap it from their body."

He took a deep breath, the words which had been lodged in his throat for so long tumbling from him as if he could no longer stop them. "Being away from you *pains* me . . . *kills* me. I did not send you here because of the *realm*. *Fuck* the realm!" he shouted. "I sent you here because the thought of seeing you hurt . . . the thought of *them* capturing you, makes me fucking crazy. I sent you here to save *both* of us, because there will be nothing left of this world if somebody hurts you. I will make sure of it."

Deya stared up at him with wide gray eyes, her mouth opened as she looked at him. "Caelum," she whispered, but Caelum was over waiting for her to respond, and he did the thing he had been dying to do for weeks now. He dragged her by the hair towards him and kissed her, hard on the mouth.

Deya let out that breathy little sigh which always made him crazed, and her head dropped back, allowing him more room to explore. Their tongues twisted together, their hot breath mingling with the heat that was beginning to build inside Caelum.

Swearing, he pulled back. "I still fucking taste him on you, Deya. Give me one good reason why I shouldn't go back down to that hall and murder him for—"

But Deya silenced him with another kiss, her hands working at the laces on his pants, her hands pulling him closer. "Let's fix that, then," she murmured.

Before he knew what she was doing, his pants were down, and his cock sprang free, already hard and ready for her. Deya sank slowly to the ground, her eyes still locked on him and his breath caught. She had never done this before, and he couldn't deny that the sight of her on her knees with him fisted in her still-gloved hand had him almost close to the edge already.

"You'll be the only taste from now on," she whispered, before her tongue darted out and licked him from base to tip.

A groan escaped him, and he stumbled back, his hands finding the wall as she took him fully in her mouth and began to move. Her lips slid over him, hot and wet, the gentle stroking of her tongue made stars appear in his vision.

"*Fuck*," he whispered, his hand coming to fist her long hair which tumbled in waves and braids down her head. He had never seen it properly loose before, and he ran his hands through it before gathering it away from her face as she moved faster and faster along his length.

Her head and hand moved in tandem, the pressure building in Caelum's core as his frost began to creep from his fingertips against the wooden wall he still held onto. He knew if he let her keep going like this he wouldn't last much longer.

Reaching down, he pulled her to her feet, taking a moment to revel in her puffy, swollen lips before devouring her mouth with his.

And she was right. All he tasted was himself now.

"Better," he growled into her kiss, before he grabbed the collar of his shirt and pulled it up over his head. Deya reached for the laces behind her dress, fumbling with it, the intricate ties at her back proving to be a hindrance. Caelum tore at the shoulders of the dress, ripping it along the seams as she worked the knots loose, desperate to kiss the skin along her neck. His teeth dragged against her collarbone and the whimper she let out made him pull at the collar of her dress with a more frenzied force.

Finally, the dress slid off her, baring her to him. She was still slender and dainty—sharp points, and elongated planes—but she was no longer emaciated. Her breasts were still small, yet round and full, peaked at attention, waiting for him.

It had been weeks since he had last seen her naked, weeks since he had been able to glide his hands along her bare skin, to run his finger up the slit between her legs and feel how wet she was for him.

Deya moaned as his finger ghosted along her skin, just enough to feel the dampness between her thighs.

"Is this all for me or was it for him?" he breathed in her ear, his hands still fisted in her hair, angling her neck as he bit her, hard on the shoulder.

"You . . ." she whispered, her voice breathy and trembling as she dug her fingers into his shoulder, too lost in everything to even remember to remove her gloves. "Only ever you . . ."

Caelum let out a grunt of approval as he released her hair, moving to grasp her by the bottom and hoisted her up. She let out a gasp as he carried her through the room, dropping her down on the closest available surface he could find.

Deya looked down at the wooden mantel he had deposited her on, the fire crackling underneath her feet. She opened her mouth as if to say something, but Caelum didn't wait for her to speak. Pushing her legs apart, he fell to his knees and dove between her thighs with a ravenous fervor that made her clutch the wood and cry out.

Caelum nipped and sucked at the sensitive bundle of nerves between her folds, his hand reaching up to grasp her breast as she squirmed on top of the mantel. The warmth from the fire was almost too hot, but the waves of cold rolling off him tempered the heat.

"Tell me I'm the only one who has had you like this," he growled, looking up at her. The absence of his mouth made her whimper with need, and he spread her wider, determined for her to feel him, to need him more.

"You're . . . you're the only one—"

"Tell me I'm the only one who has claimed you like this."

Deya fought for words as his lips brushed against her, squirming and panting with desperate need. "You're . . . the only one . . ."

"Tell me that you're mine," he growled, and slowly, he sank a finger into her. She bit down on her lip, a half moan, half scream coming from her throat as he pushed into her.

"I'm yours . . . Everything is yours."

"Good girl," he murmured, then he sank another finger into her up to the knuckle and dove back in between her legs. Deya cried out, her hands tangling in the hair at the top of his head, her legs wrapping around his neck as she began to fight release. Caelum pumped into her, his tongue, and fingers relentless, loving the feeling of her thighs trembling around him.

Every feeling was heightened—his own desperate need to be buried in her mixed with the heady pleasure he was giving her, thundering through him like a storm. He could almost feel each spasm of pleasure she took as if it were his own, making him double his efforts until, finally, she screamed out his name, her fingers digging into his scalp, her legs tensing and twitching as they tightened around his head.

He milked her with his fingers, feeling her orgasm roll through her, each brush of his tongue against her making her twitch and moan. But he wasn't done with her. Pulling her off the mantel, he turned and threw her finally onto the bed.

It had been weeks of sneaking into her room in Nodaria, having to pretend like the sight of her didn't make him crazed with longing. Having to kiss her in darkened hallways, take her in deserted libraries when there was no one around and he couldn't wait any longer.

The realization that he no longer had to hide it—that he could have her as loudly and as often as he wanted—filled him with anticipation as he clambered over her, his cock pressing against her entrance.

She panted against his mouth, her body limp from release yet still alight with yearning. Her hips thrust upwards, the slickness of her moving against the hardness of him, making him draw in air through his teeth. She reached for him, but Caelum seized her wrists, pulling them up above her head.

"Impatient," he snarled in her ear, his tongue and breath making her shiver as it caressed her. "Are we that eager?"

Deya nodded and Caelum could feel himself dripping his own anticipation. Slowly, tantalizingly, he began to rub himself against her opening, feeling it slip and slide through the wetness of her.

Gods, he had needed this. Had wanted her and missed her since the moment they had made that stupid bet on who would give in first. He didn't care that he had lost. *This* was the best consolation prize he could ask for.

"Do you want me, Deya?" he breathed, staring down at her body, stretched with her hands above her head. He leaned down and his tongue flicked over one erect nipple, making her whimper and moan.

"Yes . . . please—"

"Say it," he commanded, moving to her other breast to give it the same treatment. "Tell me."

"I . . . I want you."

It was all Caelum needed to hear.

Lining himself up against her opening, he looked down into her gray eyes as he thrust into her. The shout left her as he began to drive into her, his movements becoming faster and harder.

He released her hands, attempting to hold on, grabbing her around the back of the neck, bringing her face to his so he could press his mouth to hers as he thrust into her, the sound of her breathy moans and whimpers filling the room.

"Caelum . . ." she moaned, her hands coming to scrabble against his face. "I love you, Caelum . . . I—"

But no sooner did she say those words than Caelum shattered, his release exploding through him as he spilled into her, his body shaking, frost rippling from him in waves.

And as he slowed to a stop, his head dropping down onto her chest, his pleasure faded as his heart clenched at the words she had said.

CHAPTER 15

Deya awoke the next morning with her head pounding like the drums from the party the night before. She opened a bleary eye, expecting sunlight to be pouring through the mullioned window at the end of her room, but it was only to find it still black as pitch outside.

She had almost forgotten the Long Night, fueled only by mead, vengeance and . . .

The bed shifted, and she turned to see Caelum asleep beside her. He was still naked, the tattoos standing out starkly against his olive skin, and Deya stared at him for a long moment. She had not forgotten what they had done last night, but she was surprised to see him still in bed beside her. He never stayed, choosing to slip out before dawn so no one would catch him in her bed.

His eyes were still closed, his white hair spread across the woolen pillows, the one braid he kept twined on the side of his head falling into his face. She reached out one blackened finger to brush it away but stopped short, pulling her hands back and tucking them under the pillow.

Death Bringer.

It was stupid to remove her gloves, but she had wanted to touch him with bare hands again, hoping it was dark enough for him not to notice.

The fire crackled low in the grate. The room was still dark, with only the faintest glow of warmth as she watched the shadows flutter on Caelum's lashes.

She had said it last night. Blurted it out mid-orgasm without a thought. Aided by frostfire mead and sheer delirium from the first mind-bending climax, it had slipped from her mouth before could shove it back in.

She loved him. She knew she did—had known for a while. But she hadn't missed the look on his face after she said it, how he had lain in bed underneath her afterwards, quiet for a long while. Not pushing him on it had been difficult, but soon, she had drifted to sleep, knowing he would probably slip out of her room before she woke. To find him still here beside her . . .

His eyelids fluttered, and then two purple eyes opened to rest on her. The last time they had woken up together had been in a small cave on the outskirts of Arctos. The first time Deya had ever been touched like he had touched her. It had only ever been him for her. Kissing Espen had been a spiteful, vengeful thing for her to do. And yet . . .

Caelum lifted his head to look out the window. "Is it still night then?"

Deya nodded. "For another day, I think."

He stretched, closing his eyes again. His hand reached out and found her face, stroking it lightly with one lazy finger. Deya relaxed at his touch, each brush of his hand calming her frazzled nerves about what he must be thinking.

Finally, Caelum's eyes opened again, and he turned to look at her. "I'm sorry."

"Sorry?" Deya echoed, sitting up to look at him. "For what?"

"For leaving you here alone," he said. His finger caught a lock of her hair, and he looped it around his finger, his purple eyes watching its movement. "I should have sent someone to be here with you. I'm sorry I can't . . ." He fell silent, his jaw tensing in the way it always did.

"Caelum, it's okay," she said softly, but he shook his head, his eyes distant as he looked past her, as though trying to figure out how to put something into words.

With a deep breath, he spoke. "All my life, I've fought. I've fought to be looked at as my father's son. I fought against everyone who laughed at me for my hair or because I was a bastard. And since the day Praiton invaded the Keep, I have not stopped fighting since. It is all I know." He looked at her, and the rare softness in his face coupled with the pain furrowing his brow made Deya's heart hurt. It was as if he was imploring her to understand . . . To understand *him*.

"When Praiton attacked Nodaria, the first thing they did was come for everything Castor loved," Caelum said, his voice quiet. "He was the strongest king in the realm, yet he died trying to protect us. We were the strongest king's biggest weakness."

"Caelum," Deya whispered again, reaching for his hand, but pulling back, the stab of fear of her blackened fingers stopping her again. But Caelum didn't seem to notice.

"What you said last night . . . what you've asked of me . . . That is something I can't return." His voice was pained, and he turned away from her, as if looking at her hurt him. "Love is only a weakness to exploit," he whispered. "And, in the end, I do not know what love is. I never have."

Deya nodded, although her heart hurt. She understood what he was saying, and yet, the possibility Caelum may never say it back to her stung her deeply. She had always been empathetic, perhaps too understanding for her own good. Even then, as she nodded, alleviating Caelum's guilt, she felt a knot in her chest at the possibility that she would never be loved back.

The door flew open, and both Deya and Caelum jolted up in the bed, dragging the sheets with them. Karyna bustled into the room, as she usually did in the morning, but froze when she saw Caelum.

"Oh!" she gasped, whirling around to face the wall, her pale cheeks a bright red. "Oh, I am so sorry! I didn't know you were . . . I . . ."

"It's alright, Karyna," Deya said, pushing a forced chuckle through the lump still in her throat. "It's an honest mistake."

Karyna glanced back at them, her cheeks still pink, her eyes locking with Caelum's, who didn't look the least bit hurried to dress himself. He tucked his long, tattooed arm behind his head, elongating his muscled and equally tattooed torso, his lower region barely concealed by one of the fur blankets.

"I . . . Good morning, my lord," Karyna stuttered, averting her gaze.

Caelum raised an eyebrow. "Good morning," he said, and Deya knew by the tiniest, faintest glimmer of a smirk that he was enjoying this.

Grabbing a spare pillow, Deya thumped him, hard on the head, making him grumble as she got out of bed, wrapping one of the blankets around her.

Karyna hurried to her wardrobe, pulling out her dressing gown and helping her shrug into it. "I must say, as surprising as this is, I'm glad not to find you in here with my brother," she whispered in Deya's ear. "Espen warms a different bed every other night."

"He's your brother?" Caelum said, his hearing annoyingly attentive as usual.

Karyna turned back to him, her face still red, giving him a short nod. "Yes, my lord. Espen is my brother."

Caelum's lip curled. "Good. You can remind him not to touch what is mine the next time you see him."

This time, it was Deya's turn to go scarlet. And when Karyna merely stuttered a hasty acknowledgement before turning to tidy the room, Deya glared at Caelum.

"Could you sound a little *less* barbaric, please?" she hissed, but Caelum leered at her.

"This is what you asked for, darling, I'm just delivering," he said, grinning. Deya flushed at the nickname, never having heard Caelum use any term of endearment for her, but deciding she didn't care in the slightest, fighting back the warm glow in her heart. Suddenly, she wished

201

Karyna would leave so she could crawl on top of the nearly exposed male and force him to make good on delivering what *else* she wanted.

But it was then that Karyna noticed the torn gown on the floor. "Oh no," she mumbled, kneeling to pick the tattered garment up. "Did you really have to take it out on the dress?" she snapped at Caelum.

Caelum smirked, reaching out to grab hold of the end of Deya's hair, twirling the curled lock between his fingers again. "Would you rather I have taken it out on your brother?" he asked coolly.

Karyna blanched, and Deya jumped up hurriedly. "Okay! Karyna, could you possibly give us a minute to get changed and, uh, I'll come find you later." She gave Karyna her sunniest smile, but Karyna was still staring, wide-eyed and fearful at Caelum.

"Um . . . yes, okay," she said finally. She scuttled from the room, Deya's ripped dress still in her hands.

Deya whirled on Caelum and flicked him right in the middle of the forehead, causing him to yelp. "What was that for?" he cried.

"For acting like an ass to Karyna," she snapped. "There's no reason for it. And for your information, Karyna is the only reason Bridah hasn't been sheer misery for me."

Caelum looked up at her, rubbing the now red spot in the middle of his forehead. "About that," he said, and he gestured for her to come closer. Deya gave him a leery look, but edged nearer, her arms still crossed tightly to hide her hands. "I know Val leaving has been hard on you," he said.

Deya shifted. "How is she?"

Shrugging, he said, "She's . . . okay. Training nonstop, mostly. But she told me to tell you hello."

Her mood lifted at this. She wished to talk to Val more than anything—had even contemplated asking Caelum to take her back to Nodaria to do so—but the fact that she had asked Caelum to say hello meant she wasn't mad at her, at least.

"Anyway, that *runt* you left behind," Caelum said.

"Who, Luc?"

"Whatever his name is," Caelum said, rolling his eyes. "He's been doing round the clock research since you've left, attempting to find out about the Heart, and your powers. If *you'd like"* —He paused here, as if this whole sentence pained him to say— "I can bring him here. So, you have help in your research and at least have a familiar face."

Deya blinked in surprise. "Really?"

Caelum gave a disgruntled grumble. "I still do not trust him, but he has been in Nodaria now for over a month and so far, no information has been leaked that we know of—and I *have* planted false information around him, to see if he'd betray us. But so far, he hasn't. I also do not have the time to babysit him, so if you would prefer him here—"

But Deya cut him off midsentence as she clambered onto his lap, straddling him, and laying a slow languid kiss on his mouth. Caelum's words died as he reached up to wrap his hands around her waist, Deya threading her blackened fingers into his white hair.

"Thank you," she whispered into his mouth.

Caelum gave her a small, crooked grin. She was not used to seeing Caelum's genuine smile. It was a rare, beautiful occurrence that reminded her of a shooting star or a solar eclipse. She never took for granted the fact that *she* made him smile like this.

But his smile quickly turned into a growl as his hands began to undo the dressing gown she had slipped on.

"Take this off," he murmured in her ear, before lifting her by the backs of the legs and easing her back onto him.

Deya's mouth opened, her head dropping back as she felt him fill her again and Caelum smiled that same crooked grin as they melted back into each other, Deya's black hands wrapped around the back of his neck.

❄

Caelum had no choice but to leave later that day, but before he did, he made good on his promise to Deya and brought Luc.

Deya's old friend stumbled out of the portal in Fangdor's library, looking winded and disheveled, gasping for breath. "*That*," he spluttered, "was bloody *awful*."

Deya chuckled and shrugged from where she was sitting in her usual chair in front of the fire in the library again. "You get used to it," she told him.

The portal vanished with a *whoosh* of air, leaving Luc standing in front of her, shifting on his feet, rubbing his arm sheepishly as he looked around at his new surroundings.

"So, this is Bridah," he said, gazing around, his dark eyes wide. "Well, they definitely did not exaggerate the cold, did they?"

It was even more intense during the Long Night. The small amount of weak sunlight Bridah got at least helped somewhat. At night, however, the cold seemed to seep into Deya's bones.

At Luc's words, she nodded and pulled her cloak tighter around herself.

He moved into the room, tugging on his threadbare woolen cloak which looked thoroughly secondhand. Sitting down at the table, he finally looked at her for the first time before giving her a small grin.

"Hey, Dey."

She gave him a grim smile in return. "Hi, Luc."

The ice was thin between them still. His dark eyes darted up at her, as if unsure if he were allowed to. Deya knew Caelum still didn't trust Luc, but seeing him in his ragged clothes—which she knew Saros must have dug up from the storage of old castle uniforms—and the way they still hung loose on his frame made her sympathy grow for him. It reminded her of the way her clothes had fit her when she had first arrived at Light's Tower.

She knew what trauma looked like, and because of that, she didn't fear Luc betraying them. Not this time.

Luc cleared his throat and glanced back over his shoulder where the portal had disappeared. "I see you took care of our benevolent High King," Luc said, smirking at her.

Deya felt her face grow warm. "What . . . what makes you say that?" she cried, her hands coming to clasp at her cheeks.

Luc gave a smug chuckle. "Well, that bite on your neck is a good little indicator," he said, jerking his finger at her.

Deya's hand leapt to her throat, the flush spreading all the way down her chest. Mortified, she sprang from her chair to look in the mirror above the mantle, just to see a dark splotch in the perfect shape of Caelum's mouth stamped onto her collarbone.

"That *bastard*," she muttered, and Luc burst out laughing.

"Honestly, I should be thanking you. He almost *smiled* at me today before he kicked me through the portal." He paused, rubbing at his backside, as though remembering Caelum's boot hitting it, and shrugged in that lazy way he always did. "Plus, his complexion has never looked better."

After that, things seemed to ease between them. Deya fell back into step with her old friend as they spread out through the library, flicking through books, thumbing across the spines of old tomes and scrolls. It began to feel a bit like old times in the infirmary, a feeling that both comforted and unsettled her at the same time.

A whole afternoon passed with the subdued sounds of flipping through pages upon pages. It only took about eight hours for Luc to realize—just as she and Val eventually had—that there was very little information on the Mother in Fangdor's library. By the end of the Long Night, their eyes were beginning to ache from reading the small text by candlelight, and their heads were pounding from attempting to understand the number of tomes not in the common tongue.

"Right, I quit," Luc declared, slamming his book shut with a *thud* and a puff of dust.

Deya rubbed at her eyes, but as the dust cleared, she caught sight of the book he had tossed aside. Its dark leather was cracked in places, its cover quite unlike anything she had seen thus far. More . . . sinister.

Shadows of the Snow, Death in the Frost Kingdom.

Her mouth went dry. What Karyna had told her about *dodsbringern* seemed to echo in her mind, and for a moment, she couldn't breathe. Could there be more information on the death omen in there? Could she perhaps dispel her greatest fears about her powers?

Or perhaps, prove them right.

With an enormous effort, she tore her gaze from the book. "What do you mean *you quit?*" she said, her voice quivering with her attempt to steady it. "You can't *quit.*"

"Oh, yes, I can." Luc rose from his chair and paced the darkened library. The black sky outside was illuminated only by the blue and green glow of the Verja Aurora, casting a gentle light down onto the windowsill. Luc peered out of the thick glass, his arms tugging at his worn cloak. "You and the Manielian girl have been doing this for weeks already, right?"

Deya hesitated, but Luc seemed to guess what her lack of an answer meant. He gave her a sideways look, and it was as if they were back in the infirmary again, overwhelmed with sick patients while Luc tried to convince her to leave and go to lunch with him.

"And tell me if you even found *one* mention of the Mother Goddess in all that time," he said.

Deya shifted in her chair, huffing a piece of hair off her face as she avoided his gaze.

"*Exactly,*" Luc said. "Obviously, the answers we're looking for are not in here. We need to stop wasting our time in this place and look somewhere else." Deya felt her eyes dart back to the dark book still sitting on the desk and she swallowed hard.

"And where do you suggest we look?" she demanded, her tone sour. It wasn't as if she and Val hadn't tried to look elsewhere. They *did* nearly die in the unbearable tundra outside, all to talk to a High Priest. And for what? For Deya to be told that she would bring death upon those around her?

Her eyes drifted back to the book again. *Shadows of the Snow.* A flame of anxiety flickered in her chest, and her gloved hands squirmed in her lap.

"Your boyfriend did say Bridah's High King mentioned ancient texts and tomes all over this kingdom," Luc said, his flippant use of the word "boyfriend" making Deya blush. "Bridah has apparently remained untouched from the rest of the realm. Surely that means it's as close as it can be to the age when the goddesses walked this Earth."

Blinking at him, Deya processed what he had said. She hated to admit he was making sense. In a lot of ways, Bridah reminded her of a house which had been abandoned in the middle of a meal. All the plates and cups left, exactly where it was, lost to the power of time. What if Luc was right, and Bridah had preserved more than what the library was showing them?

As she was contemplating this, the door opened and Karyna pushed in, holding a large pot of steaming tea. When she spotted Luc, she started, a flush creeping up her pale skin.

"Oh . . . *Heil og sal,* hello," she stammered, her head dropping quickly. Deya had gotten used to Karyna's more rambunctious side of her personality, so seeing her drop back into the demure lady's maid made her raise an eyebrow.

"Karyna, this is Luc. Luc, Karyna, my lady's maid," Deya said, but her dismissive introduction didn't seem to register on her old friend.

Luc was appraising Karyna with an equal amount of fascination. His dark eyes took in her white hair, crystal blue eyes, and pale skin, and he smiled at her.

"Perfect timing, Karyna," he said, his voice jovial as he clapped his hands together. "You can help us. What is the oldest, holiest site in all of Fangdor?"

Karyna blinked, the pretty pink flush spreading across her porcelain cheeks. "I . . . I think that would be our underground temple. It is said the first son of Flykra made it himself before She was returned to the snow."

Deya's head snapped towards the small lady's maid, her attention fully captivated. "What underground temple?" she blurted, trying to ignore the smug look on Luc's face. "Why have you never taken me there before?"

Karyna gave a small, one shoulder shrug. "I worked there briefly when I first came to Fangdor, before I became a lady's maid. I never took you because it is not insulated down there. Our priestesses say that it is where the soul of Flykra lies. Our eldest and most experienced priestesses work and study there, to feel closer to our goddess. You would freeze without the proper assistance."

Deya felt herself shiver in spite of herself. After her trek to Frode, the feeling of the frigid cold also brought back other memories . . . like Frode's hand clamped over her face.

"Well, let's get some cloaks and have a poke around," Luc said, turning to Deya with an eager look. "It's obviously a dead end here. What other choice do we have? And plus," he turned to beam at Karyna, "you can give me the official tour of this place while we're at it."

Deya made to protest, but then the little dark book flashed through her mind again, and her heart quickened a beat. The breath in her lungs grew tight again, and she drew in a breath, attempting to calm herself. She did not want to go down to the temples now. All she wanted was to sneak off with that book, to satisfy the anxious curiosity that was filling her with a cold dread. But, before she could think up some lie or excuse, Karyna spoke up first.

"Neither of you are dressed for the cold in the temples," she chastised, setting the tea pot down on the table and crossing her slender arms in a stern stance. "And besides, it is too late to go down now. It is especially cold during the Long Night. The cold is strengthened at this time of the year because of Vetrnaetr."

Luc wilted at her words and sighed, shooting a grim look back at Deya, as if for confirmation. Luc had never felt Bridah's cold—not like her. While they had both grown up in Praiton, which had a full array of seasons and temperatures, they were both full-blooded Ganiean. Ganiea only knew two seasons: summer and spring. A flower was not built to withstand a blizzard. She had learned that the hard way.

"I suppose we can give it another day," Luc said, his brow furrowed.

Deya could tell he felt a bit of a coward. But she also couldn't help feeling that putting off the inevitable was more appealing than walking down into a frozen temple.

"Okay." Deya nodded, hoping she didn't look too eager to agree. "Tomorrow."

Karyna clapped her hands together and gave a small, excited bounce. "Oh good, then we can attend the festivities for the Long Night, instead! You do not want to be in the temple looking at dusty scrolls. Tonight, we feast and dance around the fire in the courtyard!"

When Luc began asking Karyna questions about the festivities, Deya found herself opening her mouth.

"Um, if it's alright with you, I think I may call it an early night tonight."

Both Karyna and Luc turned to look at her.

"But . . . there is no *early* night tonight," Karyna protested. "Oh, you *must* come, Deya! Please!"

But Deya was shaking her head with an apologetic smile. "I really am exhausted. I think I'm going to go back to my room with a few books and try to get some research done before bed."

"Dey," Luc began, his brow crinkled with worry, but Deya shook her head.

"It's fine," she said cajolingly. "Honest, Luc. Go with Karyna. Go see Bridah. I'll be fine for the night."

Luc hesitated, as if he didn't quite believe her.

Could he tell? Could he see the flutter of anxiety in her chest that she was so desperately trying to smother? Could he perhaps see the panic in her eyes?

Karyna hummed in a thoughtful tone. "I guess it is for the better," she said. "My brother will no doubt look for you. He does not like being upstaged by another male."

A strong blush spread across Deya's chest and up her cheeks, the warmth of it burning off the lingering chill that the fireplace could not combat. Luc turned slowly to look at her, a dark eyebrow arching in surprise.

"Her *brother?*" he asked Deya, a catlike smirk spreading across his face. Deya cleared her throat, and looked away, tucking a stray lock of hair behind her ear.

Karyna gave her a cheeky grin. "I will let Espen know you send your best," she said. "Or, perhaps, that the High King has come to see you again . . . just so he doesn't attempt to come looking for you in your chambers."

The redness in her cheeks grew even warmer as Luc stifled a laugh.

Deya grumbled. "Thanks a lot, Karyna."

Karyna giggled and motioned for Luc and Deya to follow her. As clandestinely as she could, Deya scooped up the stack of books that *Shadows of the Snow* was tucked into, being sure to gather as many of the other books with blackened, cracked spines that she could see. With her heart in her throat, she pulled them into her arms, the tomes seeming to thrum with dark energy, before she quietly followed after them.

They left the library, heading down the wooden stairs towards the lower levels. Luc and Karyna walked ahead of Deya, and she couldn't help but feel a squirm of jealousy as she watched the two of them laugh and talk. Luc had always been a master of assimilation. He folded into groups easily, could make friends wherever he went. Deya had always felt like she was fortunate just to be included.

Even now, as Karyna pointed things out around Fangdor to him and Luc oohed and ahh-ed, Deya couldn't be angry at him. There was a familiarity with Luc, a comfort that even his betrayal had not seemed able to erase.

They had been through so much together at the infirmary. Had laughed, had argued, had spent many sleepless nights together on night duty. There was a camaraderie between her and Luc which was embedded so deeply within her. She couldn't seem to shake it, even when she remembered the look on his face as Clarita threw her into the dungeon; even when she thought of his silence, and how he hadn't gone to see her before she was sent to Ironbalt.

From up ahead, Luc glanced back at her and smiled as Karyna jabbered on about the castle activities and Vetrnaetr. That smile made Deya sigh. It was hard to forget Luc's secret, mischievous grins. They had always made her feel included, as if she were on the inside of a joke for once instead of a lonely outsider.

And with that, she knew she had forgiven him. If only just a little.

They reached the landing where Deya's room was located, and Karyna let out a cheerful wave as she bounded down the steps, no doubt eager to begin celebrating the Long Night. Luc, however, paused and hung back, his eyes roaming the stack of books still clutched in her hands.

"Are you sure you don't want to come?" he asked cajolingly, giving her a light nudge with his elbow. "Surely it'll be more fun than more of *that*." He gave a pointed jerk of his chin towards her books and Deya smiled, shifting her grip on them as her arms began to ache.

"I'm sure it is, but don't worry about me. Go have fun with Karyna."

Luc glanced back down the stairs where Karyna had disappeared, before whispering out of the corner of his mouth, "Is her brother as cute as she is?"

"Oh, most definitely," Deya whispered back, smirking.

Luc grinned. "Think he's my type?"

"Do you even *have* a type? I thought 'breathing' was the only requirement."

Luc let out a bark of laughter, nudging Deya gently on the shoulder before following Karyna back down the stairs.

Deya cast one last glance back over her shoulder before hastening towards her room. Heart hammering in her chest, she closed and locked her bedroom door behind her. The sounds of the beginnings of the Long Night celebration rumbled from downstairs, causing the thick pane of glass to rattle in its mullioned frame. But Deya could barely hear it over the pulse throbbing in her ears.

She laid the books down onto the bed, before picking up the first one and moving to sit in the chair by the fire. The first book held nothing but ancient Bridanian death rituals performed back in the days of the goddesses. The second was all about different types of poisons found within the flora and fauna of the kingdom. By the time she reached the third book, Deya's eyes were drooping, her head swimming in time with the drums and chanting from the festival downstairs.

But then she paused. As if drawn to it, her eyes found the black leather book at the bottom of the pile. The one she had buried there, as if by hiding it, she could forget about it. Slowly, she plucked it free from between the other books. Its black spine crumbled within her grip. Its cover was gritty with dust and something that felt horribly familiar . . .

Deya scraped a black finger down the cover and rubbed the tips together, recognizing the substance instantly.

Ash.

Her breathing slowed, her chest constricting. *Shadows of the Snow. Death in the Frost Kingdom.*

Holding her breath, she lifted the cover back. It was written in the common tongue, unusual for a book so old. The way Karyna had spoken about *dodsbringern,* it seemed as if it were a well-known thing in the Frost Kingdom. As if it were a legend used to scare children. Had Frode called her a monster?

Was she?

Each section was a small folk tale about a creature and a description of its history. And all were denizens of Bridah's underearth.

One section told of beings called draugr, undead corpses who rise with the fall of avalanches, bringing plague and famine to nearby villages. Another was tales of something called an ísnykr, a horse made of ice that lures unwitting travelers to frozen lakes. There was even a section on skathis—the illustration of its pallid skin and sharp teeth making a shiver roll up her spine. Page after page of icy death, and for a moment, relief washed over her that there was nothing more sinister. But then her gaze froze on another page.

The illustration on this page was darker than any other before it. Deya recognized Flykige immediately, its stone henges crudely detailed with Flykra's likeness, but the rest of the background was shrouded in darkness. A shadow loomed out from behind the pillar, its misty hands wrapped around the stone.

Deya felt her vision begin to blur as her eyes spun around the page. She took in the shadows undulating off the clawed hand, the gleaming eyes of the shapeless creature, the mix of Brynorsk and common words swirling in her vision.

The laws of Flykra are one of nature. When one betrays the other, Dodsbringern will appear.

Deya's shaking finger traced the letters, her mind barely able to process the words with how quickly and desperately she read them.

On the eve of the first war of fae and gods, Asger, son of Flykra described a dark shadow which appeared before the battle. Asger's attack on Maniel over an attempted coup by the Ember Throne was to stake claim of Bridah's eastern springs. Skirmishes raged for weeks. Blood stained snow and sand alike. On the day Asger planned to end the Ember Kingdom, he was faced with a dark creature. With one look, Asger's army was reduced to cinders, and from the ashes, the Verja Fjords rose, encasing Asger and the Frost Kingdom within itself, protecting it both from Maniel and its own invasion.

Deya stared at the shadow in the picture. It seemed more monster than man. Her eyes skimmed the passage again. *A dark shadow* was how it was described by Asger. At that moment, her mind flashed to an image of Caelum's Shadow Sword. Was that what *dodsbringern* was? A shadow creature, just like the nyraxi that chased her last year? Like the magror?

But no, a voice in Deya's head whispered. She slumped back against her chair, her breath coming in trembling gasps. *The magror did not have that power to turn things to ash . . .*

The book slipped from her blackened fingers, which shook like the dead branches of a tree.

Only *she* did.

CHAPTER 16

Helene Sidra's spine was so rigid in her chair, Val found herself imagining snapping it in two like a piece of kindling. The Prime Minister's mouth twisted into a thin line as Caelum informed the council of the new Legion outpost north of Arctos.

Saros was spinning a small blade in his fingers, his purple eyes watching as the council burst into furious yells, one member even jumping to his feet to point an angry finger in Caelum's face.

"Your blatant disregard for everything our *duly elected* Prime Minister has said is a disgrace to this kingdom!" the male roared.

Caelum stared at him with a murderous, cold glare that made the male waver. Val couldn't help but admire the way Caelum handled himself. Gone were the days when he'd flare and lash out at everyone around him. The cold arrogance was still there, but it was much, much deadlier when wielded quietly.

"If we do not aid the Legion, we will fall *again*," Caelum spat. "Is that what you want, Councilman Mah?" The male grumbled, sitting back in his chair in a disgruntled silence. Caelum sneered. "I thought as much."

As the meeting carried on, Val's attention drifted back out the window towards the starry sky. She and Saros were there to represent the Legion in lieu of Aris's absence. The general was away much more these days than he'd ever been. She knew he had things to attend to across Krigor, but she couldn't stop the empty pang she felt when she thought about him.

The night of Vetrnaetr, when she had agreed to his impossible task, she had expected him to be pleased that his plan was going to be put into motion. Instead, Aris had seemed . . . distant. He had told her to begin training herself before promising he'd be back in a few days to help. That was all. The warmth and kindness he had shown her while she had cried for her sisters had seemed to cool back to something impassive and formal.

Val shifted, her stomach flaring with fresh anxiety—a now common occurrence whenever she thought about preparing for Mount Cinis. Since that night, she had stayed in the training ring for so many hours, she had watched the moon go through a full cycle in the constant night sky. Hours and hours of pushing her magic harder, trying to endure the heat longer. But each time it ended the same: her clothes alight, her skin burned, and her anger at her weakness building with each failed attempt.

"Except for the outposts, the Legion has kept Nodaria fairly insulated." The sound of Saros's voice brought Val back to reality and she blinked, shaking off thoughts of her last few pathetic attempts at pushing her Ember Magic to its limits.

Helene let out an abrasive scoff. "The outposts have made Nodaria a central hub of Legion activity," she snapped. "More and more Legion soldiers are camping in our fields, even walking throughout Arctos. Their presence is unacceptable—"

"If Praiton retaliates, who do you think will help defend us?" Caelum snarled. Reaching for the sword at his hip, he unlatched it from his belt and slammed the Shadow Sword onto the table, causing the entire council to jolt. All their eyes were drawn to it, as if it were the bloody head of General Morlais. But its presence was a stark reminder of where they had come from. "Stop your nonsensical whining. Having the Legion present is the best defense we have."

"But—" Helene began to protest, but Caelum rose from his seat, his purple eyes glowing.

"I'm done listening to this," he growled, grabbing his sword and strapping it onto his hip. "Let me know when you all find something more important to bother me with."

From beside her, Val saw Saros close his eyes, a small, exasperated sigh escaping his mouth, before he pushed back his own chair and followed Caelum out the door.

The council began to murmur heatedly amongst themselves, all of them casting filthy glances in Val's direction as she hurried to gather up her papers and follow behind Saros and Caelum.

By the time she made it back into the hallway, Saros was standing there, watching as the white-haired High King stormed down the black marble staircase.

"You're not going after him?" Val asked, coming to stand beside him.

Saros sighed, the same exasperated exhalation he had let out in the council meeting. "For as similar as they are, he certainly lacks his father's diplomacy."

Val snorted. "Yes, well, tact isn't exactly in Caelum's nature."

Saros's brow was furrowed, his gaze still lingering on where Caelum had disappeared. "Nodaria has always been a stronghold," he murmured. "We have fought through the rise of Praiton and crumbled when all was lost. Losing Castor was a tragedy that will stain the history of Nodaria forever. We needed someone strong—both in will and power—to take his place."

Val nodded. She remembered the day Nodaria had fallen. She had still been in Maniel, languishing in the Augusta Manor. It had been the final straw in her decision to desert. For all that it cost her, Castor's death left a stain on her own history as well.

"Though he may not seem it, Caelum is the best thing for this kingdom right now." Saros sighed. "I just wish they would see it, too."

Val glanced back over her shoulder as the door to the council room opened, and the dark-haired males and females of the council filtered out. Many of them shot disdainful looks their way or avoided their eyes altogether. Both she and Saros waited for them to clear the hall before daring to speak again.

"Having us here really is for the best," Val murmured, careful of the way her voice would carry down the cavernous halls. "Why do they think they'd be better off without the Legion?"

Saros shrugged sadly, his eyes following the council members down the hall. "They think it makes us a target. They think we are attempting to make Nodaria the mainland base for the Legion."

"That's preposterous," Val hissed. "Elbania will always be the best place for the Legion's headquarters—"

But Saros shook his head. "No, it is not. Elbania is too far from the mainland. Too isolated from information, supplies . . . help. No, the Legion *does* need a mainland stronghold. And Nodaria *would* make the most sense."

Val turned to stare at her fellow captain, her eyes wide. "So that *is* what you all have been angling for this whole time? A mainland stronghold?" It would mean dissension the likes of which she could not fathom within Nodaria. What would it mean for Caelum? If the council was angry over a few mere outposts, it would be nothing compared to operating the totality of the Pillar Legion from the Celestial Kingdom.

Saros huffed softly. "It is not something that we have formally discussed," he said. "But I cannot say it probably hasn't crossed all our minds at some point as the move with the most strategic sense. Nodaria is insulated. Mount Mors on its northern coast, Bridah on its eastern border. Ganiea's thick forests are on its west. We are more protected than any other kingdom besides Bridah. Castor always knew it, too. We had discussed offering a place to Aris long before Castor's death, but . . ."

Val's mind was reeling, processing what this could mean. She found herself looking around at the glittering black halls, imagining it replacing Light's Tower ... imagining people like the other two captains, Lycas and Elric, slithering through its corridors. A shiver rolled up her spine.

"Speaking of Nodaria's protection, the general mentioned your plan." Saros cast her a sideways glance, and Val could not place the look in his purple eyes. There was no smirk on his lips, none of the arrogant swagger he often had. If anything, the Nodarian captain looked ... concerned. "Are you sure it is wise, Val? I do not know much about Manielian traditions, but I do know Mount Cinis is not for the faint of heart."

Val's hands clenched and, in that moment, she could feel every blister and burn on her skin. Even after days of pushing her Ember Magic to tantamount heights until she couldn't take the heat anymore, her magic still fought her. She knew it wasn't enough. Knew that the only way to get stronger was to do what her brothers used to do to her.

A knot tightened in her throat at the memory.

But Saros just looked at her, his eyes roaming to the bright red patch of skin on her hands. Even though Saros always remained in a neutral middle between her and the other captains, she still found it difficult to trust him. What must he think of her after everything that happened?

"It's the only way," Val said finally, but the words were forced and strained.

But Saros gave her a small smile. "If you say so." Reaching out, he gave a gentle squeeze of her arm. "I should go tend to our High King. I get the honor of babysitting duty while the general is away," he said.

Val's heart skipped a beat at the mention of Aris, and before she could think twice, she blurted out, "Where is the general, by the way?"

The slight tremor to her words was the only giveaway that her heart was in her throat, heat prickling under her skin as Saros glanced back at her. "The general is in the south, attempting to work on something with your Sea Fae friend."

"Rayner?" Rayner had been gone for weeks on a secret mission for the Legion. He had said he'd be back soon, but she had heard nothing from him since he had left. "So, Aris is in Laenimore? With Rayner?"

Saros shrugged. "I'm not sure. He does not tell me much about his plans. Only that he goes—"

"Where he's needed," Val finished for him quietly.

Saros gave her a small grin and nodded, before turning and heading back down the hall, leaving Val to her thoughts.

The general had sent Rayner on some mission she knew nothing about. The Sea Throne had been deserted after Praiton took over and the High Queen had gone missing. It had fallen into disrepair since—a warzone where Praiton soldiers roamed, where they hunted the nymphs for sport. She had heard nothing but horror stories from Laenimore. But since when did the Legion start efforts there?

Val's feet began to move down the hall towards the back entrance, thinking she'd go back out to attempt to train a while, but stopped short as she turned the corner. A young male stood, his back to her, hidden in the shadows behind a large stone statue of a male with a telescope to his eye. He was speaking to someone, and instantly, the hair on the back of Val's neck stood on end.

A strong sense of foreboding overtook her, and before she could think twice, she pressed herself against the cool marble of the wall, before leaning around the corner, attempting to keep out of sight. Even from her new vantage point, she could only make out the glint of a silver Star Sword hanging from the young male's hip. The person he was talking to, however, was hidden from view.

Val felt herself freeze, instinct slowing her breathing. She peeked around the corner again just in time to see the young male take what looked to be a purple velvet pouch. It clanked loudly with the weight of silver as it was placed into his palm.

"See that it is done, boy," a male voice said from behind the statue . . . a voice that sounded faintly familiar to her. "But don't let that white-haired *bastard* catch you." The young boy nodded, pocketing the coin purse.

Val whipped her head back around the corner, her heart pounding in her ears, her breath coming in quick gasps. Whatever she had just seen, everything in her body was screaming at her that something was not right . . . that something was very, very wrong. Without thinking twice, Val took off back down the corridor, the only thought in her head being to find Saros again, to tell him what she had just seen . . . and quickly.

She was beginning to think that the situation in the Celestial Kingdom might be much worse than they had feared.

The next day, Deya and Luc met on the landing of the stairs, as they had planned. Luc's hair was disheveled, and he was rubbing his bleary eyes as Deya approached.

"Morning," he said, stifling a yawn with his fist. It was obvious that Luc had stayed up all night embracing Bridah's celebrations with full muster. Deya would've found it amusing, if she too weren't shrouded in a veil of her own exhaustion.

Sleep had not found her easily after reading the story of *dodsbringern*. Her mind had spun with endless horrific possibilities. Even that morning, after she had woken to the blazing sun of the Long Day, she found herself examining her blackened fingertips.

Had it grown? Was the blackness always midway down her knuckles? Had it always shimmered like a velvety night sky—devoid of all light and life? And what about the whispers that had filled her head that day with the magror? Could she still hear them? If she listened hard enough, were they still there, lurking in the shadows of her mind?

Deya curled her gloved hands into a fist and attempted to smile back at Luc. "Long night?" she asked, her voice a slight rasp.

Luc's mouth broke into a wide, gaping yawn. "The very definition of it."

Deya chuckled. "Did you have fun at least?"

"Oh, definitely." Groaning, he stretched his arms over his head, and a small smile slipped through the mask of exhaustion. "The Bridanians sure know how to party. We've been missing out all these centuries."

Deya scoffed and shook her head. Luc did love a good party. He was always invited to the feasts and festivities in Praiton. Deya usually never participated, choosing to take on an extra shift at the infirmary while she was still hoping to cull Clarita's favor.

Needless to say, that never happened.

They headed down the stairs towards the main entry hall where Karyna stood, waiting for them. Deya's small lady's maid looked as equally disheveled as Luc—yawning widely enough that tears brimmed in her slightly red eyes. She greeted them both with a groggy hello in mumbled Brynorsk before leading them towards a large wooden door off to the side of the entry hall which Deya had never noticed. The minute she opened the door, a draft drifted up the stone stairs, causing Deya to shiver in both cold and fear.

"Wow, you weren't kidding," Luc said, peering over the threshold, his teeth chattering slightly. "Bridah really is brutal."

Karyna shot them an apologetic look. "I can always go fetch you both some warmer clothes," she offered. "But I can't say it'll do too much good."

Deya leaned over Luc's shoulder, her eyes taking in the dark, stone steps, slick with ice. At that moment, a brutal breeze blasted them both in the face, as if swept off the top of the fjords themselves. Luc reached out and slammed the door shut, as if out of instinct, before turning to look at Deya sheepishly.

"Whoops," he said and Deya rolled her eyes, but was secretly glad he had done it. They were both dressed in extra layers today—thick woolen cloaks with furs, leather gloves and boots with extra socks. Luc even had a knit scarf twined around his neck. After her journey to Frode, Deya knew she could withstand the cold. If she hadn't died out in the open, she knew she could probably survive the underground temple. But it wasn't the fear of death that stopped her.

The ice had crept into her soul, had lodged into her very heart. Now, the cold felt like icy fingers clamped around her face.

Death bringer.

The memory of the book she had read last night flitted through her mind, and she shook it away swiftly. It had already haunted her nightmares all night. She couldn't dwell on it now.

She looked at Luc and squared her shoulders. "We've got to do it," she whispered. "It can't be all bad."

Luc chewed on his lip, looking unconvinced, but eventually, with an exasperated sigh, he nodded. Turning, they both faced the wooden door.

Pulling in a deep breath, Luc looked over at her. "Ready?"

She wasn't. After what she had read last night, she couldn't fight the crushing fear over what else she may discover in Fangdor. What other dark secrets were waiting for her down in the temple?

But she couldn't tell Luc this. Instead, she clenched her jaw and gave a grim nod before Luc pushed open the door again.

The frigid breeze hit them both. Luc sucked in air through his teeth and Deya closed her eyes, feeling the icy air wash against her cheeks. The memory of the skathi breathing down on her made a chill prickle the back of her neck.

With a little bow and a slight chatter of his teeth, Luc said, "After you."

There was no turning back now, no more excuses to be made. Giving a small wave to Karyna, who bid them a nervous farewell, they began the slippery descent down the stone steps, Deya gripping the walls as her heels slid over patches of slick ice and piles of gathered snow. Luc was behind her, his murmurings of "Oh, I don't like this . . . Oh, I *really* don't like this," echoing off the narrow passage as they descended further and further down. On several occasions, Deya almost slipped, but Luc reached out and grabbed her by the arms before she went crashing down the miles of stairs.

Finally, after what felt like ages, the hallway opened and what she saw stole the air from her lungs. A large, cavernous hall loomed over them, its ceilings so high, she briefly wondered if they had gone hundreds of feet underground. Icicles and frost coated every available surface, including an enormous stone carving of a beautiful female holding snowflakes in her hand. Deya had seen this female's face many times now and was always stunned at the resemblance she bore to the current Frost Princess.

Flykra's features were more detailed in the large stone statue. Her face was angular, cheekbones high, and she bore a small smile, as if she had a secret only she knew.

All around them, priestesses in fur-lined, periwinkle-blue robes sat at stone tables, writing on scrolls, or else reading books. Some were on their knees in front of Flykra, singing in a quiet, lilting tone, a haunting song in Brynorsk.

Lining the cave-like walls were short bookcases. Piles of scrolls and delicate handbound books were stacked inside small square cubbies, each shrouded in cobwebs and snow. The shelves snaked around the walls, looping out of sight behind tiny tables and around other statues and portrait displays. Deya recognized one smaller statue to the left of Flykra as a young man with a haircut similar to Espen's. From the books she had already poured over, she figured this must be Flykra's first son, Asger.

"*Gyet ég aishtoda feg?*"

Deya and Luc jumped. They had been so entranced by the sight of the underground temples that they had not heard the elderly priestess who had approached them. She was regarding them warily, her bright blue eyes narrowed.

"H . . . Hi," Deya stuttered, spinning around. "We were just looking for . . . books."

The priestess stared at them. Deya detected a slight eye roll from the elder female at the sound of the common tongue. She held her chin up, but when she spoke again, this time, it was in their language. "What kind of books would interest two outsiders in our most sacred place?"

Her accent was stronger than even Karyna's, and Deya struggled to pick out each word within the rolling consonants and vowels.

"We . . . we were looking for any books on the Mother Goddess.

Maybe about the birth of Flykra?" Deya edged.

The priestess had bristled slightly at the mention of the Mother Goddess. Deya had been worried about this. If Kindra's reaction to the Mother was any indication, the people of Bridah did not hold Mav in the same regard as Praiton did. She knew Bridah's devout practices towards Flykra most likely infuriated Decius, as each kingdom bent the knee to Praiton's forced religious practices. Bridah's belief in Flykra was strong, its magic still pure, its culture untouched by the surrounding kingdoms. United. It was a strength even Praiton probably overlooked.

"The scrolls about the birth of Flykra are found in that section over there," the priestess said finally after a long pause. "Though I do not know what good it will do those who cannot speak our tongue. They are the oldest documents and should not be touched by anyone other than a qualified archival priestess."

Luc balked behind her, but Deya refused to be beaten. Rallying, she quickly replied, "Is there anyone you know who can help us? We *really* need to look at any information you have. Please?"

The priestess stared at her; a long, cold gaze which made Deya subconsciously clench her fingers. It was as if the female could see through her, could maybe see the blackness in her soul that Frode had. The fear that she was tainted to those with more acute eyes made her crumble inside.

The priestess's gaze darted behind them towards the group of curious onlookers listening in to their conversation. When the elder female's eyes flashed towards them, they immediately scattered, darting back behind the low shelves, bending over scrolls, attempting to look busy.

"Who is tasked to watch you, outsider?" the female asked.

"Watch me?" Until that moment, Deya hadn't considered what Karyna did as *watching* her. Caring for her, maybe. But the way the priestess said it, it made her wonder if Karyna's duty was more than just tending to her needs. "I . . . I have a lady's maid. Karyna."

The priestess pursed her lips, the fine lined wrinkles around her mouth gathering like a cinched purse. "Karyna had been trained in the archives before she became a lady's maid. Perhaps, with the right supervision, she may aid you in what you seek."

Deya turned to look at Luc, but he was already heading back towards the stairs. "I'm on it!" he said. "I'll be right back!"

Luc sprinted up the stairs again, leaving Deya alone with the priestess, who continued to stare at her with the same look of suspicious disdain. With an awkward smile, Deya inclined her head to her in a polite thank you, before beginning to wander around the large room.

The commotion their arrival had caused calmed as the priestesses turned back to their work, ignoring Deya as she edged around the room. She peered into cubbies, taking in the peeling and yellowing parchment inside with cobwebs and small amounts of snow, before craning her neck to study the enormous statues at the front of the room.

Asger's statue was the most intriguing. He held a large hammer in his fist, his eyes empty carvings, yet still managed to hold a trace of intimidating focus. Snow, both real and carved, dusted his shoulders, along with an etching of the Bridanian crest on the shield across his arm.

She moved on from the statues, her breath coming out in cold clouds of mist, turning instead to a small alcove which held a collection of round tables and bookshelves cut into the stone. There, on the wall behind one of the tables, was a small oil portrait. Compared to the size of the statues, the painting was modest, accented only by its silver gilded frame. From the canvas, three white-haired girls looked back at Deya. Her breath caught as she moved closer, her eyes immediately alighting on the smallest girl in the middle.

There was something about her eyes . . . the gentle curve of them, the slight intensity of the blue irises. If she hadn't been smiling, Deya would've picked out Caelum's facial features right away. Even the way her mouth spread into a wide grin reminded her of the way he had looked the other night when he had given her that rare, beautiful smile.

"Sweet, isn't it?"

Deya started, only to find the elderly priestess standing behind her. But she was not glaring at Deya this time. Instead, she gazed up at the oil painting of the three girls, a sad, reminiscent smile on her face.

"Are these . . ." Deya asked, but the older female nodded gravely.

"The Frost Princesses, yes."

Chest tight, Deya turned back to gaze at the portrait, too. It was easy to pick out Kindra—the tallest one of the group. Even though she looked to be barely a teenager in this portrait, the hardened scowl on her face made her look much older than her two sisters.

Hedda had a softer look to her eyes than Kindra. She had a hand on top of Asti's, a motherly air to her smile. But it was Caelum's mother that drew her gaze. The way she looked ready to burst out of the canvas—a large smile beaming out of her young face—a stark contrast from the other two more understated expressions of her sisters. She was barely a child, and yet Deya wondered how much of the High King of Nodaria was mirrored in the ghost of his mother.

"No matter how many years go by," the priestess said, sighing, "this portrait still saddens me deeply. Princess Hedda was found in this very chamber . . . She was so burned we could hardly identify her."

The gasp Deya let out lodged in her throat, but that didn't stop the rise of tears that surged up unexpectedly.

"B-burned?"

The priestess nodded. "Bridah was the second kingdom attacked after Ganiea fell in the beginning of the war, as you know. We were who Praiton targeted after they sought an alliance with Maniel. Although unsuccessful, there were grave consequences to their attempt."

Deya swallowed past the lump in her throat. No matter how long she fought on behalf of the Pillar Legion, she didn't think she would ever be able to get past the soul-wrecking guilt. Praiton had crushed so many, had destroyed so much . . .

The blue eyes of Caelum's family gazed back at her, just as Castor's had in the throne room of Nodaria. The entirety of Caelum's lineage now lived only on canvas.

"What about Princess Asti?" Deya asked quietly. "What became of her?"

Another sigh fell from the older female's mouth as she shook her head. "The last I saw of Princess Asti, she was being rushed from Fangdor through these tunnels with Hedda. They made sure we had all exited the tunnels first. But what became of her . . . I do not know. Her body was not found with Hedda's . . . nor was it ever found."

Deya fell silent, but her mind was racing. It was foolish, the swell of hope that rose in her chest. Because if a body was never found, Asti could still be alive . . . Couldn't she? She suppressed a sad scoff as Caelum's voice drifted through her brain at the thought. *Optimistic fool.*

She *was* an optimistic fool. No matter how much darkness and shadow had befallen her life in the last year, she tried her best to still cling to the hope and light she yearned to have. But she couldn't help but wonder how much death and darkness needed to touch her before she, like Caelum, believed only the worst.

"Dey?" Luc had reappeared with Karyna, who bowed deeply to the priestess.

"Sister Isfrid," Karyna murmured.

The priestess then began to chastise her in rapid Brynorsk. From where Deya was standing, it sounded like a very stern lecture—most likely on letting outsiders handle their precious artifacts.

Luc edged around the two Bridanian females towards Deya and leaned down to murmur in her ear. "Are you okay?"

Many years of working together meant Luc could pick up on the slightest change of Deya's mood. Or was the sadness just hanging over her like a dark cloud?

She nodded, though, not really in the mood to discuss Caelum's family with Luc just yet. Quietly, she turned away from the piercing blue eyes of Caelum's mother.

They began their research slowly. Karyna was forced to don gloves and use a pair of thin, metal tongs to lift delicate scrolls from their individual cannisters within the cubbies. Every old, yellowed piece of parchment was filled with confusing Brynorsk letters, sometimes worded in such a confusing manner that even Karyna had a hard time deciphering its meaning.

Hours trickled past and each scroll they touched gave them a little less hope. Karyna would read out the scroll while Luc jotted down notes, and Deya searched for the next one. And the next one.

The history of every battle Bridah ever fought, the lineage of the entirety of the royal line dating all the way back to Flykra, ancient prayers—even one very long scroll dictating Flykra's intensive frost training exercises. Eventually, Karyna's voice began to grow hoarse, and even the other priestesses began to pack up, readying to leave the temples for the day.

"Well, I don't see us getting much done at this point," Luc said tiredly, rubbing at his eyes with a gloved hand.

Deya's nose twitched slightly with the dust and snow. She had been trembling for the last hour. Even with Karyna's magic keeping the cold at bay, the frigid temperatures of the temple were finally starting to get to her. The four thick layers of clothing she had on did little to dispel Bridah's chill, which settled onto her bones.

"Fine," she sighed, gently closing the delicate book in front of her. "I suppose we can continue on tomorrow."

That was all her life had become, after all. One big research project with nothing to show for it. The weeks and weeks of fruitless searching were beginning to grate on her nerves, filling her with a familiar, uneasy fluttering in her chest.

She couldn't help but worry that their time was running short. Images of dragons flying over Bridah's glacial walls floated through her head as she, Luc, and Karyna carefully packed away their materials for the night. In the end, she knew that Caelum was right. That it was no longer a matter of *if* the dragon would breach Bridah.

Now, it was only a matter of *when*.

CHAPTER 17

Caelum watched the Nodarian guards moving below, just tiny specks from his usual perch on the window of the astronomy tower. His eyes darted between the moving figures on the ground and the night sky, sweeping the dark clouds and the stars. The last time he sat here, a dragon had flown overhead. And even though no further sightings had occurred, Caelum couldn't shake the unease that had settled in his gut—especially after what Saros had told him.

Val had warned Saros of what she had seen—a solider being paid off. A possible plot brewing. But with little information to go on, Caelum was left to sit here and observe. It could be nothing. Could be something innocuous and irrelevant, and yet . . . While he had not seen any outward signs of it—even from his vantage point up above—there was something in the air. He could feel it. A prickle on the back of his neck, a tingle of nerves in the pit of his stomach.

The council meeting today had been calm . . . too calm. Councilman Mah had not so much as blinked when Caelum had reported a delivery of

Nodarian resources set to be sent to Light's Tower the next day via caravan.

Nodaria had been flourishing lately, its resources coming back in abundance. He knew they had the supplies to spare, and he never thought twice about his decision to send the excess to the new outpost he had set up in the neighboring town of Aldebaran, even when the decision was met with an uproar. But when Caelum announced the delivery of supplies to the Aldebaran outpost that day, it was silent. Helene voiced her displeasure—which Caelum overruled—and the meeting dismissed without so much as a curse aimed in his direction.

Caelum kicked his foot hanging over the ledge, dangling hundreds of feet in the air. Bits of the building cascaded from his heel, tumbling down towards the ground. His eyes moved over the formation of Nodarian troops, out towards the furthest training ring. At the moment, it was empty, but usually, it was filled with a roaring flame that could be seen from miles away.

Val had been out there every day, pushing her flames harder, faster, further. He hadn't had the time to speak to her about the plan Aris had told him he and Val were enacting. But, in his rare moments of free time, he watched Val from a distance. He could feel her frustration, see the flames sputter and fizzle.

Whatever Val was trying to do, it was failing.

A door behind him creaked open, and Caelum started in surprise. But instead of a wandering star seer or a visiting priestess, Rayner popped his head over the threshold.

"They said you'd be up here."

Caelum slid off the windowsill, staring at the Sea Fae in shock.

"When did you get back?"

Rayner's blue-gray face looked tired and worn. Dark circles lined his eyes, and his hair and clothing were disheveled. He rubbed a hand through his messy sandy blond hair and tried to put on an easy, carefree smile. It came out pained.

"Just now. I came looking for you, but Saros mentioned you might be up here." He walked into the room and collapsed onto a velvet pouf by one of the brass telescopes in the window. His body seemed to give out as he sank into the cushion, and he let out a long sigh.

"Where did Aris send you off to for so long?"

Rayner chuckled. "Oh, you know. Here and there." The exasperated look Caelum gave him made Rayner laugh again. "Don't look at me like that. I promise it was nothing extreme."

"I heard you were in Laenimore."

Rayner shrugged his wiry shoulders. "Just outside of it. As you can imagine, visiting Laenimore right now is not advisable."

Caelum had never been to Laenimore, but he had heard things. If Nodaria's state was bad when he first returned to it, he could not imagine Laenimore's.

Rayner sighed, waving a dismissive hand, as if to brush away all thought of his kingdom's decay. "How are things here?" he asked.

Caelum let out a short grunt in response and Rayner smiled grimly.

"Saros alluded to something," he said, and his face became more serious. "Caelum, what has been going on? Even I could sense something when I came in. The guards in the training field—"

"I'm aware," Caelum said. Leaning back against the black marble walls, he gazed out the open window again. The only distinguishing feature Val had told Saros she had observed was that one of the traitors carried a Star Sword. His stomach clenched at what this meant. Of *who* it meant. The coveted Star Sword was given to different esteemed members of his father's army—Saros included. For the traitor to have a Star Sword meant he came from a family loyal to the throne. But obviously not loyal to *him*.

His eyes swept the grounds, the small dots of guards moving below. A group was cloistered to the side, not bothering with their weapons or magic training.

He sensed Rayner rising from the cushion to join him at the window, his eyes following the separated faction. From this height, he couldn't recognize those congregating below, but he did recognize the Star Sword on the hip of a smaller guard.

It had taken him several weeks to remember where he had seen the soldier who he had crashed into the night he went to see Io, but it had finally clicked in his memory. Deimos, the young soldier who had answered the door of Mount Mors all those months ago, whispered below him with the other guards, carrying his father's sword proudly on his hip. Caelum could see the glint of the silver pommel from the top of the tower.

"I was assuming that things had gotten better with how many Legion troops I saw on the grounds," Rayner said. "But by the looks of it, I would say I was wrong."

Caelum didn't speak. He was busy watching Deimos. The boy was locked in deep conversation with another soldier, his posture stiff. Deimos had crossed his path many times since he had been made High King. In the beginning, the boy had bowed to him—still jumpy, but otherwise respectful. Now, however, the boy often avoided his eyes, walking past him quickly in the hallway, his face set into a grim scowl. But he never forgot the way the boy's lip curled when he had seen him in his weakened state. As if in *disgust*. He hadn't given it much thought until now. This reaction was common these days. But now, after what Val had witnessed . . .

"Caelum," Rayner began, a hint of a warning in his tone, but Caelum shook his head in a short jerk. He didn't need the lecture. This never stopped the Sea Fae from trying, however. "You are their High King," he said in a low voice. "If there is unrest, perhaps listening to their complaints—"

"All I do is listen," Caelum spat. His hands tightened into fists across his chest, still watching Deimos below. "They want to be sitting ducks for Praiton, to let them storm back in here and take us. Forgive me if I refuse to let that happen."

"Perhaps there is some credence to their misgivings. Maybe conceding a bit can help ease tensions."

"Ease tensions?" Caelum sneered. "*I* am their High King. I am doing what is right, what will keep this kingdom *safe*."

This was what he told himself, but even the words made a small, tingle of doubt scratch at the back of his mind. He was tired. *So* tired. His body ached daily from the demand on his magic, but it was nothing compared to the weight on his heart and soul. Every day, he tried to do what was right for the people of his kingdom. And every day, he doubted more and more if he was capable of *ever* being able to do anything right.

He was not a king. With every day that passed, that thought became more prevalent.

His jaw clenched, and he steeled himself again, hoping Rayner did not see the shadow pass across his face. Thankfully, the Sea Fae fell silent, giving up the fight. But Caelum didn't have the option of feeling guilty. After everything, he trusted Rayner more than he could believe, yet the Sea Fae's calm, placating nature often clashed with his own. Unlike Rayner, he wasn't desperate to please everyone he encountered.

Even if this was to Nodaria's detriment.

They watched Deimos and the others begin to disband, attempting to blend back into their ranks. The unease Caelum felt tickling his insides was more difficult to ignore—and so, unfortunately—was Rayner's warning.

"Keep an eye on them for me," Caelum said finally.

It was a mark of their friendship that Rayner only nodded.

Val's fingers burned as she dug her heels into the hard, packed earth of Nodaria's training ring. Panting, she flexed her fingers, feeling the stiffness and ache of them with each movement.

You call that a flame? the familiar voice jeered in her ear. Val ground her teeth and, with a roar, sent another tidal wave of fire exploding from her. It was as if she were trying to burn the voice from her mind, to wipe it from her very being.

And as her fires burned, so did she.

Orange flames expanded around her, throwing the dark, empty

training ring into sharper relief. Val breathed in deeper, focusing on that small flame roaring in her chest and *pushed* into it, forcing it to billow, sending its warmth shooting down her body, through her arms and legs, plunging towards her fingers. The flames surrounding her roared in response, their color accelerating from orange to white in a flash.

But then another voice whispered in her ear. Quieter and gentler than the other.

There was enough left of them to bury.

A shriek escaped her as the soft voice caressed her ear, her concentration on her inner flame snapping like a loose string. Immediately, the fire engulfed her, scorching her skin, igniting her clothes.

With a cry, Val threw herself onto the ground, rolling in the dirt as she beat the flames from her clothes, her skin screaming in pain. As the last of the flames were extinguished, Val lay there, panting, staring up at the starry sky, feeling her body ache and sting.

She didn't know what she was doing . . . why she even bothered. It was pointless to train like this, pointless to think pushing her flames as high as they could go would prepare her for what real dragon fire felt like. Nothing could match those conditions—particularly not here, out in the open air.

Heat from Ember Magic could be easily withstood if she used it in the way she was used to. Clinging to her swords. Thrown from her hands. Pushed *away* from her. But to survive a Trial by Fire—a dragon's blast of flame, the hottest flame on earth—she had to wrap the flames around her. Encase herself in a fiery cocoon. And let herself burn.

Reaching up a burnt, blistered finger, she touched her face gingerly. Tears clung to her cheeks, streaking down towards her chin.

Pathetic, the voice inside her whispered, but this time, it was not Leo's voice, or even Lorenzo's.

This time, it was her own.

She was not strong enough to endure even her own flame in her weakened state, much less the Heavenly Fire the Augusta name was known for. With her weakened magic, she could barely produce the flame, much less endure it at close range. It would've been a challenge to withstand it even when she was at her full power. And her power was nothing compared to a dragon's.

At this rate, she would die. And all of this was pointless.

After returning to the Keep with her failures burned into her skin, Val spent a full night tossing and turning as her burns screamed against the cool satin of her sheets, fearing the beginning of her training with Aris the next day.

Nightmares of her brothers' faces and her murdered friends flickered like flames in her mind, jolting her awake every other hour. By the time she dragged herself down to the great hall the next morning, she felt sick to her stomach. But the second she saw a familiar Sea Fae sitting at the table at the front of the room, her exhaustion seemed to disappear entirely.

"Rayner!"

The Sea Fae's face split into a wide grin and Val rushed to him, throwing her arms around his neck, colliding against his wiry frame. Rayner grunted with the impact, but she heard him chuckle into her hair.

"Good to see you, too, V," he murmured, tousling her bright red hair.

Val pulled back, grinning, taking in her friend. Rayner had been one of the only constants she had had in Ironbalt. Always the first to back her up in a fight, the Sea Fae proved not only loyal, but also a steadfast friend in the times when Val thought she'd lose her mind in that place. And as Rayner's scarred, burned hands gripped her wrists in a friendly squeeze, Val couldn't help but appreciate the fact that they were friends at all.

"When did you get back?" she asked as they both sank into chairs surrounding the long dining tables.

"The other day." Even though he tried to smile, Val noticed he looked tired and even a little sickly. "But I've been busy doing other things on our noble High King's orders."

Val let out a derisive snort. "Oh? And what orders does our High

King have to delegate to you?"

"That is none of your business," a cold, deep voice said from behind them. With a brush of winter wind that made Val shiver, Caelum plunked down into the chair beside her. Val noticed that he had chosen a normal wooden chair, completely avoiding the High King's golden seat at the head of the table.

"Nice of you to join us," Rayner remarked, smirking, and Caelum grunted in response. But his purple eyes narrowed at Val as they drifted up to rest on the burns peeking out from her sleeves.

"I see Aris's plan is going well."

Val flushed, pulling on the edge of her sleeve, trying to hide the blistered skin.

Rayner jerked his head to look at her. "What plan?"

The heat was draining from her cheeks, trickling down her chest like cold rain.

"It's going fine."

"*What plan?*" Rayner asked again.

Caelum was still looking at her. And if Val didn't know any better, she would think it was concern making his purple eyes flash like that.

"I hope you know what you're doing," he said after a long pause.

Val raised her chin defiantly but had to clench her hands to keep them from shaking. "Careful, Caelum," she said with only a slight tremor. "People may actually think you care about something."

But Caelum didn't laugh. Instead, his hard gaze lanced through her for a beat longer than was comfortable.

"*What plan?*" Rayner demanded again.

Caelum turned away, seizing the water jug and filling his goblet. "Val has agreed to journey to Maniel and claim a dragon of her own."

The silence that followed this statement was deafening. Rayner stared at Val, a wild fear filling those bright blue irises. Rayner was not much older than she was. Unlike Caelum and Deya, Rayner grew up in the realm before Praiton, was well-versed in the other kingdoms' lore. He knew what going to Mount Cinis meant.

"Val, you can't be serious."

Looking away, she attempted to steady her voice, even though her burnt fingers trembled as she reached for the goblet of water on the table in front of her. "Aris believes it is the only way we can win against Titus's dragon."

"But—" Rayner whirled to look at Caelum, who was watching breakfast be delivered within the hall with a steely, purple gaze. "The general must be mistaken. Val . . . are you sure—"

The door to the great hall swung open and the general himself strode into the room. Val had not heard when the general had returned to Nodaria, yet she figured it must have been at the same time as Rayner.

Rayner fell silent at the sight of Aris, and Val was grateful for it. She didn't think she could stand hearing about how Rayner didn't believe she could survive Mount Cinis. Because, if she were being honest with herself, she'd admit that she agreed.

Training had not been going the way she had hoped. No matter how hard she pushed, something still held her back. The Augusta Heavenly Fire, which her brothers had spent years of her adolescence forcing out of her, could not sustain for long—and when it did, it burned her badly. If she kept going like this, her chances of survival were bleak.

Val watched apprehensively as the general approached their table, golden armor gleaming in the lanterns sparkling with starlight, the shadows still weighing down his handsome face in the most disarming way.

"Good morning," he said, giving them each a short nod. Val noticed he hadn't looked at her long, before turning to Caelum. "Are you ready?"

Caelum's gaze flicked up to the general, a familiar glint of defiance present again. "I was ready thirty minutes ago," he replied.

Aris inclined his head again. "Yes, well, Kindra was busy preparing. I only just now received word that they are ready for us."

Val's head whipped around. "Kindra? Us? I thought we were beginning my training today?"

"We are," Aris said. "In Bridah."

CHAPTER 18

"No!" Val stomped her feet, dug in her heels, almost damn near burned Atlas Keep down as Caelum dragged her towards Castor's study again.

"Stop acting like a child."

"I am not going back to Bridah, Caelum! I won't—"

But Caelum thrust her into Castor's study and slammed the door behind them. The look on his face was one of murderous ire, but she was too crazed with panic to let it bother her. After all these weeks . . . after flinching every time she felt the draft of a cold breeze . . . after having the image of Lucia's head rolling across the crimson snow to rest at her feet . . .

She couldn't go back. She *wouldn't*. Training was pointless anyway, she knew that. She wouldn't go back to Bridah just so she could die in a few weeks.

"Why Bridah?" Val demanded, pulling her arm free of Caelum's hold.

"Why not stay here? I was doing fine on my own."

"Why don't you ask the general?" Caelum asked coldly, crossing his tattooed arms to glare back at her. "He's the one calling the shots. I'm just your bloody transporter."

Val blanched at this. She could throw a fit to Caelum, but she absolutely refused to show her hand to Aris. Especially after the particularly distant greeting she received this morning.

She opened her mouth, about ready to rip into Caelum some more, when she caught sight of his face. It had been several days since she had seen him properly—the many council meetings and back and forth trips from Nodarian outposts had kept the new High King busy. But now that he was barely a foot from her, Val could see the weariness on his face. Caelum looked gaunt and grim, as if he had barely slept for days. As if something more than just the discord in the Celestial Kingdom upset him.

At that thought, the memory of what she had seen in the hallway after the last council meeting flashed through her mind and she knew that Saros had to have told Caelum what she had seen in the hall.

"Caelum, I—"

But Caelum cut her off. "Do you think you are the only one who is forced to do things you don't want to? To go where you don't want to go?" he said in a low growl. His nostrils flared, and he looked away, as if trying to hold back what he truly felt.

"What do you mean?" Val whispered, but Caelum shook his head.

"I can't do it all," he said finally, his voice strained with a heavy frustration. "I can't take one more thing, Val. I *can't*. So do not make me have to fight you on this . . . Please."

The final word made Val pause. She had never heard Caelum speak like this. *Plead* like this. The way he said it made her think he was not just talking about sending her to Bridah, but rather something else. Something bigger. Heavier. Now, suddenly she could see the weight of the crown he bore, the one he had been trying to carry all alone, and her complaints shriveled in her throat.

Sympathy for her friend rushed over her, and she swallowed down her protests. Whatever her fear of the Frost Kingdom, she knew Caelum had much more on his shoulders to deal with. So, she closed her mouth and nodded.

Caelum let out a disgruntled sigh, his arms unfolding, his shoulders slackening. "Look," he said in a voice much gentler than before. "From what Aris told me, Bridah has the structure necessary to increase your endurance," he explained. "We don't have anything like that here in Nodaria, unless you prefer me to shove you into the oven. Which if that's the case, all you have to do is ask."

The statement sounded more like his old self, and Val shot him a sardonic, yet relieved, glare. "You're a dick," she said, and Caelum smirked that crooked grin of his.

The door opened again, and Aris and Rayner entered. The pair were conversing, and Aris had on his usual cool expression, but Rayner looked worried . . . even upset. They both fell silent the minute they entered the room, and Val wondered if they had perhaps been arguing about her.

"Ready?" Aris asked, looking between Val and Caelum. Rayner had his arms crossed, his shoulders stiff, and he looked as if he were bursting to say something but holding back.

Caelum gave a curt nod, but Val hesitated. Aris's starburst eyes turned to her, and she found she wanted to scream at the emptiness they held.

Only a few days ago, that night in Castor's office, he had looked at her so differently—with the same brazen fire that seemed to disregard all thought and rationality that he had all those years ago in his office. What had happened?

"Valeria?" he asked softly.

Val turned to look at him, and in that split second, when their eyes connected, it was like a million things passed between them all at once. Heat and tension, fear and lust . . . confusion and pain. It was all wrapped within that single, tiny look. And it was all Val could do to nod.

A portal spiraled into the room, and with a deep breath, Val stepped through it. She never thought she would get used to the feeling of one of Caelum's portals. It was as if she were being shoved through a tiny keyhole. And then, with a great, shuddering gasp, she was deposited onto the familiar floor of Fangdor's entry hall . . . and right at Deya's feet.

Val struggled to stand, and for a moment, she and Deya looked at each other. Her friend was just as delicate and petite as she had been when she had left. The furs draped over the collar of her dress made her look a bit more imposing, but the way she clasped her gloved hands in front of her, and the tremble of her lips as she looked at Val made a piece of her heart break slowly.

"Hi," Val breathed.

Deya grinned. "Hey."

And then they were embracing. Deya jumped on her with the force of a hot wind and Val felt tears burn her eyes as she crushed her friend to her chest, and her broken heart bled a tiny drop at the feeling. Deya was safe, warm, and not angry at her . . . She was *okay*.

"It's good to see you," Deya said, pulling back and beaming at her. Both of their eyes were shining with unshed tears, and Val fought the urge to laugh at the silliness of it all.

"Yeah, you, too."

Their reunion was cut short by Caelum and Aris both hurtling into the room—Caelum with a bit more practiced grace than Aris. The general stumbled, yet remained on his feet, almost careening into a tall figure standing, quietly in the corner.

The Frost Princess reached out and caught Aris by the arm, righting him with a small smirk hauntingly similar to the one Caelum had given her earlier.

"Not used to such travel, General?" Kindra teased in her rolling, melodic accent.

Aris gave her a smooth grin, one that made Val's skin tingle in an all too familiar way. "I do prefer much more . . . physical forms of movement, it is true," Aris replied, and Kindra gave a low, suggestive chuckle.

A flame flickered in Val's chest. An angry, injured roar.

Seeing Aris flirt with other females should be something she was used to by now, but Gods, how long had it been since Aris had outwardly done such a thing? With the ramping tensions in the realm, it was almost as if he had been too preoccupied to think about such matters . . . much less flaunt them in front of her.

Then, a horrible thought flared in her mind. Had something happened between the general and Kindra?

"Well, hurry, I do not have all day," Kindra said, and with a wave of her pale hand, she gestured for them to follow her.

The cold had already begun to creep into Val's blood again. She had not dressed for this kingdom—had instead dressed to withstand an intense amount of heat. The thin long-sleeved training top she wore under her cloak was not enough to combat Bridah's cold, even indoors.

Her trepidation built when Kindra led them out the back door towards Bridah's heavily frosted gardens. Even with Kindra and Caelum shielding them from the worst of the elements, Val's internal flame was already beginning to fade.

"Are you alright?" Deya whispered to her.

Gods, she wasn't. She was so far from alright. Just being here, walking through the snow with Deya was beginning to chill her very bones. Deya reached for her hand, and Val seized it, squeezing it a little too tightly.

"I'm fine," she said tensely. "Just . . . not a big fan of this place after . . ."

Deya gave her a sympathetic smile. "I know . . . but it'll be okay. We'll warm up in a second."

"Deya . . . about our trip from Frode," Val began, but Deya shook her head, turning to her earnestly and squeezing her hand.

"It was my fault," she whispered. "Please forgive me. I shouldn't have let it get so far—"

"*Your* fault?" Val gasped out a disbelieving laugh. "How in the Mother's name did you come to that conclusion? Deya, it was *me*. The skathi tricked *me*, and because of that . . . Oh, I don't know how you can forgive me—"

But Deya's shoulders dropped, as if in relief, and she laughed. Pulling Val into her side, she clutched her arm tightly, as if to hug her. "Don't be ridiculous. There's nothing to forgive. Now, can you forgive me?"

Val stared at her, dumbstruck for a moment, but then she smiled. "There's nothing to forgive."

They both smiled at each other, their arms still tightly linked, before Deya nodded ahead of them. "Now come on, we'll be there soon, I think."

Thankfully, Deya was right. No sooner did Val think her internal flame would freeze altogether, did Kindra stop on the outskirts of Fangdor's grounds. Half buried in the snow, a large, rounded dome of curious white stone protruded from the ground. It reminded Val of a turtle's shell, peeking out from the mountains of frost.

"What is this?" Val asked, shooting a hesitant glance first at Deya, then at Aris and Caelum. But it was Kindra who answered.

"This is our Hearth House." She laid her pale fingers on the handle of the stone door—a large metal latch, almost like the lock on a porthole in a war ship. "This structure has been a part of these grounds since Asger the Third. It is how we cultivate crops which need warmth, how we mine for materials that are lost to us in the snow, and of course, where we forge special weapons which require intense heat."

Kindra splayed her hand across the latch, and crystalline veins of Frost Magic spread from her palm, shooting across the surface of the door in all directions, as if drawing frost away from its center. And then she pushed down the lever and the door swung open.

A blast of soothing warmth rushed over her and Val closed her eyes, breathing it in. It smelled of fire, and earth—of sun, and trees of other lands. It wrapped her up like a warm hug, and Val's internal flame flickered weakly in response, like a dog lifting its head to a familiar scent.

Kindra made a sweeping gesture, ushering them across the earthen threshold, but the Frost Princess did not follow. "It is too hot in there for my tastes," she said, her lip curling as the heat brushed her face. "When you're finished, Caelum can get you out."

And with a final wave of her long fingers, Kindra vanished back into the snow. With a soft clang, the door sealed itself behind them, leaving them standing in the entry room of a narrow corridor.

Immediately, the heat pressed down on them.

Deya began to shrug out of her fur cloak, and even Caelum shifted uncomfortably. Val didn't know how Aris didn't so much as flinch underneath all that heavy gold armor, but the general was all business as he began to lead their group further into the Hearth House.

"Kindra was kind enough to clear out a chamber for us."

"A *chamber?*" Val repeated, wondering just how large the Hearth House really was.

Huge, it turned out. Much bigger than the exterior led her to believe. The corridor before them was narrow, leading to a series of similar steel doors stretching the length of the structure. Beside each door, a small porthole window nestled in its center like a large glass eye set into the steel.

As they began to walk, their feet sinking into the loamy earth of the structure's floor, Val was mystified by this strange, humid oasis that had been hiding here in Bridah all along.

Aris led them down the corridor, as if he had been there before. Belatedly, Val wondered if he had. After all, *he* had contacted Kindra to set this whole thing up, had known it was there, even before she had agreed to this. The new flame of suspicion and asinine jealousy flickered within her, and Val stamped at it like an errant spark.

One door was left cracked, as if waiting for them. Aris pushed it open and gestured for Val to enter. The room was empty, filled with nothing but dry soil and sloped walls and ceilings made of the same, curious white stone as the exterior.

"What is this?" Deya asked softly. Her gloved hands skimmed down the white stone, her eyes wide with curiosity.

"Kindra tells me it's an ancient, Bridanian mineral," Aris said, pulling off his thick gloves and golden gauntlets. "It's called eldsteinr. It's exceedingly rare and only occurs deep underneath Bridah's tundra. This house is the only structure made with it that I know of."

Caelum was roving the exterior of the chamber, running his fingers across the stone, as well. "Funny, never took you to be a Bridanian geological expert, General," he said snidely.

Aris smirked. He dropped his heavy gauntlets down onto the dirt floor outside the chamber with a dull thud, before turning to face Val.

"This rock will insulate your Ember Magic. It will trap in the heat, and the temperature will build with your power. To ensure you can survive Mount Cinis, you need to be able to withstand an immense amount of heat," he said. "Are you ready, Valeria?"

Val swallowed hard. In the end, she knew her routine exercises in Nodaria's training ring were not enough. Knew that if she were to have a good shot at survival on Mount Cinis, she would have to do something like this.

She was familiar with this kind of training. Her brothers had forced her into their stone vault underneath the Augusta manor, which had made her burn and burn until her skin began to blister. It was how they had forced Heavenly Fire from her. How she had been built to withstand it.

Val had not forgotten the pain and fear those years had brought her. And she was *not* ready to face it again.

But she found herself stepping over the threshold of the earthen chamber, anyway, feeling her feet sinking into the soft soil of the floor.

Aris caught her arm. "We will be right outside the door," he said softly. "If you need us."

Val nodded, but she barely felt the movement. Deya and Caelum were watching her from the hallway, their faces painted with twin expressions of concern. Their magic was not like Ember Magic—though Caelum's Frost Magic was close. It had to be tested, to be pushed to its limit.

The door closed with a soft hiss of suctioning air and Val walked across the room to stand in the middle of the rounded chamber. It was so quiet. She couldn't even hear her companions on the other side of the thick steel door. She could, however, see their anxious faces pressed against the glass of the small window.

Val rolled up her sleeves. The flame inside her gave a feeble flicker, as if trying to push past the cold from the journey there. Drawing in a deep breath, Val's fingers twitched and slowly, she began to draw in power. Fire began to roar in her veins, flooding her body, warming her very bones. Her hair rose to stand on end as flames shot up from the tips of her fingers, surging up her arms, encasing her like fiery sleeves. And, with a roar, she let her fire explode.

Flames filled the whole room, making shadows flit across the stone walls. Instantly, the temperature rose to suffocating levels. But still, the heat was bearable—nothing she hadn't been able to withstand in the past. This was slightly below what she'd use for Heavenly Fire.

A bead of sweat rolled down her forehead as the temperature began to build. Digging her heels into the ground, she steadied herself and her flames. But she knew she couldn't stop. Not yet.

Slowly, she pushed a bit harder.

The flames roared higher, and her skin began to prickle—a familiar feeling of fear that had nothing to do with the heat. No, the intrusive feeling had everything to do with the memory that burst into her mind with the fiery wall she pushed from her body. Heavenly Fire. The Augusta family's signature move. And the one that had nearly killed her.

And just like that, she was back at the Augusta Manor, Lorenzo circling her, Leo cackling behind her.

Harder. More. You are weak. Pathetic.

The voice was so *loud* . . . so overwhelming. Even when she closed her eyes, reminded herself she was far from Maniel, that her brothers were *not* there—the voice grew louder and louder, like the crackle of her own flames.

You call this fire? I'll show you fire, baby sister. I'll show you how it feels to burn.

Angry tears began to fill her eyes but were immediately seared away by the heat of her magic. She pushed through her brother's jeering, tried to shut it out, tried to picture her flames ripping through him . . . Val let out a yell as the flames grew from burning red to blinding white.

Then, pain ripped across her. The heat itself felt like it was attempting to push into her body, burrow into her very skin. And then it was just pain . . . blinding, agonizing *pain*.

There was enough left of them to bury.

The words burst into her head without warning, and she stumbled. Suddenly, her flames caught, the white of their light engulfing her as Val's subsequent gasp turned into a bloodcurdling scream. Then, like her flames, everything went white as she fell to the ground.

Her flames ripped through the empty cavern, enveloping her body as if it had a mind of its own, taking advantage of her weakness. And all Val could do was scream.

The heat . . . the fire . . . the burn. It was all too much. All too familiar.

Then, suddenly, a blast of icy air rocketed through the room, and cold hands seized her.

"Val! *Val,* are you okay?"

Val opened her eyes in time to see frost and snow explode from the person holding her aloft.

Caelum had run into the room, his Frost Magic on full blast. He was wrestling down the flames she had created until, with a low, innocuous hiss, all her flames were extinguished.

Val blinked. Frantic purple eyes looked back at her. She tried to sit up, but her skin gave a tiny shriek of protest. Wincing, she held a hand up to her eyes to find her skin was bright red and blistered in places where the flames had reached her.

"Are you okay?" Caelum asked again. Snow drifted down around them, an eerily similar moment to when he had rescued her from the skathi.

Val nodded, but closed her eyes, unable to look at him. Anger was beginning to overwhelm her.

She could not withstand the built-up heat of Heavenly Fire. And if she could not withstand that, how could she survive Mount Cinis? For all her talk . . . all her confidence and assurance that she was strong, *this* moment just confirmed what her brothers had always said.

That she was too weak to be an Augusta.

"All we could see were flames," Caelum panted. He was looking around the room, as if checking to make sure everything was put out. "We couldn't see you at all . . . So, Aris sent me in."

Val struggled to sit up, her burnt cheeks flaming. "I'm fine," she insisted, but with the way Caelum was looking at her, she knew he did not believe her.

The door opened again, and Deya rushed into the room, followed closely by Aris.

"Val! Are you okay?" Deya cried. She rushed to Caelum's side, grabbing her other arm and, together, the two of them hauled her to her feet. "Gods, you're burning up."

"I'm *fine*," Val insisted, but she knew what the others were looking at. Her body was flushed with a light burn, and movement made her skin ache. But what she was most scared of was Aris. To look him in the eye, to see his face. His expression would be proof, after all, that she was *not* the solution to their problems.

That she was too weak.

As if she couldn't resist, her eyes flicked towards the general. Aris's face was ashen. His hazel eyes roamed the scorched earth of the chamber, the frost beginning to melt off the walls . . . and finally to her burns.

Their eyes met.

"Are you okay?" he asked, his voice soft.

Val gave a short nod. "I'm fine . . . Just got a bit lightheaded." Even after Caelum's blast of ice, the room was still warm. The eldsteinr stone definitely did its job. Even now, Val could feel the heat thrumming off the walls, melting Caelum's ice from its stone surface.

"I need to go again," she said through gritted teeth.

Aris looked alarmed. He probably hadn't expected this from her. She had been scared when he had first asked her—terrified. But frustration was boiling along with her blood.

She knew what she had agreed to. Known that it was an impossible task. But her brothers' voices echoed so loudly in her mind that she could hardly concentrate. They were making fools of her again—just as they had the day they captured her.

No, she couldn't give up, even if this was an impossible task. In the end, the torment and pain she was unearthing was all to give her friends the false hope that she would survive . . . In the end, it was the only chance she had to possibly avenge her sisters.

The image of her sisters' mangled bodies flashed through her mind, and her heart hurt so suddenly that she nearly stumbled. Clenching her jaw, Val shoved the image aside with all her might, but the tears still ached in the back of her throat, demanding to be shed.

"Valeria," Aris said, and Val could hear the strain in his words. He was her general, but she knew he cared for her—if not in a purely platonic way. "Are you sure? If it's too much, we can take a break—"

But Val shook her head. "I need to go again," she insisted, but her voice was hoarse. "There's no other way, General. If I am to have any kind of hope, I need to keep going."

Aris stared at her, his handsome face unmoving. She couldn't for the life of her see behind that cool mask, couldn't tell if he wanted to push her for the Legion's sake or stop her for her own. She guessed she would never truly know.

After a long pause, Aris nodded.

Val returned to the chamber, dread overtaking her, the fear of hearing her brothers' voices again—of seeing the bloody remains of her sisters—washed over her. A terror, hot and molten, like the lava cooling underneath her feet. She did not know how much more of this training she could endure. The heat was one thing, but the memories were something entirely different.

And even though the seed of doubt in her yearned to scream at her friends not to go, they left the room so Val could begin again.

Again and again, she unleashed her flame. Again and again, the fire burned her, overwhelmed her, choked her like a sweltering blanket.

And all the while, her brothers' voices played in her ear.

Deya accompanied Val, Aris, and Caelum to the Hearth House every day for the next week. It pained her to see Val struggle like this . . . to *hurt* like this. In the middle of every training session, when her flames burned the hottest, she would fall, screaming, to the ground. Her burns were getting worse, but Deya could tell the physical was not the only thing breaking her friend.

After every collapse, when Caelum's frost had broken through the flames, it was to find Val gasping for breath, tears shining on her face while she beat her fists on the ground in fury. And all the while, Aris watched her with an inscrutable expression . . . as if he knew something the rest of them didn't.

But while she spent her evenings in the Hearth House, she spent her days deep below Fangdor Castle with Luc and Karyna, thumbing through old, crumbling scrolls written in a foreign tongue, looking for any mention of the Mother Goddess. And getting more and more frustrated with the lack of results.

Luc flung another long canister out of the cubby with an explosion of dust and snow. Karyna winced.

"Which one is that?" Deya asked tiredly.

Luc's long brown fingers flicked the lid off the canister and slid out the scroll, holding it up to Karyna for inspection.

"*Fashion of Ancient Times.*"

Deya and Luc both heaved identical groans of derision.

"Well, that's it," Luc said, chucking his quill and throwing up his hands. "That's all Bridah's most holy temple has left to offer us. The ancient version of *Fae Fashion Weekly.*"

Deya's forehead hit the table, her temples already aching. She was so tired of searching and searching with nothing to show for it. Every bit of information she had learned since arriving in Bridah had only brought more questions, more confusion . . . more fear. Between Val's ongoing struggle in the Hearth House, and the threat of dragons looming overhead, Deya's nerves were beginning to reach their frazzled ends.

"Hang on," Karyna said, shushing Luc and brushing away the quill he had thrown. "There's something here."

Deya didn't even bother to lift her head. She had been here before—even in the last hour. Karyna would see a symbol she didn't recognize and their hope that it may mean something substantial would quickly extinguish when they realized it was an old translation of Flykra, or else an ancient proper name Karyna didn't know.

But something was different this time. Karyna sat up straighter, angling the candle they had burning closer to the scrolls—while still careful to keep dripping wax away from the delicate parchment.

"What is it?" Luc asked, leaning closer.

Karyna's brow was furrowed, her ice blue eyes sparkling with concentration. "It is . . . another name. But it is familiar, just spelled a little funny." Her eyes flitted across the page for a moment before they widened and slowly looked up at them. "It says Astrea . . . the Celestial Goddess."

This time, Deya's head rose from her arms. The look she and Luc exchanged was a mixture of hope, anticipation, and wariness. To be disappointed one more time might kill her. But this was the first mention of any other goddess besides Flykra they had encountered. After hundreds of books, no other goddess had been so much as alluded to.

Luc made a jerky waving motion, urging Karyna on. "Well, c'mon, don't stop now! What else does it say?"

Karyna hushed Luc again, her eyes flitting back and forth. "The Moon Goddess prefers her clothing flowing and loose . . . to better monitor her movements while controlling gravity . . . has moonstone earrings which have been passed on to her firstborn granddaughter, Aster Hesperos . . ."

Karyna let out a frustrated sigh. "It is nothing but her commonly worn items. Artifacts passed into the lineage."

Luc let out a groan, but Deya dared to hold onto hope. Because if Astrea was mentioned . . .

"Keep going," Deya urged her. Karyna sighed, but her eyes continued to flit across the page.

"Arista . . . the Harvest Goddess and her peridot diadem . . . wore rope sandals to feel the Earth . . . Calida . . . the Goddess of Flame . . . a ruby encrusted sword along with leathers made from her fallen dragon's hide . . . Eula . . . her silver scepter . . . and—" Karyna let out a sudden gasp, causing both Deya and Luc to nearly jump out of their seats. The temple had not cleared out entirely yet, and Karyna's shriek of surprise had caused the few remaining priestesses to glare petulantly at them. But Deya couldn't care less. She bolted out of her chair and rushed to Karyna's side as the small female cried, "She's here! The Mother Goddess!"

Deya and Luc crowded over Karyna's shoulder, looking down at the ancient scroll properly for the first time. The parchment was browned with age, the delicate, primitive paintings cracked and fading, yet there was no mistaking the small illustration of the Mother Goddess. Mav was at the very bottom, underneath her daughters: her set of scales, her long, flowing white robes, and her eyes, covered with a thin gauze.

"Mav, the Mother of All, often wore common clothing," Karyna read, her excitement making her accent stronger as she hurried through the passage. "Her brass scales were a representation of the balance she brings to the realm, though she did not often carry them. However, Mav was also known to wear . . . her heart around her neck."

It was as if an explosion went off in Deya's mind. She jerked, bolt-upright, just to find Luc staring back at her with the same elated expression of realization on his face.

"*The heart!*" Luc cried. "All this time! The heart was—"

Deya stumbled backwards, her hands clutching her chest, scrabbling at her bare collarbone—where she had seen something similar nestled on

Clarita's chest every single day during her time in the infirmary. Where it had sat under her nose the whole time.

"Her amulet," Deya breathed, jerking the scroll towards her to see better. "Mav's amulet . . . my gods, how could I have been so oblivious to not have thought of it!" There, clear as day, was a crude drawing of the amulet, just as she remembered it. A simple gray stone with silver twining around it, like the arteries of a heart.

Immediately, the first person she thought of was Caelum. The joy of the discovery rushed through her, and she wished he was there. It was as she wondered how soon she could alert him that a rush of air blew over them, and a portal appeared to their right.

The priestesses shrieked in fright as two figures burst into the cavernous temple, sending loose parchment flying.

"Caelum!" Deya cried, reaching out to grab hold of the scroll to keep it from flying away as the portal closed.

The white-haired Nodarian and the general of the Pillar Legion straightened, and Caelum stood before her, his dark eyebrow arched.

"You called?"

At any other time, she would've paused to contemplate how strong this so-called bond they had actually *was*, but she was too excited to dwell on it then.

"We found it," she panted, grinning at Caelum and Aris. "We found the Heart of the Mother."

Aris's hazel eyes widened in shock, a rare moment of expression for the general. "Are you serious?"

Caelum and the general both flocked to Karyna and listened to her read out the description of the Mother Goddess again. This time, however, the realization didn't hit either of them like it did Luc and Deya. Caelum's purple eyes flashed towards her, his dark brow furrowed.

"Wear her heart . . . But what does that mean?"

Forgetting that Caelum and Aris were not raised in strict worship of the Mother Goddess, as she was, she hastened to explain. "The Mother

Goddess is always depicted with a necklace around her neck. I never gave it much thought until now, though. It's her *heart*. The amulet must be known as the Heart of the Mother. Look." And she pushed the next roll of parchment with the crude illustration towards them.

Aris blinked; his golden eyes still fixed on the parchment. Luc, however, let out an elated laugh, his hands rubbing through his dark hair. "We are terrible Praitonians to not have realized . . ." But then, he dribbled off, and—just like with their realization—horror set in at the same time.

"*Why* are they seeking the amulet?" Luc asked. "I always thought it was a myth, not an actual thing. Clarita bought her replica from the castle jeweler. There are cheap imitations all over Praiton . . . Where in Mother's name would the real one even—" But Luc dribbled off as the general pulled the scroll to face him, his brow furrowed.

For a moment, none of them spoke as they watched the Pillar Legion's general stare down at the cracked parchment in front of him.

"Why, indeed," Aris murmured. Deya, once again, found herself watching the general and wondering if there was more to what he knew than he was saying. Finally, as if coming out of a trance, Aris glanced up at them. "Regardless of *why* Praiton wants it, one thing is very certain. It is imperative that we find it first."

Chapter 19

Flies buzzed around Caelum's head and his nose wrinkled at the smell of decay that blanketed the air. Blood flowed from the body at his feet, spilling out onto the dark grass of the forest path.

Swearing under his breath, Caelum rose from where he knelt in front of the body of the dead male. A second corpse was still in the driver's seat of the caravan . . . the caravan full of supplies Caelum had dispatched to Light's Tower only last week.

Both driver and companion, dead—a long while dead, judging by the smell of them. The wagon was torn apart . . . and not a trace of the supplies.

Caelum paced around the wooden caravan. The doors to the back were wide open, the insides clean, not a scrap left.

He supposed he had been preoccupied lately with his constant trips to Bridah to help Val in what was beginning to seem like a futile effort to strengthen her Ember Magic, but also with the new discovery of what the Heart of the Mother was.

The last few days since Deya and Luc's discovery had been a whirlwind of nights with Rayner, tearing through any books they could find on this rare, and seemingly lost artifact. But even with an answer to Praiton's quest now in his grasp, he ached with irritation at the fact that he still did not know *why* they sought the amulet . . . much less why they hunted Deya.

He stepped over the body of the second merchant, careful to avoid the splatters of blood on the dirt path. Sensing movement to his left, his hand immediately grabbed for the hilt of the Shadow Sword.

"Easy," Saros said, walking towards him from around the broken-down carriage. "It's only me."

The breath Caelum released did not make him feel much better, nor did it make the situation any more logical. There were no markings on the ground, no sign of a struggle . . .

"Bandits, perhaps?" Saros murmured. The captain's purple eyes raked the scene before them, brow furrowed. Caelum could see his fears mirrored in that of his cousin's. Both were thinking the same thing.

"I do not think this was some pathetic street urchins, do you?" he said in a low voice.

Saros did not answer, but in his silence, Caelum knew what was not said.

"But why leave them here?" Caelum murmured, his eyes sweeping the destruction, tracking every drop of blood, every scuff in the dirt. "Why not hide it?"

Saros drew a finger over the surface of the driver's seat, holding his hand up to the moonlight, before saying, "If you ask me, this was *meant* to be found. This was a message."

Caelum's spine stiffened. *A message.* After what Val had seen, he had been prepared for something to happen. And yet, as unhappy as some of those within the Keep were about Nodaria's stance in the war, he had not anticipated it coming to blood.

His jaw ground together as he shifted underneath the night breeze, the smell of death sweeping below his nose. "Have you found anything else out? Anything like *who* is threatening us?"

The Nodarian captain did not respond for a moment. He was too preoccupied with studying the clean slice underneath the driver's neck. "I have only heard whispers," he said. "And all of them having to do with their anger over your new outpost in Aldebaran."

Caelum jerked his gaze towards his cousin. It would make sense. It had been his most contested decision by far, what with the outpost's proximity to Arctos. And this caravan had come directly from it.

"If they aim to dismantle the outpost, perhaps we can use that to lure them," Saros said, his voice ruminative. "Smoke them out."

As tempting as this seemed, Caelum did not know how they might go about doing this. But the way his cousin's brow furrowed as he said it, he wondered if he had something up his sleeve.

But Saros rose from where he had been crouched over the bodies and cast a sidelong glance at him. "In the meantime, I hesitate to ask if all that time you are spending in Bridah has been worth your absence or not."

Caelum's shoulders tensed. The answer to Saros's unanswered question was a resounding *no*. Val could not last more than a mere minute in the Hearth House with her flames at full power before her body caught fire, and she would collapse in screams of agony. Caelum winced at the memory of the pitiful sound of his friend's screams rebounding off the white stone walls of that fetid oven he had been spending all his nights in lately. But, more than anything, he felt sympathy for the Manielian female, whose pain did not seem to be solely the result of her burns.

When Caelum did not answer him, Saros sighed and waved a blasé hand. "Go. I will deal with this for now. You need to get back to Bridah."

It took everything in him not to argue, but as much as it was killing him to do this day after day, he knew he was needed in the Frost Kingdom, knew that Val's training was a ticking clock.

One that was almost up.

Giving Saros a curt nod, he strode towards the horse he had tied off several feet away, mounted, and flew back towards Atlas Keep. He barely registered the blurring scenery, the noise of Arctos washing over him as he blew through it. His mind kept replaying the scene, kept analyzing it for every detail.

No hoofprints. No footprints. A clean swipe across the throat of the driver. A precise puncture to the neck of his companion. Something did not add up.

He urged his horse faster, digging his heels into the beast's sides.

Last week had been an exhausting whirlwind of portals and ice. Having to balance himself, hide his weakness from those around him . . . even spitting the blood secretly into the sleeve of his tunic when arriving back from Bridah was beginning to wear on him. What with the power he needed to go back and forth from Nodaria to Bridah, he barely had the energy to make it to the meetings, leaving Saros to delegate in his stead.

Leaving the council unsupervised, especially with the threat of an uprising prickling at the back of his neck, was a risk. He knew that. He knew it wasn't smart . . . knew it wasn't safe. But what other choice did he have? In the end, Aris was right: without Val securing a dragon, Bridah would fall.

And Nodaria would be right behind it.

Dismounting at the stables, Caelum walked as fast as he could towards the Keep, his heart pounding in his chest. The hallways bustled with people. But all of them immediately dove aside, hugging the walls to keep their distance from the wave of icy air exuding from him as he stormed into the entry hall.

His jaw ground together, the heels of his boots thundering across the black marble floor as he mentally parsed the bloody scene again. Would it be foolish to hope it had been merely the work of bandits? But no . . . there had been no bandit attacks since he had regained Nodaria. And besides, the kills had been too . . . clean. Too perfect. This was, no doubt, the product of something much more sinister.

Caelum made a sharp turn around a corner, only for a shadow waiting around the bend to fall into step beside him.

"Are you planning on frosting over the whole Keep?" Rayner asked. Caelum could hear the smirk in his tone, and it clawed across his already frayed nerves.

"I'm not in the mood, Rayner."

"When are you ever." His long legs matched Caelum's strides as the pair took the steps of the grand staircase two at a time. "I heard about the ambush on the caravan."

"I thought you were supposed to be keeping an eye on things," he growled. A star seer and a castle servant hurried from their path as Caelum nearly barreled into them, refusing to slow his pace for even a second.

Rayner danced around the frazzled servants, as light on his feet as ever. "I was instructed to watch the council and the Keep, *my lord*, but I can redirect my efforts elsewhere if that's what you want."

The look he threw sideways at the Sea Fae could've killed, and yet all Rayner did was laugh. "If you call me that *one more time*, I swear on Astrea that I will shove that bow someplace you will always find it."

Rayner gave a wry chuckle. "Look at you, swearing on your goddess. How very kingly of you—"

Caelum sent a strong band of cold air towards the Sea Fae, but once again, it was expertly evaded.

"Anyway, as much as I'm enjoying this fast walk through the halls, this is important," Rayner said, grabbing Caelum by the elbow. "I have news, and you're not going to like it."

Rayner's hold on him forced Caelum to come to a screeching halt—one that he was not very happy about. "If it's about the threat against the outpost—"

"It's not that."

Caelum huffed irritably. "Well, make it quick. I should've been in Bridah a half hour ago," he growled.

"Well, maybe you should rethink spending so much time there."

His eyes narrowed. "Why?"

"Because." Rayner pulled Caelum out of the throng of the main corridor, leading him off to the side, away from prying eyes. "I've been doing my best to stay out of sight, yet still within earshot. And the council has been having private discussions . . . discussions about a vote of no confidence."

Caelum's blood ran cold. His fingers clenched so hard onto the hilt of his sword that his knuckles turned white.

He couldn't say he was necessarily surprised. The spineless cowards on the council made their displeasure well known in the last few months. Still, a vote of no confidence had never happened to a High King in any kingdom he was aware of. After all, no other ruler had been elected in the nature he had been.

Not only would it be irritatingly embarrassing, but the unrest it would lead to . . .

Grinding his teeth, frost began to crackle at his fingertips as Caelum turned back to Rayner. "How much of the council?"

"More than half," Rayner said grimly, and Caelum swore under his breath.

He knew what the council thought of him. After all, none of them had served under his father. This was what was left over after the Battle for Atlas had wiped out his father's entire cabinet. They had some loyalty to the Hesperos name, but much less to him . . . to a fucking bastard.

Caelum took a deep breath. "Helene?" he asked Rayner.

To his utmost surprise, the Sea Fae shook his head. "She was never a part of these discussions from what I've seen, but Caelum . . . as your friend, I implore you to *try* to assuage some of the worries your people have. If the caravan attack gets out, you know it will cause an uproar. Already rumors about someone spotting a dragon over the Keep have begun to spread. People are afraid—afraid to fall to Praiton again—"

"Exactly," Caelum snarled, his already short temper faltering under the surge of anger bubbling through his veins. "Which is why my position and what I do is *necessary* to protect this kingdom."

"All I'm saying," Rayner said, holding up his hands, his electric-blue eyes filled with their usual placating shine, "is that sometimes you must put the duty to your kingdom before all else, Caelum—"

"And what do you know about duty to one's kingdom?" The words burst from him—a vicious growl that made Rayner take half a step back. Caelum was too angry to care—too frustrated and overwhelmed by the fucking mess he was leaving across several kingdoms at this point. He was trying his best. Trying to do what was the best for his kingdom, but it never seemed fucking good enough. The words sprang from him with his frustration before he could stop them, and the Sea Fae's face hardened.

"I know that sometimes you must sacrifice what you want for the good of others, no matter what you may feel," he replied, his voice cold, a glimmer of pain in the words. Rayner had never said much about where he had come from before joining the Pillar Legion. But at that moment, Caelum wondered exactly what Rayner knew about sacrificing what he wanted.

The frost crackling at Caelum's fingertips subsided as he drew in another deep breath through his nose. He didn't know whether to punch Rayner or the wall. He just wanted *something*. Something destructive and violent to unleash all his frustrations.

Ever since he had been made High King, he had been drowning under the expectation of being anything other than himself. No matter what crown they put on his head, he knew, deep down, that no one would truly accept him as the ruler of Nodaria. It's not as if they ever accepted him in any other way, after all.

Rayner sighed and laid a hand on his shoulder. "Go. Get to Bridah—"

"No."

The word shocked him as much as it did Rayner, but the minute Caelum said it, he knew it was right.

It did not matter that they did not accept him as High King. He *was* the High King, whether they fucking liked it or not—whether *he* liked it or not. And if the council was brewing up a vote of no confidence, it meant he had damage control to attend to.

"You're right," Caelum grunted. "I need to stay here and deal with the caravan. And the fucking council. I'll send Val and Aris on without me."

Rayner paused, and then he gave him a small smile. "We'll figure it out, Caelum," he said gently. "We have before."

Caelum gave a stiff nod, but despite Rayner's assurance, he wasn't very convinced. He had a feeling that a vote of no confidence was only the beginning of troubled times in the Celestial Kingdom.

※

The Hearth House was becoming Val's own personal nightmare. Every day, for so many days she began to lose count, Val stood in that wretched cavern of a room and burned herself alive.

Day after day, Val pushed her flames as hard as she could. And day after day, her body would give out. Burns covered her skin—burns from magic so strong that they often did not heal fully before she was back in the Hearth House again.

And yet, no matter how strong her magic was, she knew the minimal resistance she'd built up was not enough to survive Mount Cinis.

Val staggered where she stood, her vision going white as the stone room swam. Every inch of her body screamed in pain. Even through blurry eyes, she could see the peeling blisters on her arms and hands, could feel the tears she had accidentally cried sliding down the burns in an exquisite sensation of torture.

"I can't," she breathed, shaking her head. Her knees gave out, and she collapsed to the dirt floor, hands digging into the hot earth. "No more . . . please."

"No more, please!" Val cried to her eldest brother as he prowled in a circle around her crumpled form. Flames spiraled up his hands—a billow of fire brighter and hotter than any she had ever seen. He seized her by the hair, jerking her up to face him.

"We stop when I say so," Lorenzo murmured in that cold, calm voice of his—so antithetical to his younger brother's. "And that is when you can withstand the heat of Heavenly Fire. Now, get up."

Then the sound of Val's screams filled the basement room of Augusta Manor as

Lorenzo slammed his hand of white flames against her face.

Val blinked angry tears out of her eyes and slammed her fist against the ground as the door to the chamber opened. Deya rushed in, stumbling with the weight of a large metal bucket of ice. Without Caelum to cool Val down, this was her friend's hasty decision. She would run back out into the cold during every session to shovel fresh snow and ice into the bucket. Val was grateful for her absence during this time. She didn't want Deya to see her like this.

Swooping down beside her, Deya shoveled a fistful of cold snow and pressed it against Val's aching cheeks. She flinched, almost expecting the burn of her brother's fire, but relaxed against the cool sensation of the ice.

"Are you okay?" Deya whispered. Tears shimmered in her friend's eyes and her heart gave a small squeeze of affection for Deya. She could sometimes see Deya's face through the glass window of the room as she pushed her flames harder and harder around her. She always looked petrified; caught somewhere between wanting to cry and wanting to stop her altogether. But not the general.

Aris stood in the doorway, the same unreadable look on his face, day after day. He constantly checked in on her, even going so far as to send healers and servants with ice baths when they returned to Nodaria. Yet the general kept most of the interactions almost superficial lately. As if keeping her at an even greater distance than usual. His stoicism made Val want to scream and kick with rage.

She was doing this for *him*, after all. She was setting herself on fire day after day for weeks because *he* had asked her to. The least he could do was fucking *look at her* . . . just not like *that*.

The general moved quietly into the room behind Deya.

"I'm fine," Val told Deya, but she didn't mean it. She was not fine with the memories that had come roaring forward along with her flames. And she was definitely not fine with the way Aris was staring at her. Determined not to look at him, Val began to throw snow over her body, soaking her already sweat-drenched shirt. As the ice hit her skin, a small sizzle filled the room as the snow turned to water.

"I'll go get more," Deya said, and before Val could beg her not to go, Deya rushed from the room again.

Then it was just her and Aris.

Val could almost feel the general's movements, feel his golden-green gaze on her. It made her blistered skin prickle. Biting her tongue, Val concentrated on pressing what was left of the snow against her burns.

After a moment of charged silence, Aris spoke.

"How are you *really*, Valeria?"

Val looked up at him, taken aback. The general's cool expression was momentarily replaced by the concerned look she had seen many times before. A lump rose in her throat, and she looked away, blinking back more tears.

"I'm fine."

"Valeria." Aris sank down to where she lay on the dirt floor, and although she tried with all her might to avoid his eyes, she couldn't. Val looked up at him. The faintest beading of sweat was beginning to form on his brow, even after only two minutes in the room with her.

"Let's take a break," he said gently.

"No."

Aris blinked. "No?"

Val shook her head, the lump that had risen in her throat choking her again. Her body screamed in pain and every time she moved, she wanted to cry. Because this pain felt all too familiar . . . It was weakness.

"It's not working," she whispered, tears welling again. "It's been weeks, General. *Weeks* and I can barely withstand the heat of Heavenly Fire . . . nothing more. I need to push my magic further, or else . . ." Or else she would be just what her brothers had said. Or else she would let down the whole Legion . . . Or else she would never avenge the lives that had been taken from her.

Val shook her head, words failing her as furious tears bubbled up her throat. Traitorously, a few escaped her eyes and streaked down her face.

Aris didn't say anything for a long moment. Then, slowly, he reached out a hand and caught one of her loose tears with the pad of his thumb.

He winced at the heat of her skin, but still, his touch lingered. It reminded her of that day he had carried her up the stairs of Light's Tower . . . of the way he touched her bare skin . . . how he had looked at her when she had risen from the bathing pool, her clothes clinging to her body—

"Why do you cry when you release Heavenly Fire?" he murmured, his words slapping her viciously back to reality. "Is it just from the pain?"

Her heart clenched. "I—" she began, but the words died on her tongue.

They had never spoken about it . . . what Leo had done to her that day in Maniel. But she had known by the look on Aris's face that he had deduced what she had never been able to say aloud.

Thankfully, he didn't wait for her to answer.

Reaching out a large, calloused hand, Aris cupped her cheeks, using both thumbs to wipe the tears from her eyes.

"Is it possible that something is holding you back?" His question made her jerk in surprise, and she blinked up at him, as if a trance had just ended. Had he seen her struggling with her magic this whole time? Had it been so obvious?

He was so close to her that the heat from his body added to the heat from hers. The feeling of his hands on her face was more soothing than the ice and Val yearned to relax into his touch, but right before she let herself, he released her and rose from the ground.

He held a hand down to her and she saw the skin of his palm was blistered. Slowly, Val took it, and he pulled her to her feet. For a moment, they stood there, Aris staring down at their clasped hands, as if surprised to see it.

"You think about *them*, don't you," he said, not letting her hand go. It wasn't a question.

Swallowing through the tightening in her throat, Val was only able to nod.

Aris's eyes were trained on their linked fingers, his thumb absentmindedly smoothing across her skin. "I looked into strength building exercises for Ember Magic before we began this," he said, his thumb brushing her knuckles, making her heart thud loudly in her ribcage. "I know this is a common practice in Maniel. I wondered if this . . . if this may have been used against you."

Her eyes burned, but still, all she could do was nod again.

"Valeria," Aris said, and this time, his voice was no longer cool and impassive. A slight shudder of anger hung on each syllable. "What did they do to you?"

Blinking violently, Val tilted her chin to the ceiling, willing the tears to stay in. She had never spoken about this. Not to anyone. Not even to Lucia, Katia, or Atria. It was her secret shame, her deepest wound. To stand in front of Aris of all people and admit this . . .

"They . . . they burned me, until I could withstand Heavenly Fire. Only then was I worthy enough to be considered an Augusta."

Aris's grip on her hand tightened. "And what else?"

No. She couldn't tell him that. What would he think—

"Valeria," Aris said, and his voice was a low furious rumble, a thundercloud above their heads. It was a sound so unlike him that it shocked her to her core. *"Did they touch you?"*

A cold, piercing spike of pain in her heart sent waves of shame and sadness rippling up her body. She closed her eyes, but she refused to let the tears come this time. She wanted to stamp it away, beat it from her mind. She was angry at herself for crying, angry at herself for caring . . . for letting her brothers affect her, even now.

Val drew in a deep, wavering breath and a single, hot tear rolled down her cheek. She didn't know what it was that made her fall apart like this in front of Aris Calatos. Was so hopelessly confused as to why this male could get the truth out of her when no one else could. But the words broke from her in a choked, pained voice.

"Only Leo," she gritted out, so quietly she prayed Aris didn't hear. "And only a few times . . . But please, General, I—"

But Val broke off as her tears choked her and she felt Aris's hold on her hand stiffen. She was too scared to look at him, too terrified to see the truth register on his face.

What would he think of her now? Now that he knew that she was soiled . . . ruined by her own flesh and blood.

Suddenly, Aris tugged on her hand, pulling her closer. Val gasped, her tears momentarily stopping as the general extended her arm, rotating it so her palm faced the ceiling. A long, golden finger traced down her hand, all the way down the tender, burnt flesh of her forearm.

Aris's hazel eyes were fixed on the movement, as if hypnotized by it.

"Do you remember that time at Light's Tower . . . when I helped you to the bath? We talked about how incredible our bodies are with how they adapt . . . how they strengthen with our magic."

Val remembered. She remembered everything—especially how he was touching her the exact same way he had then. A slow, languid movement, the lightest touch on sensitive skin. Only this time, the skin was bright red, blistered and peeling . . . broken.

But when Aris finally looked up at her, there was nothing of what she expected to see in his eyes. No disgust, or judgment—not even pity. Instead, there was something else on his face, something that made her heart race and her body flush.

"You are still perfect," he whispered.

Val's breath caught. For one, heart stopping moment, they looked at each other. He was a hair's breadth away, his hand still clamped onto her arm. The ache from the pain of finally admitting her past became a different ache then. A dull, furious roar—a *demand*.

It wanted the male in front of her. Wanted him so bad, it was as if a fire had been ignited in her chest—taller, hotter, *brighter* than the one she had been forcing out of herself all evening.

Aris's gaze was locked onto her face, those peridot eyes traveling down towards her mouth. Fingers tightened on her skin, which was now heating with a flush of her barely contained flame of longing.

"We adapt, Valeria," he breathed. "The pain of our experiences strengthens our bodies . . . our souls."

Val wet her lips, unable to look away from the general's mouth.

"Let us try your fire one more time," Aris murmured, a small jerk of his hand bringing her to his chest, their bodies touching—the thin, damp fabric of her clothing meeting the cold touch of his golden armor. "You *can* do this, Valeria. I know it more than I know anything else."

If it had been anyone else, she would've said no. If it had been anyone else, she would've given up and walked away. But when the general asked her, all she could do was nod.

Aris led her back to the center of the chamber. Val rolled her neck and flexed her sore and stiff fingers but froze when she saw Aris begin to remove his heavy gold armor.

"General, what—"

Aris stripped off his gauntlets, then the pauldrons, before shucking off the large gold breast plate. It was like watching a bird emerge from an egg. Val had never seen Aris take off this armor, and it was a strange, almost bewitching practice that made her throat run dry.

Chucking the pieces of heavy armor into the outside hall, Aris turned back to face her wearing nothing but the plain white cotton tunic and his brown breeches and boots.

"I said we'd do this together, didn't I?" he said, giving her that small smile that made her knees weak.

Val shook her head, panic building. "General, *no*. It's too dangerous . . . Your body isn't made to withstand this kind of heat! You'll die—"

"Don't worry about me," Aris said, and turning, he closed the door of the chamber with a finite hiss of air, sealing them in. "I will leave when conditions get too hot. I know my limits."

Val hesitated. While having Aris with her in the chamber may be a comfort, the fear of hurting him held her in a chokehold.

But the general moved closer, and at that moment, the absence of his armor made everything seem closer . . . more personal. Intimate.

"Trust me, Valeria," he murmured. "Can you do that?"

At that question, all the memories of Aris washed over her like a gust of hot air. Remembering how he had supported her, stood up for her . . . kissed her. Then how he had tossed her aside, ignored her, *lied* about her. That moment in the entry hall of Light's Tower seemed so long ago, so far away, and yet the pain she had felt at his words was still palpable. Like a bruise that ached if she pressed it.

But seeing Aris standing in front of her, exposed, willing to risk death rather than leave her side . . .

In that moment, Val let herself do the thing she had refused to do for the last thirty years.

She forgave him.

With a deep breath, Val nodded and the tension in Aris's shoulders eased, as if he too felt the weight being lifted. Whatever was between them, whatever had happened back then, it all seemed to pale in comparison to where they were at that moment.

Aris positioned himself in front of her, his stance widening. "Right, you'll have to help me understand, Valeria," he said, and his tone was suddenly businesslike. "In Ganiea, our Earth Magic comes from our core. From here." He placed a hand on his lower abdomen. "Our magic flows from the base of our spine for those more inclined to Plant Magic, and in the core of our stomachs for those with healing abilities. Where does your magic lie?"

Val hesitated. Her Ember Magic never seemed to come from a singular place. It was all over her, flooding her body, zipping through veins, brushing sinew and bone—filling up her very being. But, she supposed, if she had to guess a place . . .

Her hand touched her chest, right underneath her collarbone. "Here," she said softly. "My fire comes from here. Our internal flames—our life forces—are here." Even as she spoke, as Aris's eyes shifted to rest at the space above the swells of her breasts where her hand lay, Val's internal flame gave an insistent, almost needy flicker.

"What does it feel like now?" Aris's voice was soft, matching her own. It was almost as if the suffocating heat was pressing them closer.

"It's . . . flickering," she breathed. The fire within her had been sputtering for months now, as if fighting to stay alive. It was nothing like that demanding roar it once was, before she had returned to Light's Tower. Before she had lost everything.

"And what about when you push your magic?" Aris asked. "What then?"

"It . . ." Val's brow furrowed as she mentally swept her body, digging into her memory. She had never taken much note of her internal flame, just as she had never noticed how her heart felt to beat, nor her lungs moved to breathe. "It feels like it fights back. Like it's resisting. I push it to grow but it does not want to." The memory of her sputtering flames and the burns covering her body filled her mind. She had felt it for a while; could not deny how, lately, it felt like her magic was fighting against her—as if something held it back.

Aris hummed thoughtfully and she could see the information processing behind his eyes. "Curious," he murmured, more to himself than anything. "And tell me, Valeria, when does it feel its most powerful?"

Val felt herself flush as she looked away hastily. "When . . . when I'm happy. Or when . . ." She remembered the last time her flame had roared the strongest she had ever felt. It had been when he had pressed her into the wood of his desk with his hands and mouth. The memory made her face burn.

Aris's gaze darkened, as if he too guessed what she held back from saying, and suddenly the air was so thick with building heat Val could barely breathe. But Aris did not look away, nor did he evade the subject like he so often did. Instead, the feral glint in his gaze seemed to sharpen, a lethal point articulating his movements.

"I believe your endurance—your *power*—is linked to this internal flame, which is your very soul," he said. "Your memories, your pain and fear, it has been suffocating that part of you. Weakening it. You need to push through it. *Feel* it."

Her heart dropped straight down into her stomach, and she began shaking her head. "No . . . I can't, General, I—"

"I'm right here, Valeria," he murmured. "Right here . . . Nothing will hurt you. I'm right here."

Val's hands were shaking, her throat and chest burning with fear. But Aris's words seemed to calm her, as if stroking her internal flame with a loving caress, calming the wild flickering.

"Try," Aris breathed. "*Try.*"

Val's heels dug into the ground, Aris's words echoing in her ears.

Pain. Fear.

Those two words were so closely linked to her brothers. To the paralyzing terror she had carried with her since she was a child . . . to the bone-breaking anger she carried with her now. During the last few weeks of training, she had always tried to close her mind off to her brothers. But what if Aris was right?

Val sucked in a breath and concentrated as hard as she could on her two brothers. And then the flame in her began to roar.

Fire exploded from her, rippling up her arms, bursting out into a band around her. Aris leapt back just in time, hitting the steel door of the chamber.

"That's it, Valeria," he said. "Give it more. You can do this."

Val ground her teeth and slowly, like someone turning the burner of a lamp higher, she leaned into the flames. The fire went from bright orange to a dazzling white. Heavenly Fire was coming out of her, and for a moment, Val thought she had won. But then it started again—louder and more vivid than before.

"You feel that heat, baby sister?" the voice in her ear crooned. *"Feel that touch you? You like that, I know you do."* Pain seared Val's sides as Leo dragged fiery fingers down her ribs, across her bare skin . . . down. *"That's power, baby sister."*

That's power."

"*No*," Val cried. She screwed her eyes shut, as if fighting back against the memory of Leo's touch raking across her flesh. "*Get out of my head . . . GET OUT OF MY HEAD!*"

The flames spluttered, the brightness of the light flickering back to red and orange. Fingers pulled at her hair, the flame inside her screaming along with her.

No, no, no, NO!

"Valeria!"

Suddenly, hands were seizing her wrists before, with a sharp curse, they released her, as if too hot to hold. Val's eyes snapped open, and Aris's face swam into her vision, pushing out the image of Leo on top of her with a fistful of fire from her mind.

"Valeria, *focus!*" Aris shouted over the roaring of the flames around them. "I'm right here! Push through it!"

Val gave a mangled scream, the flames around them flaring as high as the domed ceiling. The sleeve of Aris's tunic caught fire, and without even blinking, the general ripped the shirt off, tossing it out of the ring of fire before grabbing hold of her again.

She could see the wince of pain on his face, before her vision flickered, swaying like the dance of fire around them. But those peridot eyes held her steady, held her in the moment.

"Your brothers cannot hurt you," Aris shouted over the roar of the flames. "They will not hurt you. I will *kill* them if they hurt you again. *You will kill them if they touch you again.*"

The scream that exploded from her mingled with her tears and her pain, the aching in her chest making the fire in her billow, mirroring the flames around them. Slowly, the blaze began to accelerate, turning back to its blinding white.

"*Show me*, Valeria! *Show me* that you will not let them stop you!"

Val yelled with the effort, leaning into her flames, pushing past the voices and the terror of her past. But just as she thought she had finally had the nightmares beat, a new memory burst into her mind—one so hot that it made her stumble.

"You are stronger than this. Braver than this. More powerful than them. You are Captain Valeria Augusta! Do not ever let anyone make you feel like you're lesser than that!"

Lucia's words rang so clearly through her mind it pierced her heart like an arrow. Val stumbled, her flames sputtering. Then, Katia's face came to her, laughing on the floor of her bedroom, holding one of her favorite romance books and tittering over who she found to be the best kisser in the Legion. Then her face became Atria's, waving a large sword in the air, reenacting a battle with her usual spunk and gusto, the feeling of Val's smile and laugh still fresh on her face . . .

"No," Val whispered, because these memories were even more painful than those of her childhood, more excruciating to watch. And as they morphed from happy memories into the image of their mangled bodies, a scream split from her that rocked the rafters of the Hearth House.

Fire flooded the entire room, sending Aris flying to the ground.

And Val screamed and cried as her flames burned from white to a blinding, colorless shimmer of gas and light, flaying every inch of her with an agonizing heat the strength of which she had never felt before.

And all the while, her internal flame roared inside her . . . before it flickered and faded.

Val hit the ground, screaming, panting, and sobbing. Stamping out the flames clinging to what was left of her clothes, she shrieked in pain as she took in the blisters forming on her skin—bright red, angry, and bloody.

"*Dammit,*" she cried. "I don't understand . . . It should've worked. It *should've worked!*" But even as her tears sizzled into steam, she knew she could not deny the reality of the situation. It was over. She had tried to do what Aris asked. Had tried to face what blocked her heart . . . and she had failed.

She flinched as hands touched her, her eyes squeezing shut as ripples of memories and heat washed over her.

"Valeria . . . open your eyes. It's okay . . . it's okay."

Aris. It was as if Val had forgotten the general was even there. Her eyes snapped open, and horror seized her by the throat.

The general's skin was bright red, but it was not as severe as hers. It seemed as if he had avoided the worst of her flames. He knelt over her, his bare chest shining with burns and sweat, breathing hard as he pulled her into his arms.

"I'm sorry . . ." Val sobbed. "General, I'm sorry—"

"Shh, no, you did fine, Valeria," he panted, giving her a smile that seemed laced with pain. "It's okay."

A sob burst from her, as if exploding from where she had held it back for so long. Her hands moved almost instinctively, reaching up to touch Aris. Her blistered fingers brushed his chest, looking for burns, terror at what she had done coursing through her. But the perfectly sculpted muscle of his chest was only slightly burnt and red—hard lines shimmering with sweat, streaked with scorched earth. She felt him stiffen under her touch, as she dragged her fingers along his chest, down the well-defined recess of his stomach. He opened his mouth to speak, but then the door to the chamber burst open. A gust of cool air washed in, and Val's burns smarted with the sensation.

Deya flew into the room, her face ashen, her gloved hands still clutching the ice bucket.

"General . . . you're burned—"

But Aris waved her off, getting to his feet, only wincing slightly with the movement. "I'm fine, Deya. I—"

But Deya's gray eyes burned with a horrified fury as she took in the sight of them both, and as Val's hazy mind refocused, only then could she see what Deya could.

Val's clothes were burned to almost nothing—barely covering her bleeding, blistered body. And while Aris's burns weren't as bad as hers, he looked no better. In fact, Val noted the sway in the general's balance, as if he was struggling to remain upright.

"You both need healing," Deya said. "*Now*. I'll go get Luc . . . Don't move!" And, dropping the bucket, Deya flew from the room.

The sight of ice sloshing onto the hot, steaming earth was the last thing Val saw before her head hit the ground. And all went black.

※

Deya watched the warm glow emanating from Luc's hands as they roved up and down Val's body. She itched with impatience as the burns slowly scabbed, her black hands curling into fists as resentment for the dark, insidious power that had replaced her Healing Magic surged through her.

She thought nothing would scare her more than running back into that chamber to find Val burnt worse than any corpse she had ever seen. But then she saw the general.

Something about Aris seemed indestructible. And yet, to see him burnt, scorched, and close to fainting . . .

Luc dropped his hands with a sigh, slumping back against the table beside Val's bed. "That's about all I can do for now," he said, panting slightly. "I know I'm not as strong as you, Dey, but that was some powerful Ember Magic . . . Stronger than I've ever seen."

Deya didn't speak. She was staring at Val, who was motionless in the small infirmary cot that she had brought her to. Fangdor's infirmary was not as well equipped as Praiton's. Even with the aid of Luc's magic, there was not much to treat the burns that were too severe to heal.

She yearned to do something—*anything*—to help her friend. But this time, it was her turn to sit and stare . . . and wait.

The door behind them opened and Aris emerged, pulling on the last piece of his armor over now unblemished skin. Aris's burns hadn't been as severe as Val's. Luc's magic had been able to ease the tender redness, and now he looked none the worse for wear.

"How is she?" Aris asked, his eyes trained on Val.

"Mending," Luc said, with an apologetic shrug. "Honestly, General, I'm not sure how you survived in that room with that much fire. You should be as charred as a roast ox after that."

Aris shrugged, but his gaze did not leave Val. "Got lucky, I suppose."

But Deya wasn't fooled. She watched the general move into the room, noted the pall of worry hanging over him. When she had burst into the chamber of the Hearth House, she could've sworn there was something going on between Val and the general. Even in Val's delirious, overheated daze, there was no mistaking the look in her eye . . . nor the one that was now in Aris's.

"How are *you*, General?" Deya asked. The sharpness of her tone made Aris blink, tearing his gaze away from Val, as if remembering himself.

Clearing his throat, the cool smile slid back onto his face. "I'm well, I promise. A little water and I'm good as new."

A little water and half of Luc's energy to heal you, Deya thought bitterly. Ire for the general flooded her and she clenched her fists a little too tightly. On the surface, she was annoyed the general had risked his life like that, waiting until she was out of the vicinity before throwing himself into a ring of fire. The general was the linchpin of the Pillar Legion. Jumping into that chamber with Val was reckless. But another part of Deya was angry at the general for a whole other reason.

Her eyes moved back to her friend, lying motionless on the bed. Her blisters had scabbed, and she already looked much better than she did when Deya first saw her, but a small, terrifying voice scratched at the back of her mind.

A voice that was telling her that Val would not survive this plan the general had devised.

Suddenly, a loud *whoosh* of air filled the room. Bandages and sheets fluttered in the wind of the portal which had ripped into view in the corner of the infirmary. Deya's heart gave a joyful leap as Caelum fell into the room.

"Caelum!" she cried, half rising from her spot beside Val's bed.

"Where have you been? What's been going on—" But the look on his face stopped her dead in her tracks.

She couldn't help but notice him stumble slightly as he dismounted from the portal, his face paler than usual as he straightened his broad shoulders into a rigidity Deya recognized.

"Sorry I'm late," he said gruffly. And even though he barked it out in his usual passive aggressive tone, Deya could feel a tremor in her gut, as if a large thundercloud was rumbling in her chest.

Aris looked around, surprised. "Caelum, what—"

"We have a problem."

Movement caught Deya's eye, making her whip around. Val was rising from the bed, her expression screwed up in pain but otherwise focused on Caelum. "What *kind* of problem?" she asked, her voice thick with the effort of standing. Deya rushed to her side, helping to ease her into a sitting position, but she waved her off.

Caelum's purple eyes roved over Val's still bright red skin, before turning to the general. "The situation in Nodaria has . . . escalated."

Aris's shoulders stiffened. "Escalated *how?*"

Caelum drew in a deep breath and Deya could see the ripple of aggravation and worry move through him—could feel it in her own body, like a breeze brushing against a flower's leaves.

"The council is pushing a vote of no confidence."

The silence that fell over the room following that statement was deafening. Even Val stilled in her shift to get comfortable in her burnt skin. Aris recovered first.

"A majority?" he asked, and although his voice was calm, Deya knew better. His spine was rigid, and his large hands flexed inside his gloves.

Caelum gave a stiff nod. "I've left Rayner and Saros behind, but I do not think we have much time before things get worse."

And it was as this ominous statement hung in the air, a loud shout echoed from outside the hall. Collectively, everyone within the small Bridanian infirmary froze, their eyes darting towards the door.

Deya felt her skin prickle, the same feeling of intense foreboding that had been creeping up her insides like the black stain on her fingertips overwhelmed her. She rose from Val's bedside, instinctively moving towards Caelum, who reached out a hand and pulled her towards him.

The shouting outside grew louder. The cacophony of clanging weapons and clinking armor mixed with the sound of the voices, until, without warning, the door to the infirmary banged open.

A gaggle of Bridanian soldiers streamed in, clad in furs, holding their weapons . . . and all with the same look of terror on their faces.

"Please," one of them said hastily upon noticing their group. "Someone said Princess Kindra was in here . . . has anyone seen the *hersir*—"

Deya felt Aris straighten beside her, the dim candlelight making his golden armor shine in its full, impressive effect.

"What's going on?" he asked. Deya always admired the general, how he took charge of every situation, commanded it with his whole presence. It was a rare trait, indeed. Even the Bridanian guards latched onto him immediately, as if relieved someone could take charge in lieu of Kindra.

We need to find *Hersir Kyandra* right away. It is our southern border," the soldier panted. His war paint was smeared down his face, along with a thick red substance.

Blood.

Blood covered his hands and knees, soaked into the fur lining his clothes. And as she watched, one crimson droplet splattered onto the stone floor.

"There has been an attack."

CHAPTER 20

Fear and panic flooded Val's insides as, immediately, the group leapt into action. Aris sent Luc sprinting out of the infirmary with an order to find Kindra, before he and Caelum hurried after the soldiers. And, since the thought of staying behind and waiting for news was the worst thing she could imagine, Val went after them, Deya at her heels.

Val winced with every movement as she hurried to keep up, her skin still tender from the burns. The memory of what had happened in the Hearth House was a haze now, nothing but a fiery nightmare. How long had she been unconscious?

Her eyes instinctively sought the back of the gold armored general up ahead. He seemed unhurt; his perfect olive skin not even reddened. Val flexed her own stiff fingers and thanked the gods she hadn't harmed him. But even with this comforting thought, panic was billowing inside her chest.

The Nodarian council was moving to push Caelum out. Ever since the day she had seen the soldier being paid off, she had feared the worst.

Saros had told Caelum, and she knew they were keeping an eye on the situation, but she could not help but fight the sick, dark wave of anxiety that crept through her chest that this was only the beginning.

Especially now with an attack on Bridah.

The sun had just begun to set in the Frost Kingdom. Vetrnaetr had come and gone, and the remaining vestiges of the festivities had been cleared. And as Caelum, Aris, Deya, and Val tore through the castle, they did not see a single soul.

They hurried out of the courtyard, past the city walls, and through over a mile of snow and frost, none of them speaking besides Aris, who peppered the soldier with questions as they walked.

"Where did the attack come from?" the general asked. He was striding through the snow, long legs moving so quickly the soldier struggled to keep pace.

"I am not sure," the soldier panted. "I was on perimeter duty in the southwest. I only heard the screams . . . and when I got to them . . ."

The whole group froze. There, about a dozen yards away from them, was a stain of crimson snow.

"Fuck," Caelum breathed.

Bodies were scattered across the ground, some burned, others mangled. But, past the splatters of blood, Val saw something much more alarming.

A large, molten hole had been blasted through the wall of the glacial fjord. She stumbled to a halt, all the air leaving her lungs.

From beside her, the general knelt to the ground by the bodies. "Scorch marks," Aris breathed. Rising, he rubbed a mix of ash and blood between his fingers and turned to the Bridanian soldier. "Did the attack start with the blast?"

"I-I do not know," he stuttered. "By the time I got here, the battle . . . the battle was finished."

Val was frozen, staring up at the molten hole, her mind reeling. Slowly, she dragged her eyes from the gaping maw, sweeping the carnage around her.

Aris was right. Scorch marks littered the powdered snow and Val's nose twitched as the smell of burning flesh mixed with the metallic scent of blood and death. This scene was all too familiar, the magic so strong in the air that there was no denying it . . . even to herself.

A figure moved beside her, and a warm hand touched her elbow, jolting her out of her own horror. Deya stood by her side, gray eyes wide as she took in the scene around them.

"Is this . . . Is this from what I think it is?" she breathed.

Caelum was pacing around the bodies, rolling a few over with his foot to examine the injuries. Bloodied footprints followed him as he walked. "Ember Magic," he whispered to Aris.

The general was still crouched, his fingers rubbing together the blood and soot, as if in a trance. "It certainly looks like it," he said, and when he rose from the ground, his gaze met Val's. At that moment, the memory of the Hearth House came back to her. Aris gripping her wrists as she burned—grounding her, protecting her. But now, those peridot eyes were wide with alarm. "The hole is what concerns me. It looks as if it was caused by something much bigger than an Ember Magic wielder."

Caelum's gaze jerked towards the general. "You mean—"

But it was Val who said it, the word leaving her before she could even think.

"A dragon."

All their eyes flickered towards her. Val had moved in a trancelike daze around the bodies, taking in their wounds, the burns. No, there was no mistaking it. The magic here was stronger than any normal Ember Magic wielder, stronger than anything she had ever felt before.

This magic was not from a fae. This magic was from a beast. A large, *powerful* beast.

One that she could no longer outrun.

"Caelum," Aris said. "Get Deya out of here. It's not safe. I'll wait here for Kindra. She and Ulf need to seal up this hole quickly."

Deya opened her mouth, about to protest, but Caelum swooped

down on her, wrapping an arm around her waist from behind.

"Don't even think of arguing," Caelum snapped, before he began dragging her back towards Fangdor, leaving Val and Aris alone, staring up at the melting glacial wall.

For a moment, neither of them spoke. Val could feel every burn on her body, every spot that had blistered and scabbed, healed and burned again over the last few weeks of fruitless training. What had happened in the Hearth House today weighed between them—a stone, hot and heavy, the same size and intensity as the fire ball which had blasted through Bridah's walls. Because, even with weeks of training, even with Aris locked in a fiery hellscape with her, pushing her through the worst of her fears, she *still* could not withstand her strongest flame.

But standing there in front of the biggest threat to the remainder of Krigor, she knew that failure was not an excuse. Deep down, she knew she had been running from this. Training with vain hope that what she was preparing for would never come. That she could keep running from it forever.

"Valeria," Aris said finally. His gaze was still locked on the wall, but Val could see it. His hands were clenched into fists at his side, and every word looked like they cost him a great effort to say. "Our time has run out."

Val closed her eyes, and she felt the burn of tears in her throat. "I know."

"But I will not ask you to do this. I can't—"

"You don't have to ask me, General," she said. Aris's head jerked to look at her, his hazel eyes widened with alarm and . . . horror. "I made a promise. As you said, I am our only hope."

Aris stared at her. "Valeria . . . are you . . . are you sure?"

She wasn't sure. If she was ready, if she was strong enough . . . if she would survive. But she knew she had no choice but to try.

"Give me tonight to prepare," she whispered. "One night. And then I will leave for Mount Cinis."

The fear hung over them on the entirety of the walk back to Fangdor, both Deya and Caelum lost in their own silence. Deya kept thinking about the molten hole blasted through the Verja Fjords. If Val was right and it was the result of dragon fire . . .

It meant Bridah was no longer the safest place in Krigor.

It also meant that Val was out of time.

Caelum and Deya returned to the empty library to sit in silence. Waiting. She could feel Caelum's heartbeat, feel the nervous energy as his leg bounced, his hands running over the black hilt of the Shadow Sword.

Is it as bad as I think?

Caelum glanced over at her, alarmed. It was obvious he had heard the words she had spoken in her head.

Yes.

His silent answer enflamed her already frazzled nerves, but she and Caelum spoke no more.

Finally, after a quarter of an hour, the door to the library was thrown open. Kindra and Aris strode through the room, both covered in snow. Aris's golden cheeks were pink with cold, and his hair was mussed.

Caelum leapt to his feet as they entered, and although Deya wanted to, she found her legs too shaky to stand.

"So?" Caelum asked.

Kindra's pretty face was set into a worried scowl—so like Caelum's—as she shook her head. "It is as we feared."

"What happened?" Deya asked, her voice a quiet tremor. "How did they blast through the fjords? They've never been able to in the past."

But it was Aris who answered her. "Dragon fire."

"Titus has had that dragon for decades now," Caelum said. "Why now? What's changed?"

Kindra sat down, hard, in a chair. The Frost Princess stared at the floor, her ice-blue eyes unmoving. It was only then that Deya saw her hands were stained with dried blood.

"A dragon's bond with its rider strengthens over time, as does their shared magic," Kindra murmured. "It is possible that it is finally strong enough to penetrate our Frost Magic. But I do not know how."

"Were you able to seal the hole?" Caelum demanded.

"Not fully." She ran her bloodied fingers over her face, smearing the markings under her eyes, mixing the blood and the paint. "*Faor* is away, attempting to find a way to fortify the walls once again. He has been searching ever since your first warning about the dragon. We have sent an urgent owl, but do not know when it will reach him. My magic is only strong enough to seal it with a thin layer of ice. It will not withstand another attack." Her fingers clenched around the battleaxe she held, her gaze stormy and furious. "Bridah is compromised."

A loud silence followed this statement. Aris stood, rigid, by the fireplace, his golden-green gaze fixed on the fire. Caelum, however, was looking between the two war commanders and Deya could feel his burning panic. It was only then that she noticed who was missing.

"General, where's Val?"

Aris was still staring at the fire, as if he weren't seeing anything at all. "Valeria has gone to ready herself. She has decided to go to Mount Cinis tomorrow."

Deya's head whipped around. Even Caelum's nervousness melted into shock and then settled on anger. But it was Deya's terror that broke through first, and she sprang to her feet.

"You're *letting her go*?" Her legs were no longer numb, but they still shook with her own indignation. "General, after today, you *know* Val is not strong enough! You know she cannot—"

"This is her decision," Aris said, and the sharpness of his tone made Deya fall silent. Aris never snapped, but this was the closest he had ever come. The general stared down at the stone floor, his brow furrowed, his teeth bared. When he spoke again, Deya could sense the slightest tremor in his words. "Valeria insists she needs to try, and I cannot say she is wrong. Bridah being breached is the worst-case scenario. If she does not do this, it is only a matter of time before Bridah falls—especially if whoever escaped into the walls attempts to attack while Ulf is still away."

"What do you mean *escaped?*" Caelum demanded. "Are you saying that whoever attacked those guards are . . . They can't be *loose* in Bridah—" And in a rare moment, Deya could see Caelum's fear. Almost like an errant breeze, the words crept into her mind, a secret she wasn't supposed to hear.

I can't leave her here. I can't . . .

"We do not know," Kindra snapped, rising from her chair in a furious motion. "If Titus has finally trained his beast to melt the fjords, our situation is most dire. Especially if there are intruders within our walls. I have every Berserker under my command tracking the scene, attempting to locate any invaders. But, in the meantime—"

All eyes fell on Deya. Her shaking legs threatened to give way as she turned to Caelum, as if for help.

The white-haired Nodarian whirled on Aris. "We cannot leave her here," he hissed, vestiges of his former ire pushing through. "Bridah is not safe. Let me take her back—"

But Aris held up a hand. "No." His gaze had not left the fire, still staring at it as if it were about to tell him a secret. The general's mind was at full work. She could see it in the furrow of his brow, the stillness of his broad shoulders, how his large hand clenched on the hilt of his golden sword.

Caelum let out a full growl now. "What do you mean *no?* We moved Deya here to *protect* her! If Bridah is not safe—"

The general snapped his attention away from the fire to look at Caelum. The intensity of his gaze made the Nodarian High King fall silent, seething. "Deya is to stay," he said finally. "She will not leave Fangdor. Kindra can arrange to have full time security for her. But the Frost Kingdom is still the safest place."

Deya sat, listening to them all decide her fate, feeling as if she should have some say in this discussion. She knew Caelum's desperation to have her back in Nodaria had everything to do with the wild fear she felt blooming in her chest—a fear entirely separate from her own. It was Caelum's panic over his inability to ensure her safety himself. The dark fear crowding his mind began to overtake hers as well when Aris turned to face her.

"If there are intruders in Bridah, we have Ulf, Kindra, and her Berserkers. But if all that fails, we have you."

The color drained from Deya's face, and she curled her blackened fingers into fists on her lap. "M-me?" she stuttered.

Aris nodded. "Like it or not, Deya, you are not helpless. In fact, *you* are your own greatest defense. If it comes to it, are you prepared to defend yourself—as well as Bridah?"

All eyes were on her, and the weight of their gazes pressed down on her windpipe. But all she could see was black. The blackness of her fingers, the blackness of the magror turning to dust . . . the blackness of the shadow creature in the book she had found, the violent whispers that had invaded her mind, the black claws clutching her face.

Dodsbringern.

Deya felt her head shake back and forth, her gloved hands digging into the arms of her chair. "N-no . . . I can't . . . You can't expect—"

But by the way Aris and Kindra were looking at her, they *did* expect it. If the worst happened, she would have to protect Bridah. Possibly with her own soul.

At Deya's silence, Aris inclined his head and turned to Kindra. "The Legion must act quickly," he told her. "I will reconvene with Caelum and our troops in Nodaria and devise a plan while Valeria prepares to head to Mount Cinis. If Titus intends to attack Bridah with that beast, we must have the proper precautions in place." Kindra nodded, and Aris looked at Caelum. "Are you ready?"

But Caelum did not answer him. Instead, his purple eyes were fixed on Deya, his form still rigid, fingers curled into fists. All it took was a moment—a moment to search within herself for the string that bound them.

Panic. Fear . . . Regret.

Caelum stood in front of her and feared it would be for the last time. Deya gazed back at him. *Go,* she urged him. *I'll be okay.*

But Caelum's face grew more pained at her silent words. *I can't leave you. I won't.*

You must, though. Work with Aris and the others. Stop the dragon before it comes to this. I'll be okay.

His eyes shut tight, and he drew in a deep breath. Then, he turned and ripped the air apart. The portal spun to life in front of the fire, making the flames sputter and flare.

Aris gave Deya a nod. "We will send a portal for Valeria when she is ready. We'll be in touch, Deya. Please, listen to Kindra. Stay safe."

Deya nodded, and the general stepped through the portal. As he moved to follow Aris, Caelum paused. He glanced back over his shoulder at her, and Deya felt a strange sensation—as if a finger were brushing her cheek.

Be here when I get back.

※

"Kindra, let me see her."

"No." The Frost Princess's grip bit into Deya's arm as she marched her through the dark and quiet halls of Fangdor back towards her room. Deya pulled angrily against her icy hold, but Kindra was *much* stronger than her.

"If Val is in the Hearth House, she shouldn't be there alone! I should go down and help—"

"No." Kindra gave another jerk of her arm, yanking her around the corner of the corridor. She shoved open the door to Deya's room before pushing her through it. "You are no longer allowed to leave this castle, Little Bird," she said. "My nephew will have my head if I allow one dainty toe of yours across that threshold."

Deya glared at her, breathing hard. She had fought Kindra's hold all the way from the library, kicking and bucking like a wild mare that had been bridled.

"But Val—"

"Will most likely be portaled back to the Celestial Kingdom within the hour," Kindra replied. "Be calm, *Smafugl*. Until we can reach *Faor*, we are wide open to attacks. Rest now and be on your guard." And with that, she turned and disappeared back into the shadows of the darkened hall, slamming the door behind her.

Deya paced the worn wooden floorboards of her room. Back and forth she went, wringing her gloved hands together. She couldn't escape the unease that had settled on her at the thought of her friend embarking on such a risky mission, of the possibility of intruders within the Frost Kingdom . . . At the chance she would have to use the dark powers locked within her.

Sitting down hard on the edge of her bed, Deya tried to steady her breathing. But, instead, her gaze locked onto the dark, crumbling book on her bedside table. The dusty tome seemed to taunt her, as if images of *dodsbringern* would crawl out of its yellowing pages and laugh at her. Angrily, she turned her back on it.

She was sick of being held hostage by this power. Sick of having to hide and worry . . . And yet, the thought of Caelum seeing her stained fingers, of the shadows that had crept into her mind after the magror, of what she could be . . .

She pushed it from her thoughts. Afterall, her mind was no longer a safe place. It was now one she somehow shared with Caelum—a baffling connection, the intricacies of which she had yet to unravel. Whatever the cost, she had to block him out. If he heard . . . if he knew . . .

Deya stopped in front of her window where a bushel of snowdrop flowers nestled in a small vase. Karyna liked bringing her flowers, often swapping them out every few days to keep them fresh. She stared at them for a moment, the delicate white petals glistening like pearls in the waning moon outside her window.

Slowly, she took off her gloves.

She had dodged training sessions for weeks in Nodaria. Made up excuses, faked illness, stayed in bed—hells, she even bedded Caelum to distract him from forcing her to go to training one day. How long could she keep this up?

Squaring her shoulders, she faced the vase and held up her hand.

The unsettling churning of darkness and pain rose through her core. It twisted along the normal channels of her power—as if running a shadowy hand across the suffocated warmth of her Healing Magic—before, with a jerk of her fingers, Deya pulled back on the leash of her power.

The snowdrop flowers began to wilt, the delicate green stems turning brittle and gray. Petals began to decay; ash filled the air—and the blackness crept farther and farther up her hand. And then it began. Whispers filled her head like the flutter of death's wings. They swirled in her head, clouding her vision, and for a moment it was as if Deya could feel it. A dark claw attempting to seize her mind. Trying to seize *her*.

With a gasp, Deya ripped her hand back, cutting off the churning darkness, attempting to shut it back inside herself before the shadows could go further, before it could hold her further.

But something was wrong.

The wildness of her panic seemed to feed the dark wave of power. It bucked against her control, pushing back—

"*No*," Deya murmured. "*No, no, no*—" Desperately, Deya grabbed at her own hands, wrestled with her panic. Tears of terror began to fall down her face, when suddenly the door burst open.

"Dey, I just wanted to make sure you were oka—" Luc froze midsentence as Deya jumped a foot in the air . . . and her magic exploded.

"*Luc, move!*"

Luc dove for cover just as the wave of blackness surged across the room . . . looking for life . . . looking to *kill*. The black wave rippled through the air, swallowing everything in sight. Every living thing in its path disintegrated—the other flowers Karyna had brought her, the hanging pine garlands draped over her mantlepiece and doorways. They wilted and decayed . . . crumbled before her very eyes.

With a strangled yell, Deya fought with all her might against the wave of impenetrable pain and darkness exploding out of her, when—with a great effort—she slammed the door shut against it. The whispers faded. The shadows fled.

And all was still.

Panting, tears streaming down her face, Deya gasped for breath. Ash thickened the air, dusted every surface, choking her with its familiar, bitter taste. And when she looked down at her hands, it was to find the blackness now coating almost the entirety of her fingers.

A sob burst out of her, and she shoved a black hand over her mouth, stifling the sound.

From across the room, Luc slowly rose from the floor. Ash covered his dark hair and clothes, his eyes wide and terrified. He took in the swirling particles in the air, watched as they fell and settled on top of him and Deya like snow . . . and then, he saw her hands.

It was all too familiar. The expression on Luc's face was just like it was that night in the dark hallway of Stonehall Castle. Just like then, his face was pale, still reeling from a secret he was not supposed to know.

Deya looked up at him, her black hands trembling, tears falling. With a voice that shook with every word, she whispered her biggest fear: "Are you going to tell?"

Shock creased Luc's features before they crumpled. "Dey . . ." he breathed.

The tears were beginning to blind her now as she shoved her shaking hands under her arms. The stain was so bad that she could still see its darkness, even with her fingers curled into fists. Luc moved slowly across the room before sinking down beside her. His hand touched her shoulder, and the jolt it elicited caused the floodgates to open.

Deya buried her face in her blackened, traitorous hands, and sobbed. All her fears, all her frustrations . . . they poured out of her in an uncontrollable wave—just as that awful power had.

Hands touched her, then suddenly she was being pulled into Luc's side. "Shh," he murmured into her hair. "*Shh* . . . Dey, it's okay. It's okay."

His murmured consolations soothed her, and soon, her tears began to abate. Finally, it was just them, sitting on the floor, staring at Deya's hands together.

After a long silence, Luc asked, "Does he know?"

Deya didn't have to ask who he meant. She shook her head. "No."

He stiffened against her, but his hands still rubbed along her arms, still comforting through his unease.

"Dey . . . Maybe you *should* tell him—"

"*No.*" Deya said it so vehemently she could tell it took Luc aback. But she knew without a doubt she couldn't tell Caelum. He didn't think she noticed the look on his face every time he caught sight of her prophecy. She'd often see him staring at it when he thought she wasn't looking—a cloud of worry on his face, *fear* in those purple irises.

Caelum feared—just as she did—what her prophecy meant. The memory of his hatred for her was still too recent to forget. She couldn't bear the thought of him looking at her like that again, as if she were a threat, a danger to the realm . . . a bad omen.

"How long has it been like this?" Luc asked, his voice barely a whisper.

Taking a deep breath, she closed her eyes. "Since we took back Nodaria."

Luc nodded, processing. "This power . . . you mentioned to me before that your Healing Magic is gone. Is this what replaced it?"

Numbly, Deya nodded. "I'm scared," she whispered finally. "I . . . I don't know what this is. I don't know what *I* am."

Luc didn't speak. Instead, with trembling fingers, he laid his hand on top of Deya's. Jumping, Deya glanced sharply at him, only to see his grim, determined face.

"I won't tell," he said softly. "I won't tell a soul. I promise."

Tears welled in her eyes again, but she swallowed them down, only able to give him a grateful nod.

"We'll figure out what this is," he said, but with the way he said it, it almost sounded like he was convincing himself more than her.

She didn't know whether she was stupid to believe Luc again—to trust him. But as he held her blackened hands—after they nearly incinerated him—she couldn't help but believe in him.

And at that moment, she was grateful to have him back on her side.

CHAPTER 21

Val finished packing her last thin linen top into her worn satchel with the same feeling one might have when burying a loved one. She wasn't even sure why she bothered packing. Her thickest leather armor—which had become soft and worn from battle and blood—was to be her only defense against the fire and heat of Mount Cinis.

It was her last night in Nodaria. Her last night before Caelum transported her back to Elbania to depart from the Legion's port on a ship that would take her to uncertain doom. Her last night before she was to set foot back on Manielian soil for the first time since she had been captured.

There had been a constant, simmering flame of anxiety burning under Val's skin since she had left Bridah. Even when she had returned to the Hearth House one more time—with the vague excuse to Aris that she wanted to train before she returned to Nodaria—she had merely stood there in the center of that blasted chamber and screamed herself hoarse. Screamed until her throat burned like the rest of her, screamed until tears fell down her face and made the still tingling, aching skin burn all over again. Screamed until that fucking flame in her heart quieted . . . Until it became nothing more than a molten simmer of panic in her chest.

Snapping the clasps closed on her satchel, she paused when she caught sight of her dual swords laying against the wall by her bed. The handles were dull bronze, the steel of the blade nicked and chipped, made even more obvious by the flickering of the fireplace. A knot tightened in her chest at the thought of the golden swords she had lost that day in Maniel. How Leo had kicked them into the wall of flames, never to be seen again.

Val grabbed the shoddy swords, holding them up towards the firelight. She had taken them from the large stock of weapons in the armory at Light's Tower. These swords had probably passed through many hands, never having a single master for long. They had most likely endured dozens of training sessions, maybe even a battle or two, but had never truly belonged to someone. No matter how long Val used them, they never felt right. No, they would always be borrowed.

A small knock sounded at the door and Val paused, lowering the swords. "Come in."

The door creaked open, and the general stood in the doorway, still wearing his golden armor, yet looking tired and windswept, as if he had not stopped all day. "I wanted to see if you were ready," he said. Although his face was its usual placid calm, Val could see the pallor in his complexion, the permanent furrow to those straight brows.

"About as ready as I'll ever be," Val said with a grim smile that only slightly trembled with the effort. Aris did not return the smile, though. Instead, he watched her from the doorway, as though too afraid to enter.

"Valeria, I . . . I wanted you to know that you don't have to do this." The words sounded strained, and when Val turned to look back at the general, it was to find him staring down at the floor, his jaw tense, his shoulders stiff.

The anxious simmer in her chest heated, making her body hum with an unpleasant feeling of dread that was both foreign and familiar to the hot panicked fear she had been feeling all day.

"I know I don't have to, General. But I must."

Aris looked up, and the expression on his face made all the air leave Val's lungs. The hazel eyes looked pained . . . *tortured*. As though standing there in front of her was costing him something great. He drew in a deep breath, then, finally, he said, "I was not lying to you when I said I *do* think you are capable of this, Valeria. Because I do. I believe you are capable of greatness. I always have."

That flame in her chest flickered, that ever-present fear mingling with another feeling, another flame. It was *yearning*. It was *pain*. It filled her body, almost sweeping out every other thought and feeling she had.

Blinking through the confusing mix of feelings now swirling through her, Val gave the general a small smile.

"Thank you, General," she murmured. "For believing in me . . . For *always* believing in me."

His fingers dug into the wood of the door frame, his boots still not crossing the threshold into her room. They looked at each other, the silence pressing in around them. She wanted to scream at the general to spit it out, to say what it was he was so clearly holding back on. She wanted to seize him by the collar of that gold armor and drag him into her room, rip off his clothing, and finally finish what they had started that night in his office all those years ago.

It may very well be one of her last nights alive. And she wanted to give in. But before she could succumb to the brazen madness churning within her, the general wrenched his eyes away.

With a curt nod, he said, "I will see you in the morning, Valeria," before turning and closing the door behind him, leaving Val aching with feelings that she wasn't sure were entirely her own.

Val slept poorly that night, tossing and turning, unable to switch off her mind . . . her dread. All her life, she had heard stories of Mount Cinis, of the beasts that were so integral to their goddess Calida that she was often depicted with a small dragon draped over her shoulders. Calida's children were always said to be the blood of the dragon, which is why only the royal families had ever tried to conquer Mount Cinis . . . and only ever the males.

From all her hours researching dragons these last few weeks, she knew that female dragons were rare—only used for breeding, and discarded after it bore enough broods to ensure the species would continue. The only dragons worth a damn to the Manielians were the bulls—the biggest, most powerful of beasts. Val could only guess how large Titus's dragon must be. Judging by the size of the hole it had blown through Bridah's walls, it had to be enormous.

Bitterly, Val realized that Maniel would always be like that. Prioritizing male power. . . the females just used to cultivate more power for them. And when Val fell asleep that night, it was with the pitiful realization that she may relate to a dragon more than she ever thought she would.

The next morning, Val walked down the quiet halls of Atlas Keep and entered Castor's library for the last time. She was supposed to meet Caelum and Aris, but it was to her utmost surprise to find neither of them there. Instead, Saros sat at the table by the fire that she usually occupied, sorting through a couple sheaves of parchment, all with the Legion's crest on them.

"Good morning," the captain said, shooting her a small smile.

Val didn't feel much in the smiling mood, yet she did her best to return it. "What are you doing here?"

Saros sighed, and leaned back in his chair, rubbing a hand across tired, purple eyes. "I was attempting to find our merchant log to pinpoint when our supply caravan was attacked. You can understand how I feel slightly . . . uneasy about it."

"Of course," Val said. She shifted in her leather armor, feeling each strand of her long, thick ruby hair weighing on her shoulders. But it wasn't just her uncomfortable traveling clothes that were dragging on her. This had been the first time she had seen Saros since that day when she saw a soldier being paid off by an unknown traitor. The memory still sent a tingle of anxiety crawling up her spine.

"Any news on the soldier I saw?" she asked, edging into the room. "Do we know who was paying him off?"

"No," Saros murmured, his hand still rubbing anxiously at his mouth. "Though I have my theories. The attack on our caravan was indeed troubling, and while it is possible it isn't connected, I have a sinking suspicion that it is." There was a long, tense pause, before the captain sighed and stood up again, gathering the papers in front of him. "Regardless, Rayner and I are keeping a close eye on it, I assure you. We will get to the bottom of things. I just hope it is not too late when we do."

"I thought the general would've sent Rayner off on another mission by now," Val said, dropping her heavy satchel on the floor, her brass swords clanging as they hit the hard marble. "It's rare to see both of them in one place for so long . . . especially the general."

"Ah, well the general is very much in demand," Saros said, chuckling slightly. "As you probably well know."

Val felt her face flush. Saros probably didn't even mean it in the way she interpreted it, but her mind immediately flashed to all the priestesses she had ever seen leaving the general's bed chamber at Light's Tower, all the rumors from any newcomers about their desire for him. She immediately felt sick.

"Yes, well, I'm sure the Star Seers have already had their way with him," Val muttered, giving her satchel a bit harder of a kick than she intended.

Saros glanced over at the sound of her foot hitting the pack, and he arched a dark eyebrow. "Oh, I wouldn't say that," he said coolly. "It's been a long time since he has, shall we say, *galivanted*."

Val froze from where she had reached down to rub at her throbbing toe. "What do you mean?"

"I mean exactly that," Saros said, shrugging. "In the last few decades that you've been gone, the general has very much withdrawn into himself. No more fornicating with the priestesses or healers . . . or anyone for that matter. At least, from what we have seen, the general only seems to have thoughts of war these days, and it's been like that for a long time now." He gave a wry chuckle. "I admit it has made things easier for those of us in the Legion, with the general no longer in competition. But still . . ." He gave another lazy, one-shouldered shrug, gazing out the window at the moonlit courtyard below. "I had forgotten he used to be like that, but it does not surprise me, given his history—" Saros stopped short, as if catching himself, before hastily turning away.

Slowly, Val straightened. "What do you mean? What about his history?" It felt like a forbidden question. Like, if she didn't whisper it, lightning would strike her down for even asking. But she had always wondered about Aris's past—what had happened in Ganiea, why he was so guarded, so calculated . . .

Saros shook his head, gathering papers, still not looking at her. "Nothing. Forget I said anything."

"*Saros.*" Val moved towards him, her heart pounding so hard in her ears that the image of the dark-haired captain swam in her vision. "What is it? Tell me."

Finally, Saros stopped moving. His hands loosened on the papers he was holding and slowly, his head dropped backwards to look up at the ceiling. He let out a long sigh.

"It is not exactly common knowledge. I should not even know—"

"*What?*" Val demanded, a million thoughts racing through her head, a thousand guesses, fears, and hopes—

"The general was once betrothed."

All the air whooshed out of Val's lungs. The flame inside her, which had been hiding beneath embers and ashes, suddenly roared to life in a furious, jealous blaze.

"B-*betrothed?*" she stammered.

"Yes." Saros sighed. "It did not last very long, though, what with his role in the fall of Ganiea."

Val's hand shot out to grab hold of the chair nearest her, beginning to feel a little lightheaded. "What do you mean his *role* in the fall of Ganiea?

Saros, what—"

He sighed again and rubbed a hand his face. "You see, when the general was appointed as the captain of the King's Guard back in Ganiea, it was his duty to protect King Makis and the royal family. But, when Praiton began the siege of the kingdom, Aris was nowhere to be found. Apparently, Praiton had targeted his betrothed's village in Lavalthon and he had raced to her aid, completely abandoning his post and his duties."

Cold was creeping up Val's toes, inching towards her head—a stark contrast from the hot flutter of panic in her chest. "How do you know this?" Val breathed.

"I'm not supposed to," Saros admitted, looking sheepishly down at the carpet, as if too ashamed to meet her eyes. "Petrus, the captain from Burningtide, was in the Ganiean army at the time. He had kept it to himself all these years out of respect for the general but accidentally told me about it many moons ago over one too many mugs of mead."

Saros made to move towards the door, but Val was still rooted to the spot, her mind reeling. Aris abandoned his post . . . He had let the High King fall, had left Prince Minos and the rest of the royal line be taken just to save—

"But what about his betrothed?" Val demanded, whipping around, her heart pounding. "What happened to her?"

Saros paused at the door of the study. "She died," he said sadly. "In the end, the general was too late. That's the tragedy of it, I suppose. It was all for nothing."

And with one last shrug, the Nodarian captain disappeared from the room.

Val collapsed into the chair beside her, too stunned to think straight. She had known Aris blamed himself in some way for the collapse of Ganiea, but she had always assumed he was being gallant, or else simply too hard on himself. But all along, he *had* been to blame—at least partially.

And what about this betrothed? Who was this female that was so important to Aris that he had abandoned his friends, his *duty* . . . his kingdom. Ever since she had known him, Aris had always been about the mission of reclaiming Krigor above all else. She had always suspected that the cool mask he kept permanently in place was to keep everyone else at a distance. But in those times when she had seen it slip, she wondered why he had fought so hard to hold it in place.

Especially around her.

The door opened behind her, and Caelum and Rayner entered. Both stopped when they saw her looking pale and shaken in the chair by the fire.

"You alright, V?" Rayner asked gently. His scarred hand reached out and touched her shoulder, squeezing reassuringly, but Val barely felt the pressure over the roaring in her ears.

"I'm okay," she said, but the words felt hollow and neither of the males seemed to believe her.

Caelum was watching her with a particular interest, those intense purple irises—brighter and more indigo in color than his cousin's—appraising her quietly.

"What?" she grumbled, sitting up in her chair, shifting uncomfortably at Caelum's scrutiny.

But the High King didn't break his gaze, even as she angled away from him. "Val, are you sure about this?" he asked finally.

Val blinked, taken aback. It was alarming to her how much Caelum had changed since their first introduction in Aunecia all those months ago. Now, free of the snarling and snapping, it could almost be construed that Caelum had something more than just a black lump of coal for a heart, like she had previously thought.

"Whatever that fucking ass of a general has asked of you, you don't have to listen to him, you know. You can say no." The vehemence with which he said these words made Val rise from her chair to better see the anxiety painted across his face . . . the concern.

"Caelum—" she murmured, but Rayner stepped forward then, reaching out and grabbing her wrist.

"Caelum's right. Whatever Titus and Praiton has planned, there's got to be another way. We'll find it, Val. No one would blame you if you chose not to go. We'd rather you be safe—"

But before Rayner could finish his sentence, Val threw her arms around both males in a tight, suffocating hold. They grunted under her strength, and she heard Caelum grumble in irritation, but still she held fast, sniffling slightly.

"Thanks, guys," she whispered, her voice thick with tears. She tightened her hold on them both, breathing in the scent of a faint winter wind and a salty sea breeze, trying to memorize it, burn it into her memory.

For everything that she had lost, she had gained something. These two—and Deya—*cared* for her. *Worried* for her. They were her friends.

After a moment, Rayner's free hand came up and wrapped around her waist, squeezing her back. With a sharp thrust of Rayner's elbow into his ribs, Caelum grunted and grudgingly patted her on the back with an awkward hand.

She released them, wiping her eyes, attempting to staunch the tears she could feel burning up her throat as she looked at her two friends.

"Rayner, you know I have to do this," she whispered. "If not for me, then for them." Rayner's face grew sad at that, but Val held strong. "But, above all, you know that there *is* no other way." She took in a deep, shuddering breath and squared her shoulders, before looking at Caelum. "Give Deya my love," she breathed, a tear falling, which she quickly dashed away. "And take care of her for me. We all know how you feel about her, no matter how much you try and hide it."

Caelum's face colored, and he grunted in irritation, before giving a short nod in agreement.

Footsteps sounded behind them, and they all turned to see Aris walk into the room. Time seemed to stop for Val as their eyes locked, and it was like looking at the general for the first time all over again. But this time, he looked different to her. He was not just a cool, calculated war leader, someone who made cold plans that prioritized victory above all. He was someone who had failed. Who had lost someone—someone who was *afraid* to lose someone again.

She saw herself in him as clear as day, and her internal flame roared to life at the sight.

"Are you both ready?" he asked, looking at Val and Rayner without even a greeting.

"Both?" Val asked, confused.

"I've asked Rayner to accompany us." Aris was still not looking directly at her as he adjusted the golden gauntlet on his arm. "It's more than a day's journey to Maniel from Elbania. I'm afraid Caelum can't portal us directly there due to the limitations on his magic. The closest we can get you is by boat to the shores of the southernmost point of Maniel where it should be an hour's walk to Mount Cinis. We need all the powerful Water Magic users we can get. So, Rayner volunteered his services, along with about a dozen other Laenimorians at Light's Tower to power one of the smaller ships there."

Rayner gave her a small smile. Knowing Rayner, he had only offered his help to stay close to her. Val smiled back, grateful.

Aris nodded to Caelum and the white-haired Nodarian turned and pulled apart the air, sending the familiar purple disc spiraling into the office.

Rayner and Aris stepped into the portal first, and as Val shouldered her bag again, a hand seized her wrist, stopping her from stepping into the portal after them.

"Caelum—"

"You better come back," he said, and even though he wasn't looking at her—as if he were too stubborn and embarrassed to meet her eye—she could feel the tightness of his hold. "If you don't come back, it'll break her heart. And I'll have to kill you for that."

Val smiled. "Careful, Caelum. I may think you actually care about something."

Caelum shot her the smallest of glances, his mouth still locked into that familiar scowl. And yet, the corners of his lips twitched slightly.

"You blasted harpy."

"You heartless prick."

Caelum gave her the smallest of rare smiles and squeezed her wrist. Then he let her go, and Val stepped into the portal.

Deya stared out the window of Fangdor's library, her eyes sweeping both ground and sky, looking for any sign of trouble. The afternoon light was weak, yet it made the newly fallen mound of snow outside sparkle like freshly mined diamonds.

Today Val was leaving to board a boat to Mount Cinis. And she never got to say goodbye.

"Do you perhaps have demon blood in your family?" Luc asked from across the room. He was sprawled out in an armchair, feet thrown up on a stack of books as he thumbed through another sinister looking tome. They were in the same dark corner of the library Deya had found the story on *dodsbringern* in but had not yielded any further results.

Deya shot him an exasperated look. "Are there even such things as demons?"

Luc shrugged. "According to this book there is. This chap claims our realm is only one of three, and that we're all built on top of each other like layers of fabric. The demon realm is supposed to be underneath the human one. Maybe a demon slipped through the veil into our world, and had you?"

Deya fought a shiver when she remembered the Praiton soldiers who called her "demon girl" when she first escaped from Ironbalt. Having demon blood was too much of a horrific concept to even consider. There would be no escaping the evil she was destined for if that was the case.

"I'm going to say probably not."

Luc nodded and slapped the book shut, tossing it into the growing discard pile by his chair.

In the time since they had discovered what the Heart of the Mother was, it had seemed to fly completely out of their minds. Deya knew it was pointless searching for its whereabouts here in Bridah, but she couldn't help but feel a restless itching in her chest whenever she thought of it. That, coupled with the ever-present feeling of dread, as though waiting for an invisible axe to drop, had left her permanently shaken and shut down.

The broken bird she had thought gone from her chest was born again, and its tiny wings fluttered anxiously in her ribcage. Deya laid an ungloved hand over her sternum, closed her eyes, and breathed.

Breathe in . . . Hold five seconds . . . Release.

The door opened, and a servant entered, toting a tray of tea that Luc had requested. Deya caught herself staring at the male servant absentmindedly, taking in the scarf wrapped around his face, obscuring his features. She had noticed that the inhabitants of Fangdor had been eerily calm about the attack on the wall. It wasn't until Kindra had told her that—while she had secured both Frostheim and the border—they were keeping the attack quiet to avoid chaos erupting within the kingdom. Only then did their lack of panic make sense. Even now, the servant pouring their tea was calm and steady, an eerie contradiction to the anxious paranoia that was pulsing through her and Luc. The servant set the tray down with a light clatter, and with a bow to them both, he was gone.

Luc sighed and rose from his chair, stretching his lanky body as if attempting to touch the ceiling. "Well, I don't know where that leaves us, Dey," he said, reaching towards the tray of tea. "Remind me again . . . You always said your mother was from Ganiea, right?"

Deya reached for her own tea, her soul feeling particularly heavy. "That's right. She came to Praiton right at the start of the war."

Luc nodded, sipping his tea, digesting this. "And what about your father? Where was he? You've never really mentioned him."

"I . . . I don't know much about him," Deya admitted. It was true, after all. Athena had rarely mentioned Deya's father. No matter how much she asked her, her mother had always deflected the question. "My mother only ever told me that he was from Ganiea, as well."

Luc let out a troubled hum, his finger absentmindedly twirling the teaspoon around the rim of his cup. "Well, if you ask me, the answer must lie with your parents. You say that this magic unlocked itself at Ironbalt, but it had to have been something that's always been in you, especially if it's detailed in your prophecy."

Deya's spine gave an uncomfortable tingle at the mention of the prophecy. Last night in her room, Deya had told Luc everything. The blackness on her hands, the prophecy branding her back, even what Frode had called her . . . all her worst fears.

The trepidation of trusting him again was second only to her fear of facing this alone. After months of dealing with it by herself, it felt good to have someone in her corner to worry along with.

Deya placed her bare fingers on the table, studying their stark contrast with the bone white porcelain of her teacup.

"Maybe," she mused. "But if that's the case, how am I supposed to find out? My mother's in Praiton. I can't very well ride over there and *ask* her, can I?"

Luc sighed gustily again—a familiar sound to her. "No, I suppose not," he huffed. "And I doubt there's any Ganiean genealogy records in Bridah . . . or anywhere other than Ganiea."

One blackened finger tapped anxiously against the rim of the cup—a fierce, staccato rhythm. "No, you're right. They're only in Ganiea," she murmured.

"So, what about the Heart? If it's the amulet, what did Frode mean when he said it was her daughters?"

But Deya sighed, her chin hitting her palm despondently. "I don't know," she said, too anxious to admit that the same question had been troubling her for days now as well.

"Maybe we can get Karyna to go back down to that temple to look—"

But Deya shook her head again. "Kindra will not let me go unaccompanied anywhere. She says the temples are unsafe because they have passages leading out. Besides, what are the chances we find anything having to do with the Heart's whereabouts or its uses in Bridah?"

Luc let out another disgruntled sigh, drooping back in his chair in frustration.

So, this was it. Another dead end. Another wall leading to more and more questions. Deya rose from her chair, pacing the dark room, walking towards the library's large, mullioned window. It faced out, over the back courtyard of Fangdor. If Deya squinted, she thought she could see the vague outline of the Hearth House from where she stood, and she instantly felt a pang of worry for her friend. Where was Val now? Was she, perhaps, already crossing the Gray Gap towards Maniel? Was anyone with her, or was she alone and scared?

A prickle at the back of her neck made all her hair stand on end and Deya slapped a hand over it. The feeling of being watched and followed crept over her like the blackness on her skin.

In the handful of hours that had passed since the hole had been discovered, they still waited to hear from Ulf. In the meantime, Kindra and her Berserkers swept the entire city of Frostheim, but there were still no signs of any intruders.

And while this could mean that Bridah was safe, Deya was not so convinced. Neither was Kindra, it seemed. The Frost Princess patrolled the borders all night and now, during the day, Deya was constantly followed by one or two of Kindra's soldiers—never Espen, thankfully. But still, she could not shake the feeling that to relax was to die, like a creature exposing its vulnerable underbelly to a predator.

Luc's eyes followed her across the room, watching as her black fingers scraped against the wooden frame of the window.

"Dey?" Luc asked hesitantly, but Deya didn't respond. She was staring out at the frost coating the bannisters outside, wondering who was out there . . . Who was looking for her.

And when they would strike.

"You're worried about another attack, aren't you?" Luc asked.

The snow was swirling, gathering in piles on the sill outside. It was quiet. So quiet.

"Aren't you?" she asked softly. "Can't you feel it, Luc? Like something is watching us. Like something is waiting."

This time, Luc did not reply. And the silence built around them, suffocating the room, just like the sparkling white powder of the snow outside.

Eventually, they gave up on their fruitless search and said goodnight, Luc heading towards his room, while Deya was escorted by two burly Berserkers to hers. On the walk back, Deya kept alert, her ears perked, eyes scanning the dark, quiet halls of Fangdor. But there were only a few servants, their faces swaddled with thick scarves, sweeping the light dusting of snow which had settled on the baseboards.

But when Deya entered her room, it was to find Karyna weeping by the fireplace.

"Karyna!" She rushed to the young girl, who wiped her eyes and rose hastily from the hearth. "What is it? What's wrong?"

"Oh, Deya, I'm sorry, please forgive me!" Karyna gave a loud sniff, using the sleeve of her blue gown to swipe at her running nose. With her red eyes and shining face, she looked much younger than usual. "I am so embarrassed. I was lighting your fireplace and I . . . I . . ."

"What's wrong?" Deya asked, kneeling beside the young girl. "Please, don't apologize. Just tell me what it is."

Karyna sniffled, drawing in shuddering gasps as her tears abated. "I . . ." Hesitating, she looked up at Deya. Her ice blue eyes shone with tears, her pale skin red with fear and firelight. "It's just that, servants talk, you know how it is. And, oh, is it true, Deya?"

"Is what true?" she asked, but by the way Karyna was crying, she feared she already knew.

"Is it . . . is it true that Bridah has been breached? Are we . . . in danger?"

Deya closed her eyes. Judging by the state Karyna was in now, it was clear that Kindra had made a wise decision to keep the attack quiet. Karyna was more than just panicked, she was *petrified*. The way she clung to Deya's hand as she gazed up at her . . . and Deya wished she could give her any answer but the truth.

With a deep breath, Deya nodded. "Yes, Karyna. It is true."

A small squeak of terror escaped her, and Karyna fell back onto the floor, staring into the fireplace, her eyes wide, unseeing. The flames danced in her blue irises, the shadows casting her pretty features into sharp relief. After a moment, she drew in a shaky breath. "I was not alive when Maniel and Praiton last attempted to invade us. But I was a child when the High King of Maniel first got his dragon and attempted to breach the wall. I lived on the outskirts of Frostheim with my *faor* and *maor*. They burned our house down and killed both my parents."

Deya's breath hitched, and she reached for the girl's hand again. "Oh, Karyna, I'm so sorry."

Karyna wiped at her eyes again, her voice still thick with tears. "Espen carried me and Niel to safety. Niel was only a babe at the time, a newborn with barely a month of life. The dragon attempted to break through, but only the soldiers in red came before Ulf raised the glaciers that now surround us. The Berserkers managed to end it quickly. When the battle had finished, and Ulf had heard of my parents' deaths, he took all of us in. Niel and I were raised by the priestesses and servants, and Espen was molded into a future warrior for the kingdom."

Karyna reached down towards the hem of her dress and pulled it up. Deya froze. A blossom of red mottled her leg from ankle to knee. The burn was raised and uneven, the skin shiny and unnatural.

"When we fled, one Manielian soldier grabbed hold of me and . . ." Karyna's eyes shone, and she touched the skin lightly with a finger. "They didn't know if I'd ever walk properly again. Espen killed the soldier. Smashed him to bits with *faor's* axe. We both grew up that day."

Deya didn't know what to say. She held Karyna's hand and tried to swallow her own tears which had welled up. Anger churned within her as she stared at the scar on Karyna's leg.

The last time Bridah had been fully breached was when Princess Hedda had been killed . . . when Caelum's mother had disappeared. But this battle was many years after. News of the battle Karyna spoke of had not reached her in Praiton. She did, however, remember Val telling her of her capture, how the Legion had been there to protect the wall, and how the invasion had only stopped when the glaciers rose.

The hand that was not holding Karyna's curled into a fist. Here it was again. Another inescapable, undeniable moment where Praiton had burned lives to the ground. Had left behind nothing but ashes.

A memory of a silver hooked whip flashed in her memory, and for a moment she could feel them dig into her skin, could see the spray of blood, could remember the feel of her cheek pressed against the grimy stone floor. Could still taste the inevitability of her own death on her tongue.

"Ulf is a good king," Karyna whispered. "I do not know much of the realm's other kings, but I am sure none are like Ulf. And they . . . they mean to kill him, don't they? That is why they are coming, yes?"

Deya's mouth opened but dread was filling her chest. Because they *weren't* coming for Ulf, at least, not this time. No, she had a sneaking suspicion that this time, they were coming for *her*.

"There is no reason to worry right now, Karyna," Deya said hastily. "Once Kindra reaches Ulf with the news, and the Berserkers on alert, Fangdor is still safe—"

But Karyna was shaking her head. "That's just it. My friend who works in the scullery overheard *Hersir Kyandra*. They have not been able to reach the High King. The *hersir* fears that, wherever the High King is, messenger birds cannot reach him. That he is far away on a mission."

"What do you mean they cannot reach him? What kind of mission?" Deya demanded, but her throat had gone dry, her heart skipping a beat as if she had tripped going down stairs. Not being able to warn Ulf at this time was a terrifying notion. The same image of an animal rolling onto its back flickered through her mind.

"I do not know," Karyna said, shaking her head. "But he said it was to fortify Bridah, but for that I assume he has to go far into our mountains, where our deepest secrets are kept."

She knew Kindra had mentioned this, but were they aware it was this severe? Had anyone told Caelum of this? Or Aris? Both were probably much too busy preparing Val to leave for Maniel. Should she send a raven? Had Kindra already put them on guard? Deya's mind was racing, wondering what Ulf was off to do.

Numbly, Deya patted Karyna's hand, swallowing down her own fear. "It's okay, Karyna," she said, but she did not believe her own half-hearted reassurances.

Because if Ulf was far away and unreachable, Fangdor and the city surrounding it were now wide open.

CHAPTER 22

Val watched the water of the Gray Gap slap against the side of the small boat as it prepared to leave the Legion's port. The boat was slightly smaller than an average carrack ship, yet it was already teeming with over a dozen Laenimorians, all preparing the boat for push off.

The breeze brushed against her face, and Val closed her eyes and breathed in. There was something special and unique about Elbania's sea breeze. She had thought it the first time she had ever come here.

Before she had been banished, she had never left Maniel's borders. Her life smelt of desert sun, hot sand, and smoldering embers. But here, the air felt open and free, the breeze a cool caress from the mountains, with the forest hiding Light's Tower from view.

"Something smell good?"

Val's eyes snapped open. Rayner idled up, a teasing smile on his face. He leaned against the rail beside her, following her gaze out towards the sea. "Just . . . trying to remember home," she said. She leaned down, bending over the wooden railing of the boat and plopping her chin onto her hands.

"You didn't want to go inside the Tower?"

Val scoffed. "Are you kidding? I'm still wondering why Caelum couldn't teleport us to Dritus and have the ship meet us there, so I didn't have to come back here for this." Being on Elbanian soil again had her feeling melancholic on top of anxious. The area around her was nothing but memories of hikes with her friends—training with Lucia in the mountains, swimming with Atria in the sea, cooking with Katia over the fire.

"Caelum can only portal places he's been before," Rayner said, but his voice was gentle. "You know this is the only way."

Val grunted, sick to death of that phrase.

The only way.

The only way to save Krigor was to take a boat to her death. The only way to get to her death was a day-long boat trip where she would have nothing to do but sit and wait—a prisoner on the execution block.

Rayner gripped her shoulder. "Well, try to relax some. I'll attempt to make time to come see you, but I've got to get below decks with the others—"

"Wait, you're not staying with me?" Val cried, shooting up in alarm, but Rayner was already walking towards the stairs leading below deck.

"I'm sorry! I'll try to get away, I promise," he called over his shoulder.

"Wait—!" She made to follow him, but he was lost in the push of the other Laenimorians heading to their posts below.

Anxiety tightened its grip around her throat, that damned flame in her flickering, spreading its hot warmth across her chest. She had hoped Rayner would be with her for the journey, that he would distract her from what awaited her at the end of it.

But it seemed that she would have to do this alone.

Dazed, Val began to wander the small ship, walking back towards the cabins, her mind in a haze. Without Rayner, how was she to pass a whole day and a half of paralyzing panic?

Someone shouted an order to begin to pull up the gangplank, and a few soldiers rushed forward to pull the board up on deck, when they suddenly stopped.

"Sorry I'm late."

Val whirled around at the sound of the familiar voice.

Aris strode onto the ship, and as the soldiers behind him hurried to pull up the plank, he stopped in front of her. For a moment, Val couldn't hear the wind, nor smell the breeze she had been inhaling like it was an anchor she could hold onto. Instead, she was only aware of the familiar peridot eyes and the burning ache in her chest that always seemed to accompany the sight of the general.

Val cleared her throat, attempting to push past that irritating, all-consuming feeling. "What are you doing here?" she asked. She crossed her arms, held her chin high. Aris smiled and she let out a small laugh, knowing what he was about to say before he opened his mouth. "Let me guess, a general goes where he's needed?"

Chuckling, he moved past her, his arms behind his back, armor glinting in the late afternoon sun. "If you already knew, then why did you ask?"

"Oh, I don't know." She moved to stand beside him. "Just in case it was for some stupid, noble reason. I wanted to make sure you knew you didn't have to."

But the look Aris gave her made her heart stick in her throat. "I know. But I wasn't going to let you do this alone."

With an abrupt jolt, the ship pushed off from the shore of Elbania, moving at a brisk pace out across the Gray Gap. The wind buffeted around them as they both moved to the wooden railing she had previously abandoned, and for a moment, they both stood at the bow, watching the boat sail away from the Exile Continents.

The wind picked up speed as the Laenimorians below intensified their magic, and Val had to squint against the cold wind as it roared in her face.

"Why don't you go below deck?" Aris asked. His short, usually well-styled hair was being blown in all directions, and Val resisted the urge to run her hands through it and smooth it back down. "It's getting a little cold out here."

But Val shrugged. "I think I'll stay up here for a while. You know"—She gave Aris a dour smile— "enjoy the cold while I still can."

Val expected him to laugh—or at least crack a smile—but, instead, the general's expression fell for the briefest of moments, as if remembering what they were on this boat to do. Then, it stiffened back into its usual mask. It was like watching a linen shirt be steamed—the wrinkles of expression melting seamlessly back into his handsome face.

"Right," he said with a brisk nod. "I'm going to go check on them down below. I'll come find you in a bit, okay?"

Val nodded, but inside, all she felt was hollow as she watched the general walk away. Many suns ago, they had stood on a boat, just like this, and he had apologized to her for everything that had happened between them. At the time, she thought she would never truly forgive him. But now . . .

Val sat on the deck, watching the sun turn a bright orange before melting into a vivid pink as it slunk below the horizon. She had always loved watching the sun set over the water—used to come out to the shore with her sisters to watch it. Being born in Maniel meant limited access to the water and, even now, it still remained a novelty.

Eventually, as the sun set, she began to head towards the stairs of the cabin area, when she crashed into a hard, golden body.

Aris grabbed her before she tumbled down the stairs, seizing her around the waist as she reached for the wooden wall.

"I was just coming out to find you," the general said.

"Well, you found me," Val gasped. Her heart was still pounding somewhere in her lower belly from the falling sensation. This was made only worse by the maddening reaction her body had just from the general fucking *touching* her. Gods, this was getting annoying.

Aris smirked and slowly, he released her as she righted herself.

"Have you eaten?" he asked, falling into step beside her as they descended the stairs. "You probably should. There are no cooks onboard, but I'm sure—"

But Val smiled and shook her head. "It's okay, General. I'm not feeling too hungry. I'm just going to turn in for the night if it's all right with you." Even though she knew there was no way in hells she was going to sleep. Sleepless nights upon a warship were nothing unusual to her—but this time, the fear tasted much different. It boiled in her gut, eating up any sort of appetite she might have had otherwise.

Aris seemed to know what she was thinking, because his eyes drifted down her body, as if taking in the slightly gaunter features of her silhouette. "Are you sure? I worry you haven't eaten much since—"

"General," she said, cutting him off with a laugh as she stopped in the wooden, torch-lit hallway of the ship's sleeping quarters. "I assure you, I'll be all right." Although Val could not describe it, something between her and the general felt awkward and charged. As if there was something he wanted to say but couldn't. Everything about him was stiff and polite—almost distant.

This demeanor was nothing new for the general—and had been happening much more frequently lately—yet she wanted to scream in frustration at the way those hazel eyes never seemed to linger on her long, as if they were afraid to. And even though his concern for her wellbeing seemed genuine, she yearned to have the male who used to look at her like he could see right through to her soul.

Aris opened his mouth, as if about to say something, when his eyes drifted behind her. His brow furrowed.

"What is it?" Val asked, turning, but then she saw what he was looking at.

The size of the ships within the Legion's fleet varied depending on the mission they were taking it on. Val had been on ships the size of a small fortress, with dozens of doors for private sleeping quarters, as well as a mass, shared barracks for crew and staff.

This carrack ship, however, was much more condensed—honed mostly for getting a small group somewhere quickly.

Which meant there was only one door to a single cabin in the hallway that they were currently standing in.

Val turned back to Aris, her mouth opening. "There's . . . only one cabin."

Aris swallowed. "Yes, it appears so." His gaze drifted towards the wooden door behind her, and he seemed to lose himself in his thoughts. Shaking his head, as if to ward off flies, he said quickly, "You take it, Valeria. You need the rest. I'll bunk with the rest of the crew in the barracks."

"No, General, absolutely not," she insisted. "The cabins are given to those of the highest rank onboard. *You* take the cabin, and I'll head to the barracks—"

She made to move past him, but Aris seized her wrist, pulling her back.

"*Valeria*," he said, and this time his voice held a hint of derision. Val heard the slightest crack in his golden armor and leapt on it.

"*General.*"

"You are being stubborn."

"And *you* are being ridiculous."

Aris's brow rose, and she could see the hint of that same smirk that made her knees weak pulling at the corner of his mouth. He still hadn't let go of her wrist.

"What will it take for you to stop arguing with me for *once* and take the damn cabin?" he said through slightly gritted teeth, pulling her even closer to him.

Val smiled demurely and felt herself fall into him as the ship bucked and swayed underneath them.

"Only a damn miracle, General."

His fingers bit into the skin of her wrist as his grip tightened on her, his gaze moving down her face again—but this time, it lingered on places that made her skin tingle.

"What happens if I make it an order?"

"Then I'll disobey."

His eyes rolled up to the ceiling, but that's when she saw it. The smile broke free of the mask, and Val felt a small glow of victory at the sight of it.

"*Why*," he hissed, "do you enjoy *vexing* me so much, woman?"

She smiled a catlike grin. "I'm a simple girl, General," she purred. "Please allow me the small pleasures in life, it's all I have."

The ship rocked violently, sending them lurching off balance. The general flung out a hand to catch himself on the door of the cabin as Val stumbled and crashed into him again.

Grasping his shoulders, Val straightened as Aris's free hand curled around her waist. For a moment, they both looked up, still gripping each other as the ship rolled over the churning sea.

"Why won't you take the cabin, Valeria?" Aris breathed. His mouth was tantalizingly close. Val found herself staring at it a little too much.

Absentmindedly rubbing at a smudge on the general's breastplate, still unable to avert her gaze from the one place she really wished to touch, she murmured, "Because you know exactly what they'd say if I sent the Legion's *commanding general* to the shared barracks and took the captain's quarters for myself." Wrenching her eyes from his mouth, their gazes locked, and Val saw the derision in his expression lessen slightly.

"You know perfectly well that I am not going to send you to sleep in a rope hammock surrounded by yelling deckhands when you're about to . . ." Aris trailed off and his fingers tightened on Val's waist for a second before, suddenly, they were gone. Aris stepped back, as though putting space between them could erase the tickling undercurrent of electricity thrumming in the air.

Val smoothed down her clothing, feeling the annoyingly familiar flush his proximity created before chancing a glance back at him. "How about a compromise then?" she asked. And before she knew what she was doing, the words were out of her mouth. "We share the cabin."

The proposition hung in the air between them like one of Caelum's air-sucking portals. The swaying, creaking of the ship was the only indication time moved on at all, and that they both weren't frozen at the very thought.

Aris blinked before his head tilted the smallest centimeter, as though considering her. Then, after a long moment: "All right . . . but you take the bed. I have some work to tend to before sleep, anyway, so I won't disturb you." But even though his tone was back to being distant and business-like, she wondered if the slight flush creeping up his cheeks was only a trick of the light.

The dark cabin was modest and rudimentary. It was obvious that this ship was not meant for long excursions. There was a small bunk off to the side and a simple desk in the center of the room—which Val crashed into immediately upon entering.

"Easy," Aris chuckled, grabbing her elbow as Val bounced off the edge of the desk, swearing under her breath. "Let's get some of these lanterns lit."

They moved around the room, lighting the candles within the lanterns and the iron stove in the corner, constantly bumping into each other in the small quarters.

"What kind of work do you have at a time like this, General?" Val asked, flicking her fingers so a tiny flame shot out of the tip of her nail. She held it against the wick of the candle by the bed until it caught.

Something warm and hard pressed against her backside as Aris scooted past her to reach the candle to her right. "Just provisionary plans," he said, striking a match against a small box. "We've lost a lot of outposts in the last few months, and the loss of the Nodarian supply caravan is proving to be a bit of an issue at some of our more remote posts."

Finally, all the candles were lit. Now, bathed in the warm glow of about a dozen tiny flames, the room looked even smaller than it did when in complete shadow. They were only separated by the desk, with little room on either side. Even though the bunk in the corner was small, it seemed to take up all the available space.

"Are things in Nodaria really that bad?" she asked, sitting down on the edge of the bunk.

Aris sighed, pulling out the chair in front of the desk and sinking into it. "The council pushing for a vote of no confidence is concerning." He leaned back and closed his eyes. "This recent movement is interesting to me, though. The council has always opposed Caelum, but to move to vote him out is . . . odd. He is Castor's son, the only surviving heir to the throne. Nodaria has always been very traditional in that way. It is how it has been done in this realm since the goddesses' time. All the goddesses only produced sons, so it became the eldest son of the old royal lines to become High King. Making a move like this tells me that there is something else afoot. Another plan . . . another successor."

Val sat up, a hot heat of anxiety pricking her nerves at Aris's words. "Another successor? Are you saying that this . . . this is a coup?"

Aris opened his eyes, but he didn't look at her. Instead, he stared up at the wooden ceiling, his brow furrowed, deep in thought. "I think it may be the beginning of one," he murmured. "But it doesn't make sense to me . . . Caelum is the strongest person Nodaria has to sit on that throne. He *is* their greatest protection. Unless . . ." Aris trailed off, and for a moment, darkness clouded his face. Then, with a blink and a shake of his head, it was gone. "Never mind," he said quickly, dropping forward in his chair and giving her a small, tired smile. "I'm just thinking out loud. I shouldn't have said anything."

But even though he had tried to brush off his musings, they still left Val unsettled. She wasn't sure if Saros had told Aris what she had seen that day in the hall of Atlas Keep, if he knew the depth of the severity in Nodaria. But Aris was a master strategist, an expert in tactics and military maneuvers, and had superior instincts. The chances that there *was* credence to his musings were high.

Val suppressed a shudder. The last thing they needed right now was a coup on Nodaria.

"Anyway," Aris said, jerking his chin at her. "*Rest.* And *that* is an order, Valeria."

Val gave a low growl which made Aris chuckle as he turned towards the desk, rifled through its drawers to extract a roll of parchment and quill, and began to write.

Feeling dismissed, Val pulled off her boots, dropping them to the floor with twin thuds. Hesitating for a moment, she chanced a glance at Aris. When she saw he was busy at work, she hastily undid the laces of her leather corset vest and tossed it beside her boots before clambering into bed.

She wasn't tired, not even a little. The ceaseless rocking of the boat, the scratching of Aris's quill, the maddening, suffocating *nearness* of him barely a foot from her kept her wide awake, shifting back and forth on the thin mattress.

Since she had departed that morning, what Saros had told her about Aris had played over and over in her mind. She yearned to ask him about it all, wanted to find out more about the female who had managed to claim him when no one else was able. All these years she had wondered . . . had always craved to know what was behind the general's mask. In the end, it was the same as what was buried within her.

Shame. Regret. And the blood of dead loved ones staining their hands.

Val opened an eye, losing against the all-consuming urge to look at him. The general had his chin in his palm, the quill still dangling loosely from his fingers. But his eyes were closed. For a moment, Val thought he was merely thinking, but when she saw the quill droop between his slackened fingers, she knew better.

"General."

Aris started, his dark lashes fluttering open. "Yes?"

"You were sleeping."

"Just resting my eyes."

"Now you're *lying*."

Aris turned his sardonic gaze to her and swiveled in his chair to face her fully. The size of the room meant that when he did this, his knees were a centimeter shy of touching the wooden frame of the bunk.

"And *you're* disobeying orders. Why are you not asleep?"

Val shifted on her back, looking up at the wooden ceiling—anything to avoid looking directly into those starburst eyes. "We're quite the pair," she said. "One who can't sleep and the other who can't keep their eyes open."

Aris gave a wry chuckle and quickly stifled a yawn with his fist. "Be that as it may, you really do need your rest, Valeria."

"So do you, General." She sat up, leaning up on her elbow to look at him directly. This, however, put her alarmingly close to him. Her fingers almost brushed the wide curve of his knee, and she could see herself reflected in his golden armor.

She didn't know what possessed her to say it. All she knew was that the tiny flame inside her was roaring, demanding her yield to what it wanted—what *she* wanted.

"You can't possibly sleep in that chair," she said hesitantly. Slowly, she scooted over until she was pressed against the wooden wall of the ship. Aris watched her move, his expression unreadable. "We could always . . . share the bunk. I promise I won't kick you or anything," she added, anything to distract from the flush that was beginning to creep up her face.

Aris stared at her for a moment. His hazel eyes had darkened at her suggestion, but there was something else brewing behind them. Just like her, he knew this was a bad, *bad* idea. The longer he stared at her, the more Val regretted asking. The general was much too pragmatic to agree to this. What had she been thinking—

"Are you sure?"

Val's heart began to thud in time with the flickers of that pesky flame, but she found herself nodding, holding her breath.

Aris paused, before rising from the chair, and reaching towards the straps of his breastplate. Val watched him slowly remove the golden pauldrons, then the gauntlets, and finally, the large breastplate was lifted over his head and placed on the floor by her boots.

She didn't think she'd ever tire of seeing Aris in his tunic and breeches. The way that the neck of his tunic fell open, revealing a light smattering of hair on his defined chest, how each hardened plane of muscle that was usually concealed by gold and steel was suddenly on full display to her underneath the thin linen.

He sat down on the edge of the bunk, and Val scooted as far against the wall as she could, even turning on her side and putting her back to him. But even with all of this, the general was much larger than the bed allowed. After a few moments of fumbling and shifting, the only way he could situate himself on the mattress without falling over the edge was curling around her, his chest to her back, his hands rigid at his sides.

"Are you all right? Do you have enough room?" Val asked, turning her head back and almost gasping at his proximity.

Reaching up, he brushed strands of her hair out of his face and cleared his throat, looking pained. "I'm fine, Valeria. Please, just . . . go to sleep." The previous levity of the mood had shifted, and Val found herself too afraid to even breathe, lest she press herself any further against him.

She could feel him on every inch of her backside. The heat from his chest was warming her back and she had a feeling that if she dared to arch her spine, her bum would rub right against something she really should *not* be thinking about right now.

Aris was shifting rigidly behind her, obviously attempting to get comfortable. A few times, she felt his hands accidentally nudge her as he tried to put them someplace out of the way. The problem was, there was little room between them and Aris's refusal to touch her meant that his arms were probably pitted against him.

"If it's more comfortable . . . you can put your hands on me," she whispered. "I don't mind."

Though she couldn't see him, she could feel him stiffen at her words. "Valeria—"

"Or don't," she said quickly, the heat in her cheeks threatening to burn her. "It was just a suggestion."

There was a long pause. Then, large, warm hands slid around her waist and her whole body tensed. A shiver rolled up her spine as Aris's calloused fingers brushed over the thin fabric of her undertunic.

Gods, why did she suggest *any* of this? Had she gone mad? She had spent *years* resisting the general. Years telling herself that he was a smarmy lout who was not worth her time. And yet, she had always known it to be a lie. After everything Saros had told her, everything that Aris had done for her in the last few weeks within the Hearth House, she knew he was so far from what she had told herself he was.

To hell with being safe and cautious. To hell with her damned pride and what assholes like Elric and Lycas would think of her.

There was a high chance that she would die tomorrow. And she was done running from what she wanted.

Aris's hand was frozen in place on the delicate curve between her hip and ribcage. Her whole body was aching for it to move, to feel his touch on her. Instinctively, Val wriggled, arching her spine a little.

Aris's hands tensed, the stillness of his body around hers told her he was barely breathing. But in the movement, his hand inched slightly higher. His fingers were now resting lightly underneath the swell of her breast, and the feel of it was starting to make her body tingle with a crazed desire.

Val closed her eyes, attempting to block out the heat that was pooling in her and the ache that was beginning to throb between her legs. As Aris's fingers brushed against her again, her breath caught, her nipples pebbling against the linen of her shirt, and she bit back a small whimper.

Aris's breath was tickling the hair around her face and Val, nearly dizzy with desire, arched her spine once again. This time, she pushed her ass backwards into him, and there was no mistaking the low, tortured groan that escaped the general.

Val twisted at the noise, turning over her shoulder. There was a feral darkness to his hazel eyes, a tortured shadow she had only ever seen once before. And the sight lit a fire in her so strong that the heat was beginning to roll off her body in waves of unfettered yearning.

"*Valeria,*" Aris said through gritted teeth. Their foreheads were nearly touching, and Val could feel his fingers tighten on her waist.

"Yes, General?" she breathed, accidentally brushing against him again. Aris closed his eyes, and this time, when his hand gripped her, they were so close to where she desperately wanted him to touch her that she nearly cried out.

"If you move like that *one more time*, I . . ." His words trailed off; his eyes pinching shut again. Never had she seen the general look so conflicted. Yet she was certain—*so certain*—that the desire she felt screaming inside her was echoed back to her in the general's face. She could *feel it*. Like a second flame intertwining with her own—a suffocated fire of fervent desire, a flame dying to breathe.

And with that realization, Val arched her back again.

Aris's hands shot forward, seizing Val by the throat, pulling her towards him so their foreheads were together, their lips so close she could feel the ghost of their touch. What was more, she could feel something hard now pressing into the base of her spine.

"*Valeria*," he growled, his breath brushing over her lips. His other hand had moved as well, now cupping the bottom of her breast—not fully touching her, yet just enough to make her want to scream with want. "*What are you doing?*"

Val was practically panting. "I . . . I don't know," she whispered truthfully.

Aris gripped her throat harder, and her vision began to blur before, with a strangled curse, Aris flew from the bed. He moved across the room in a flash, pacing the worn wooden floorboards of the cabin in a frenzied stride.

"General?" Val rose from the bed, but Aris held a hand, stopping her from coming any nearer.

"Please, Valeria. Just . . . stay there."

"Why?" Val demanded. Maybe it was because her whole body felt hotter than it ever had in the Hearth House, or maybe because she was still fucking *burning* to feel his mouth on hers finally, but suddenly anger was beginning to overwhelm her. "What's wrong—"

"We shouldn't be doing this, Valeria. Not again. Not *now*." He ran a hand through his hair, still pacing manically across the small room.

Tears seared her throat. The feeling she had experienced all those years ago when Aris had kissed her and stormed from the room was beginning to creep over her again—shame, confusion, embarrassment, rejection . . . it was all swirling around her like embers on smoke.

"*Why?*" Val cried, cheeks burning as she stood in her undertunic, her breasts heavy, her nipples peaking through the thin linen. She folded her arms across her chest, anything to hide herself from the male who had rejected her again. "Why not *now?* I don't know what's going to happen to me tomorrow, General, but I know that right now . . . I—" Val's words died on her tongue because tears were threatening to spill now.

She wanted to tell him that she wanted him more than she wanted to live. Wanted to tell him that she had thought about him every day in Ironbalt, had ached for him every moment since he had come back into her life. She wanted to scream at him that she didn't understand why she sometimes felt like she could *feel* him, as if he were an extension of her very heart and body, but it all seemed too ridiculous to say out loud. She could not lay her heart at this male's feet for him to stomp on it once again.

The general was standing, frozen, watching her. The mask had fallen from his perfect face, and Val could see the cracks underneath, the tortured conflict behind those dazzling eyes. She wanted to know what he was thinking, what was going through his mind as he stared at her, jaw clenched, chest heaving. It looked as if he were calculating something, running numbers in his head—an expression she had observed on him many times before in previous battles. But what risks could he possibly be weighing *now?*

Shaking her head, Val blinked back tears. "Never mind. Forget I said anything."

As she made to rush past him, she saw it. The pained look on his face shattered. Suddenly, with a tortured groan, Aris caught her by the wrist and pulled her, hard, into his body, before his lips came crashing into hers.

She stumbled backwards into the desk behind them, a small breathy moan escaping her. Heat exploded between them as their hands gripped and tugged at each other. Aris seized the hair on the back of her head, dragging it back, nipping at her bottom lip, a frenzy of teeth, tongues, and fire. Val gasped into his mouth as she was pressed into the edge of the desk again, her heart beating in her ears, heat pooling in her belly.

The taste of him made her want to cry—like finally sipping water after years dying of thirst. She clawed at his shirt, desperate to feel his skin as he pushed her backwards onto the desk, sliding her onto the smooth surface, sending his parchment and quill flying to the floor.

Half crazed, Val grabbed for his tunic. Aris broke free of their kiss, just to wrench it impatiently over his head before diving back for her mouth. Tipping her head back, Val opened her mouth for him and when she felt his tongue slide against hers again, they both let out twin tortured moans.

"Gods, Valeria," he breathed into her mouth, muffled by his refusal to stop kissing her. "What you fucking do to me . . ."

She lunged for his lips again, too consumed, so needy for him that she did not want to think too long or hard about why he still looked pained, as if some invisible force was compelling him to touch her like this, kiss her like this . . .

Pulling back, Val slid fully onto the desk, staring up at the general. Aris was shirtless, breathless . . . gorgeous. He was panting, not a flicker of gold to be seen in those dark, fathomless eyes as he stared at her like a starving man.

"What do I do to you, General?" she whispered. Her hands reached for her own tunic, pulling it up, revealing an inch of skin.

Aris's expression was feral. "You know perfectly well what you do to me," he rasped. "You've *always* known."

Her shirt moved up another tantalizing inch, revealing the undersides of her breasts, and Aris's hands balled into fists.

"You've done well to hide it."

He let out a humorless, frustrated laugh. "Valeria . . . You don't understand, I can't—"

But then she pulled her shirt all the way up, revealing herself fully, and Aris's words were lost as he stared at her. She smoothed her hand over herself, still not looking away from him, wanting to see how far she could push him, how much she could make him lose control. She *loved* watching him lose control. It felt like a gift, a secret, a sight just for her, a talent only *she* had.

"What don't I understand, General?" she breathed, and as her fingers reached up to cup herself, she saw the general break. And then he was on her again.

Large, rough hands ripped her shirt off over her head, and suddenly Val was flat on her back across the desk, hitting the wood so hard that a gasp of air escaped her lungs. But the gasp quickly turned to a moan as Aris's hands cupped her breasts before devouring them with his mouth. His tongue teased and lapped at a peaked nipple and Val almost melted into the desk, her hands scrabbling at the wood, heat spilling from her body.

More, more, more.

And as if the general heard the words shouting in her head, he reached for the laces of her breeches.

"Gods, you're beautiful," he whispered, more to himself than to her. "You'll fucking ruin me." His hands seized the waistband of her pants, and slowly, agonizingly, he began to slide them down her hips until they dropped to the floor.

Now spread out on the desk in front of him in nothing but the small strip of lace covering her, Aris stared down at her naked body, and the look in his eyes was nothing like she had seen before. It was not just hunger and lust . . . it was something else. Something indescribable. Like seeing the moon beside the sun, like touching a star with the tip of a finger . . . like swallowing fire and trusting it would not burn.

Slowly, he hooked a finger under the strip of lace and began to move it down her hips until it joined her breeches on the floor. And then she was bared to him—in a way, she always had been. Because she had always been an open book for this male to flip through, to peruse when he'd allow himself.

She was always *his*. Had always been only *his*.

"You are perfect," he breathed, but he wasn't touching her. As if he were too afraid. But he looked—*Gods,* did he look.

Val sat up on her elbows, reaching for him, suddenly feeling too exposed, too naked before him while he was still mostly clothed. She seized him by the waistband of his pants, pulling him forward, working at the laces while his gaze never left her.

"What is it, General?" she whispered, her lips coming to drag across his neck, her teeth scraping skin, hearing the sharp intake of breath it elicited. "It's like you've never had me on a desk before."

Aris swore softly, his gaze moving downwards to watch as her fingers deftly unlaced his breeches, before pushing them down, desperate to see him, to touch what she never thought she would.

"Trust me, Valeria. I have never had you in the way that I've wanted you."

And when his breeches hit the ground, Val froze. Because Gods, had Katia been right.

She shoved the memory of her friend from her mind, focusing instead on the glorious sight before her. Reaching out, she wrapped a hand around the general's length.

The touch sent an electric jolt through the room. It was as if the world shifted on its axis, as if the sea itself had felt the ripple of this touch that was so different from any they had ever had.

The flame in Val was roaring out of control—heat was spilling from her, fire crackling in her veins, demanding, wanting—

And then the general's mouth was back on her, and Val was thrust down onto the desk again, his body pressing into her. She wanted to cry from the relief of feeling his skin on hers, from still holding the long, hard length of him in her hand, like a trophy she had been dying to win.

With a little jerk, she dragged the head of his cock against the soaking apex of her thighs and the general stumbled, breaking their kiss to groan into her mouth, a sound of simultaneous want and misery.

"*Valeria,*" he panted as she dragged him over herself, arching her back and mewling with need every time he brushed against the sensitive bundle of nerves. "Valeria . . . I need you to stop me."

She froze, looking up at him. Their foreheads were together, lips still touching, but the look on his face . . .

"Stop you?" she gasped. "Why the hells would I want to stop you?"

But Aris shook his head, wincing again as her hand that was wrapped around him shifted, pressing him into the slick folds of her, causing him to let out another tortured moan.

"*Please*, Valeria . . . tell me to stop."

Val's free hand reached for his face, smoothing across his cheek, pushing back so she could stare into his eyes. And, when he looked at her, even through the fear and pain, she saw something else.

Val had never been in love. But if she had to put a name to what she saw in his eyes, it may have been that. It was the same way Caelum looked at Deya—like he hated how much he cared, how much he wanted her . . . loved her . . . was *scared* of it. That was what she saw in Aris's face as she pulled back and gazed into those starburst eyes.

"Do you want to stop?"

Aris closed his eyes, his face screwed up in agony. "No, of course not . . . but Valeria, you don't understand—"

But Val wasn't interested in his excuses. She grabbed his chin, angling him back to her mouth, feeling his lips brush against hers as she whispered, "Then don't stop . . . I want to feel you. I want to feel you inside me, Aris."

He froze, and his eyes snapped open. The shock on his face almost made her stop, wondering what she had said to have made him react that way.

"Say it again."

Val blinked. "Say what? That I want you inside—"

"No. My name. Say my name again."

Val stared at him, and the flame in her chest ached at the way he was looking at her then. As if the battle was done . . . as if he had lost.

"Aris," she breathed. "Aris, please—"

With a strangled moan, Aris slammed his mouth back into hers, kissing his name off her lips, kissing her as if he were throwing caution to the wind. Slowly, Val coaxed the tip of him to her entrance. And, with one sharp pull of her hand, he thrust into her.

The fire in Val exploded—the second flame she had felt flickering beside her own was swallowed whole, becoming one, large, uncontrollable pyre. Her body filled with heat and her hands grasped Aris by the back of the neck as he slowly began to move inside her.

It was as if something in Aris had broken, as if her speaking his name had been his undoing. Before she could even adjust to the feel of him filling her, his movements began to increase, faster and faster until he was slamming into her. Val screamed with each thrust, hands gripping the edge of the desk, and she could feel fire bursting from her fingertips, burning through the wood underneath her.

And as they began to move together, everything blurred. The fire, the sounds of the ship, the water pushing underneath, the mix of their moans and frantic breathing, the fire inside of her . . .

And as the pressure built within and she shattered, it was with the feeling that she was exploding into flames, bursting into sparks . . . and when Aris came undone a second later and collapsed on top of her, it was with the same feeling that everything had suddenly and irrevocably changed.

CHAPTER 23

The darkness of Atlas Keep seemed to muffle Caelum's footsteps as he walked the silent halls. Nothing but the stars in the ceiling and floors followed him as he went, except for the lone soldier walking ahead of him. As his boots struck the marble floors with each heavy stride, he clenched the Shadow Sword in one hand and a small, sheaf of parchment in the other.

It wasn't even dawn yet. Sleep had evaded him as he tore through books in his room, too preoccupied with everything to rest. After all the portals he had made in the last few days, he *should* have rested. Even now as he walked, the starlight in the halls blurred in his vision and he swayed slightly as he went. He needed to rest, but he didn't. And then the guard ran into his room to deliver the note.

The guard claimed the note was from Saros, informing him that an outpost outside Arctos had been attacked, urging him to come quickly.

This warning set off alarm bells in his head. The captain had told him he was following a lead today. After he had sent Val, Rayner, and Aris through the portal to Elbania this morning, the Nodarian captain had disappeared, and Caelum had been too preoccupied to ask where or why.

When he had arrived at the council meeting that afternoon, it was to find no one there. He had sat and waited for a whole half hour like a fucking idiot, growing more and more livid with each second that passed until, finally, he had stormed from the room.

He hadn't seen Saros all day, and now this letter had appeared on his doorstep. He was not fooled.

He knew the letter was not from Saros.

And now, as he followed the soldier out of the Keep and towards the bridge leading to Arctos, he couldn't help but feel as if he were walking straight into a trap.

There was nobody here to back him up. Aris was gone. Rayner was with Val. Saros was off investigating gods knew what, and even though he would've sooner swallowed his own blade than allow Deya to accompany him anywhere dangerous, she was also hundreds of miles away. Even their connection had gone quiet, although he'd occasionally give the thin string within him a tug, just to ensure it was still taut . . . just to make sure she was still on the other side.

Yet, it was quiet on her end. Not a stirring of emotion nor a single word had slipped through the bond. And it was beginning to worry him.

"Do you know which outpost it is?" he demanded of the soldier walking ahead of him.

"Past Aldebaran, my lord."

Caelum growled and quickened his pace, nearly overtaking the soldier. It was just as Saros had predicted. The traitors, whoever they were, had targeted the outpost he had spent weeks attempting to build. The outpost was much farther away from Atlas Keep than he wanted to be—especially now. He debated portaling there, but was still drained from transporting Val, Aris, and Rayner that morning. Frustration flooded his core, the permanent dizziness that now swirled in his head making him sway. His portal magic was getting stronger, but it still was not at Castor's level. And he was pushing himself too hard. Too quickly.

No, he needed to save his magic. After all, he did not know what awaited him in Aldebaran.

Caelum's eyes darted towards the soldier who had summoned him. He was walking at a brisk pace ahead, his head down, eyes hidden underneath his helmet. The hair on the back of Caelum's neck prickled—a sensation that had been happening much more often these days.

In that moment, he was certain of it. This *was* a trap.

His hand tightened on the hilt of his sword, and he felt it hum underneath his touch, as if it too, could sense the blood that would soon wet it. And like his sword, Caelum felt a small thrill of satisfaction as he followed the unwitting soldier through Arctos and towards the small village outside it.

The words Saros had said to him that day over the murdered bodies of the caravan drivers pricked the back of his mind.

Smoke them out.

They were idiots if they thought they'd be able to ambush him and destroy an outpost. A bunch of low rank soldiers who could barely swing a sword? Caelum smirked slightly to himself, his eyes still locked onto the back of the figure in front of him.

Let them try. Besides, it would make it easier to cull the traitors from the ranks. Let them expose themselves to him with this pathetic ruse. So, Caelum followed quietly behind the soldier, his hand poised on his sword, waiting.

They moved over the bridge out of Arctos, and across the quiet moonlit paths he and Deya had walked down so many months ago. It had been barren then, but now the dark green grass was lush and overgrown, the black-blue leaves of the trees flowering with white blossoms.

But it was then that Caelum smelt smoke.

"What is that?" he demanded, but the soldier did not answer. The outpost came into view, except it was not the quiet stone fortress Caelum had spent weeks watching be built, had spent days filling with supplies. Instead, it was a bonfire. Bright orange flames billowed out of the small loophole windows, and thick black smoke filled the air, obscuring the entirety of the upper half of the tower. And burning all the supplies in its wake.

"*Fuck!*" Caelum cried, and, drawing his sword, he hurried into the flaming village.

Immediately, smoke stung his eyes, the acrid smell burning his throat, making him cough. He stumbled towards the building, the heavy wooden doors of the main entrance thrown open, smoke billowing out. The first floor was not yet alight, but he could see the flames trickling down.

"The attack started on the second floor, my lord!" The soldier had followed Caelum into the mayhem and was pointing inside the dark entrance of the outpost. True to the soldier's word, flames blew through the upper floor, bursting out of windows, swallowing the top half of the stone structure. Fire rippled from the spare haybales stacked around the stone tower, creeping from its epicenter outwards.

Caelum hastened towards it, his sword drawn, all the while keeping his eyes peeled for signs of blood and blades. Yet no invaders approached him. There was no carnage, no attack. Only smoke and fire.

Grinding his teeth, Caelum made for the entrance. His fingers twitched and cold, wintry air blasted from him. The bitter breeze suffocated the roaring flames with frost and snow, and when Caelum kicked the door to the outpost wide enough to allow him in, it was with a flurry of snowflakes.

The tower inside was filled with the sounds of fire, smoke so thick wafting from upstairs, Caelum had to hold his breath as he moved further inside. Only the faint orange flickers from the fire upstairs lit the enclosure. There was nothing in there but a few haybales and . . .

Caelum paused, a canister catching his eye. Stooping, he reached down and picked up the large jug. No sooner did his hand touch the handle than a familiar, searing bolt of pain rippled across the back of his skull. Everything went white, but unlike the time it happened with Val in Bridah, this time he was ready for it.

The vision appeared to him in rapid flashes. A soldier in Nodarian armor holding the jug filled with a grain alcohol, tossing the liquid around the outpost and on the haybales and supplies upstairs. The same soldier lighting the match, running from the village . . . the same soldier drawing his sword within the dark tower.

Caelum let out a dark, soundless laugh. "Are you sure you want to do that?" he asked softly. The tip of the blade pressed into the back of his neck—the point so sharp he could feel it cut skin.

"Don't move and I'll let you live," the soldier said, but Caelum only sneered.

"Yet you can't even hold your sword steady," Caelum said and, slowly, he turned to face his attacker. "Can you, Deimos?"

The young boy's sword shook, nearly grazing Caelum's nose, but still, he did not move. He stared down the blade of the silver Star Sword that had been the young boy's father's. He still remembered the day General Pallas had been given it. Had remembered the look of pride he had when Castor had bestowed it to him, the way he cherished it when he trained with the others.

"What would your father think of this," Caelum said, his voice still soft and menacing. "His sword being held in the face of Nodaria's ruler. I think he'd rise from the grave to smite you, boy."

Deimos's face was pale and at Caelum's words his hand shook even harder. "Shut up!" he said. "Don't move! If you move, I'll—"

But the magic was already beginning to crackle at Caelum's fingertips. Frost was creeping from his toes, his eyes beginning to glow their usual, sinister purple.

"You'll *what?*" Caelum snarled. And then, he lunged.

But no sooner had he leapt for the boy, his Celestial Magic about to tear him apart, when something hard and cold seized him by the neck. Caelum gagged as the chain cut into his windpipe. His hands scrabbled at the binding, attempting to pry it loose, but before he could regain his balance, two pairs of hands threw him to the ground.

Caelum surged, bucking against the chain. The Shadow Sword was knocked from his hand, and just as he raised his arm to send his attackers flying into the air, a manacle was clapped across his wrist. The male holding the chain around Caelum's windpipe gave an almighty pull, and he was slammed into the ground, the force of the blow knocking the wind from him. Stars popped in his vision and before he could move, another manacle was slapped onto his other wrist.

"We got 'im!"

There was whooping and cheering, the sound lighting a fire of fury in Caelum's gut. He struggled upright, but the chains pulled him back. The fucking assholes had strung the heavy iron taut, locked to two hooks protruding from the ground. He struggled against it, the chains only allowing him enough slack to move an inch off the ground, just enough to look at his attackers.

Panting, shaking with an explosive rage he had not felt in weeks, Caelum roared and yanked at the chains. When they did not give, he wrapped his hands around the links and reached for his Frost Magic. It swelled in his chest, filling his veins and then . . . it stopped.

"Ain't no getting out of here, *my lord*," the male sneered. "Your bastard magic won't work here."

Panic flooded his insides as he tried again, this time reaching for his Celestial Magic. Again, it rose from his core . . . before stopping dead in its tracks.

No.

But there was no mistaking it. Blocking out the jeering of his captors, he could hear it now. The smallest, tinny ringing in his head.

Faerivaine shackles.

But *no* . . . it *couldn't* be. No other kingdom had access to these chains. Faerivaine was a Praiton invention, a creation they coveted and protected. The only way this pathetic lot would've gotten faerivaine chains was if . . .

No.

"What the fuck are you doing?" Caelum snarled. He bucked against the restraints, choking slightly as the one still wrapped around his neck pulled him back. "If you don't let me go right now—"

"Then what?" The other male laughed uproariously. "I promise you, bastard, there's nothing you can do to us now. You're *useless*."

Caelum's eyes turned to Deimos. The young male was standing between the other two, his face stricken. But when their eyes locked, his jaw set, and his chin tilted up defiantly.

Caelum was not fooled. Even through the thick smoke filling the room, he could see the tiniest quiver to his chin, the shaking of his hands—which were balled into fists at his side.

The other two males laughed still, slapping each other's hands in idiotic congratulations, guffawing at their own dumb luck that they had trapped the High King of Nodaria. They turned towards the door and Deimos hesitated for all of a second, before slowly turning to follow them.

"*Deimos!*" Caelum roared. The sound made all three stop dead. Because it was not just anger in Caelum's voice.

He strained against the shackles, his own sheer strength bending the iron with the force. He pulled himself into a sitting position and blood dripped from his wrists as the chain cut into his skin. And when he looked at them through the smoke, they flinched back as his eyes blazed with sheer power. "You know full well this will not hold me," Caelum snarled, and for a moment, all three faces went white. "And when I break free . . . I will rip all three of your spines out. And I don't need magic for that."

For a moment, none of them spoke. Even the two gloating buffoons were petrified for all of a moment until one broke the tension with a shaky laugh.

"Right, *my lord*. Big words from a bastard chained to the floor. All you'll be doing from here on out is burning. Maybe, if there's anything left of you to collect when we come back, I'll feed your ashes to my pigs."

Then, the males turned to leave and, with a flick of a match from his pocket, one tossed a careless stick of fire onto the straw-strewn floor. And then the rest of the outpost went up in flames.

Deya woke to the sound of a loud crashing noise outside her room.

Sitting, bolt-upright, she lurched from the bed, listening. Fangdor was quiet, nothing but the whistling winter wind disturbed the peace of the wee hours of the morning. But Deya sat, rigid in her bed, her ears straining down the hall of the castle.

She could've sworn she heard a crash. Was it a servant knocking something over? Was it merely an accident?

Gingerly, she pressed a hand to her chest, feeling the nervous flutter of her heart beating against her ribcage. She didn't think it would ever get better . . . the dread, the anxiety, constantly living in a quiet fear of Praiton coming for her. Even now, a year after she had left Praiton—had escaped Ironbalt—she still had dreams that would wake her from a dead sleep with a cold sweat and a terrified scream.

Sometimes it was watching Oswallt die on the whipping post. Other nights, it was Clarita, looming over her in the darkness of a blood-stained prison cell.

You're safe. You're safe.

She repeated the words to herself over and over, hand still clasped against her chest. Closing her eyes, she breathed to the rhythm of the rapid fluttering, attempting to ease the fear.

You're safe. You're safe.

Had the crash been a part of her dream? It wouldn't be the first time this week she had been woken from a bad dream. Even before the crash had woken her, she was tossing and turning, trapped in a fitful nightmare. But this time, it hadn't been any of her familiar traumas. Instead, she had dreamed of being trapped in a burning building, of having flames licking her skin, of straining against tight shackles bound to the floor . . .

Deya shivered at the memory, rubbing at the goosebumps that had risen along her bare arms. It had felt so *real*. Her wrists even ached slightly, as though those iron shackles had really bitten into the skin around them.

Then, suddenly, another crash came from outside her door.

And this time, she knew she had not imagined it.

Deya leapt from the bed, her hand immediately grabbing for the dagger she kept under her pillow. Her white knuckles clenched around the dagger, the pearl of its handle clashing with the blackness on her fingers as she crept towards the door, her ears straining for any sense of the noise.

Kindra had told her not to wander at night—had even posted two burly Berserkers by her door to make sure no one came in . . . and that she never went out. Deya had thought this to be a little excessive, but, as she slowly pushed the door open a crack and saw no one standing outside her door, she changed her mind.

The hallway was dark and deserted. Moonlight filtered in through a few lancet windows lining the wooden corridor, but otherwise no movement disturbed the darkness. But there was *something* wrong. She knew it.

Sounds of a faint commotion drifted towards her. Clattering and clamoring, almost wet noises, and . . . a chilling growl. Deya tightened her grip on the dagger. Dammit, why did she not insist on keeping a sword with her? This dagger wouldn't stop much—could do nothing but maybe buy her a little time.

Slowly, Deya stepped a foot out into the hall. The crystal floors glistened as she tiptoed over them in her slippered feet. She was virtually soundless as she crept towards the sounds of the scuffle, leading towards the main stairwell.

Her room was at the end of a long corridor of other chambers meant for guests, but, for her safety, Kindra had placed her there alone, ensuring that no one had access to her but her guards and lady's maid. Now, alone and unprotected, Deya wished she hadn't been put there by herself. Luc's room was on the floor below, and she did not know where Karyna slept.

Who was she to alert if the source of the noise was more sinister than just a servant dropping a broom?

She inched along, her heart beating so hard she was scared that someone would hear it. The sky outside was brightening, waking from its own sleep. Weak morning sun was beginning to spill from the gray sky, illuminating the hall. Shadows still hugged the corners of the wide corridor, yet the lightening hall calmed her.

It couldn't be anything, right? Not with daybreak threatening the horizon. Not when the castle was about to be filled with people, when breakfast should be beginning in only a few hours. It was with these thoughts that she turned the corner . . . and froze.

There, across the hall leading towards the stairwell, were two large, shadowy figures. But they were not shaped like any fae-like creature she had ever seen. Instead, they stood on all fours, long, talon-like nails digging into the crystal floors and tearing at a mass between them. And that's when Deya saw the blood.

Rivers of crimson stained the glass floor, wending its way down the hall, like fingers reaching towards her. Deya stumbled back, letting out a small squeak of terror before she could stop herself and suddenly, the heads of the two hellish creatures whipped around to look at her.

Everything seemed to slow as Deya gazed into the faces of the creatures who haunted her vivid nightmares. Their large talons struck the glass floor, leaving red stains in their wake. Half man, half canine, grisly and hairy, shadows rippling from their hides like smoke.

Nyraxi.

And when they moved towards her, Deya saw what they had been feasting on.

It was the guards from her door.

The nyraxi closest to her let out a low growl, its ghoulish face curling upwards to reveal a mass of jagged teeth, all tinged with blood.

And then, they pounced.

Deya turned and ran for her life. Her slippers slid on the slick ice floor, sending her careening towards the ground. The pearl dagger flew from her grip and skittered into a corner.

No!

But she didn't have time to mourn its loss. Frantically, she scrambled to her feet and sprinted the opposite way. The sounds of the nyraxi charging after her shook the walls of the castle, made the windows tremble in their panes. Deya ran as hard and fast as she could, her legs fumbling under her nightgown. Heart beating wildly, she bent her head and sprinted, pell-mell back towards her chamber.

She fell onto the wooden door, the nyraxi roaring behind her, a hairsbreadth away. Throwing herself over the threshold, Deya slammed the door, hard behind her, forcing the deadbolt into place. There was a sickening crunch as the nyraxi's hard bodies collided with the wood and Deya screamed, throwing her weight against it, praying it would hold.

The creatures pitched themselves against the door, crashing into it over and over, desperate to get at her. Deya dug her heels into the floor, breathing hard, heart hammering, the wings of anxiety taking flight in her chest. The tiny bird she had locked in her ribs that she thought had flown away was flapping with more fury than she had felt in a long time.

Please, Deya thought desperately. *Please, someone come . . . someone help . . .*

But Ulf had left Frostheim, and her guards were dead. But what about Kindra? What of the other Berserkers? Where were they?

Deep, guttural growls sounded from the other side of the door and Deya lurched as one of the nyraxi slammed into it again. She yelped as the long talons pierced the exterior, sending chunks of wood flying.

Squeezing her eyes shut, she reached into herself. She felt past the glowing orb of Healing Magic in her core, past the sinister black shadow that suffocated it, and yanked, hard, on the string twined around her ribcage, right by her heart.

Caelum . . . Caelum!

She had never tried to reach him like this before. This bond was still so new, so foreign to her that she had been too afraid to see it for its uses.

But at that moment, she gripped that invisible string like a lifeline and tugged on it over and over.

CAELUM!

But there was no reply. The bond had gone silent.

Breathing hard, Deya looked frantically around the room as the door jolted beneath her spine. The deadbolt wobbled in its frame, as though threatening to break from the door.

Thinking fast, Deya lunged for the heavy wooden armoire that sat on the wall. Seizing it by the rough wooden edges, she pulled as hard as she could. The armoire groaned with her weight, dragging inch by painful inch across the floor.

The nyraxi were pounding against the door in unison now, their snarling louder than before, filling her ears, making her slip in her haste as she pulled and pulled at the heavy chest. When she had gotten it halfway in front of the door, she sprinted to the other side and pushed it into place.

Now, the sounds of the door rattling were muffled by the large wardrobe. It jolted with each crash, the doors springing open, her pretty winter dresses shaking on their hangers. Backing up slowly, Deya watched in trepidation, begging for it to hold. Eventually, the banging stopped, the quiet and stillness returning—but she was not fooled. She could still hear their low growls, could still see the shadows of their movements under the large armoire as they paced in front of her door.

She was trapped. Cornered . . . and alone.

With a shaking hand, she reached for one of the hangers spilling from the wardrobe and withdrew it. If she was going to die, she would not do so in her dressing gown. She didn't reach for one of her usual Bridanian dresses, though. Instead, she pulled out something she had specifically requested Kindra bring to her. It was a pair of brown woolen breeches, a thick, dark blue linen shirt which cinched at her wrists and crisscrossed over her chest, and finally, a brown leather corset adorned with a myriad of buckles and straps, which she tightened around her ribcage. Pulling on her worn, familiar boots, Deya backed into the corner of her room, her eyes still locked on the door.

She had been so panicked before, the adrenaline still pumping in her veins, that she had not stopped to think. But now that the danger was temporarily at bay, she was able to focus.

How had nyraxi gotten into Fangdor? And what else had come in with them?

Deya stopped backing up when her spine hit the wall beside the lancet window, her heart pounding, her mind spinning. The castle was still quiet. Was it possible that only these two beasts threatened the Frost Kingdom's castle?

But a sinister voice scratched at the back of her mind, and when she blinked, the image of a dozen corpses lying in crimson snow beneath a large hole in the glacial wall flashed through her mind. No, something told her that these nyraxi were not the only creatures within Fangdor Castle.

And she feared that they were also not the worst.

CHAPTER 24

The moan that came out of Val's mouth was sinful. She arched her back, her hips lifting off the table as a tongue teased her, caressed her . . . drove her to the brink of fucking madness.

"Valeria . . . *stay still*," Aris growled. A large hand shot out and grabbed her by the hip, pinning her to the desk she was currently spread out on like a banquet.

"I can't stay still . . . Not when you do that—" But her words ended in a muffled scream as Aris sucked on the sensitive bundle of nerves between her legs and she bucked off the table, only to be held down by the general's other hand.

"You're being very difficult," he murmured, looking up at her with dark, slightly manic eyes. And in that moment, the sight of him between her legs almost had her unraveling all over again.

"It's your own damned fault," she moaned, her hips lifting back towards him, aching to find his mouth again. But Aris just watched her squirm with a cocky smirk, still close enough to her aching heat that she could feel the warm caress of his breath. And it was making her *mad*.

"Is that any way to talk to your general?" Aris breathed, the smirk growing wider as a flush of longing flooded her body again.

Val let out a plaintive whimper which quickly turned into a stifled scream again as Aris slowly sank a finger into her. She was beginning to see that the general definitely had a sadistic side to him.

Neither of them had slept a wink. She didn't know where the boat was nor how long they had been locked inside this cabin, clawing, licking, and fucking each other until neither of them could think straight.

It was like being in a dream. A beautiful, wonderful, intense dream that was equal parts strong as it was delicate. And as Aris clambered over her naked, quivering body—the savage, feral look still in his hazel eyes—Val felt a twinge of worry over what was going to happen when the dream finally ended.

"I seem to remember," Aris breathed, his fingers still buried in her, his lips drifting down her neck, biting her collarbones roughly, "you telling me that I would never taste you."

The memory of those words brought with it a sharp stab of pain. How she had said it to him in a blind rage, how broken his expression had looked when she had said it. It was definitely not the same look that was on his face now as he thrust a second finger into her, making her gasp, her mouth gaping open in a tortured moan.

"I'll have you know, Valeria," he whispered against her neck. "That you taste fucking *exquisite*."

The words made the roaring wildfire inside of her spring to life again and she wrapped her legs securely around the general's waist and swung her hips, deftly switching their positions. Throwing him down onto the desk, she mounted him with a sultry, teasing look.

"Now that's not fair," she purred. "You've been having all the fun." And with that, she bent over and wrapped her lips around the generous length of him.

Aris let out a guttural noise that stirred something deep within her as she took him into her mouth. His hands came to tangle in her long hair, his head dropping back onto the desk.

"*Fuck.*"

When Val released him, Aris let out a low growl before seizing her by the hips and putting her back on her feet. She didn't even see him slide from the desk and come up behind her before she was pushed face first onto the hard, wooden surface. Val laughed but the laugh quickly turned into a yelp of pleasure as he slapped her firmly on the ass. Looping his arms through hers, he seized her by the hair roughly, pulling her back with a force that made her whole body tingle, before thrusting into her again.

This was what it had been like all night. Half rough fighting and half furious, frenzied fucking. Since their first time—what felt like hours ago now—Aris had been like a man possessed. Thought and reason had not seemed to return to him. He moved in a manic fury, flipping her from position to position, taking her on every available surface, as though he were afraid that—if he paused to think too hard—reality would set in.

Val couldn't deny that she felt the same way. The more she surrendered to the mind-numbing bliss Aris's hands, mouth, and cock were giving her, the less she thought about what would happen when this boat reached land . . . which should be any minute now.

When they finally slowed in their frenzied love making, they both collapsed, panting against each other in a sweaty heap on the floor beside the smoldering desk. Val had been unable to control the explosion of flames that had burst out with each orgasm Aris had drawn out of her, and as a result, the desk looked as if it were being held together by mere embers and a few splinters.

"I thought you commanded me to sleep, General," Val panted, and Aris gave a dark laugh as she poured her head into his naked lap. "Or are you breaking your own rules?"

"Trust me," Aris said, his breathing still ragged. "Breaking my own rules is *exactly* what you make me do."

For a moment, neither of them spoke. Aris's hands absentmindedly combed through the sweaty strands of her ruby hair, the mirror rhythms of their uneven breathing and erratic heart beats echoing in her ears. Val could feel them—like twin flickers of the same flame.

"What are you thinking?" she whispered, looking up at him. And although they had just spent hours getting to know each other in the most intimate way possible, that one question filled Val with more self-conscious anxiety than she'd expected.

But Aris's hazel eyes looked far away, as if he were staring into space. He shook his head. "Nothing."

The primal, wild glint was starting to fade from his eyes and there was no mistaking the look that was replacing it. It was stone-cold, sobering reality.

"Hey," Val murmured, sitting up and grabbing his chin and pulling him back to her. "Hey, don't get quiet on me."

It felt like plunging her hands into a cold, icy lake, attempting to pull Aris back to the surface. When their eyes met, she saw the look in them soften, and his hand reached up to grasp her fingers against his face.

"Don't think about it," she whispered.

Aris let out a small, humorless laugh. "Think about what?"

But Val didn't want to say it. To put it into words, to give it life and shape within this room felt like shattering the illusion. Because, deep in her heart, she wanted the general to acknowledge *this*. The way everything felt different. Like they had gone too far, like something had solidified.

Everything had changed.

It felt stupid and childish to want this male to *acknowledge* what this was between them. And if he did, then what? After she came back from Mount Cinis—*if* she came back—was she going to become his? Was this the start of something? And, if it was, why did it feel so horribly like the end of something instead?

"Aris," she whispered, drawing his attention back to her. "When I get back . . ." But when the hazel eyes looked at her, it was with the same tortured look, as if something in him were crumbling. And then he was shaking his head.

"Don't think about it," he breathed, and then he was pulling her into his lap, and kissing the words out of her. But this time, their kiss wasn't frantic and frenzied. It was slow, and languid . . . A goodbye.

The kiss began to get heated, Val fisting his hair, Aris gripping her bottom so hard it made her want to scream. They were just starting to lose themselves in each other again when a loud knock sounded at the door.

Val and Aris sprang apart like shrapnel.

"*Shit!*" Val hissed. They flew around the room, crashing into each other several times as they hurried to put on clothes and attempted to hide the obvious evidence of sex that was now all over the small cabin.

And by the time Aris had managed to throw his tunic and breeches back on and wrench open the door, Val was still only in her tunic and underpants. With a small shriek, Val made to dive out of sight behind the door, but it was too late.

"General?"

Val froze at the familiar voice, her pants still in her hand. Slowly, she looked up.

Rayner stood there, his bluish gray skin turning a splotchy purple as an embarrassed flush crept up his face. His eyes darted between her and Aris, obviously adding two and two together. It was only then—with the door opened and fresh air now drifting into the room—that Val noticed just how smoky the small cabin had become.

Aris leaned against the door as if for support, disheveled and still slightly out of breath.

"Rayner," Aris said, and Val felt a cold chill creep over her. The general had straightened his shoulders, his posture going back to a tall formality, and that look . . . The mask slid back into place as if it had never left at all. "What is it?"

"Uh . . ." Rayner seemed to have forgotten what it was he had come here for. He was still staring back and forth between Val and the general as if he were trying to scrub his brain free of the image. "Land is in sight,

General. We're estimated to arrive in about ten minutes. You're needed on deck."

Aris nodded, his hands smoothing down his hair. "Right," he said. And, with one blank look back at Val, he strode from the room. The look crushed something in her heart, and as she stood there in front of Rayner, she tried not to let it show on her face.

The dream was officially over.

Rayner cleared his throat, and when Val looked at him, it was with the shock that Rayner hadn't cleared his throat at all. He was *laughing*.

"And what are you laughing at?" she demanded haughtily. Her tone just seemed to make Rayner lose hold of his stifled laughter, causing it to burst out of him in an explosive bark.

"I was trying to find you earlier. When I told you to find something to keep you occupied, I didn't mean the general," he said, still trying to hold in his laughter.

Val flushed. "Rayner!" she cried. "I . . . It . . . Oh, never mind. Why are you down here anyway? I didn't even hear the signal that land was approaching."

Rayner pressed a knuckle to his mouth, his shoulders still shaking. "You probably had a hard time hearing it over the sound of the general fucking you through the hull of the ship," he muttered.

Val jabbed him so hard in the ribs he nearly flew into the wall, but it didn't stop the uproarious laugh that exploded from him again that made Val blush from her toes to her hairline.

"Shut up," she snapped indignantly, pulling her breeches on with as much dignity as she could. "I swear, you're spending way too much time with Caelum."

Rayner chortled. "Probably."

But Val turned to face him, and the look on her face sobered the Sea Fae instantly.

"Rayner, please don't say anything," she whispered. The taste and feel of tears were burning in the back of her throat, but she pushed them down, determined not to fall apart. "I don't know when the general wants this out . . . *If* he wants it out. So just . . . don't tell anyone about this, okay? Please?"

Rayner's expression softened. "Don't be silly, V," he murmured, reaching out and squeezing her wrist. "I'd never." He gave her a small smile in the way that only Rayner could—like he held her soul in his hand, and that it was safe within his grasp. "To the grave. I promise."

At that moment, the sound of a loud foghorn filled the air. Val froze, her eyes snapping to the ceiling of the boat where the sound had come from.

She hadn't stopped to think about what land approaching meant. She had been so consumed with thoughts of the general that she hadn't realized.

Rayner glanced over at her, no doubt taking in the color draining from her face.

"V," he whispered. He reached out and laid a gentle hand on her arm, making her jump from the sudden contact. "V, have you thought all this through?"

Val glanced sharply over at him. "Thought what through?"

"This." Rayner jerked his head towards the interior of the cabin, at the smoldering desk, her clothes strewn about the room, Aris's armor still lying on the floor. "This thing with the general . . . and what you're about to do."

A cold puddle of fear was beginning to seep through her, paralyzing her in place. Because the truth was, she *hadn't*. She had been acting out of instinct—out of the sheer, delirious desire to *live* while she still had the chance to. To yield to the darkest desires of what she wanted.

The reality was, she had done something stupid and reckless, and if that look Aris had given her was any indication, he believed he had done the same.

"V," Rayner said again when she didn't speak, "Are you prepared for this?"

Val turned to look at him, and a tear escaped, rolling down her cheek as she shook her head and whispered the truth.

"No."

Rayner didn't say anything. Instead, he looked at her, as if waiting for her to continue, but the words were stuck in her throat. The flame inside of her felt different now, bigger, as if it contained more than what it had before she got on this boat. And the heat of it, the constant roaring in her chest . . . She knew what it was that she secretly wanted.

She wanted Aris. Was willing to give up everything for him—her captaincy, the Legion, even her life. But she was about to step off this ship and attempt to do what practically no one had been able to accomplish.

She would lose her life trying to claim a dragon. And not only would she lose her friends, but Aris, too. But if she lived . . .

"Hey," Rayner said, jerking her out of her reverie. "You know you can do this, right? If anyone can, it's you."

Val gave him a weak smile. "Thanks, Rayner," she whispered. She only wished she believed him.

She dressed hurriedly and joined Rayner up on the deck. Twining her sweaty, sex-matted hair into a thick plait, Val stood on the bow of the ship, watching the rocky black shores of Maniel come closer. The air surrounding the shore shimmered ominously, a ripple of heat that blurred her ability to see any further than the craggy black sand ahead.

Her fingers dug into the wooden railing as she stared at it. Even from here, she could see dark, billowing clouds of smoke undulating into the air from the volcano beyond. It was barely morning, but no daylight could penetrate the thick smog that clung to the horizon. The blackness obscured the sun, casting the entire area into shadow. But, from the shores, she could see it. Rivulets of bright, burning lava flowed down the mountains and rock, spilling into the ocean, sending waves of steam and heat pouring into the air. Although she was looking for it, she didn't see any dragons. Not a wing, tail, or scale. The beach stood empty and deserted. Quietly burning.

All too soon, the ship crashed onto the shores. The Sea Fae around her hurried to ready the gangplank. But only for her.

Rayner stood beside her, a steady, comforting presence. But it did little to alleviate the numb terror spreading through her. A blue finger brushed her hand.

"V?"

Val stood motionless, staring out at the black shore in front of her. Smoke curled in her vision, the acrid smell of burning rock filling her head until she was beginning to feel faint. The weight of everyone's expectant eyes pressed down on her like a heavy pressure against her chest, and she staggered backwards.

"I got her, Rayner." A soft, familiar touch drifted around her waist, and before Val could regain herself, she was being pulled away from the prying eyes, ushered into a quiet corner of the boat.

Val was gasping for breath, her vision still white, legs shaking.

"*Breathe*, Valeria. *Breathe.*" And with those words, Val stilled. Blinking the smoke from her vision, she looked up.

He had put the golden armor back on. It looked almost bronze in the thick, black smoke that hung in the air above them. Aris squeezed her shoulders, shaking her slightly, trying to rally her.

"Aris," she whispered. "I—" There were so many things she wanted to say. So many things she yearned to ask him. But the look on the general's face shattered her pounding, anxious heart. The mask was back in place, marred only by the set of his jaw and the furrow of his brow.

"I know, Valeria. But it'll be okay. Just remember—" He leaned forward and suddenly, his forehead was against hers. He closed his eyes and drew in a deep breath, as if he too were trying to savor this last little shard of their daydream together. *"You are stronger than you think."*

Val closed her eyes and breathed in deeply. The feel of Aris's forehead pressed against her own stilled her frantic heart. Grounded her. She could feel his breath caress her mouth and she tried to memorize how this felt. To imprint it into her mind so that, no matter what happened to her, some part of her would always remember. But before she could even process it, it was gone, and Aris was pulling back.

The general took her hand and walked her halfway down the gangplank, stopping as Val's toes reached the end of the wooden board.

"We will have to go back out to sea," Aris said. "If any Manielians are nearby, they'll surely attack, so we must stay out of sight of their shores. You still have the flares?"

Val felt for the sticks of explosives in her pockets and nodded.

"If you feel you cannot make it, or if something happens, *use them*." He paused and for a moment, Val saw it on his face. His brow was so furrowed that all she wanted was to reach out and smooth the valley of worry out with her fingers.

"I will, General," she said softly.

Aris looked up at her, a flash of pain flickering in his eyes again. Stiffly, he nodded.

Val turned to step off the gangplank but was stopped short. Aris had not let go of her hand.

She turned back. "General?"

But he wasn't looking at her. The muscle still feathered in his jaw as he tightened his hold on her wrist, staring past her into the fiery waters under the small precipice on which they stood.

"Aris," she breathed. At the sound of his name, the general closed his eyes. His fingers squeezed tighter for a second before, with a deep, choked breath, he let her go.

"Good luck, Valeria," he whispered.

And with that, Val stepped off the gangplank.

❄

The wall of heat hit Val with the force of a punch. Instantly, the hot rocks began to burn through the soles of her leather boots as she made her way across the rocky shores. Behind her, she could feel the boat she arrived on creep back into the mist of the horizon, circling back around.

Leaving her.

Taking a deep breath, panic still hazing her vision, Val drew her twin swords. The bronze hilts were already hot, as if they had baked in the sun all day. If it was already this warm, how was she supposed to survive closer to the volcano?

Taking a deep breath, she pressed on. Rivulets of glowing molten magma slithered down the hill, hiding amongst the black rock, proving to be a dangerous maneuver as she attempted to evade the pools of lava that hid beneath the terrain. Thick smoke filled her nose and mouth, making her choke and struggle for air. If this was only the beginning, she shuddered to think how bad the conditions would be closer to the mountainside. But still, she kept moving.

The sky above grew darker and darker, the tar-like smoke swallowing the blue of the sky, undulating from the black mountain that loomed into view in front of her. She had seen pictures of Mount Cinis—crude illustrations which filled Manielian books—had even heard it depicted in songs they'd sing around fires, usually in Materín, a language only the nobility still understood. Unlike Nodaria and Ganiea, whose ancient language fell by the wayside, Maniel gave their ancient tongue to those they deemed the most powerful and thus, most worthy: Those sired from Calida's blood.

She could still remember sitting beside her brothers in front of their private tutor, forced to recount their family tree until they reached as far back as Calida. The Augusta line was born from her third son, who had shamed the line by birthing a daughter.

Daughters diluted power. Or so she had always been told.

For a moment, she thought about Lucia. The Niro family had been small, with Lucia being their only child. Her parents kept her away from the Ember Court, yet Lucia's sharp features and penchant for fighting had drawn too much attention. They had forced her into priestess-hood to rid her of her stubborn, independent spirit.

Val felt an ache in her chest that had nothing to do with the intense heat that was beginning to press down on her like a fiery hand.

It should've been Lucia. It should've been Lucia who led the Fireflies, Lucia who led the regiment. If it *had* been Lucia, they would all be alive right now. She knew that.

A sharp pain pierced her chest, and her eyes burned with smoke and heartache as she thought of her best friend. Of the weakness that killed her. Of the friendship that doomed her.

As Val moved closer towards the mountain, her skin began to itch with the heat, sweat beading in all the places that her leather armor touched. She had always been comfortable in hot climates, but this . . . this was hotter than what most Manielians considered comfortable.

She vaguely knew that she had to find a dragon willing to let her attempt to claim it. What that looked like or how she would do it, however, was another story entirely. All her research on dragons had only told her vague things. Powers they had—the ability to see long distances, heavily armored scales and self-healing properties, even the ability to create illusions or visions. But none of these details would help her claim one.

Val quickly found out the shoreline of Maniel which housed Mount Cinis was nothing but a large valley of flowing lava and slate. The toes of her boots were smoldering, and she could feel the heat licking her skin from underneath her leathers. Everywhere she looked, a thick blanket of mist hovered in the air, and it wasn't until after nearly a quarter of an hour of walking that the valley opened up . . . and there it was.

Mount Cinis stood out amidst the steam and smoke. Bright, glowing rivers of orange flowed down its slopes. Sparks flew from its churning molten depths, and the glow of its caldera lit the surrounding area with a sinister, red light. It stretched on for miles, its black hills curved upwards towards the sky. What little foliage existed around it had turned gray and brittle with ash, leaves giving off a fiery luminescence as magma nestled within its hold.

But it wasn't the rivers of lava that made Val stop dead in her tracks.

All around her, huge, scaly creatures lounged in the flowing lava. Like large dogs rolling in muddy puddles, everywhere Val looked, a dragon rested. Enormous wings fluttered with sleep; large, vicious spiked tails swished in quiet anticipation; and bright, terrifying slitted eyes turned to look at her with a sinister, hungry glow.

Even though Val was hotter than she had ever been in her life, she felt frozen as she stood at the apex of the smoldering valley. She could feel it—like a solid wall of impenetrable heat standing between her and the entrance to Mount Cinis. It felt like stepping into a roaring oven, sticking her head into a fireplace . . .

Slowly, carefully, Val stepped forward and gasped. Heat pressed in all around her—a suffocating, all-consuming squeeze that made her stagger. All the pores in her body seemed to open and ache as the heat went from simply uncomfortable to all around unbearable.

Tears sprang to her eyes as she took another step and yelped as her foot sank into a puddle of lava. Stumbling back, swearing, she looked down at her foot. The sole of her shoe had melted back, the dark leather turning black and oozing slightly. Thankfully, her bare foot was not poking through the leather, or else she might not be able to continue.

She had to be careful. One more wrong move like that—

At that moment, large, seismic thuds sounded behind her. Val froze, her spine rigid, the hands holding the two swords falling to her sides as the feel of a hot, sizzling steam washed over her, burning the skin on the back of her neck. With bated breath, Val turned.

Twin yellow eyes stared back at her. The pupils were slitted like a cat's, the enormous dark orbs drinking her in. The dragon was easily the size of a large house. Its mahogany-colored scales glistened in the shimmering heat, and for a moment, Val wanted to reach out and touch it. She had never seen a dragon before. It was breathtaking and terrifying all at once.

For a heart stopping moment, Val stood and stared into the dragon's eyes. Its large nostrils flared, as though smelling her. Smoke began to curl around its mouth, and she knew what was about to happen a split second before it did.

Val threw herself out of the way just in time for the dragon to open its mouth. A fireball glowed within it before a stream of fire burst out, grazing her already burnt foot as she tumbled to the ground. Her swords flew from her hand, spinning into the air before landing in a pool of fire.

Panting, elbows smarting from the fall, she looked up to see a large, spiked tail flying towards her. Val shrieked and rolled, but not fast enough. The spike of the tail licked her shoulder, and she screamed in pain. Droplets of her own blood flew through the air, sizzling as they splattered into puddles of lava.

The blood spilling from her arm not only seemed to entice the dragon more, but all around the fiery clearing, large scaly heads were lifting, noses tilted towards the sky as if they could smell her.

Val froze, her hand clamped across the gushing wound as the feeling of hundreds of glowing, catlike eyes zeroed in on her. All of them were rising onto enormous, glistening haunches, wings flapping, hackles rising. And a low, steady thrum of growls began to fill the air.

Her limbs were poised, but still she was frozen. If she dared to move too fast, would that spur them to chase her? If she stayed still, would they leave her alone? But everywhere she looked, dragons were creeping closer, large claws sinking into puddles of lava, wings flapping as they moved.

Val's breath sawed out of her, her heart pounding in her ears. The dragon that had originally approached her was swishing its tail, the end like a spiked bludgeon. It let out a grumbling roar when it realized it had not hit her like it intended, its yellow eyes searching for her, its nose sniffing the air. And when it found her again, several feet away, bleeding and shaking, she knew that she had no other choice.

She ran.

All around her, the sounds of the dragons' roars filled the valley, and heat began to beat down on her as wings took flight. Val ran without direction, without aim or goal. All she could think of was to get as far away from the dragons as she could, to hide—

A wave of fire exploded to her right, narrowly missing her. Val dove to the side, rolling as a screeching mass of scaly wings beat above her.

Another spiked tail swung towards her and this time, the thick sinews of the tail caught her around the middle. The air flew from her lungs, spikes tearing into her side as she was launched through the air. With a scream, she slammed into hot rock, the coals burning every inch of her as she slid to the ground, clutching her aching side.

Blinded by pain, soaked in sweat and blood, she could barely see as she lifted her head, her vision beginning to swim. In her haste to outrun the dragons, she had run closer to the bubbling volcano. The heat was suffocating, thickening the air, making it hard to breathe, to see . . .

A shadow passed over her, strong gusts of hot air thrust her back to the ground, making it hard to raise her head. But as Val looked up, the sight above her made her blood run cold. A bull the size of a large warship hovered over her head. Its scales were the color of the black obsidian rock burning beneath her, and its eyes . . . its eyes glowed a sinister red.

For a moment, she stared at the beast, immobile except for every nerve ending in her body screaming in pain and warning. The great beast opened its mouth, and a bright, brilliant ball of fire welled in its throat, temporarily blinding her. Before it let loose.

Val dove, pain from her many injuries washing over her as she rolled out of the line of fire, the flames licking at her heels. Even as she gasped in pain, she knew she could not stop. Zigzagging between pools of lava and rustling beasts, Val raced towards the volcano, the heat slowing her, pressing itself down onto her like a hot, heavy hand. The large beast roared above her, giving chase.

It was hotter than the Hearth House. Hotter than Heavenly Fire.

Sweat dripped into her eyes and her legs began to tremble, but she could not stop. The bull above her was still sending jets of roaring flame down at her, forcing her to keep running, to keep going . . .

Go, go, go!

But the small voice in her head was beginning to get fainter as her vision grew foggier. Her legs were starting to leaden and slow, as if she were moving through a thick, syrupy ocean. It wasn't until she hit the ground, throwing herself behind a large black rock to avoid the dragon fire raining down on her that she could see where her blind panic had brought her.

The black mountain rose from the lava, the molten rock spilling down the sides towards the ground. Fog obscured the top of the volcano from view, giving it the illusion that a waterfall of fire was falling from the sky. Even from where Val lay, the lava slithered under her, brushing her skin, burning it in an agonizing, searing heat that seemed to blend into one overwhelming pool of pain and flame.

She was fading. Fast. Her vision was growing white, and her skin was beginning to blister. And as a sob escaped her chapped and bleeding lips, a memory drifted back to her mind. The taste of Manielian desert sand choking her . . . her brother's knee against her back . . . and his voice in her ear . . .

What's wrong, baby sister? Didn't you miss me?

Val screwed up her face against the memory, tears washing over the burns on her cheeks as her fury pushed her to crawl frantically towards the shelter of a narrow rocky ravine. She dove for the crack in the black rocky earth, throwing her bleeding body between the tight spaces of the boulders. She tumbled headfirst into the small crevice and threw her arms over her head as the shadows of the dragons flew over her.

Fire rained down on her hiding place, a blast of flame overwhelming the crevice she was encased in. Val screamed, the blaze licking her knuckles and singeing her hair. But buried beneath the rock, the dragons above could not reach her. And although flames caressed her face, burning and smiting any skin it could touch, she was safe from the worst of it.

Panting, Val's bleeding body collapsed onto the ground, rolling onto her back to stare up at the smoke-ridden sky. Darkness was beginning to crowd her vision as Leo's face danced in her mind again. The image of him holding her down, thrusting fire into her face . . . the echo of her screams quickly turned into the screams of her sisters and Val let out a hopeless, despairing sob.

Her internal flame was dying . . . she could feel it. The heat had seeped into her body, burning her so thoroughly that her life's flame was fading, even as she tried desperately to keep it alive. Without her flame, she could not survive any longer. She knew that. There was no use. No point. Here she was, crawling across lava and molten rock, when she knew she was one degree away from death.

Her tears were evaporating in the heat of the dragons' fires as they circled her—carrion birds impatient for her death, roaring for her blood as Val's breathing began to slow.

She would not avenge her sisters. She would not make her brothers pay. The Legion would have to go on without her. In the end, she knew this would be the result.

And as Val lay there, she found herself thinking about Aris. How he had circled her in the Hearth House, how he had told her that her power was linked to the internal flame that was now sputtering out inside of her, too overwhelmed to do anything more than flicker.

His face flashed through her mind and her heart clenched, her fingers digging into the rocky ground below her. And at that moment, when she thought of Aris, she felt a molten anxiety flood her—one that had nothing to do with the dragons above.

What was that feeling? Why did she suddenly feel a restless, anxious regret pounding in her heart?

Why did she feel like her heart was breaking?

From up above, a smaller bull dove for her, no doubt catching the scent of her blood on the wind. Val barely had the strength to roll over, stuffing herself further into the crack she was encased in, only just avoiding its long, sharp talons by an inch.

Desperately, she tried to focus and clear her vision from the blinding whiteness that was beginning to encroach on all her senses and thoughts. Searching desperately within herself, she urged her flame to *go*. To *work*. To *save her* from this inevitable death. But all it did was flicker feebly.

What else had Aris said?

Your memories, your pain and fear, it has been suffocating that part of you. Weakening it. You need to push through it. Feel it.

Feel it? She could not feel it—could not look too deep at the wounds still fresh in her heart. The way it felt to say goodbye to Aris. To walk away from him. The way Lorenzo had burned her over and over, the way Leo had held her down and tortured her . . . How he had cut her sisters to shreds.

At the thought of her sisters, her heart let out an earnest, keening ache. The flame inside of her wilted at the thought, and Val gripped her chest, tears stinging her eyes. She fought so hard not to think of them. Had thought pushing it away to be the only way she survived the pain of it.

But then, realization hit her like a jet of fire and her eyes flew open.

In the Hearth House, she had tried to push past the memories of her brothers, but even then, her magic failed. Could this be why? That it was not the memory of her brothers that she had to overcome, but her sisters? Was that what was at the heart of her power? The pain of her loss? The pain of her guilt?

Val attempted to raise her head, out from the crevice of the rock she cowered under, only to be blasted by another surge of dragon fire that seared past her face, causing her to scream and drop back below the ground.

Feel it.

Through her blinding pain, Val closed her eyes and tried to do what she had avoided doing ever since learning of their deaths.

She tried to feel it.

Mentally, she reached into her chest and thrust her hand into the small, weak flame, just as she had done in that ice cave with Deya. And then, with a deep breath, she let her mind go.

"Captain. Captain." *It felt as though invisible hands were pushing her, pulling her up from where she lay, curled underneath the flaming rock.*

No. No. To unfurl herself would be to expose herself. She shouldn't move. She couldn't.

But the hands were insistent, and finally, Val opened her eyes.

Three pairs of amber colored eyes looked back at her, all different shades. Katia's soft honey-colored irises, Atria's orange orbs that matched her equally bright orange hair, and Lucia's golden eyed stare, as sharp and focused as a dragon's.

Val blinked, trying to clear the haze that clouded her vision, yet there was none. In fact, Mount Cinis was gone, replaced with a familiar grassy pasture.

"You fell asleep," Katia said, smirking as she nudged her. "You nearly missed dinner."

"Nearly missed . . . ?" Val sat up, breathing in the cool fresh air of Belston Gardens atop Light's Tower. But strangely, there were no headstones here, as if they had been cleared away.

"Come on, it's roast beef tonight!" Atria cried, leaping to her feet, seizing Val's hands, and pulling her up. Val rose in a daze, her eyes drinking in her three friends. It had been so long since she had seen them. They had never appeared to her like this. Clearer than any dream, softer than any nightmare. It was as if she could reach out and touch them . . .

Without thinking, Val reached out a hand and touched Katia's shoulder. She stopped, her smile fading as Val's other hand reached for Atria, grabbing her fingers, feeling the warmth of her skin. Then, she looked up to find Lucia watching her. Why was it that Lucia seemed sharper than anything else around her? That even in the sway of the tall grass, the rustle of the girls' ginger hair, it was Lucia who seemed to be the brightest of anything Val could see.

"Come on, Captain," Lucia said softly, holding out her hand. "It's time."

"Time?" Val whispered. The two other girls stood beside Lucia, watching her, their playful smiles now ones of somber understanding. "Time for what?"

Lucia smiled. "For us to go."

Val stared at her hand, at the many marks and calluses that adorned it, at the jagged scar she herself had given her best friend during a sparring match many years ago. It was the shape of a sharp L, and it stared at her as Val's vision swam with tears.

". . . Go where?" Val whispered and her voice shook.

Katia gave her a small smile and she could see her eyes glisten, as if she too were holding back tears. "You've held on for long enough, Val. It's okay."

A lump rose in her throat, and Val struggled to draw breath, but the pain stuck in her chest, ached in her heart. Tears began to fall, thick and fast, as she shook her head.

"I'll hold on forever. It's okay, I don't mind. It's my fault . . . all my fault—"

"No." Atria took her hand again, and the small girl smiled up at her, although her eyes were lined with water, too. "It is not your fault. We would've come for you no matter what. For anything."

Val crumpled, falling to her knees, tears falling, breath coming out in jagged gasps as her sisters sank to the ground of the empty graveyard beside her.

She could not breathe, could not see. The pain ripped her open, tore her apart, burned her hotter and stronger than any dragon fire ever could.

She felt the hands of her sisters wrap around her, felt the cool heat of them—comforting and familiar, entwining around her like a silk shawl against a cold wind.

"We will always come for you," Lucia whispered. Val lifted her chin to look at her, and the older girl's pretty, angular face—so like that of a fox's—crinkled into a rare, beautiful smile. "We are stronger when we are together. We can conquer anything, as long as the four of us are together."

Val closed her eyes and willed herself to stop crying. Three sets of hands laid on top of hers and she squeezed them, hard, as if the pressure would somehow make this easier. As if, somehow, letting them go would be any less painful.

"Go," Lucia whispered. "We're here. We're always here."

And when Val opened her eyes, the flame inside her felt stronger, bigger . . . Whole. She looked up from where she was still lodged inside the crevice, only to see a black cave staring back at her. It was carved into the side of the volcano, something she had missed with the amount of flames roaring around her.

Val tensed, bringing her body slightly up off the ground, testing her muscles, surprised to feel that they were not as weak as they had been a moment ago.

What was that vision? A daydream? An illusion brought about by heat exhaustion? Perhaps it was a delusion of death? Whatever it was, Val rose from between the rocks, her heart still aching, everything within her still crying out for her sisters, but otherwise feeling lighter.

And then, she ran for the cave.

The dragons who had been lurking by the rocks, waiting for her to move, roared to life. Fire exploded on all sides, enveloping Val, but with a scream, she sent out Heavenly Fire—a band of white-hot flames around her like a shield, pushing out the dragon fire. It was not strong enough to withstand it, but it was enough that, as she pelted towards the entrance, it kept the flames at bay. Until a large, spiked tail crashed into her path.

Val screamed and made to duck, but was sent flying backwards, the spikes ripping into her stomach. She crashed into the ground, stars bursting in her vision, body screaming with pain. Hands fisted against the now gaping wound on her stomach, she got to her feet again and continued running.

It was all she could do. Keep going. Keep moving and hoping she would make it. The cave was the only shelter, and everything in her told her to get there—for what or why, she did not know.

Fire rained down around her. Talons reached for her—like eagles attempting to snatch up prey—but Val dodged and rolled, the heat soaking into her skin, sinking into her chest, into the fire which was roaring with the dragons. *Pushing, pushing* . . .

Val stumbled forward, and suddenly, the dark, cool shelter of the cave overwhelmed her. She fell to her knees at the dark entrance, flames still clinging to her hair and clothes, so weak and dizzy with pain she could barely move. Outside, the dragons roared with outrage as they clawed at the entrance, sending jets of fire streaming uselessly into the dark hole. The entrance was much too small for the enormous bulls outside, and for a second, Val allowed herself a moment to breathe.

Until she heard a low, rumbling growl.

The sound seemed to echo around the cave, filling up every inch of space around her. She stiffened, her hands still clenching the wound on her stomach which was gushing blood. It dripped onto the dark floor of the cave and for a moment, her eyes watched the crimson splatter before, slowly, she looked up.

The flashes of fire from outside lit up the interior of the small, dark cave. There, sitting on a pile of what looked to be bones, was another dragon.

Val froze, her eyes taking in the bones. Some had tumbled free of the pile to rest by her knees—some animal, some looked even fae. Fear gripped her as she looked up at the dragon, which was staring right back at her.

But something was different about this dragon. Its dark, rust-colored scales lacked the sheen and luster that the ones outside had. In fact, this dragon looked much smaller and scragglier. Large cuts and scars covered its smaller body, and, when it rose onto its haunches and flexed its wings, Val felt a pit rise in her stomach.

A large, golden spear was pierced through both of the dragon's wings. It was lodged right behind its shoulders, holding the wings together, stopping the beast from flapping them. One large foot moved towards her, crunching onto the bones as it neared. Its wings attempted to rustle, but the injury caused the dragon to squawk slightly in pain.

Val was still on her knees, still faint with agony—with heat and loss of blood. She struggled to hold the dragon in view as her vision swam. The scaled beast moved into the firelight, and finally Val was able to see its full size.

It was smaller than a carrack ship, its scaly, spiked head more pointed and delicate. But it was the eyes . . . The eyes were different than all those that had looked at her hungrily, like she was their next meal. There was something about the dragon's golden, cat-like gaze that seemed almost familiar to her . . . It then occurred to her what this dragon was.

It was the female—the lone brood beast that a dragon colony kept.

She had stumbled into the dragon's nest.

It was obvious now. This dragon was abused, malnourished, and hiding in this cave, where the others could not reach her. She did not know where the spear had come from, nor what had trapped this creature here, but she could not help but feel an ache of sympathy for the beast.

The female edged around the large pile of bones, pinned and shredded wings attempting to flutter.

Its golden eyes locked onto her, still on her knees. And when smoke began to unfurl from the corners of its mouth, Val knew.

She looked at those familiar eyes, thought about how they had crinkled when they smiled in her vision. And something in her fluttering heart stilled. Her flame ignited.

So, when the dragon opened its mouth, Val closed her eyes.

CHAPTER 25

Caelum pulled at the chains binding his hands to the floor, but it was no use. Smoke burned his eyes, and the air soon became thick with the acrid smell.

Fuck.

Fuck, fuck, fuck.

Even though he knew it was pointless, he still gave a furious jerk of the chain with his fists, just to let out some of his anger.

This was his fault. He had walked into this, thinking there would be no way a couple of lower-level grunts could possibly overtake him. The thought had been laughable only moments ago. But he had never anticipated this.

Faerivaine shackles.

He hadn't yet dwelled on what these soldiers having faerivaine meant. But there was no doubt about it. This was more than an ousting. This was a coup.

Fire crackled around him, eating up the dry wood of the outpost's jousts in a furious blaze. A loud cracking noise overhead sent Caelum twisting out of the way as a crumbling beam collapsed from the ceiling. It crashed to the ground, stopping just short of crushing him by the weight of a sturdy rafter stopping its descent. Sparks flew at the impact, flames roaring higher, and Caelum let out another strangled curse.

He had to act. *Now.* Before there was nothing left of him but a pile of ash.

At the thought of ashes, Caelum's heart gave a tight squeeze. He thought about reaching for Deya, to warn her of what was happening in Nodaria, but paused. Was the bond considered magic? Something faerivaine would cancel out? Or was it truly what the old stories said—a full twining of their souls? Two becoming one.

Caelum felt inside of himself, a mental finger stroking the string that was linking them together but stopped. What would telling Deya do other than worry her? There was no way for her to help him that wouldn't put her in danger.

No, he couldn't worry Deya with this.

He dropped his touch from the bond and, with a deep breath, closed his mind to it.

He had to protect her. If she were to reach for him now, she would feel the prickle of heat on his skin, the beading of sweat on his body, the bleeding aches of his wrists where the chains cut in . . . even hear the tinny, high-pitched ringing that had haunted them in Ironbalt now reverberating in his head.

Caelum closed his eyes, and slowly, his mind shut out the bond. He was on his own.

Another fiery beam crashed to the floor and the consequent explosion snapped him out of his stupor, bringing him back to the very real danger he was currently in.

His eyes roved the chains, taking in his situation. Both of his arms were spread as far as they could go, the chains pulled taut, not allowing for much movement. Then there was the loop wrapped around his neck, limiting his oxygen. It contorted him into a backwards bend, his knees splayed with only enough slack to rise partially from the ground.

Laying on his back, he rotated his neck back and forth, attempting to slip free of the loop. After several tries, he finally worked it loose enough to slip out. He gasped for air, relishing in the release of his throat, but his relief was short-lived. Even though his neck was free, his arms were very much trapped.

Sparks flew overhead as debris began to rain down from the ceiling. With each collapse, dust and fire would ricochet into the air, burning his eyes.

Sitting up, Caelum strained desperately at the restraints on his arms. With full use of his body weight, he threw himself in one direction, then the next. The chains didn't move. The shackles around his wrist were only a tiny bit loose. If he strained all the way to one side, a sizeable gap would appear, but none big enough to fit through . . . At least, not with all his fingers.

Caelum paused, and then closed his eyes, and drew in a deep, aggravated breath at the realization of what he was going to have to do.

Fuck.

The fire was beginning to get unbearably hot. His skin was tender and sore, the heat suffocating him as he looked up above his head. The beam that had partially fallen was smoldering, the cracks in the wood glowing with embers. It was leaning against the rafter above, its end just close enough for him to reach.

With a deep breath, Caelum swung his body towards it and, with a sharp kick, sent the rest of the beam crashing down towards him. He threw his body to the side and closed his eyes as the beam fell from the ceiling onto his chained hand.

He let out a roar of pain, and for a moment, the agony of his shattered bones was kept at bay by the sheer fury he felt over having to be in this position at all. And it was that anger that pushed him to pull at his crushed hand. The sound of his furious yell echoed around the burning building as—with an almighty wrench—he yanked his broken hand free of the shackle.

For a moment, he could only lay there panting, before another beam crashed from the ceiling. Pulling himself to his feet, he was able to see the mangled, limp tangle of fingers that was now his left hand before he wrapped the chains around his arms and pulled.

With the full weight of his body, the final chain snapped free, and—still dragging the chain—Caelum ran towards the Shadow Sword, hidden in darkness that seemed to abruptly clear, and seized it, before sprinting from the building. He was barely clear of the entrance before the roof caved in, imploding into a pile of flaming rubble.

Panting, Caelum stared at the burning building for a moment, before turning to look around. The structures around the outpost—a few workbenches, a stable, and a small armory—were all still in flames, yet there was no one around. Those stationed at the outpost looked to have all fled.

Swearing, Caelum made towards a workbench smoldering nearby, seized a metal poker and began to pry off the manacle on his good hand.

He was seething, nearly dizzy with fury and pain. The hand was nothing—a minor irritation. It would heal, but it would definitely slow him down. Even now, attempting to fumble the poker into the clasp of the shackle with his mangled hand was proving difficult.

He was going to rip those soldiers' throats out. And he was going to *like it*.

Finally, the poker found the ridge in the shackle and, with a great deal of wincing and swearing, Caelum managed to pry the manacle open and whip out his hand. Kicking the chain into the fire roaring beside him, he panted and steamed like the smoke around him, before his eyes darted across the horizon.

From where he stood, he could see the top of Atlas Keep's roof. There was no sign of a struggle, but he knew it was in danger. They had tried to dispose of him, and he knew now that it was not the outpost they were after. It was his kingdom.

With a shout, he pulled the air apart. A portal sprang forth and his body buckled with the effort. Spitting out a mouthful of blood, he struggled to hold the portal open. It was smaller, the edges of it were fuzzier than normal. This portal was probably the last he'd be able to summon until he could rest. But it was no matter. He didn't need portals for what he was going to do next.

Caelum threw himself into the suffocating darkness, and a second later he was spat out into the quiet of Atlas Keep's moonlit courtyard.

Stumbling to a stop, he drew the Shadow Sword from its scabbard, his eyes darting around. His breath was coming out in jagged gasps, and his abdomen ached. Blood filled his mouth, but he spat it to the floor, struggling to stay focused.

The Keep's courtyard was a rounded, open enclosure. The ground was padded with rock and neatly manicured with foliage and flowers. At its center, a large statue of Astrea stood. Erected in stark white marble, Astrea held her hand to the sky, as if reaching for the stars.

It was quiet. There was no rustle of wind, nor buzz of insects. Only the deafening silence of prey being hunted . . . of a target being watched.

"Your stupid plan did not work!" Caelum roared. His words rent the silence, echoing around the courtyard. Panting, he gripped his sword tighter and willed himself to stay standing. "Come fucking get me. *I dare you.*"

As sudden as a cloud drifting in front of the moon, Caelum felt the presence before he saw it. A streak of a shadow, and then a blade pressed against his neck.

"You speak boldly, bastard," the voice hissed in his ear. "But if you insist—"

Caelum whirled backwards, Frost and Gravity Magic exploded from him, flinging the assailant and his blade away. The figure didn't fly backwards and hit the ground as he intended, though. Instead, he landed lightly on his feet, a smirk on his face. As he straightened, Caelum was able to see more clearly.

A green cloak draped around the male, a silver pin holding it to his chest—a dagger through a set of scales. Caelum recognized the uniform from the description Deya had given them the day she had been attacked. Cold, paralyzing dread seeped through him as the Silver Dagger assassin gave him a roguish grin.

"I'm impressed, bastard," he said, pulling a second sword from his belt. "It took you less time to escape the trap than I thought."

All around him, Caelum felt movement. Figures emerging from shadows, glints of silver twinkling in the moonlight. His eyes darted around, trying to get his bearings while not taking his eyes off the male in front of him.

He was surrounded. Green cloaks filled his peripheral and hastily, he tried to count, but found it was impossible to without turning his head. A dozen? Maybe more?

Caelum's breathing slowed. A cold frost was beginning to creep up from his toes, spreading up his arms, the telltale crackling beginning to snap at his fingers.

"Why are you here?" he snarled. His feet began to move, slowly backing up inch by inch. The movement was slight enough that the Praiton assassins didn't seem to notice as their leader let out a sharp laugh.

"Isn't it obvious?" he crowed. Absently, he flicked an invisible piece of lint from his blade and smirked. "It appears you are not very popular with your people, *Your Highness*."

Caelum's lip curled, the fury that was beginning to flood him cold and bitter. He had to stall. He could barely keep sight of the assassin in front of him as he edged slowly backwards. A few seconds . . . a few seconds to catch his breath . . .

"Tell me who fucking hired you," he growled. "*Now.*"

But the assassin merely smiled, and Caelum felt the sword in his hand hum, as if it wanted the male's blood on it as much as Caelum did.

"You know who hired us, bastard."

And as Caelum inched slowly backwards, his heel hit the marble of Astrea's statue as the assassin leered.

It happened in an instant. The second Caelum's foot hit the statue, the assassins around him moved. With a roar, Caelum flung out a hand and frost exploded from him, but they were too quick. Green cloaks whirled around him, dodging the icicles shooting from his grasp, evading his attempts to seize them with his Gravity Magic.

The first flaming blade came for him. He ducked, parrying as the blade sent a chunk of the statue's marble bust flying. But he was barely able to recover before another blade was thrust his way. He dodged and parried, ducking the assassin's blades and their low-level magic. Flames and vines streaked past him, grabbing at his ankles, seizing his wrists.

With a growl, Caelum ducked one blade, slashed at the assailant with his sword, whirled to face the next, throwing the assassin into the air, before crashing the body back to the ground. Over and over, he ducked and slashed, dancing around the green cloaks and silver blades, before, finally, he was backed into a corner.

Panting, covered in blood and frost, he raised his sword.

"Something wrong?" the same male sneered. He was out of breath, too, blood now staining his green cloak and flecking his cheeks. But the annoying smile was still plastered across his face as he spun a small silver dagger, flames licking up his blade like a flickering candle. "You're moving slower than I thought you would."

Caelum snarled as his hand gripped the hilt of the Shadow Sword. He had cut down six of them, but there were more than he had anticipated... more than he could count.

His magic was weak, his left hand useless, his body giving out. There were several wounds on his body—gashes and cuts he had been too angry and preoccupied to notice in the moment.

Chest heaving, his heels pressed into the corner of the courtyard's low brick wall and frustration beat like a drum in his ears.

He had vowed to never be weak again. He had sworn to himself that, if Praiton crossed Nodaria's borders again, he would wipe them from the face of the earth. Never again would he be that little boy who cried while his family was cut down. Never again would he allow his home to be burned and conquered.

This time, he'd fight with everything he had.

This time, he'd die fighting.

"You will not invade my kingdom," Caelum growled. "I will kill every single one of you before I ever let you within these walls—"

"Let us?" The assassin laughed and the sound sent a chill down Caelum's spine that had nothing to do with the Frost Magic threatening to burst from him. "Don't you understand, bastard? We are not invading . . . We were *invited*."

His heart skipped a beat. It *shouldn't* have shocked him—Deimos's ambush, the faerivaine shackles, all of it was proof that *someone* had opened Nodaria's borders to Praiton assassins. *Someone* had brought them here on purpose . . . But why?

Breathing hard, Caelum demanded, "Who brought you here?"

The assassin laughed, gesturing at the coalition around him, as if inviting them to share in the joke. "Look at the bastard, demanding answers," he laughed. "Enough with your questions." The smile faded, and all that was left in its place was a sinister gleam, a small, twisted smirk that made the hair on Caelum's neck stand on end. "Nodaria will fall today . . . just as Bridah falls now."

A burst of cold, sickening panic washed over him, as if someone had dropped a bucket of ice water over his head. Caelum froze, his hand almost dropping his sword at the assassin's words.

"Deya," he whispered before desperately, he dove into his core, mentally fumbling for the string that bound him to the girl he had denied loving, denied feelings for, denied his claim.

Because love made him weak.

But before he was able to grab hold of the bond, the assassin moved. With a clean, arcing strike, he slashed his blade across Caelum's chest.

A jolt yanked Deya from her terrified reverie as the door to her bedroom rattled with the force of another blow.

Gasping, Deya grabbed at her chest, her heart quickening.

For a moment it had felt like *something* had grabbed hold of the bond. She seized hold of the line again and yanked on it, just as she had done over a dozen times since the nyraxi had trapped her in the room.

Caelum . . . Caelum, help! Bridah is under attack! Bridah is under attack!

But there was no answer. The bond was silent.

With a shriek of frustration, Deya sank to the floor, her eyes burning with tears. From outside, she could hear the obvious sounds of screaming. The castle was no longer silent. Shouting, banging, the sounds of an obvious scuffle . . . and the screams. The screams filled Deya's ears, making her freeze on the floor, her hands clasped over her head, trying to block it out.

Angry tears fell from her eyes, her fingers digging into her scalp, willing the screams to stop, willing it all to be a bad dream.

You're safe, you're safe, you're safe.

But was she ever really safe? After months of convincing herself Praiton, Ironbalt, and even Clarita were all a bad dream, her body had never forgotten how it felt to be at their mercy. Every flinch, every tremor, every freezing, fitful moment where she found herself locked in perpetual indecision . . .

It was a curse. A curse without measurable form yet still plaguing her as surely as the blackness engulfing her hands. She would never be free of Praiton, would never be free of the wretched *softness* that had left her open to them in the first place.

And as the sound of pain and death reverberated through the wooden halls of the place that had opened its arms to her, protected her . . . *accepted* her, she struggled to swallow the cold, jagged truth.

That Bridah was under attack because they were coming for *her*.

Deya's tears slowed, and she looked down at her blackened hands, as though she was seeing them for the first time. Her breath coming out in ragged gasps, she held her hands to the light.

The blackness was halfway to her knuckles now, as if she had donned half a glove. Slowly, she squeezed her hand into a fist.

What did she fear? Why was she scared of this?

There is a darkness in you, Dodsbringern.

Was she afraid of that? Was she scared to be powerful like her friends—to be strong like Caelum, courageous like Val, decisive like Rayner. Would any of them hesitate to join the fray outside? Would any of them cower on the floor like this while people died on the other side of the door?

Deya drew in another jagged breath. Tears still glistened on her face as she slowly rose from the floor and began to push back the heavy armoire from the door.

She told herself she wasn't scared. As she pushed back the wardrobe and faced the door, she told herself that the darkness should not scare her. Especially if she used it to save others. She thought of Caelum then—at the way his gaze would harden when he looked at her prophecy and what he would say if he saw her hands. With a deep breath, she pushed open the door.

The nyraxi were gone, but commotion still echoed down the hall. Howling and snarling, tearing and shrieking . . . The nyraxi had found a new, more available target.

Deya began to run, her feet soundless as she flew down the hall. The thought of Luc flashed through her mind. Maybe if she could make it to his room downstairs, they could get out of here together. But first, she had to find a sword, had to find something that wasn't the dark magic within her to defend Fangdor.

A soldier—dressed in a familiar green cloak—barreled around the corner. Deya screamed, her feet skittering to a stop, attempting to turn back as his sword narrowly missed her.

"*She's here!*" he yelled. Deya gasped and ducked as his blade swung over her head. She danced past him, barely catching her balance before she took off around the bend of the hall. Her feet flew over stains of blood and bodies of servants, her chest aching with each corpse she passed. The wooden walls streaked with blood blurred in her vision as she sprinted down the echoing halls.

Careening around a corner, she crashed into a small end table underneath a set of decorative Bridanian swords. Not pausing to think, Deya ripped the sword from the wall, just in time for the soldier to round the bend and for Deya to thrust the blade into his neck.

The sword was blunt, but just sharp enough to pierce into the soldier's soft flesh. For a moment, he stood in front of her, his mouth gaping in surprise, before he collapsed in a pile at her feet.

Panting, Deya gazed down at him, her eyes roving the body. The familiar silver pin glinted up at her, splattered with blood, and Deya froze, fear locking her muscles into place.

The Silver Daggers. *Here? Of all places?*

But she was barely able to wrap her head around what it meant when footsteps thundered towards her. When she looked up, it was not only the Silver Daggers that were headed her way, but soldiers in red armor. Blood red, with pointed pauldrons and spiked helmets. Red hair and tanned skin.

Deya's blood ran cold.

Manielians.

A jet of fire streaked towards her and Deya screamed, rolling to the ground, her sleeve aflame. Swearing, she attempted to stamp it out, but the soldiers advanced on her as she scrambled to her feet, holding the Bridanian sword. The blade was shorter, blunter and heavier than she was used to. It felt awkward in her hands, and when an assassin whirled his blade around her, she struggled to keep up.

Knocking the blade free of an assassin's hand, Deya stabbed

outwards, impaling the male in front of her. It caught in his chest, and, as she struggled to pull it free, the Manielian converged on her. The slash of his blade was too quick for her to fully evade. She dove aside, but the flash of silver sliced into her arm. With a scream and a shower of blood, Deya fell to the floor.

"Give up, girl," the Manielian panted. "Just go quietly and you may still live."

Shoulder aching, Deya crawled across the floor to the other fallen red soldier, reaching desperately for his sword. Seizing it by its gilded hilt, Deya jumped to her feet just in time to dodge another blow before, with a yell, she slashed the blade across the only unprotected part of the red armor charging towards her—his face.

The soldier fell to the ground with a bone-chilling scream, and Deya flicked blood from her eyes, panting. The scream held her in place, her hands on her knees, the violent noise jarring her. She never thought she'd ever get used to taking a life. Yet why had she not stopped to realize it had gotten easier?

Her hand tightened on the Manielian's sword. Looking down at it, she noticed the gold hilt and an emblem of a dragon. If the insignia was any indication, this was not the normal Manielian army. But she wasn't allowed a moment to ponder this before the sounds of screams filled the hall.

Without thinking, Deya ran towards it.

Bodies were everywhere. Servants and cooks, priestesses and soldiers. Her chest was tight as she looked down at the faces—faces she vaguely recognized. People who had smiled and greeted her. People who had helped her and waited on her.

Tears burned in her eyes as she moved through the hall. Blood stained the crystal floor and as Deya skittered down the stairs leading to the entrance hall, she stopped.

On the steps leading towards the lower floor, a small body lay in a pool of its own blood. For a moment, Deya felt like she was falling down a long dark hole as she looked at the head of white hair now stained red. The hallway seemed to shrink, squeezing in around her until there was nothing left but the heartbeat in her ears, the tears in her eyes . . . and Niel's body on the floor.

"*Niel*," she whispered. The small boy clutched a sword in his limp hand, as if he had tried to fight. Deya made to move towards him, but found her feet could not move. Instinctively, she reached for her Healing Magic but found only darkness. As she got closer, though, she could see the young boy was far from what her Healing Magic—even at its strongest—could help with.

Deya choked on a cry, clapping a hand over her mouth. But she had to keep moving. Sounds of battle and blood were still raging down the hall and, with a small sob, Deya hurried past Niel's body, saying a silent prayer to a goddess that wasn't hers to guide his spirit to safety.

And as she ran down the steps, something else was welling in her chest, pushing past the pain and the fear. It was angry and black, overwhelming and powerful—a dark wave churning inside of her, clouding her vision and all thoughts. So, when a group of soldiers ran into her path again, there was nothing left of the terror that had paralyzed her before.

Her lips curled back into a snarl. Then she lunged for them.

Her stolen sword tore at their bodies, the scarlet armor and green cloaks of her enemies melting into the wave of fury that was churning in her. And all the while, the dark magic bubbled up inside. A pot about to boil over, a dam about to burst—a monster she could not control.

Deya battled her way down the stairs, sword flashing, rage pounding in her temples. The Silver Daggers were harder to deal with than the Manielian soldiers. Small daggers slashed her, overwhelmed her, the fire of the Manielians causing her to dive for cover, scorching her exposed skin.

All she could think of was getting to Luc, finding help, finding *someone* who wasn't dead . . . and the image of Niel's body dripped through her mind like the blood falling into her eyes.

Deya bounded down the stairs, dodging a Silver Dagger, and slashing for a Manielian soldier, before careening into the hall of the lower floor. She could smell smoke hanging heavily in the air. It was beginning to fill the wooden halls, and the telltale heat of fire was starting to rise to the upper floors. Luc's room was only a little further down the corridor—

A yell jerked her focus from the empty hallway. It had come from the opposite end of the hall, across the landing. And that's when Deya heard the snarling.

As if out of instinct, her feet began to move. Faster and faster, she flew towards the shadowy black creature gripping someone's leg in its fanged mouth. With a scream, she sliced the head off the attacking nyraxi, sending it spinning into the air, and soaking a trembling Luc with its putrid black blood.

Panting, Deya kicked the body aside, staggering slightly under her own fear and adrenaline, before she gazed down at her old friend. For a moment, she and Luc just looked at each other. Then, Luc sprang to his feet and seized her in a hug so tight it knocked the air from her lungs.

"You're okay . . . Shit, Dey, I'm so glad—"

"I'm okay, I'm okay," Deya panted, and for a second, she clung to Luc and tried to hold the pieces of her breaking heart together. She couldn't stop—if she let herself stop to think about what was happening, she'd break. Already, the lump rising in her throat as she crushed Luc to her—as if the pressure of his body on hers could suffocate the ache in her ribcage—was beginning to overwhelm her. Pulling back, she rallied herself.

"We have to keep going. We have to find Kindra and get out of here—"

"What about Karyna?" Luc asked. "She sleeps on the first floor with the rest of the servants. Where did they all come from? Was it from the first floor?"

Deya thought of Niel and swallowed the tears that threatened to spill. "We'll find her," Deya said. She reached down and seized Luc's hand. "How's your leg?"

Luc looked down at his bloody leg but shook his head. "I'm fine. It didn't get me too bad."

Deya released a breath, relieved and nodded. "Do you have a sword?"

Hesitating, Luc looked around before spotting a dead soldier further down the landing. Hurrying to the corpse, he picked up the sword and returned to her side. "I'm not much of a fighter," he whispered. His brown eyes were wide and frantic, face still flecked with black splatters of nyraxi blood. "But I'll try my best."

Deya gripped the hilt of her sword, her knuckles whitening. "I have your back."

Luc stared at her before giving her a grim smile. "I know. I have yours too."

They began to move down the landing, back-to-back, swords raised. Smoke was filling the air, stinging Deya's eyes, making it difficult to see. Someone had lit the lower levels on fire. As they descended, she could hear the crackle of flames, see flickers of bright orange light.

A shadow moved to Deya's right and she whirled just in time as a nyraxi came barreling towards her only to be met with Luc's blade. But as they reached the entrance hall, it was to find the source of the flames, and the center of the battle. Berserkers had most of the Silver Daggers and Manielian forces locked in combat within the entry and great halls. All around them, frost and fire battled, axes and swords flashing.

"This way!" Luc cried, and using the chaos of the battle as cover, he seized Deya's wrist and began to run with her, through the fray, towards a side hall that Deya had never been down. The minute they crossed the threshold, Luc froze, Deya nearly crashing into him.

"What is it?" Deya asked but Luc had gone white as a sheet. Blinking she turned, following his gaze. Through the smoke and sparks, several soldiers were standing over a body, laughing. They were passing it back and forth like a rag doll, before a red armored soldier dumped it to the ground, pulling a bloodied sword loose from its small frame.

All the air seemed to leave Deya's lungs. The same falling sensation swooped through her stomach, the edges of her vision beginning to grow red, and then black. Blood was pounding in her ears, crowding her eyes, ringing in her head.

As if in a trance, she stepped forward.

Breathing hard, her fingers began to twitch. Her heart was pounding, and all she could see was black . . . All she could feel was the churn and bubble of the power inside of her, banging its deadly fists against her chest, begging to be let out.

And as Deya gazed down at Karyna's bloodied and broken corpse, something inside of her quietly snapped.

Deya reached into her core, pushing aside the trapped Healing Magic and the now useless string tying her to Caelum—shoved all of it away without a thought before seizing the leash holding back the cloud of death.

Then she ripped the door off her power.

A dark wave rippled across the room, and a tide of destruction erupted from her. The soldiers looked up just as the blast overtook them. They screamed; some dove out of the way but Deya's lip curled into a snarl, her fingers twisting as she forced the wave towards them.

Careful to avoid Karyna's body, she stalked towards the soldiers who fled from her, scrambling like rats for shelter, but she did not let up. She reveled in watching them cry and flee, reveled in watching as her magic devoured them—a tornado of decay reducing them to dust before her very eyes.

"Deya!"

Somewhere behind her, Luc was shouting her name, but she could barely hear him over the roar of her own power, the screaming in her head, the thrill of watching them disintegrate before her, of watching them beg for mercy . . .

One of the soldiers who had run from her fell, tripping over the corpse of another innocent. Frantically, he turned, watching as Deya stormed towards him, hand outstretched.

"*No!* No, please!" he screamed, but Deya raised her hand. Her fingers curled, and she was only vaguely aware of the blackness—vaguely aware of it spreading up her hands, spiraling upwards like veins. She only wanted to watch as the screams of the soldier melted with his body, turning into ash on the wind—

"Deya! Stop!"

Hands seized her, and Deya whirled around, snarling, her hand snapping forward and closing tightly around the windpipe of the person who had touched her.

It was Luc.

Her friend's eyes widened, his hands coming to scrabble at her black fingers, but Deya could barely see him through the haze of blackness, barely feel his resistance through the wave of death churning in her.

"*Stop!* Deya, *stop!* It's me! It's Luc! You can control this! Please, stop!"

Her fingers twitched across his throat, a black nail scraping against his jugular. She watched as the skin died under her touch. Luc let out a blood curdling scream, and it was as if someone had lifted a curtain in her mind.

Deya blinked. The blackness clouding her vision cleared, and terrified brown eyes looked back at her, his face turned gray with fear and . . . and . . .

At that moment, her power gave an almighty jerk, as if wanting more, *needing* more. With a panicked yelp, Deya shoved as hard as she could against the blackness rippling from her body, and ripped her hand from Luc's neck, before slamming the darkness back into its cage.

And then everything was quiet.

Deya hit the ground with a gasp of tears, blinking back into her body, into herself. Where snow once fell from the rafters, now only ashes swirled down around them. The entire hallway was covered in the ashes of the bodies she had decimated. Only she, Luc, and Karyna remained intact.

Luc stood, swaying, his hands still clutching his throat, gasping for breath. Even from the floor, Deya could see a thin line of blackened skin where her nail had pierced him.

"Luc . . . I'm so sorry. I don't know what—"

But Luc shook his head, his back hitting the wall as he quieted his breathing. "It's okay. I'm okay."

But his reassurance did nothing to dull her horror. Dazed, Deya looked down at her hands. The blackness was no longer confined to her fingers, but now reached her palms, spiraling up the back of her hands, creeping towards her forearms. Slowly, she looked up at Luc, who was now staring down at her, horror on his face. It was the expression she had always feared her friends wearing when they looked at her.

"I—" she began, but her apology was interrupted by the sounds of running footsteps. A burly Berserker tore into the hall, his boots slipping on the thick layer of cinders that now carpeted the floor. It took Deya a second to recognize that it was Espen. His face was covered in blood and soot, and the large battleaxe in his hand was dripping red as he dropped it with a loud crash the minute he saw the body in the corner.

"No . . ." he breathed.

Deya rose, attempting to pull down the sleeves of her tunic. "Espen—"

"*No!*" Espen yelled and his voice broke. He ran to his sister, throwing himself down in front of her, gathering her broken and bloodied body into his arms. Tears fell from his eyes, and Deya and Luc stood and watched the Berserker who seemed too big to be broken collapse in front of them.

He looked up, catching sight of Luc and Deya for what seemed like the first time.

"You," he whispered to Luc, his voice cracking. "You are a healer. Fix her. Please."

Luc's chin wobbled and Deya bit back her own tears as Luc shook his head. "I don't think—"

"*Please!*" Espen roared, his shattered sob making both of them flinch. Espen closed his eyes, his grip tightening on Karyna's body as he drew in a deep, rattling breath. When he looked back up at them, it was with the look of someone who had lost everything.

"Please," he said again, quieter this time. "Please . . . try."

Luc and Deya moved towards him and the small, shattered body he held. Cradled in Espen's arms, Karyna looked even smaller than she was in life. She and Luc both knelt to the ground and Espen opened his arms just wide enough for Deya to look at her. She choked on the sob, but it splintered out of her before she could stop it.

Karyna's white hair was stained red—just as Niel's was—and her blue gown was soaked with her own blood. Her icy eyes were still open, staring up at the ceiling, unseeing.

Beside her, Luc's hand shook, tears filling his own eyes as he placed his palm on Karyna's chest. He closed his eyes as his hand began to glow, his brow furrowing before he flinched backwards. Tears spilled down his face, and, with a shaky jerk of his head, he pulled back.

Karyna did not move.

"I can't . . ." Luc rasped; his voice thick with tears. "I can't. Espen . . . She's gone. I'm sorry—"

But Espen had fallen silent. He gathered his sister tighter in his arms, cradling the back of her head into his shoulder. He held her as if he could still protect her from what had already befallen her, as if he could singlehandedly stop her spirit from leaving this world.

At that moment, Karyna's story she had told Deya the night before drifted back to her mind, and she found herself wondering if Espen had held his little sister like this the night they had fled their village. The night he had saved his siblings . . . just the same as now on the night he had lost them both.

"Go," Espen said, his voice ragged yet soft. "Go. Leave me."

Deya felt Luc rise from beside her, but she found she could not move. Karyna's head sagged over Espen's shoulder, and Deya stared into the empty ice blue eyes, feeling like the world was melting away from underneath her. As she stared into her friend's vacant face, she wondered how much death and tragedy she would have to face before it took its permanent toll. At that moment, she felt the pain like water running over a stone. It smoothed over her sides, washed over her vision, until it was nothing but numb and cold.

Karyna's bloody face became Oswallt's. And then became nothing at all.

Reaching out, Deya laid her blackened fingers over her friend's eyes. Gently, she shut them forever.

Deya stood and, without another word to Espen, she and Luc headed back into the fray.

"Hang on a minute," Luc said, grabbing Deya and stopping her. "Are you okay? I . . . I've never seen you like that before."

The battle raged on just on the other side of the threshold, and Deya felt like she was walking through a hazy dream. She had lost control. Lost control of her power . . . of *herself*. For a moment, it had felt as if something dark and sinister had sunk its claws into her and had refused to let go. Seeing her friend in that state . . . The lump of tears for Karyna felt lodged in her throat and her chest ached with the pain of a million losses, but she couldn't focus on it now.

"I'm fine," Deya said, still not looking at him. "We don't have time. We *have* to find Kindra."

Luc watched her for a second, as if he wanted to argue, his finger still running down the black mark on his neck. Then, he nodded. "I think most of the Berserkers are fighting in the courtyard. She might be there."

With a deep breath, they turned towards the entrance to the hall, before running back into the fight. They were immediately besieged with a wave of flames blasted their way by a group of Manielian soldiers. Ducking and weaving, Deya and Luc lowered their heads and barreled through the battle.

It didn't take long to find Kindra. The Frost Princess was standing at the foot of the stairs leading to the battlements. She was whirling her battleaxe with the precision of an executioner, frost exploding in a wave, freezing all those who challenged her, before the axe broke them into an explosion of ice. For a moment, Deya was reminded of Caelum, how he had shattered the Praiton general at Burningtide the same way, and wondered if this was a strength only the royal family had.

Kindra's ice blue eyes landed on them as they sprinted towards her. "Kindra!"

The Frost Princess swung her axe over her head, forcing Luc and Deya to dive to the ground as she knocked a green cloaked assassin they hadn't noticed clean off his feet.

"What are you doing out here?" Kindra demanded. Frost had crept up her face, sealing in her sharp features with crystalline patches of hard diamond. "Don't you know they are looking for *you?*"

"Where is Ulf?" Deya cried, ducking again as a jet of fire rocketed past them. "We can't possibly fend them all off without him!"

Kindra snarled and, with a whirl of her axe, a large glacial wall erupted around them, shielding them from the battle. Hurrying towards them, Kindra shoved two thin sticks into Deya's hands.

"Listen to me," she hissed. "They mean to dismantle us, as they always do. The dragon fire, all the flames, Fangdor burning . . . It strengthens them and puts us at a severe disadvantage." She swore and frost exploded from her, intercepting a jet of fire that had arced over the glacial wall she had created. Bending back towards them, she spoke quickly. "*Faor* is away, deep within the mountains across our land and I do not know if he has even received our news. The highest point of Fangdor is the outlook tower located in the west wing, as high as you can go. Get to it and set off these flares. It is the only way to contact him and the Legion now."

Deya stared at her, paralyzed as her cold, black hands clenched the flares, her heart pounding.

"*Go!*" Kindra roared, and with that, the glacial wall surrounding them exploded. Icicles shot out like daggers, wiping out the green cloaks and red-armored assailants around them. Seizing Luc's hand, Deya pelted back towards the castle.

They ran through the entrance hall and towards the grand staircase, darting between Berserkers, Silver Daggers, and Manielian soldiers. Frost and fire flew over their heads, swords clashed, and sparks flew, but Deya could only focus on putting one foot after another and clutching the flares so tight she worried they'd snap in two.

"Where's the west wing?" Luc cried. He seized Deya around the middle, spinning her out of harm's way as a nyraxi went tearing by. Deya stabbed at it, sending it snarling over the railing of the staircase.

Deya pointed to her left, and they both turned and sprinted up the stairs and down an empty corridor. The sounds of the battle fell away and only their heavy breathing filled the air around them. Bodies cluttered the hall, but the fighting had moved to the lower floors. Or so Deya thought.

Rounding the corner, Deya spotted the door leading to the stairwell. Picking up speed, they began to dash down the hall before, suddenly a large blast of heat roared over them. Deya screamed and Luc yelled. Fire engulfed them—a wave so hot the flames were white as pure light. It knocked them both to the ground, Deya thrashing, attempting to stamp out the flames still clinging to her clothes.

"Well, well, well, look what I've found." A tall figure was walking down the hall towards them. His gait was a swagger, long, tanned limbs swinging loosely while he twirled a small golden dagger between his fingers. But he was not in red armor nor a green cloak. Instead, he wore the uniform of the Bridanian servants. Reaching up, he unwrapped a familiar scarf twisted around his head, obscuring his features. The scarf fell to the floor, revealing shaggy, dark red hair, slightly manic amber eyes, and a gruesome scar that twisted up the right corner of his mouth, giving him a lopsided, terrifying sneer.

Deya's fingers tightened on the flares in her now burned hands as she dragged herself backwards, away from the male. From beside her, Luc was struggling to rise, his hands grabbing at Deya's clothes, trying to pull her up.

There was something familiar about this male . . . something she couldn't quite place. But what she *did* know was the hallway had gotten considerably warmer since he had entered—so warm that sweat was beginning to bead around her collar and hairline.

Luc and Deya staggered to their feet, gripping each other. Deya's legs were itching to run, and from the way Luc clutched her sleeve, she knew he understood her intent.

The male smiled, bringing the left side of his mouth equal with the scarred right as he let out a wheezing giggle.

"Are you going to run?" he breathed. "I love it when they run."

Deya seized Luc by the sleeve, their feet moving backwards in tandem.

The male's smile stretched even wider, until his scarred mouth resembled a scarecrow's grin. "Run little, rabbits. *Run.*"

Deya and Luc whirled around and ran as fast as they could towards the stairs just as a jet of white-hot flames enveloped the hall.

CHAPTER 26

Val had spent weeks researching dragons and Mount Cinis, desperately trying to learn how to possibly claim one. Every book she had come across had been fairly vague on exactly how to win a dragon over. Only one book had mentioned something called *Verís Ignis*. Val had known this to mean Trial by Fire in Materín, but no text had expounded on it further.

But as Val knelt in front of the battered female dragon in front of her and watched as it opened its enormous mouth, she suddenly understood.

The fire glowed deep within the dragon's throat, then, with an almighty roar, fire exploded from its gaping maw.

Then everything went white.

It was pain as Val had never felt before. Her skin felt like it was peeling from her body, her screams melting with the leather of her armor and the steel of her belt and buckles. Light overwhelmed her, swallowed her, wrapped its fiery arms around her neck and threatened to pull her under. For a moment, as Val's vision blurred and everything in her body threatened to collapse, she saw a pair of golden eyes glaring at her through the inferno.

And her own flame roared to life.

It was as if something inside of her had fortified itself against the fire. The pain lessened as Val concentrated with all her might, fighting back against the pain, against the scorching flames, against the memories that had terrorized her, the grief that had bound her.

As if it sensed this, the dragon's fire seemed to lessen. Even though she felt faint, Val found herself wondering if the dragon was holding back—wondered if it had been, all along.

Just as Val felt as if she was going to burst, the fire stopped.

She crashed onto the hard, black rock of the cave floor, limp and flaming. Gasping for breath, her skin ached with the flames still rising from what was left of her clothes. With all the strength she could muster, she lifted her head.

Through the haze of her vision, a large dark shadow moved. Heavy footfalls thumped towards her, and Val could hear the snuffling sounds of the dragon breathing her in. A strong gust of warm air washed over her like a gentle caress against her burnt skin and shivers rolled down her spine. Blindly, Val reached out a hand, as if to shield herself from what was to come.

Would it eat her? Attack her? She had barely survived the blast of fire—the blast she knew had been her true test. But she was still here . . . still alive.

Val's hand reached into the empty air, and for a second, it hung there before a hot, scaly nose pressed against it. Starting, Val looked up, blinking back the fog.

The dragon had leaned into her palm, its golden eyes staring at her, unblinking in the darkness. The look in its glowing yellow orbs was appraising. It was mad to think that, even without a word, the dragon could say so much with just a look.

Slowly, Val dragged her elbows underneath her. Pushing herself to her feet, she stood on shaking legs. Her knees buckled and she staggered but the dragon pushed forward, catching her with the weight of its large head. Surprised, Val pulled back and stared down at the dragon she was now *touching*, leaning on as if it were a support rather than an enormous beast that could incinerate her with a single breath.

Sharp, golden eyes peered back at her, and its wings fluttered instinctively. A ripple of pain flashed through the dragon's eyes and Val glanced back at the large golden spear pierced through the thin skin of its fluttering wings.

"How did this happen?" she murmured, mostly to herself. But the dragon blinked slowly, as though trying to speak to her. It jerked its head, its tail coming around to nudge her gently.

Getting the hint, Val moved around the dragon's enormous flank, her hand trailing across its scaly body. It was so hot that steam rose from it, its scales thick and sharp, glistening and shifting colors in the dim light. When she reached the spear, it was to find it wasn't a spear at all, but a glaive. Its curved, golden hilt twinkled in the light, the carvings intricate and ornate. Val traced a finger over it, recognizing the obvious signs of Manielian royalty, her touch lingering on the engraving of a phoenix etched into the solid gold.

She did not know who, but someone must have come here and attempted to conquer the female dragon. And something told Val that the dragon had not held back for its owner, like it had for Val.

Seizing the hilt of the glaive, she slowly began to pull it free from the dragon's wings. The dragon roared in pain, bucking as the sharp blade gave way, tearing anew into the skin.

Val hissed through her teeth, feeling its pain as if it were her own.

"It's okay . . . It's okay. I got it—"

With a quick pull, Val ripped the glaive free, and the dragon screamed in pain. Dark red blood splattered her as the dragon spread its wings and roared in agony.

"I'm sorry!" she whispered, grabbing for a shred of her own singed clothing and attempting to dab at the wound. "I'm sorry, but it was the only way! It can heal now, though."

The dragon let out a pained snort, its head jerking. But Val knew it understood.

"Right," she said, and, without thinking, she strapped the bloodstained glaive to her back. Laying a hand on the dragon's head, she looked into its eyes. "Can you come with me? Can we leave here?"

The dragon stared at her, its golden gaze cool. It did not make any indication it agreed, and Val found herself getting frustrated. Time was short. She had to get back to Bridah quickly . . . preferably with a dragon.

"Come *on*, didn't I pass your test?" Val demanded. "Aren't you supposed to be mine or something?"

The dragon gave an indignant snort, hot air coming out of its large nostrils, singeing her slightly. Val cursed.

"Well, if you were only hoping I'd get that glaive out of you, then fine. Let me go find another dragon then—" But the words felt childish. She knew she would not survive the fire from the bulls. Even this dragon had held back—she knew it as surely as anything. If it hadn't, she would've perished just the same.

She hadn't chosen this dragon. This dragon had chosen *her*.

The dragon's large tail whipped forward before jerking backwards into the cave.

"What is it?"

Val leaned around it, following the direction the tail pointed. Moving around the large body, Val walked back towards the pile of bones, peering into the nest it had left, and gasped.

Nestled beneath the mountain of white bones were two large eggs. They were smooth and glossy, their shells a dark tortoise color. Both eggs trembled slightly, smoking like the dragon's hide.

Whirling around, Val looked at the dragon. It stared back with that same, impassive gaze.

"These are yours?"

The dragon didn't move, but Val could almost hear the answer in her head. She reached for the eggs but was stopped by a large, spiked tail thrashing towards her. Val ducked, narrowly missing being bludgeoned with it.

"Are you kidding me?" Val snapped, rounding on the dragon who gave an irate roar, its tail wrapping protectively around the two eggs. "Do you want to go or not? We can take the eggs. I promise I'll take care of them."

The dragon glared at her, its nostrils flaring. Its large haunches rose and fell with its massive breaths, and Val stood and stared it down.

"Do you really want to stay here being beat up by that lot for the rest of your life?" she asked softly. "Take it from someone who knows . . . It's no way to live."

It stared at her, unmoving. Then, its large body seemed to relax. Slowly, its tail unfurled from around the eggs, and with a jerk of its head, it lowered its body to the ground. Val recognized the acquiescence.

"Thank you," she whispered. Moving towards the eggs, she lifted them gently from the nest. They were heavy and hot—almost too hot to hold with her bare hands. Dragon eggs were rare, and not much was documented on them. Even as she hefted them into her hands, she felt like she was holding something more valuable than all the gold in the realm.

Unsnapping her satchel—which was scorched in places but had avoided most of the dragon's fire when she had dropped it at the cave's entrance—she carefully loaded both eggs inside, feeling the weight of them sag against her shoulder.

She walked back to the entrance of the cave to stand beside the dragon, looking out of the narrow opening into the black, fiery valley of Mount Cinis. Dragons circled the cave, the large bulls lurking around its opening, flapping their enormous wings and pacing in a restless movement in front of the entrance.

Waiting.

"They're going to try and stop us, aren't they," Val whispered. It wasn't a question. She could taste their thirst for blood.

The dragon flexed its wings beside her. Blood still dripped from the wound, but when it turned its golden eyes towards her again, it was with a different expression.

A grateful one.

"Do you have a name?" Val asked her.

The dragon tossed its head. Val took it to mean *no*.

"Would you like me to name you?"

She blinked at her softly and nudged her arm with her nose. Val smiled. She remembered, in all her readings, someone mentioning that Materín, Maniel's ancient language, was the tongue of dragons. It was the reason each child born into nobility was gifted with a Materín name as well as a common one. And as Val looked into those familiar golden eyes, one came to mind.

"*Lucéria,*" Val whispered. "Your name is *Lucéria.*"

The dragon did not react. Instead, she bent her legs, lowering her head down to her, and Val realized what she was doing. Gingerly, she clambered onto the dragon's broad back. The scales scraped her legs, and the heat of her body warmed her immediately. Careful to place the satchel with the eggs securely between her body and Lucéria's neck, she struggled to get comfortable and find a firm place to hold on.

"Can you fly?" she asked in Lucéria's ear. She grunted and flapped her wings, as if anxious to do so. "Right," Val said and, without thinking, she whispered the word in Materín. "*Laos.*"

Fly.

At the word, Lucéria let out a roar and, with a jolt, launched herself out of the cave. Val screamed as the dragon crashed through the cave's entrance, sending chunks of rock flying. She grabbed hold of the dragon's neck as they lurched out into the open. The minute they cleared the entrance, the circling bulls reacted.

They swarmed them.

All around her, a chorus of screeches and roars bombarded them. The bulls dove for Lucéria, their sharp talons snapping at Val, tearing at her skin, ripping at her clothes. Val screamed and sent a blast of fire at them, but the dragons flew through it like it was nothing more than an errant breeze.

Lucéria screeched, her shredded wings flapping desperately as she ran on her two feet, attempting to gain speed. The bulls blew fire, scorching both Val and her steed, threatening to drown them.

"*Laos, Lucéria! Laos!*" Val screamed.

Then finally, with a tremendous roar, Lucéria's legs lifted from the ground. And they were off.

The dragon tilted and fell, struggling to remain airborne. Her tattered wings beat a desperate rhythm, taking them up, up, into the bands of dark smoke, over the black mountain, its sparks and lava shooting from below.

The bulls followed, roaring after them, refusing to let their brood leave the nest. Val could feel Lucéria's desperation, feel it in the frantic beating of her wings as she dipped and fell, as though fighting with the air.

Val turned where she sat, still clinging to the dragon's scales, and pulled the glaive from her back. She whirled it over her head, sending fire sling-shotting from it. The bend and give of the glaive contorted her flames, letting it curve like a fiery wheel as she sent it spinning towards the bulls.

The great beast underneath her was grunting with the effort to keep airborne as they cleared the volcanic valley. Val cradled the satchel containing the eggs, still swinging the glaive at the bulls overhead, screaming if they happened to get too close.

The dragons snapped at Lucéria's feet, tearing into chunks of the already scarred body. Val screamed at them and kicked her foot down, but it was no use.

Just as they cleared the range of mountains bordering Maniel and Zulon—so close to being free of the volcano that Val could smell the cool, fresh air—a dark shadow fell over them. Val froze, looking up slowly, her knuckles turning white as she gripped Lucéria's ridged back.

A dragon loomed above them. It was bigger than any she had seen in the valley, bigger than any she could have possibly imagined. It filled the sky, blocking all sun and light with its enormous body. Ancient and weather-beaten, its immense black wings beat in the air, knocking Lucéria down a foot with each flap.

When Val looked up at it—stared right into its bright red eyes—the same eerie sense of understanding crossed her mind, as if, somehow, this dragon knew what she was doing.

She was stealing its property. And it would not stand for it.

"*GO!*" Val roared and she dug her heels into Lucéria's side. The female dragon let out a tree-rattling roar, and sped up, but it was too late. She was too small compared to this monster, too small to defeat it . . . and too small to outrun it.

As they sped away, Lucéria's wings beating raggedly, blood from both their wounds fell through the air like scarlet rain. When the bull opened its mouth, Val knew it was no use.

The fireball welled in slow motion within the dragon's throat. The light blinded her before, with an almighty roar, the bull released an explosion of blinding flame. But just as the fire was about to overtake them, Lucéria turned, flipping in midair before she wrapped her wings around Val.

The fire blasted them, Val screaming as the wave of flame washed over them, but Lucéria's tattered wings protected her from the worst of it. They plummeted from the sky, Val clutching the two eggs to her chest, the smell of smoke hot in her nose, fire in her hair.

And they fell.

Down, down, down before crashing, hard into the desert ground.

CHAPTER 27

Deya sprinted towards the stairs, dragging Luc behind her as a jet of white-hot flames shot towards them. Tripping over the first step, they tumbled up the landing and began to run, taking the steps two at a time. From behind them, the red-haired male cackled, not even bothering to chase after them.

"Who is this guy?" Luc cried, panting as he stumbled up yet another step.

Deya shook her head, struggling to breathe through the stitch in her side. "I don't know. Is he even following—" But before she could finish the sentence, flames raced towards them, chasing their heels up the steps, filling the narrow stairwell. Deya screamed and sped up, the white flames licking her heels.

And then it hit her.

White flames. There was only one Manielian family capable of producing white flames. She had seen it over and over again within the Hearth House. Suddenly, the blood-red armor made sense.

This wasn't just any Manielian specialty unit.

These were the Blood Riders.

Deya and Luc cleared the landing, collapsing onto the wooden floor, coughing up smoke, their clothes flaming. A laugh echoed from below.

"That's right . . . Smoke out the rabbits! Don't give up, vermin! Keep going."

"He's absolutely fucking raving," Luc spluttered, but Deya was barely listening. Seizing Luc by the collar, she dragged him to his feet and took off running again.

If this was who she thought it was, there would be no winning against him. Val had not told her much that day in the ice cave, but she knew enough to guess that this was Val's brother. Leo. The one who had killed Val's sisters. The one who had *enjoyed* it.

The unhinged laughter followed them up the steps, a sinister sound that made Deya's skin crawl. Fire blasted up the cavern again, and this time, Deya and Luc didn't outrun it. Flames washed over them, making them cry out in pain. With a yell, Deya threw herself up the last flight of stairs, desperately holding the flares out of the way. If they ignited, they would be doomed.

"Did I get you?" The wheezing voice was getting closer. The slow *thud, thud* of his footsteps up the stairs echoed off the walls as Deya and Luc scrambled to their feet, gasping in pain. "Don't tell me you're giving up already? We were just starting to have some fun."

Luc was groaning, his hands and face bright red with blisters. Deya could feel her own raw, aching skin as she struggled to her feet. She looked up at the stairs, desperately trying to remember how far they had already climbed, how much farther there was to go—

"Dey, listen. You go," Luc said, wincing as he turned to her. "I'll distract him. Just get to the top of the tower and send off the flares—"

"Are you kidding?" Deya panted. "I have a better chance than you! You wouldn't last a second against him."

Luc shook his head. "And neither would you."

Deya didn't reply. They both stood, panting in the hall, skin blistered and burnt. She knew Luc was right. The only thing she may be able to do was buy him time to reach the top of the tower. But she knew she would not last against Leo in a sword fight. And as for her power . . .

The thin black line across Luc's neck was still visible even underneath the redness of his burned skin. The magic inside of her felt like it had reluctantly retreated, but it still sat, boiling at the surface. She was too afraid to unleash it again, too afraid that the same, dark hold that had dug its claws into her downstairs would do so again.

If she faced Leo, she'd have to do it without magic.

The sounds of Leo's footsteps drew nearer and, before Deya could open her mouth, Luc seized her hands.

"*Go.* I'll hold him off. *Go!*"

"Luc, no—"

"Dey." Luc clutched at her hands, his scorched and burnt face grim with determination as he gazed at her imploringly. "You and I both know you're worth ten of me," he whispered. "If they get you, we're all doomed. Please. Let me do this for you."

Deya stared at him, her heart hammering in her chest, the stone of tears that had been lodged in her throat since she had closed Karyna's eyes surging upwards again.

"*GO!*" Luc shouted again. And, with an almighty shove, he pushed her up the stairs.

Deya began to run, the tears she had held back starting to fall as she heard the faint sound of Leo rounding the corner, of Luc squaring off, of Leo's derisive laughter at the sight of Luc preparing to fight him.

Deya took the steps three at a time, throwing her weight up, feeling her knees scream in protest as she went. And all the while, she tried to block out the noises from below. Swords clanged, and she heard a pitiful yelping noise . . . and then the sounds of flame.

Pausing, Deya hesitated, wanting to turn back, but the heat building in the small landing was becoming unbearable. Sweat and blood dripped into her eyes and her heart ached as the sound of flames blended with

Luc's screams and Leo's laughs.

What was she doing? She couldn't leave him . . . couldn't lose him too.

Flames began to creep up the stairs and, with a choked sob, Deya tore herself from the step and began to climb again. This time, Leo's footsteps were faster. Luc had bought her time, but not much. She hurtled up each step, trying not to think about how she didn't know if Luc was alive or dead, thinking that the staircase might never end, until—

There. She could see it. Only three landings above, a large wooden door stood at the top of the stairs, waiting. Deya's sore, aching legs picked up speed, seizing their second wind, climbing faster and faster.

Something seized her by the ankle. Deya shrieked as she was pulled off her feet, the flares flying from her grip. A hot hand yanked her backwards, scorching the skin through her boot. Desperately, she threw her sword forward, slamming it into the wooden stairs. It wedged tight into the cracks, and she held onto it with all her strength, stopping her from being pulled down further.

A low laugh sounded from behind her, and Deya turned to see the leering face of Val's older brother looming through the flames, his hand clenched around her foot.

"You thought that runt would stop me?" he drawled. "His screams were *delicious* though."

His words hit her like a slap to the face, and a desperate, aching pain shot through her heart.

Luc. Was he okay? Did he kill him?

With a yell of fury, Deya struck out with her other foot, aiming right for Leo's face. The male ducked, but it was enough. She ripped the sword free of the step and whirled it around. Leo rolled to avoid the sword, releasing her long enough for Deya to sprint for the steps.

She scooped up the flares, wrapping them to her chest as she pelted, flat-out, towards the wooden door. Vaulting up the remaining stairs, she reached out a hand. Her fingers brushed the brass knob when, suddenly, she was slammed against it with a force so hard stars popped in her eyes.

Deya gasped, her vision going black as she crashed into the door. Blood flowed from her nose, and a sinister giggle tickled the hair at the back of her neck.

"Right," Leo wheezed. "Playtime's over, girly."

Deya spat blood from her mouth, watching it as it splattered onto the wood of the door. And then she was struggling under Leo's full weight pressing her into the wood. A glint of gold flashed out of the corner of her eye and Deya felt the tip of the sharp knife press into the side of her neck.

"Go on," Leo whispered in her ear. "Scream. No one will hear you. No one will come help." His wheezing giggle hid the sound of Deya's hands as they scrabbled over the wood of the door in front of her ... searching.

The tip of the knife pressed harder into her neck, and she let out a strangled scream that made Leo laugh excitedly.

"That's it, pretty girl. If we weren't told to keep you in one piece, I'd enjoy cutting you open to see if your blood is as black as that magic you have."

Deya's skin crawled. A cold fear was melting through her, like ice on hot stone.

"You're ... you're Val's brother," Deya gasped. She had to keep him talking. If he saw her hand searching for the door handle, she was done. Thankfully, Leo was much too interested in the jagged line he was carving into her neck, making her thrash.

"Oh, you've heard of me?" The knife cut into her skin a little deeper, and Deya bit her lip to swallow the scream. "Are you friends with my traitor sister, little girl?"

Deya's hand brushed the cool brass of the door latch.

"Yes."

The lopsided face cracked into a twisted smile. "Excellent. I love cutting her friends to bits."

At those words, fury bubbled up in Deya's stomach—a rage so hot that the black magic in her gave a vicious roar.

"*Fuck* you," Deya snarled, and she yanked, hard on the door latch.

The wood beneath her fell away, and she and Leo tumbled to the ground, crashing onto the stone parapet of Fangdor's outlook tower. Frigid cold air blasted over them as Deya rolled over the threshold, scrambling to her feet, juggling the flares in her hands. A hand grabbed her by the leg and fire exploded. Deya screamed and she careened back to the ground.

Flames billowing around him, Leo rose, the sounds of his manic laughing filling the cold air roaring around them. Deya scrambled on her hands and knees, attempting to outrun the ring of white flames that was beginning to encircle her, still cradling the flares protectively to her chest.

"Sneaky little thing, eh?" Leo drawled, still wheezing with delighted laughter. "Tell me, little girl. What do you think you're going to accomplish by coming up here?"

Deya could feel him stalking behind her as she struggled to her feet. A sharp blade pierced the back of her leg, and she fell screaming back to the ground.

"What was that?" The blade plunged even further, stabbing through muscle, and hitting bone, pinning Deya to the ground with a howl of anguish. "Can't hear you with all that noise."

Pain was blinding her, but even with the blood pouring from her nose and the feel of the dagger in the back of her leg, Deya dragged herself forward, digging her fingers into the layer of snow on the ground. She focused on the white flames flickering before her. Their hot waves melted into her vision, a beacon that she crawled towards, inch by agonizing inch.

"Are you going to pitch yourself into the fire?" Leo laughed, and a hand seized her by the collar. Deya screamed, the skin of her fingers tearing at snow as she attempted to cling to the frosty ground. She was hoisted clean off her feet, the flares falling from her hands and rolling away. Yelping, she tried to grab for them but was yanked up and held, dangling in the air, the knife still embedded in her leg.

Face to face with Leo, Deya took the moment to look at him—*really* look at him. Traces of Val were in every feature of his face. The shade of amber in his irises, the sharp slope of his cheekbones, the warm tan of his skin . . . there was no doubt who he was. And yet Deya saw nothing else of her friend in the fiend that held her up like a ragdoll. There was none of her warmth in his bloodthirsty eyes. None of her kindness and softness, none of her fire and light.

In another world, he may have even been handsome, but the twisted, crazed look in his eyes gave his features a terrifying, distorted effect.

He hoisted her into the air, and Deya tried to kick him, crying out when the dagger lodged in her leg sent a ripple of pain up the back of her thigh. Leo held her aloft, his other hand gripping her throat, and he licked his lips as he stared at the blackness on her hands.

"My, how interesting you are," he rasped, watching as her black fingers scrabbled at his hand, desperate to pry it loose. "No wonder they want you so bad. Gods, what I could do with you . . ." The softness of his voice and the way he looked at her made fear grip her insides. Lights popped in her eyes as he tightened his grasp. She kicked and struggled, but she was only flailing. Her head began to spin, her vision going fuzzy.

"What did my baby sister tell you about me, little girl?" Leo murmured. His thumb reached out and pulled on Deya's lower lip and she cringed away, whimpering and choking for air. Leaning closer, his hot breath steamed over her as he whispered, "Did she tell you about how I killed her little friends? How I chopped them to bits and left them in a ditch for their beloved Legion to find?"

Deya's stomach roiled. The way he said it . . . like an artist admiring his work. Blind, disgusted rage enveloped her, and she punched his fist, too dizzy from lack of oxygen to respond, and he laughed even harder.

"Gods, I wish they'd let me have my way with you," he purred, his free hand coming up to pull at her hair. "What do you think would shatter my baby sister more? Finding only your head . . . or bits of you scattered in the wind?"

Deya's hand fell limp to her sides as Leo's grip tightened. Fury was pounding in her spinning mind as the oxygen left her brain, and the insidious power in her screamed to be unleashed. She wanted to *destroy* this male. Wanted to watch as his body withered in front of her, wanted to seek revenge for her friend and all he had done to her. But she couldn't. The shadows were still screaming for blood in her mind, a stark reminder of what may happen to her if she unleashed it again.

There was only one other way.

With the last bit of energy she could muster, Deya reached for her injured leg. She tore the dagger loose from where it was embedded and, with a strangled yell, plunged the curved, golden dagger into the neck of the male in front of her. A spurt of scarlet flew through the air. It mingled with Leo's yell as he dropped her like a stone, howling in pain and rage. Deya hit the ground, not even bothering to look back to see if she had killed him. She flung herself forward, seizing the two flares which had fallen into a snowbank, and, still wincing with the pain of her injured leg, she launched herself towards the white flames.

A searing, all-consuming agony licked her body as she shoved the flares into the roaring fire Leo had left behind. The sound of the Manielian's screams still ringing in her ears, Deya held the flares to the white-hot flames, and waited.

Then, with a loud *boom* that shook the ramparts around her, both flares exploded into the sky. Red and blue light filled the air and for a moment, Deya could only slump against the rampart wall as she watched the glittering sparks light up the sky above them.

They rose, higher and higher, before they disappeared into the clouds above.

Deya sagged against the wall, relief flooding her. But the feeling was short-lived. No sooner had she dropped the now extinguished flares than a shadow fell over her. Deya froze, the hair at the back of her neck prickling, every nerve ending in her body screaming at her to move, to run . . .

Slowly, she looked up.

If she had thought Leo was the worst thing she would face today, she was wrong. Hovering above her was a large, black dragon. And its eyes were fixed right on her.

※

When Aris had given Caelum the Shadow Sword, he had not known what possessing a weapon made of the bones of shadow creatures meant. The first time he had seen the sword since Morlais had fallen, it had seemed smaller than when the Praiton general had wielded it. And when Caelum had bonded with it, its very essence had changed.

While Caelum tried not to think too much about it, it was clear to him—even from early on—that the sword had some semblance of sentience.

But as the Silver Dagger's leader swiped his flaming blade across Caelum's chest, he felt the black sword humming in his hand. As if jerked by an invisible string tied around his wrist, the Shadow Sword flew through the air and blocked the assassin's fatal blow. Then, with a dexterity and ease he had not expected, the sword spun in his hand before piercing through the assassin's shoulder.

For a moment, the flames froze around him as he grunted, blood bubbling up his mouth. Then, all at once, the flames around his knife and the light in his eyes flickered and dimmed, as if life itself had been drained from him.

Eyes widening, Caelum watched as dark shadows rippled across his sword, surging down the hilt, wrapping itself securely around him and the struggling assassin, wrapping them together. He stumbled backwards in shock, attempting to pull the blade loose. It was as if the sword was *feeding* power into him.

His depleted stores of energy seemed to refill, the heady sensation of power bursting inside him. Faintly, he could feel the broken bones of his left hand shifting back into place, the painful throbbing receding. The assassin stared at Caelum over the blade that still impaled him, and for a split second, he felt the shadows ease. The second of release was all he needed.

Pulling his sword free from the male's shoulder, he kicked out, sending the assassin flying to the ground. Then, with a furious roar, Caelum plunged a hand into the burgeoning magic of snow and star churning within him. Then he let it explode.

All around him, the assassins rose into the air as one. Caelum clutched the Shadow Sword tighter, stumbling under the effort of holding the bodies aloft. Shadow and mist circled him, his vision darkening as he took one step, and then another. His hands rose and the screaming, squirming figures he held above them thrashed under his hold. Cold winter wind began to howl through the dark courtyard. Snow and sleet whirled around him, covering the dark grass, frosting over the damaged sculpture of Astrea.

Slowly, Caelum walked into the center of the courtyard, his teeth gnashed as his fingers curled, the controlled movement not mirroring the wild howling of the winter wind. The sound was so loud, people were beginning to come out of the Keep. Figures poked their heads out of windows, servants and citizens alike were stepping out, watching as their High King staggered into the center of the courtyard.

His glowing, violet eyes found the Silver Dagger's leader again, whose pale, terrified face shone back at him through the swirling snow, blood still dripping from his wounded shoulder.

"Who's laughing now, asshole," he snarled. Holding the Shadow Sword aloft, he whipped it upwards, just shy of taking off the assassin's nose. The male cringed away, a pathetic whimper escaping him. Caelum's lip curled. "Ced. "Oh, I promise, you'll *wish* I let this sword kill you." Slowly, he traced the tip of the sword against the assassin's cheek. "It would probably be more merciful than I will." And with that, Caelum raised his hand and clenched his fist.

The blistering cold wind accelerated. In a chorus of choked gasps, the air was sucked out of every assassin's lungs as the gravity around their throats constricted. Frost burst from him, winding around his victims, crystalizing icicles creeping up their bodies, trapping them.

Caelum moved around the circle, not letting up, the Shadow Sword's power fueling his own. And then, with one gentle snap of his fingers, the assassins plummeted to the ground and shattered into ice and bloody slush.

One body remained . . . One, which Caelum kept suspended, waiting. The assassin's leader was close to blubbering as Caelum prowled underneath him, spinning his sword in his hand.

"Now," he growled, reaching up and seizing the assassin by the collar of his green cloak and wrenching him down. "*Tell me.* Who hired you?"

The assassin stammered. "It-it was Mah." He raised his hand over his face, his body still held aloft by Caelum's magic. "It was all Mah! The attack on the caravan, trapping you in the village, waiting until you sent the Legion general and the captains away . . . Even the attack on the girl with the dark magic—"

Caelum froze and his grip tightened on the male's collar. Inadvertently, frost spiraled up from where his fingers held the green fabric and rocketed up the male's body, encasing half his face in solid ice.

"*He* ordered the attack on Deya?" Caelum demanded, fury and panic gripping him. It was as if someone had lit a match in his mind, sparking the memory of what this male had said only a few moments ago.

Nodaria will fall today . . . as Bridah does now.

"What is happening in Bridah?" Caelum shouted. *"Tell me!"*

But before he could open his mouth to respond, an arrow whizzed through the air. The speed of it rustled Caelum's hair before piercing the assassin's neck. The male fell from the sky, hitting the ground with a thud, and Caelum roared in fury, whirling around, searching for the person responsible

Deimos stood by the doorway to the Keep, his face ashen as he lowered the bow.

Caelum moved towards him so fast he barely had time to comprehend what he was doing, when the young boy's face went white. Without warning, he was hoisted into the air, dropping the bow to the ground with a scream.

"Sorry I'm late." Saros walked down the steps of the Keep, one hand raised, holding Deimos aloft, the other dragging a large, sweaty Mah by the collar. The councilman was bound and gagged, his face pale underneath the blood and dirt.

The Nodarian captain stomped down the steps, his dark travel robes billowing behind him as he deposited Mah at Caelum's feet. With a sharp kick to the councilman's back, he said, "I caught him attempting to board a ship in our harbor . . . A Praiton ship." Saros gave the male another hard kick and he toppled over, landing, face first at Caelum's feet.

Mah looked up at him, rage burning in his dark purple eyes. Caelum's lip curled in disgust, fighting the desire to plunge his sword into the traitor's neck. But he held back. His whole body was screaming with panic, a wild fear overwhelming him like the shadows from his own sword. *What was happening in Bridah?*

Bending, Caelum ripped the gag out of Mah's mouth.

"*Talk.*"

The councilman glared up at him and spat on the ground by Caelum's feet.

Caelum's jaw flexed. "Right." In one swift motion, he slammed the blade of the sword into the councilman's arm. This time, no shadows swarmed him, like it had with the assassin, but Mah let out a howl of pain, tears springing to his eyes as Caelum leaned his weight onto the hilt. "I'm not playing with you, Mah," Caelum snarled, grabbing the male by the collar and hoisting him closer. "Why were you working with the Silver Daggers?"

Mah let out a sharp laugh, his pale face reddening with the pain of the blade still embedded in his arm. "You damned bastard," Mah spat. "You think that just because we *gave* you the Hesperos name that you have a right to this kingdom. A right to *endanger* us—"

Out of the corner of his eye, Caelum saw the rest of the council appear in the crowd of onlookers, Helene Sidra among them, her thin face stricken.

"So, what was your aim, Mah?" Caelum leaned harder on the blade, watching the wince cross Mah's face. "To kill me and take the throne?"

"No." Mah's doughy face was beginning to turn purple—with pain or rage, he didn't know. "*You* would not protect us, so *I did*. In exchange for Nodaria's safety, I made a deal."

Caelum's eyes narrowed. "What *kind* of deal?"

"You and that girl in exchange for Nodaria's safety." Mah glared up at him. "Praiton promised to leave us be if we handed you over. All they would do is put a representative here, but they wouldn't attack us. We'd be *safe* with you off the throne. True, it was a bit more difficult when you shipped her off to Bridah, but we found a way—"

A white-hot feeling of dread and fury washed over him, and his grip tightened on the hilt of the sword. "So, you chose to sell this kingdom and its people to Praiton? To bend the knee to their rule?" he roared.

Mah strained against Caelum's grip and sneered. "I chose to do what you would not! To protect our people—"

"*Traitor!*" The shout came from the crowd, and Caelum looked up. To his surprise, it was to see Helene Sidra storming towards them, her pinched face twisted with indignant rage. But she wasn't looking at him. Instead, she was glaring down at Mah in disgust.

"Traitor!" she shrieked again. She hiked up her black starry robes, barreling towards them, shaking her finger down at her fellow council member in malediction. "We do not make deals with Praiton! No matter the circumstance!"

Caelum stared at the prime minister, shock momentarily freezing him in place. Helene looked nearly deranged as she glared down at Mah, who wilted underneath her fury.

"If you were half a Nodarian, you would *die* before bending the knee to Praiton!" she cried. "We remain free or not at all! And if that is beneath the bastard son of our late High King Castor, *so be it.*"

Something strangely like gratitude surged in Caelum's chest. Helene had never been his biggest fan, but to see her standing there—*defending* him—took him quite aback.

He looked down at Mah again before, with a snarl, he ripped the sword out of his arm. Mah screamed in pain, but Caelum ignored him. Shaking the blood off the black sword, he looked up and took in the crowd around him. They were looking at him with the same wariness they usually did, but there was something else, too . . . Something alarmingly like fear.

Caelum glanced over at Saros and jerked his head at him. With a loud *thud*, Saros dropped Deimos to the ground beside Mah. The boy had enough sense not to run. Instead, he stared down at the ground, terror on his face.

Snow still covered the courtyard, and as Caelum stood above the two traitors of the Celestial Kingdom, he could feel the quiver of the crowd, almost sensed the apprehension as to what he would do next.

Slowly, he raised the Shadow Sword. The dark, insidious ripples of shadows flickered like flames up the hilt, twining around his fingers, creeping up his forearm. It was like a whisper in his ear, a small voice urging him to do what was necessary. What a *king* should do.

Pointing the sword towards the two traitors, Caelum said, "You two are accused of treason to the Celestial Kingdom. Do you deny it?"

There was a moment of silence. Mah glared up at Caelum in cool defiance, but Deimos remained quiet and petrified, wide eyes locked on the ground.

Looking up at the rest of the crowd, Caelum shouted, "Does anyone else wish to see Praiton on the Celestial Throne again?" His voice echoed across the silent courtyard. The inhabitants of Atlas Keep remained frozen on the snowy steps, staring at him. A terrified shiver ran across them, and Caelum knew how he looked. He could feel his eyes glow with rage, could still feel the flames of shadow caressing his hand in an almost loving whisper of power from the sword clutched in it.

Blood. It wanted blood.

"If we give in to Praiton, we will fall *again*," Caelum roared to the silent crowd. "Take a look around you." He gestured to the remains of the Praiton assassins littering the courtyard and the blood that stained the layer of white snow. "Let this be a reminder to you all that those who come to claim us will be met with blood . . . and little mercy."

His eyes fell back onto the two in front of him. Deimos was quivering so slightly Caelum almost missed it. He clenched the sword tighter and raised it above their heads. And, in that brief moment, when he felt the crowd flinch back, even saw some of them cover their eyes, Deya's voice drifted into his mind.

You never want people to see the best side of you.

He stopped. A surge of irritation flooded him at the memory of Deya's words. In that moment, he thought about Deya, about how her softness and kindness had been the thing that drew him to her, like a plant starved for light would find the sun. And when he glanced up and sensed the terror of his own people, he faltered.

Then, with an irritated exhalation, Caelum swung the sword . . . and cut Mah free of his bindings. The councilman flinched and closed his eyes as Caelum's blade sliced by him but blinked in surprise as the ropes binding him fell away.

Stunned silence followed this movement, before, with an angry grunt, he re-sheathed the Shadow Sword.

"As citizens of the Celestial Kingdom, sparing your lives is my only act of mercy," he said, his voice still a soft, venomous drip. Deimos's head jerked upwards, his wide eyes staring at Caelum in naked relief. Caelum looked away. "You will be banished to the Exile Continents. You are to live out the rest of your days there."

And as he made to turn away, he felt exasperated irritation at himself for this one act of uncharacteristic kindness, and knew that Deya was the reason for it all. But, in the brief moment he turned his back to the two traitors, a swift movement of black fabric caught his eye.

In almost slow motion, Caelum turned just in time to see the large councilman rise from the ground, pulling a silver blade from the depths of his black and purple robes. He was on Caelum before he even realized he had risen, the knife flashing before his eyes.

Saros yelled and leapt forward. The crowd screamed, and even Deimos rose in shock, but it was Helene who got there first. The diminutive prime minister shot forward like a small arrow, seizing Mah by the temples, her purple eyes rolling into the back of her head. The jerk of her tiny hands stopped Mah short, the knife inches from Caelum's nose, before his face went blank.

Then he began to scream.

Mah fell to the ground, thrashing and kicking, his eyes rolling, mouth foaming. Helene clutched the male by the head, her thin fingers digging into his scalp, holding him steady as her head fell backwards.

Caelum had seen star seers give prophecies, had seen them read the cosmos and minds—even knew personally how it felt to receive a vision—but he had never, in all his years within Nodaria, seen *this*.

Finally, Helene released Mah. Her eyes rolled forward with a gasp, and, with one more pitiful moan from Mah, the male dropped to the ground, his eyes open, his face blank . . . Alive, but empty.

Caelum stared at Helene for a moment as the female rose, brushing back the few flyways that had escaped her tight bun, as if all she had done was merely swat a fly.

Caelum had known about Helene's lineage. The Sidra family went almost as far back as the Hesperos line. He had only heard talk of this special ability they had—a rare mutation only within that family. The ability to destroy minds.

Saros slowed to a stop beside them, staring down at Mah with wide-eyed fascination. Looking up, he opened his mouth, as though about to say something, when a loud noise interrupted him.

The night sky above them was suddenly lit with a distant red light. All around, the crowd pointed and whispered, and Caelum whirled around and looked up at the dark sky.

A red explosion of sparks streaked through the air like a shooting star. For a moment, he almost wondered if he had imagined it when, just as suddenly, a blue burst of light zipped past it. Caelum stared up at it, watching as the twin lights twined through the air, disappearing into the clouds. A hand seized him, shaking him roughly.

"Emergency signals!" Saros cried, jerking Caelum back to the present, back to the horrifying reality of what he had momentarily forgotten.

Bridah.

Deya.

"Go!" Saros cried, shoving him in the back. "Go to them! Quickly! I'll deal with things here."

With the last vestiges of the power given to him by the Shadow Sword, Caelum pulled the air apart. And, without a backward glance at the crowded courtyard, he hurtled through the portal.

CHAPTER 28

Val was dead. She had to be. So why could she still smell smoke? If she were dead, surely her body wouldn't still hurt this much? Every bit of her felt broken, and when she moved, she wanted to cry from the pain.

Something hard nudged her, and she flinched, moaning.

Why couldn't it just let her die? Hadn't she felt enough? *Suffered* enough?

The nudging became more insistent, until something sharp jabbed her in the leg. Val yelped and tried to sit upright, nearly throwing her bag off her lap, but was stopped short by the blinding pain that followed the movement.

She was lying in a large, smoldering crater in a deserted clearing. From where she lay, Val could see a long, deep scorch mark where they had hit the ground and slid across the desert sand. Gingerly, she struggled to sit up and her ribs screamed in protest. With a gasp, she grabbed at her aching side and felt her heart skip when her hand came away bloody.

Blinking back fog and blood, Val looked around. A large, heaving mass of scales and wings was collapsed beside her. Almost as if she could sense Val looking at her, Lucéria opened her eyes and shining golden orbs stared back at her. Only then did Val realize that it had been Lucéria's tail that was prodding her.

The small dragon seemed too injured to rise, and yet she tried, attempting to inch closer to Val, her catlike eyes locked onto the bag in Val's hands. Remembering what was inside it, Val looked down.

The two eggs sat in the leather satchel, still quivering . . . still whole. She let out a gust of air and collapsed back onto the ground, tears springing to her eyes as each broken bone in her body ached in pain.

Lucéria let out a tiny grunt, nudging her again with her tail. Val waved her away. "Stop it! They're fine . . . Stop *poking* me."

The dragon gave an irate snarl and prodded her again and Val let out a small sob. There was so much pain . . . Part of her wanted to lie here . . . die here. She didn't know if she could move again after she had been burnt and beaten, walked through emotional hell, and then thrown from the sky.

The image of her fallen friends flashed through her mind, and she felt tears that had nothing to do with her pain roll down her face. Turning, Val looked at Lucéria.

"I can't," she whispered. "You can barely fly and I . . . I can barely move." If she was being honest with herself, she wondered how close to death she truly was. Fae healed quickly—it took a lot to kill them. But at some point, the body became too damaged to repair. Val hadn't looked at herself since she had woken—she couldn't. She was afraid of what she would see . . . what she could already *feel*.

Clutching the eggs to her chest, she closed her eyes and gasped for breath, her lungs pressing against her broken ribs. Faintly, she could feel the blood of the deep gash in her side trickling down, spilling onto the sand underneath her.

She had gone too far. It was over. The magic it took to survive Lucéria's flames, as well as the others, had drained her. Now, there was nothing left inside to heal her.

She would die here . . . where no one would find her.

Faintly, she could feel the crest of the rising sun, its gentle rays beginning to break over the dunes. It had been so dark on Mount Cinis, she had no idea what time it was, nor how long she had been there. And as daybreak came, Val closed her eyes again.

Another nudge to her side roused her, and Val did not have the strength to stop Lucéria this time. The touch was gentler, almost pleading.

"Go, Lucéria," Val whispered. "Go. I release you." She opened her arms, so her bag lay open on her bleeding chest. "Take them. There's no need for you to stay. You're free."

Lucéria rose from where she lay, her scaly legs shaking with the effort. The dragon was also battered and bleeding, her tattered wings looking even worse than before, but still, the creature rose, and Val watched her, marveling at the fact that she got to see one of these magnificent, terrifying creatures even once in her life.

The dragon moved towards her, but instead of taking the eggs and leaving, she pushed her nose against Val's shoulder, nudging her again, keeping her from falling into blissful nothingness. Val groaned.

"*No,* Lucéria. I can't—" But the dragon pushed at her again. The flame inside Val was so weak she could barely feel it. Even when she closed her eyes and sank into it, it felt as if she were on a boat on a distant sea, the feel of the waves rocking her gently . . . The feel of her heart breaking.

The dragon pushed her again, and this time, when Val opened her eyes, it was with the intention of shouting at her, of telling her to get away, to let her die in peace, when a streak of red sparks caught her eye.

Despite every agonizing movement, Val sat up, her eyes locked on the sky.

"*No.*"

The red burst of sparks sailed into the air, hovering above her head. It was distant, barely a streak, as if the Mother herself had dropped a brush of red paint. But Val recognized that flare. The Legion's flare systems were designed to alert allies from anywhere within the realm. Strong enough to be seen from the opposite end of Krigor, it was the last act of desperation. A final cry for help.

Red. One for war.

She held her breath, praying the second would not come. But a moment later, the blue flare tore through the sky and Val swore so hard that tears burst into her eyes with the pain.

Blue. One for Bridah.

Slamming her fist into the ground, Lucéria jumped in alarm as tears fell from Val's eyes. She was too broken to move and yet *she* was their final hope. Here she was with a fucking *dragon,* and she was *dying.* Her friends were in danger, Bridah was being attacked, and she could do nothing but sit here and bleed out on the fucking floor.

Val gritted her teeth and took a deep breath. Lucéria watched her carefully, those familiar golden eyes tracking her every move. It was almost as if she could hear her old friend's voice in her head when she looked at the dragon.

You are Valeria Augusta. Get the fuck up.

Val planted both hands firmly onto the ground. With a scream, she pushed herself into a sitting position and gasped at what she saw. Her splintered bone was protruding from her leg. The white of the bone grizzled with blood was all she could see before she gagged, turning and spilling the empty contents of her stomach on the ground beside her.

"Oh, *fuck*," she moaned, tears and bile stinging her. But it was not the time to be squeamish. She was a seasoned warrior, for gods' sake. She had cauterized wounds, amputated limbs of fellow soldiers. She could set a fucking compound fracture.

Carefully setting the satchel with the eggs on the ground by Lucéria's feet, she pulled the scorched leather gauntlet off her wrist and shoved it into her mouth. She looked up at the dragon, who gazed calmly back. Then she cracked her leg in half.

The pain split through Val in a blinding ripple. Her vision went white, and her screams melted into the pain. Gasping, gnashing her teeth so hard into the leather she almost bit through, she burned the broken skin, sealing it shut, before pulling off her belt and tightened it around the limb.

This would have to be enough . . . just to get her moving again . . . just to get her to Bridah. She screamed through the pain as she bound her leg as tight as she could before, with a deep breath, tears glimmering in her eyes, she turned to Lucéria.

"Can you fly?"

The dragon blinked slowly at her and rustled her shredded wings. Blood splattered onto the ground from the movement, but Val knew the answer.

Carefully, she tried to stand. Her leg stuck out in a rigid angle, and even with the belt stabilizing it, the pain was unbearable. A large scaly head suddenly appeared under her arm, helping her stand. With a grateful smile at the dragon, she hoisted herself back onto Lucéria's back. Tying the eggs tightly back around her, she attempted to seat herself as securely as possible without the aid of her left leg.

"We have to get to Bridah. As fast as possible," she told Lucéria. "Can you do that?"

The dragon snorted in response and, before Val even had the chance to secure her hold on her mount's ridged back, the dragon launched herself into the sky. The air blasted Val in the face and she nearly slid off Lucéria's back. Without her leg, holding on was almost impossible. She was forced to throw herself against the scaly back, wrapping her arms around Lucéria's neck.

The dragon was moving faster than before—faster than any ship or carriage could ever take her, and Val watched as the barren wasteland of Dritus flashed by underneath them. Yet Val found herself looking out towards the sea, desperate to catch a glimpse of the Legion ship she had arrived on. But there was nothing on the distant horizon.

Had Aris seen the flares? Had they already left for Bridah without her? Could it be that they thought she had failed?

Did Aris believe she was dead?

Val pushed the thought from her mind, her heart aching for the general, the strange feeling of restless anxiety that she felt whenever she thought of him surging back again. Wherever he was, she hoped he'd make it to Bridah in time.

Lucéria sped over the tops of trees, over dunes and rocky ground. Dritus became Zulon—the barren desert ground broken up by nothing but dilapidated huts of war refugees and small villages, the shadow of Burningtide nothing but a speck in the distance.

Lucéria's small frame allowed her to narrow her body into the wind, picking up speed as they zipped along. All the while Val's chest was aflame, the prickling feeling of panic washing out the pain of her broken body.

Was Deya okay? Would she make it in time? What awaited her in Bridah?

The thought of the large hole in the glacial wall and facing what may have caused it filled her with a hot, molten dread.

A large blast of cold air suddenly hit her in the face, and Lucéria veered off course. Finally, Val could see why Bridah had been impenetrable. A wall of ice towered over them. It was so tall that Val could not see the top of it. It glistened in the sun, standing in defiance of heat and light—a solid, impregnable wall of diamond.

Lucéria pulled upwards, as though attempting to go above. The wind howled down on them, pushing them backwards. For a moment, the small dragon fought it, but soon gave up and allowed herself to be pushed back down.

"You have to go around!" Val shouted over the roaring wind. After the heat of Mount Cinis, her teeth began to chatter as the familiar winter wind washed over her exposed wounds, freezing the sweat still clinging to her body.

They flew along the edge of the Bridanian walls, looking for an opening. Val's mind was racing. How were they to get in? She couldn't remember where the breached wall was, and even if they could find it again, was it still open?

After nearly ten more maddening minutes in which Val was ready to throw herself off Lucéria and climb the rest of the way, the dragon began to rear. It was as if she could sense something nearby . . . something that frightened her.

"What is it?" Val asked but even as she said it, her nose twitched at the acrid smell of smoke and her heart sank. Sitting up higher in her seat, her eyes combed the wall of ice, looking . . .

"That way!" Val shouted, pointing straight ahead. The hole in the glacier that Kindra had temporarily resealed had been blasted apart again. From the sky, Val could see soldiers marching through it . . . all clad in blood-red armor.

Everything in Val's body went cold. A numb, tingling panic set in, her chest becoming tight as she struggled for breath.

It couldn't be them. Not here. Not now.

But before she could think of turning back, Lucéria dove for the opening and Val clenched the spiked ridges of her back so hard that her knuckles turned white.

Lucéria swooped through the opening, her tattered wings tucked into her body. And as she entered the Frost Kingdom, it was to find a bloody war of frost and flame. All around the damaged walls, Blood Riders and Berserkers clashed. Fire and ice exploded in bursts, swords collided, and bodies littered the ground.

Val urged Lucéria forward. There was nothing she could do from up there. Having Lucéria use her flame would only hurt the Bridanians. She had to get to Deya, had to find her—

But then, as Lucéria veered over the battlements and into the heart of Bridah, Val felt all the air leave her lungs.

Fangdor was burning, its inhabitants fleeing from it, screaming. Bridanian soldiers and Berserkers were struggling to protect it. But it wasn't the burning walls Val was staring at, horrified.

A large, black dragon hovered over the top of the highest tower of the castle. It was blasting jets of fire down at someone. And, as Val and

Lucéria flew closer, Val could see a small, dark-haired female with a thick braid hanging from the battlements.

"*Deya!*"

Without thinking, Val made to squeeze Lucéria's sides, to spur her on, but almost yelled in pain as her broken leg protested.

"Go!" Val shouted, squeezing with her other leg. "Go! We need to save her!"

The dragon obliged and they sped up. Fire licked under her heels as they rocketed past the burning villages of Frostheim, smoke burning Val's lungs.

The large dragon was trying to pluck Deya from the battlements, and Val's friend clung to the wall, hiding between a small corner of the wall and rampart. Lucéria let out an almighty roar and Deya's head jerked up to look at her. Her face split with a disbelieving gasp, and Val's heart swelled with relief.

Seizing the horned ridges of Lucéria's back in a tighter hold, Val thrust forward, urging the steed down. The bull seemed to notice them just as Deya did. It let out an enormous bellow that shook the burning ramparts of Fangdor. Lucéria responded with an earsplitting shriek, and no sooner did they near the small alcove where Deya hid than the black dragon dove for them.

Lucéria swerved, barely missing the dragon's talons. Val screamed, feeling herself sliding with the movement, unable to hold on tight enough with her injured leg. The bag containing the eggs rolled over her shoulder and Val made a desperate grab for them, just barely managing to secure them. Lucéria let out another loud roar and dove lower, Titus's bull following close above.

A jet of fire ripped past them, singeing Val's left side and Lucéria turned sharply, nearly colliding with a turret.

"*Cautus, careful, Lucéria!*" Val screamed as the dragon's large flank bounced off the smoldering building, nearly upending Val from her seat. "I can't hold on enough for that! You need to—"

But no sooner did she speak than a large, forked tail whirled towards them. Val, distracted, didn't duck in time. Lucéria spun in midair, her large wings coming to wrap around Val like a leathery cocoon as the bull's tail whizzed over Val's head, missing her nose by inches.

Lucéria shot up into the sky, zigzagging around the crumbling castle, weaving between turrets and smoking ramparts. Lucéria was small—much smaller than Titus's bull, allowing her the advantage of agility. Unlike Mount Cinis, where there were no obstructions and few places to hide, the burning castle of Fangdor provided enough obstacles for her to squeeze and weave through, leaving Titus's bull roaring in outrage.

Struggling to right herself on her mount, Val pulled on the horned ridges again, guiding her back towards the tower where she prayed Deya still hung.

"*Go!*" Val urged her. Lucéria obliged. The dragon pulled upwards, her wings beating hard, the unevenness of her rhythm bouncing Val in her seat. But she rose, higher and higher, past the smoke and flame until—

Val saw her. Deya was clinging by her fingernails to the ledge, her feet scraping the curve of a window casing, struggling to find purchase. Urging Lucéria towards her, the small dragon tucked its wings together, her back legs pulling underneath her as she shot towards Deya.

The bull, sensing what they were doing, let out an almighty roar and blasted after them, fire raining down. But Val held on, ducking her head as the fire swallowed her and Lucéria. With one great push, Val thrust the dragon's horned ridges left, forcing them to curve upwards along the wall. They were now running parallel to the wall Deya hung onto, flying higher and higher until they blew clear over it and Val knew she only had one chance to get this right.

Titus's dragon screeched above them, talons reaching and fire pouring down around them, and Val—with a strange intuition she did not know she had—dug her heel into Lucéria's side, turning her around, aiming her towards Deya. The small dragon dove, rocketing towards the ground like an amber arrow. Val watched as the walls flashed past them, counting, waiting . . .

The split second after Lucéria sped past Deya, Val seized her friend's wrist. She tore Deya free from the wall, and Deya landed, behind her hard, on Lucéria's back before they plummeted towards the ground.

"*You did it!*" Deya shrieked. She was clutching Val so tightly that the pain from her broken bones and injured side was beginning to make her faint. But even through the joy and relief on Deya's face, Val didn't miss the glimmer of terror.

"What's going on? Where's Ulf? What's happened?" Val gasped, but before Deya could answer, Lucéria veered upwards sharply. Val and Deya came tumbling out of their seats, rolling to rest in the soft, cold snow. Gasping through deflated lungs, Val wanted to scream as her body collapsed in on itself, watching as Lucéria flew away, unaware that she had thrown them from her back.

"Shit, Val, your leg." She was faintly aware of Deya scrambling around her, as if looking for something. Hands pulled at the hastily tightened belt around the break and Val's head swam with agony through her closed eyes.

"It's fine, Deya . . . I'm fine, I promise—"

But she could feel Deya fumbling around the ground and was faintly aware of the feeling of her belting and setting the leg with a hard piece of wood she had scavenged from the burning rubble around them.

"There, that should hold you until we can get you healed—"

But Deya barely finished her sentence when a burst of fire billowed above their heads. Without thinking, Val threw herself over Deya, shielding her as the flames licked her already burnt back. And when she looked up, she felt her body go cold.

A male landed in front of them in a burst of white flames. He was staggering, blood dripping from a deep wound in his neck, yet his scarred face was twisted into a smile. His mad laughter cracked the air.

"Deya," Val whispered, pulling her friend to her feet. "Run. *Run!*" And no sooner did Deya sprint out of sight, did her brother pull his golden knife from the curve of his neck with an almost sickening reverence.

"Hello, baby sister," Leo purred. "How interesting to see you free of prison and here of all places." Blood followed him in a grisly trail as he staggered towards her. Val struggled to rise, using the glaive she had pulled from her back to hoist herself up. She watched as her brother's feet crisscrossed and swayed. But she was not fooled.

Leo was more dangerous when he was injured.

The scar on his face that she had given him all those years ago stared back at her. A permanent reminder of that day, of the small victory she had managed before he had ripped her life from her . . . Before he had murdered her sisters.

Val stood in front of her brother and felt a murderous rage fill her like wildfire.

"What are you doing here, Leo?" she said. Whatever Deya had done to her leg, she was now able to put more weight on it, though she couldn't bend it.

Leo let out a wheezing laugh. "I'm here for your delicious little friend, of course. And to burn the Frost Kingdom to the ground. If you would like to burn with it, baby sister, I'm only happy to oblige."

Val gripped the glaive tighter, readying herself for what she knew was coming. Leo's fingers twitched, flames twirling up like snakes twisting around them. She could almost taste the fire.

"You're not getting Deya," Val snarled, sounding much braver than she felt. "Leave now, or you'll be sorry."

"Will we?" Another voice cut through the roaring winter wind surrounding them. A voice colder than the snow underfoot and the ice in the air. And Val froze as she heard footsteps crunch towards her. Slowly, she turned.

Lorenzo was walking calmly towards her, golden sword in hand . . . and Deya clenched by her braid in the other. The small female was being dragged through the snow, her eyes shimmering with tears, bright red burns on her face and arms.

"Lorenzo," she breathed.

Val's eldest brother was just as tall and imposing as he had been in all her nightmares. His red armor was streaked with blood and soot, and even though the evidence of his role in the fight was all over him, he still managed to appear cool and calm.

"*Val*," Deya whispered, and Lorenzo jerked her by the hair, making her yelp.

"Lorenzo, let her go," Val said, her voice wavering. Leo laughed softly behind her, staggering closer, trapping her between them.

Lorenzo's face did not change. "This girl is going to be turned over to the High King and given back to Praiton." The sharp golden blade in his other hand reached towards Deya, touching the fresh burns he had given her, making her flinch. "And you, *Vilaya*, will be dead."

Val slowly began to back away, trying to keep both her brothers in sight, wincing with each step on her bad leg. "If you don't let her go right now, it will be you who will be dead, *Laurus*."

The cold mask on her brother's face didn't budge. From behind her, she could feel Leo prowling closer, could hear the flames flickering on his fingertips like a whisper of wind.

"You are in no condition to fight," Lorenzo said calmly. "You can barely stand. And yet you think you can take on both of us?" His lip curled, the first flicker of emotion she had seen from him yet. "Are you stupid as well as weak, *Vilaya*? Pity. This could've been easier for you. Quicker. I was not planning on making you suffer."

"I was," Leo wheezed, and his gasping cackle made Val's skin crawl. "Oh, Lorenzo, just cut her friend up a bit. Praiton won't mind if she's in a few more pieces, will they?" His eyes gleamed at Deya, who shrank under his gaze, her hand still attempting to pry Lorenzo's fingers from her hair. "We can start by cutting off those pretty black hands of hers. Aren't those curious . . ."

Val started, and her gaze jerked back to Deya. She would not have noticed it if Leo hadn't said, but he was right. Deya's hands *were* black, from fingertip to palm, dark veins crawling up her forearms. For a moment, Val stared at Deya, her mind racing. Tears filled her friend's eyes, and she looked away, as if ashamed . . . as if she had hidden this from them all.

But before Val could even react, Leo lunged. Two golden swords flashed towards Val and, with a speed that surprised her, Val whirled the glaive above her head. It caught Leo's swords, and his amber eyes widened as he took in the new weapon before his face split into a hideous grin.

"That's right, baby sister," Leo giggled. "*Fight* for it. Your blood tastes better when you struggle."

His swords slashed again, one swinging towards her leg, the other slicing for her head. Val dove back, crying out as she landed on her broken leg, the glaive dancing around her. The top of the glaive caught one sword, the bottom meeting the other, and suddenly she and Leo were locked together.

Flames exploded from both Leo's blades, and it was all Val could do to keep up. She had forgotten what it was like to fight Leo, forgotten how the manic bloodlust translated to his swordplay. He moved in an unhinged symphony, each hand acting independent of the other in a chaotic barrage that made it impossible for her to guess his next move.

Sparks flew as Val spun the glaive, stopping Leo's swords, struggling to remain upright when, with a scream, flames exploded from the glaive like a fiery whip, forcing Leo to leap back, laughing maniacally. A blur of movement flashed in her peripheral and Val whirled in time to stop Lorenzo's blade from plunging into her back.

"That glaive . . ." His eyes were wide as they ran up the gilded hilt, lingering on the intricate markings. "Where did you get that?"

But before she could even respond, a loud, screeching roar rent the air and Val felt herself smile. A blast of hot flames rained down on them, and Val's brothers dove aside.

Lucéria exploded into view. The small dragon circled above them, screeching and raining fire down on them, chasing her brothers from Val. Taking advantage of the momentary distraction, Val dove for Deya, who had been trapped in a ring of fire by Lorenzo. Pulling Deya to safety, Val watched as Lucéria landed in front of them, tattered wings extending to their full length as she stood between Val and her brothers.

Lorenzo gaped, staring up at the dragon, the shock on his face vivid. Lucéria let out an earth-rattling roar, and Lorenzo stumbled backwards. Even Leo was temporarily stunned into silence.

"Like I said, brother," Val said, limping out from behind Lucéria. "If you do not leave this kingdom now, *you* will be the one dead." Fear pounded through her like a ferocious drum, but Val ignored it as she leaned against her dragon and stood in front of her brothers for the first time with her chin held high.

For a moment, none of them spoke, until Leo exploded in a burst of wheezing laughter.

"You call that a dragon?" He wiped a trickle of blood from his face, licking it from his fingers with a wild sneer. "That's cute, baby sister, but I hate to break it to you . . ." Raising his fingers to his lips, Leo whistled high and loud. A moment of trembling silence followed before a large shadow filled the sky and the enormous black bull crashed to the ground, roaring so loudly the noise nearly upended them. Leo burst into uncontrollable laughter. "Ours is bigger!"

Val stumbled backwards, the desire to shield Lucéria from the monster in front of them almost making her forget her broken leg. She could feel the small dragon's hesitation, could feel her recoil from the gigantic bull the size of half the castle. It loomed above them, stories taller than Lucéria, its red eyes gleaming in the winter light.

"That is not your dragon," Val snapped, her hands clutching Lucéria's neck for support, glancing quickly backwards at Deya, who crouched behind the female dragon, staring up at the bull with sheer terror on her face.

Lorenzo stepped forward, drawing his second sword now, shaking the shock of seeing Lucéria from his face. "Do you really think the High King would come to this battle himself?" he asked, coldly. "He sent me to lead this siege. And for now, Drazáth answers to me."

Val's grip tightened on her glaive, feeling Lucéria's hot, scaly flanks rise with her breathing. She felt herself brace, knowing what was coming, feeling it in the air . . .

"So, *Vílaya*," Lorenzo said, flicking a drop of blood from one of his golden blades with the cool arrogance of a seasoned killer. "Let us see who wins in a battle of fire and blood."

CHAPTER 29

When Lorenzo lunged for her, Val was barely ready. Throwing the glaive forward, she caught the twin blades, before quickly having to block again and again. It was soon apparent to her that Lorenzo was not holding back. This time, he fought to kill.

Fire flew from his swords—white hot and vengeful—causing Val to send her own flame roaring back at him. And then Leo joined the fray.

All Val could do was anticipate the next move. Her brothers moved so quickly around her, fiery blades flashing like the wings of a flaming hummingbird, hitting every inch of the golden glaive so hard Val could feel it in her teeth.

To her left, the sounds of the dragons doing battle filled the air. Drazàth had leapt on the smaller dragon like a lion set on its prey. The sounds of Lucéria's agonized screeching distracted Val as she danced around in a flaming circle, fending off blow after fatal blow from her brother's swords. The sound was like a stab to the heart as she fought the urge to rush to her dragon's aid.

From out of the corner of her eye, she saw Deya pick up a sword from the ground and run towards her to help, only to be blasted back by the flames of their battle. Higher and higher the Augusta flames raged as the three of them danced and spun within the fiery ring.

Leo's sword swung for her back, while Lorenzo's twin swords lunged for her neck, and Val pinned them both with a swirl of her glaive, the sharp end inches away from Lorenzo's face.

"You think we can feed her to the dragon, brother?" Leo giggled, leaning over Val's shoulder, his hot breath in her ear. "Or just her little friend?"

"*Fuck* you," Val spat. Leo leered at her and, before she could react, a jet of flames shot from Leo's mouth like a dragon's, blasting her full in the face. Val screamed, her glaive dropping, just barely able to avoid the clash of her brother's blades as they converged on her.

Blindly, she rolled, dodging the stabs of their swords, attempting to blink through the pain of her burnt eyelids. Then, a small figure raced past her. Deya swung her sword for Lorenzo's back, who barely noticed her in time to block it.

"Deya, *no!*" Val cried, but Deya did not listen. She launched herself into battle, taking on Leo next, who laughed uproariously at her.

"You have a death wish, little girl," Leo cackled, and before Val could rise to stop it, Leo reached out a fist and struck Deya so hard in the stomach that he sent her flying in a stream of flames. Val screamed, watching as Deya soared through the air and crashed into a snowbank several feet away. The dueling dragons were still locked in battle, their large legs clawing at each other, their wings and tails beating the ground, nearly crushing Deya's crumpled form as they went.

"*No!*" Val shouted, and made to rise, but a glint of gold sliced into her arm, sending her reeling back, gasping in pain. Blood showered down onto the snow around her, and she blindly scrabbled for her dropped glaive. Her fingers brushed the cold handle of her weapon, but boots stalked towards her, kicking it from her reach before she could grasp it.

Lorenzo stood above her, the gold sword in his hand slick with her blood, which he held above her head. "You will lose this battle." His cold voice held her in place. She was on her knees again. On her knees in front of her brothers. She knew she could not best them—not in her condition. But she would be damned if she didn't try, this time. She would go down fighting.

Lorenzo's lip pulled back, as if he was too disgusted to look at her. "Nothing this weak could ever be considered my blood," he said coldly.

Val scrambled backwards but hit a wall of flames conjured by a jeering Leo. Reaching desperately inside herself for her power, she felt nothing but aching pain. She was tapped out . . . done for. When he raised his sword, Val closed her eyes and braced herself for death for the second time that day.

Suddenly, a blast of cold air exploded from above, extinguishing the flames circling her. A black blade whirled through the air and an unseen wave sent both Val's brothers careening backwards.

Caelum dropped from a portal to the ground in front of her. Covered in blood and bruises, the Shadow Sword clutched in his hand, Caelum spat out a mouthful of blood with murder in his eyes.

Val let out a broken laugh of relief, tears springing to her eyes at the sight of him. Caelum looked back at her over his shoulder as she fell back into the snow, a half-dazed smile on her face.

"Welcome to the party," Val gasped, attempting to pull herself into a sitting position.

"Sorry I'm late." The white-haired Nodarian rolled his neck, wiping blood from his lip with his thumb. "I portaled in via the great hall and it took me a little while to get here."

Val let out another drunk laugh as she pulled herself to her feet. "You look like shit," she told him, and Caelum smirked.

"Right back at you."

Val's brothers were rising to their feet, neither of them laughing now. Lorenzo's fury was rippling from him in waves of heat, burning the snow from his body.

Caelum glanced back at her. "Deya?"

"She got hit. I think she's okay but . . ."

Caelum snarled and he turned to look at the approaching figures, the anger rippling from him in waves of cold wind.

"Caelum—" Val began, but the Nodarian High King silenced her with a single look.

"It's okay. I've got your back." And Val felt her heart swell, tears filling her eyes as the white-haired male spun his sword as her brothers came nearer. Val stood, grabbing the glaive, moving to cover Caelum from behind.

"Which one do you want?" His lip curled, his back pressed against Val's as they moved backwards in a circle, keeping both Augusta males in view. "Scar face or this twat?" He jerked his chin at Lorenzo who was stalking towards them, a cold, steely glint in his amber eyes.

Val watched as Leo laughed in that never-ending, nerve grating giggle as he stagger-stepped towards them and her grip tightened on the glaive.

"Give me Leo," she snarled. "I owe him one." Leo cackled, blood still flowing from his neck, twin swords flashing in the light.

Caelum smirked. "With pleasure."

And then they moved as one. Val launched herself first, sending the glaive jabbing towards Leo. He ducked, his swords scissoring towards her. Val spun the glaive, the ends blocking the sword as the it rolled across her body, then swinging the blade towards Leo. Flames spiraled from the tip of the golden blade as she swiped and jabbed at Leo, whose smile slid from his face, replaced with a gnash of teeth and a snarl.

Val knew Leo's style. He was all about close contact, aiming to draw her near and overwhelm her with his blades and knives. But the glaive whirling around her body kept him at bay, kept him constantly moving. Without Lorenzo at his side, she had forced him on defense.

To her right, she could see Caelum fighting Lorenzo, the two males battling so hard sparks and ice flew. Caelum couldn't seem to be able to grab hold of Lorenzo with his Gravity Magic. The male was always two steps ahead, meeting Caelum's magic with fire and his steel. The Manielian warrior had a much different tactic than his brother. The golden swords—twin blades passed down through generations of Augustas—and Caelum's large black sword meant one thing: Lorenzo was trying to keep Caelum close, overwhelm. Keep him too distracted to concentrate on using his Gravity Magic.

Caelum, impatient and hot-headed as always, charged towards him, and Val could only keep half an eye on them as she desperately tried to fend Leo off.

The four of them battled, Val whirling the glaive and thrusting it towards her brother, Caelum slashing and dodging Lorenzo's attacks. Twirling her glaive, Val caught Leo's hand, sending one of his swords flying. Victory singing in her heart, Val went for the kill, when a horrible, ailing screech broke the silence. Through the swirling smoke and fire, the sound of a wounded dragon broke her concentration. And in that moment, when Val whirled towards Lucéria, Leo acted.

Val had barely caught a glimpse of the bull seizing the smaller dragon by the neck and flinging her towards them, before she was cut down by her brother's blade. She fell, screaming, faintly aware of her dragon being thrown into the air and crashing to the ground feet from her.

"Lucéria!" Val shrieked, and she made to run towards her, but Leo, laughing loudly, dove for her, sword raised. Without warning, an arrow took Leo in the shoulder, stopping him short and sending him flying to the ground. Val gasped and looked around.

Rayner stood on top of the burning castle, his bow drawn, nocking another arrow. Val's heart soared. If Rayner was here, that meant . . .

"Go!" Rayner shouted, and Val scrambled to her feet as Leo let out a scream of fury and ripped the arrow from his arm, his sight now on Rayner.

Val ran towards Lucéria—a bleeding mass of panting scales crumpled on the ground. Her heart ached, the pain in her leg and body practically blinding her, but she could not stop. Throwing herself onto the dragon, her hands flew to the bleeding wound on the side of her neck.

"*Lucéria!* Are you okay? Can you move?"

The dragon let out a plaintive moan, and jerked her head, as if to warn her. Val turned just in time, whirling the glaive again to catch Leo's sword inches from her neck. He was panting, covered in blood, eyes glazed in manic glee.

"You may have your little friends helping you," Leo wheezed, leaning his full weight on the sword, bending Val backwards on her bad leg. "But you will die today, baby sister. And I will cut your pretty body up into bits—"

Val jabbed her glaive, sending her brother flying backwards in a wave of flames. Screaming with mirth now, Leo pulled another knife from his belt and hurled it at her . . . only for it to be blocked by a large, gold longsword. She hadn't even seen him coming, but suddenly the general was standing in front of her, a slew of Legion soldiers streaming past him, fury lining every inch of his beautiful face.

"If you touch her," Aris snarled, and Val stared at the general, never seeing him this murderous before. His whole face had contorted, his jaw rigid and teeth clenched as he charged towards Leo. "I will end you."

Leo was bleeding heavily now, but at the sight of the general, his jagged smile vanished. Instead, anger filled his twisted features, and a hot dread swept through Val at the sight of it.

"*You,*" he snarled, and for a second, his face was more than just gleefully murderous. It was *fury*. Dark, thunderous rage . . . Directed wholly at Aris.

The general squared his shoulders, his blade pointed directly at Leo. He did not back down. Instead, he stood between Val and her brother, not a hint of fear on his handsome face.

Leo's lip curled and the expression sparked a memory in her. All throughout her lonely childhood, whenever Val had managed to make a friend for herself, Leo had chased them off. It was always with the same expression on his face.

He was jealous.

"*She cannot be yours,*" Leo growled. "*Only I touch her!* You will *die* for this, scum!"

And before Val could even fathom what he had just said, Leo lunged forward with the grace of a drunken bull, and Aris caught his blades with the length of the golden sword. It was not often Val got to see Aris fight, but she found herself in awe as the general whirled the sword much like she had her glaive, fending off each of Leo's frenzied attacks. Yet the chaos was too much. Aris was too close and Leo's movements too fast. He pulled a small knife from his pocket as his blades and flames flew towards Aris in an out-of-control frenzy, making the general duck and move, unable to wield his large sword . . . when Leo's thrown blade struck him. It slashed up Aris's right arm, forcing him to drop his sword, blood spraying the ground . . . and Val's hand ached in pain.

She gasped, dropping the glaive as she clutched her right hand, the throbbing pain as raw as if she herself had been cut. Yet there was no wound. Slowly, she looked up at Aris in question, their eyes locking for the first time since she had left him on that boat, and there was something in his stare . . . Something like an apology. But she wasn't given a moment to wonder what this meant. Leo, sensing weakness, sprang towards the general, and without thinking, Val threw herself towards him.

She tackled her brother, stopping him just short of Aris, throwing him to the ground and wrestling him underneath her.

"*That's right,* baby sister, *that's right!*" he cried, his face lit with a wild mania as Val wrestled him underneath her, struggling to pit his hands to his sides, to keep the knife away from her. "*Cut me up!* Go on! And when I win, I'll hold you down, just like I used to . . . hold you down and make you watch as I cut up the Nodarian bastard, then your little friend and the Sea Fae . . . the fucking general . . . and then I'll feed their bits to your dragon while I hold you down and fuck—"

But Val wouldn't let him finish. Rage filled every inch of her, a billowing, out of control barrage of heat and fury. And when she looked down at her brother, she felt the pain in her chest—the beaten part of her that had been locked up and shoved down deep inside—explode in a shower of sparks.

"You will never hurt my friends again," Val snarled. And then she thrust her hands against his face, wrapping her bleeding, burnt fingers around the tan skin, covering the jagged scar. And, with a scream that set the flame inside of her roaring, Val let her fire loose.

White-hot flames exploded around them, swallowing Leo whole. For a moment, his face froze as the flames engulfed him, as if realizing what was happening. His gloating, jeering laugh faded with the roar of the fire and melted into a blood-curdling, agonizing scream.

Distantly, she heard Lorenzo shout for his brother, heard Caelum take advantage of his distraction to lift him into the air and send him spinning into the wall of Fangdor with a crash, but she did not let up.

She sent everything surging down into her brother. The pain, the rage, the grief, the broken, beaten parts of her soul that *he* had damaged—the home and childhood that *he* had stolen from her—she sent it all surging down into him with an explosion of white light. For a moment, all the pain welled to the breaking point . . . and then it was gone.

The flames stopped, and Val—spent and empty—teetered to the ground and fell beside the burnt and charred body of her brother . . . who was quiet at last.

CHAPTER 30

Deya rose from the bank of snow she had fallen into, gasping in pain. Clutching her stomach, she felt the throbbing sting of the burn where Leo had punched her. Ashes filled the air, but this time, it was not from her.

She was able to open her eyes just in time to realize that Aris, Rayner, and Caelum had appeared, that they were all fighting; to watch as the large dragon threw the smaller one to the ground as if it were no more than a ragdoll . . . and then to see Val launch herself at Leo. White flames exploded into the sky, and as Val's eldest brother screamed as he watched Leo go up in flames, the large black dragon screeched with a mirrored rage.

Deya saw what was going to happen before it did. The enormous dragon descended upon them as Val's flames stopped, large wings beating above. It shrieked, enraged, and Deya saw smoke unfurling from its mouth as it looked down at Val, Aris, and the small dragon. It spread its wings, hovering above the ground, and opening its mouth wide, smoke and spark undulating from it.

Deya moved without thinking. Rising from the snow, she sprinted towards the dragon, her gaze zeroed in on the low rise of its tail as it scraped against the ground. Ignoring the pain filling her whole body, she lowered her head and ran as fast as she could. Without thinking twice, she launched herself towards it, managing to grab hold of one of its spiked ridges protruding from its back.

She heard Caelum scream her name, the string tying her to him blazing to life like the wick of a candle, but Deya ignored it. Racing up the dragon's back, struggling to remain balanced as it beat its wings, Deya could only think of one thing: saving her friends.

In that moment, she didn't care if she survived. She did not care what it meant to her hands or her soul. What good were any of those things if she lost the people she loved the most? And as she threw herself towards one of the dragon's rippling wings, her gaze found Caelum's—as though drawn to him. He was standing, frozen, and Deya saw his blazing purple eyes find her hands . . . and she saw it. The terror on his face. The fear.

But Deya didn't let herself dwell on it. She seized the leathery wings and, with one last look at Caelum, she closed her eyes and ripped open the door to her power.

Immediately, the dark, insidious shadows that had slunk back inside of her stormed out again. The overwhelming flood of power crashed through her, the sound of the dragon's agonized screams singing in her ears and veins like a sweet, melodic song, fueling her strength. Its wings began to decay, large holes burning through it as it roared and bucked in pain, sending its flame shooting harmlessly into the sky, away from her friends.

She did not have the power to destroy a dragon. But she did have the power to stop it . . . at least somewhat. Faintly aware of the blackness clouding her vision, spiraling up her hands, she clung to the dragon's wing with her life and screamed with it.

It was then that a strong, unbearably cold gust of ice and snow whirled around them, nearly sending Deya flying from the bull's back. Squinting through the blistering wind, Deya saw a bright, crystalline creature galloping towards them.

Just like Frode's bear, the creature was made of pure ice. It stormed into the fray behind the dragon, the Blood Riders freezing in its path. Almost the size of the dragon, its large antlers caught soldiers and sent them spinning into the air, a stream of powerful snow following it. It was only then that Deya saw who rode atop it.

Ulf had come at last. The large male had his arms outstretched, a murderous look of fury on his usually kind, ruddy face. A brutal, uncontrolled frost filled the air, jagged icicles rained from the sky, swirling around him, obliterating the roaring flames the dragon had left in its wake as easily as if he were blowing out a candle. And in that moment, Deya understood why Ulf was considered the most powerful High King in Krigor.

Ice burst through the ground, skewering green cloaked assassins and Manielian soldiers alike. Those fortunate enough to dodge them were frozen solid in Ulf's wake, and the dragon, still bucking in pain, let out a scream that rocked the entirety of the snowy grounds.

As snow swirled around them, pushing down on them in an unbearable barrage of cold, Deya held fast, her numb fingers clenched to the wings, and the power exploding from her in uncontrollable waves of darkness and rage.

Almost there . . . almost there.

The dragon screamed as its wing withered away, and, with a violent twist of its body, it rolled sharply. Her grip slipped from the wings, and suddenly she was airborne, careening through the air in a blast of snow and ash.

She was an inch away from slamming into Fangdor's stone wall when she felt herself freeze in midair. The scream dying in her throat, Deya looked down just to see Caelum sprinting underneath her before she dropped like a stone into his waiting arms.

Tumbling to the ground, gasping and aching, both Deya and Caelum looked up. Suddenly, a pair of amber wings flashed in her peripheral, and, to her shock, the small female dragon rocketed up in the sky. As if sensing its chance, the small dragon let out a fierce roar, and with a flash of sharp teeth, grabbed the larger bull by the neck, ripping a chunk of skin and scale free of the thrashing body.

The dragon was shrieking in pain, blood spilling from its neck, its wing in tatters. Val's remaining brother rushed towards the dragon, screaming orders to retreat. A white-hot jet of fire was issued into the sky before, with a shower of blood and ash, the dragon careened into the air, attempting to take flight. Unbalanced by its ruined wing, harried by Val's dragon, the larger bull crashed into everything in its path, barely able to lift itself off the ground, before it finally burst through the hole, fleeing the Frost Kingdom with a flick of its black scaly tail.

The battle was ending. Troops were retreating—Manielian soldiers fleeing through the smashed hole of the Bridanian wall, Praiton assassins disappearing with a swirl of their green cloaks. Faintly, she could hear Val's remaining brother call the retreat again, fleeing with the rest in a flash of white flames.

And as ash and snow fell around them, Deya lay in Caelum's arms panting, the adrenaline dwindling from her body, the feeling of all her cuts, bruises, and burns coming back with full force. Turning, she looked up at Caelum . . . only to find him staring down at her hands. Deya's heart sank.

"You came," she said softly.

Caelum's eyes didn't leave her hands. They roved from the dark cuticles, down the blackened veins disappearing into her sleeves. Slowly, he set her down on the ground and rose, rubbing his face, not looking at her as he began to walk away.

Panic building in her, she hurried after him. "Caelum—"

Caelum stopped, but he did not turn back. From the part of his face she could see, his jaw flexed, the vein in his temple flaring underneath the blood and soot on his face.

"How long?" he demanded.

Deya froze. "How long what?"

"How long have you had this?"

Deya's black hands curled into themselves, and the nervous flutter of her heart pounded against the angry fear she could feel shivering up the bond that tied them. She looked down at her feet, tears welling in her eyes.

"Since your coronation."

Caelum whirled around. "Since my—" he exploded, before breaking off angrily and turning away, his hand rubbing his face and neck. He stood for a moment, panting amid the dying chaos and burning embers of the battle, and Deya held her breath.

Terror coursed through her, stronger than when she had faced Leo, stronger than when she had even faced the dragon. To lose Caelum to what she always knew he suspected . . . what he feared.

Caelum's shoulders were rigid as he stood, his back to Deya. She could almost see his mind moving, attempting to process it all.

Finally, he looked back over his shoulder at her. "Why?" he demanded. "Why didn't you tell me?"

Taken aback, Deya blinked. "I . . . I was afraid to," she whispered. Afraid was an understatement. She had been petrified to tell him—to tell any of them. Petrified to have them think she was evil, or corrupt . . . Terrified to have Caelum look at her the way he did when they had first met.

But the expression on his face was not the look of unfettered loathing he had once had for her. Instead, it was pure, unmitigated terror. As if he were . . . *worried* for her.

Caelum let out a dry, humorless laugh. "*Afraid?* Afraid of what? Me?" The flippant way he said it would've been dismissed by anyone else, but Deya felt the tug on her heart—the small pull of the string between them. He *hurt* at the idea of her being afraid of him. And in that moment, Deya felt her shoulders drop, the tears she had been holding released, and she reached for Caelum.

"No, of course not," she whispered, taking his hands in hers—jet black fingers brushing against his olive skin. "I was scared you'd be afraid of *me*."

Caelum stared at her, shock slackening his jaw. "Why the hells would be I afraid of you?" he snapped, sounding much more like his usual self now. "I'm not fucking scared of *you*, Deya. I'm scared of *this*; of what it's doing to you! This is why you refused to use your magic, wasn't it?"

Deya nodded and Caelum swore, before reaching out and pulling her roughly into his chest. He crushed her into him, and she breathed in his scent, felt his cool touch, and let herself collapse into his arms, tears of relief and grief finally washing over her.

Everything that had happened in the last several hours came crashing down as she held Caelum . . . the most solid thing she had ever had in her life, like a piece of string wound tight in her fist. Caelum's hand came up to cup the back of her head and she felt him kiss her hair.

"I love you," she whispered against his chest. She felt him stiffen at the words, and her heart ached at his silence. But, although he didn't say it, she felt him tighten his hold on her, as if it was the only way he knew how to respond.

"I'm sorry I didn't get here sooner," he whispered.

Deya shook her head, tears falling thick and fast now. "I called for you. I was calling for you the whole time."

He sighed and his grip on her tightened, his fingers weaving into her hair. "I closed out the bond. Nodaria was being attacked. I didn't want you to worry—"

"*What?*" Deya cried, pulling away from him, shock and horror driving everything else from her mind, but Caelum sighed and rolled his eyes.

"It's a long story," he muttered irritably. "Come on. I'll tell you while we walk."

Caelum took her hand in his, and they made their back towards Fangdor, picking their way across the bodies and still smoldering bits of debris littered across the snowy ground. Val and Aris had disappeared, and Val's dragon circled above them, hovering over the hole the invaders had escaped from, screeching plaintively into the sky, as if to warn them off of ever coming back.

Caelum told her about the attempt to overthrow him from the throne, about the Praiton assassins, and Mah's plot. How it had led to the carnage that was now the Frost Kingdom. As they walked, Deya tried not to look too hard at the bodies they passed by. Part of her wanted to look amongst the dead for Luc, the other wanted to cry at the possibility that he was even amongst them. Instead, she shut it from her mind, and eventually, as they entered the great hall—the large wooden doors hanging off their hinges—Rayner appeared in front of them.

Without words, they ran to each other, and Rayner swallowed Deya in an enormous bear hug that made her gasp for breath. Tears pricked her eyes again as she held the Sea Fae tightly, standing in the destroyed remnants of Fangdor Castle.

"Thank Gods you're okay," Rayner whispered in her ear.

Deya spluttered with a wet laugh, tightening her grip on him. "I missed you. Thanks for coming to our rescue."

"Wouldn't have missed it," Rayner chuckled. Pulling back, he glanced over at Caelum. For a moment, the two of them stared at each other and, quietly, they both moved forward and embraced. Caelum clapped the Sea Fae stiffly on the back and Rayner squeezed his shoulder, smirking at him in that affectionate, teasing way of his.

"Glad to see you're okay, Your Highness," Rayner teased.

"Shut up," Caelum growled, but Deya didn't miss the slight twinge of relief in her chest at the sight of Rayner from a heart that wasn't hers.

All around them, Bridanians were moving about the castle, picking up charred debris, carrying bodies out into the courtyard, sweeping up and moving on. Deya felt herself wondering where Espen was, if he had happened to find Niel's body on the staircase, whether he and Karyna were resting beside each other now, and where—

"*Deya!*"

Whirling around, Deya's heart soared at the sound of the familiar voice and, choking back tears, Deya flew across the room towards it. Luc was limping down the stairs towards them, his brown skin badly burnt, but otherwise okay. Deya ran so fast she nearly tripped as she threw herself into her friend's arms, who winced with pain as she crashed into him.

"Sorry," she mumbled, tears bubbling out of her.

Luc laughed, coughing weakly with the effort. "S'alright," he mumbled, squeezing her tightly before they both pulled back and smiled at each other.

"Gods, how did you survive that?" she whispered, clutching him tighter. The image of him running down the stairs to face Leo and his consequent screams still swam in her head. She couldn't lie and say she wasn't surprised to see him up and standing.

"He just burnt me a bit," Luc said, wincing and grabbing at his ribs. "Threw me down the stairs, though. But in the end, it was nothing I couldn't heal myself. All things considered, I definitely got off easy."

Deya released him and looked down at his burnt clothes and blistered skin already beginning to heal. His dark eyes were warm when they looked at her, yet she saw them drift slightly towards the blackened fingers that were still clutching his arm.

"You did it," he said softly. "You saved the day again. Destroyed a dragon all on your own. They're going to call you Deya the Dragon Slayer soon. "

"Definitely not on my own," Deya said, looking down at her black hands again, trying not to think about the dangerous, seductive whisper the power seemed to hiss into her ear when she had clutched Luc's throat in her fist. "Val's dragon helped."

And in that moment, Deya seemed to realize that the Manielian female was nowhere to be seen. As Caelum and Rayner came towards them, Deya turned to look at them both.

"Has anyone seen Val?"

Rayner paused, looking back over his shoulder at the broken doors leading out towards Fangdor's snowy grounds. "I think the general took her," he said, his voice heavy with something Deya couldn't quite place. "She collapsed after the dragon fled, and I saw him carry her into the castle. She's probably being healed."

Deya paused, her heart clenching at the memory of how badly mangled Val's leg was . . . and how horrifically burned the rest of her was, too.

A flurry of snow blasted its way through the open front doors, and Kindra walked in, dripping a combination of blood and sweat onto the cracked and dirty floor of the entrance hall. Her ice-blue eyes landed on them, and she headed towards them, her great battle-axe hanging from her hand.

"Kindra," Caelum said, nodding at her stiffly. "How is everything?"

The Frost Princess turned and spat a glob of blood onto the floor, and Caelum's nose crinkled, his eyebrow rising slightly. "Bad," she snapped, but Deya could see the crease of sadness in her pretty features as she looked around at the destroyed entrance hall. "We've lost many," she said softly. "But it is over now. *Faor* is sealing the hole for good. Between the dragon and the new frost sprite he has found, Bridah is more secure than ever."

"Frost sprite?" Deya asked. "Was that what he was riding on? Was that what he was out looking for?"

"Yes," Kindra said, tapping the edge of the axe's blade against her foot. "Frost sprites are spirits. They hide between the fabric of our world and theirs. The *Eiktaerner* is a spirit of the gods. It is said that he was Flykra's steed. *Faor* has been searching for him for many years now. With his protection, we should be safe from anything the Praiton scum could throw at us." She spat onto the floor again.

Rayner caught Deya's eye, and she remembered he had not yet had the pleasure of meeting Caelum's aunt properly. She wondered if he could see the family resemblance. Judging by the small smirk on his blue-gray face, he obviously could.

"Come," she said, jerking her head over her shoulder. "There is much to discuss. I hear from your general that we were not the only kingdom besieged. We shall reconvene."

Caelum glanced at Deya, as if asking her to come, but she squeezed his hand, nodding towards Kindra, who was waiting expectantly.

"Go," she said. "I'll stay with Rayner. I'll be alright."

Caelum hesitated, and she knew he was reluctant to let her out of his sight again. But then, to her utmost surprise, he crossed the distance between them and there, right in front of everyone, he leaned down and kissed her. His lips were hot on hers, and his hand came up to cup her cheek. When he pulled back, Deya stood, stunned, as she took in the purple eyes looking back at her. With a slight cough, and one last squeeze of her hand, he followed after Kindra.

Rayner chuckled as she stared after Caelum's retreating back. "About bloody time," Rayner mumbled, and he took her arm, shaking her out of her stunned trance. "Come on. I'm sure we can help clean up."

The aftermath of the battle was spread throughout the Frost Kingdom's castle and out into the grounds leading towards Frostheim. Deya, Rayner, and Luc began to help the remaining castle staff carry the bodies of the fallen out into the courtyard where they were laid to await burning. A large pyre was being built outside and Deya's heart ached as she carried body after body down the steps and laid them to rest in the snow, awaiting their time to become ash.

As she carried the last of the dead down the stairs, she stopped when she saw Luc standing in the corner of the courtyard, looking down at something. Putting down the last body—a small priestess that she did not recognize—she made her way towards her old friend. A tear fell down Luc's face as he pulled his cloak tighter around him to ward off the frigid chill. And as Deya approached, she saw what he was looking at.

Karyna and Niel lay together in the snow. Their eyes were closed, and short of the dark stains of blood on each of their bodies, they looked at peace, as if they were merely sleeping.

Without thinking, Deya reached out and took hold of Luc's arm, who jumped, but relaxed upon seeing it was her. Wiping his face clumsily, he sighed. "I didn't know," he said finally, his voice thick, his nose stuffy. "What our kingdom was capable of. This . . . this was not necessary. Karyna didn't deserve this. And Niel . . . He was just a bloody child, Dey."

Deya nodded, tears clouding her own vision as she looked down at her lady's maid.

"I know," she whispered.

All around them, family and friends of the fallen moved between the bodies, some crying, some laying flowers. Deya could hear the same phrase echoing around her, the same whispers of the melodic, rolling lilt of Brynorsk she had gotten used to hearing now.

A shimmer of blue robes moved out of the corner of her eye, and Deya turned to see the older priestess she had met down in the temples.

"Sister Isfrid," Deya said. The old female looked up, and Deya saw her eyes were misty.

"*Heil og sal*, I am glad to see you have survived," she said, nodding politely at them, but then her eyes traveled down to look at the two bodies at their feet, and her face crumpled. "So many lost. So many to be returned to the snow," she whispered. Leaning down, she touched Niel and Karyna with two delicate, wrinkled hands.

"*Fraom ao naesta leifi*," she whispered to them, before rising and straightening her robes.

"Sister," Deya said, stopping her before she could walk away. "What . . . What did you just say to them?"

Sister Isfrid's face was sad as she turned back to her. "It is our farewell," she said. "Our goodbye to those returning to Flykra. *Fraom ao naesta leifi*. Until the next life." And she turned away, leaving Luc and Deya standing amongst the dead, snow and ash falling around them, and their hearts as heavy as ice.

"Come on," Luc said finally, nodding back towards the castle. "Let's go find Rayner."

And as Luc made to usher her away, Deya paused. Bending down, she touched Karyna and Niel's chests, just as Isfrid had done. Their bodies were cold, the blood stiff against their clothing.

"Fraom ao naesta leifi," she whispered. "Thank you for being my friend. Until the next life." And, with one final look at her small lady's maid and her brother, Deya rose and followed Luc back to the castle.

Val sat beside the charred corpse of her brother, her knees to her chest, watching Lucéria circle the now sealed glacial wall in the distance. The dragon had not come down since Titus's bull had fled, as if the smaller dragon was determined to stand guard until she was sure it never would. Her satchel sat at her feet from where she had retrieved it from a deep snowbank, thankfully unharmed. Both eggs felt cold, so Val had set a fire warming beside them as they trembled weakly within the worn leather.

Flexing her hands, she felt the smallest sting of the remaining burns. She had been thoroughly healed by the combined power of two of the Legion's combat medics, and yet there were some burns that had not gone away. And though her leg had been set back in place, it still ached, and as she looked at herself, she wondered if her body would ever truly heal.

Val's eyes drifted back to the corpse next to her. There was barely anything left of Leo. If it hadn't been her who had done it, she would not have been able to tell that this burnt body was her brother. Shifting, Val tore her eyes from him, feeling a lump of guilt and sadness rise in her throat. She dashed it away, tears of rage surging upwards to replace it.

She should be happy . . . relieved. She had avenged her sisters, avenged the girlhood he had stolen from her. There should be nothing but peace within her. But there wasn't. In the end, there was nothing that could bring back what she had lost. And as she sat next to the charred corpse, she bit back anger at the slight twinge of irrational sadness at the loss of her brother.

A shadow fell over her, and Val knew who it was without even looking up, could feel it like the cold wind, and she stiffened immediately.

Aris sank to the ground beside her, his golden armor dirty and scratched, soot and blood still on his face.

"I was looking for you."

Val's jaw tightened. "Well, you found me."

Aris nodded his head, a tense, awkward silence falling over them. They both watched the dragon circle the battlements, Lucéria's screeching cry echoing across the pink horizon as the sun sank slowly.

"You really did it," Aris said, his gaze following the red dragon.

Val picked at the burnt skin on her hand and shrugged. "I would say she did most of the work," she mumbled.

Aris looked over at her, surprised. "She?"

Nodding, Val spoke to the ground. "Her name is Lucéria." She could feel the general's eyes on her, but she wouldn't look at him.

It was then that he noticed the eggs nestled by her feet. His eyes widened. "Are those—"

She nodded, reaching out to brush her fingers against the smooth surface of the eggs. "Yes. They're hers."

Aris blinked, and for a moment, the war general in him threatened to come out. She wondered if he was contemplating what having three dragons would mean for the Legion, before she scoffed derisively.

"Incubation times for dragon eggs are wildly unpredictable," she said stiffly. "It is unknown when or even *if* they'll hatch. Most eggs are unborn. I would not be plotting a dragon unit for the Legion just yet, General."

The general's handsome face colored underneath the soot and blood. "Valeria, I wasn't—"

But Val shook her head. She felt the ache in her chest, the pain in her heart, and as her eyes drifted involuntarily towards the general, she caught sight of the still bleeding cut on his right hand . . . the one she could still feel a ghost of pain on her own.

Val shoved the hand under her arms and stood, seizing the satchel containing the eggs and making to leave him, when Aris rose, reaching for her.

"Valeria, wait—"

Val knocked his hand away and whirled to face him. "How long?" she demanded.

Aris froze. "How long, what?"

"How long have you known?"

The handsome face froze, the olive skin paling underneath the blood and dirt. Then, he looked away, as if too ashamed to meet her eye. He spoke to his shoes.

"Since the first night. When we kissed in my office."

Val stared at him. She felt like she was falling from the sky again, the hot flames of pain and betrayal chasing her down to the ground like a dragon's fire as she stared at the general in horror. She had not been able to get Leo's words out of her head.

She cannot be yours. You will die for this, scum.

She hadn't understood what he meant. But now . . . now she didn't understand how he had known.

"You've known since then," Val stammered. "All this time . . . That was why you left, wasn't it? That was why you stopped that night. Because you *felt it.*"

Aris was still staring at the ground, his brow furrowed, pain lining every bit of his face. But he did not reply. In his silence, Val knew the answer. Tears filled her eyes, and she didn't know whether to scream or hit him as hard as she could.

Turning from him, Val struggled to steady her breathing. "But why now?" she demanded, spinning back to face him, fury burning through her skin and clothes. "Why act on it? Obviously, you don't plan on committing to it, do you?"

Aris flinched, his eyes closing. "Valeria, I can't . . . You know I can't."

Val let out a harsh bark of laughter. The sound splintered out of her as a fracture tore through her heart. The noise cracked, and tears blurred her vision as she looked around them, at the crimson snow, at the bodies covered with ash, at the dragon flying in the pink and orange sky.

"Then *why*?" she pleaded, tears burning her throat. "Why awaken it? Why bring it to life if you have no intention of honoring it? Especially on the night before I was—" But Val froze, realization slamming into her harder than any of her brothers' blows. Aris stood, frozen, watching her realize it, pain welling in his eyes. "You didn't think I would come back," she whispered. "You thought I would die before it had a chance to develop, didn't you?"

"Valeria—"

"*Didn't you?!*" Val roared, and Aris closed his eyes. Beside her own fractured heart, she could feel its twin pain. Both hearts were breaking, and yet only one was responsible.

"It wasn't like that," Aris whispered, his voice choked. "Please, Valeria, you need to understand—"

"Understand?" Tears were falling down her face now, blinding her, the general turning gold in the blur of her tears and his armor. "You shag me because it was your last fucking chance to do it, and you woke up *this* all for a fucking one night—"

"No!" Aris moved towards her, seizing her by the still burnt arms, shaking her imploringly. "It was not just one night, Valeria, please!"

"You thought I would *die*!"

"Yes!" he yelled. "*YES,* and I was terrified at the idea that I would let you walk off that boat without ever having a chance to hold you . . . to *be* with you . . . to know what it would be like to live a life I don't deserve to have for even a moment." Aris was breathing hard, and Val stared at him as she watched the general fall apart. The strongest male made of gold was melting. And she was melting with him.

"It was a moment of weakness," he said, shaking his head. "I have always cared for you, always *wanted* you, Valeria. And I could not stop you from going on that mission. I *couldn't,* no matter how much I wanted to. It was the only way we could win this war. It was part of the plan—"

Val scoffed, jerking her hands out of his grip. "*The plan,*" she spat. "Yes, I was part of your big plan, General. Is that why you're refusing this? Because of *the plan?*"

Aris stared at her, defeated. "Valeria," he whispered. "I am the general of the rebellion. I cannot sacrifice this cause for my own selfish wants. I can't . . . I *won't.*"

Shaking her head, Val looked at him in disgust. "Is this because of what happened in Ganiea? Is this because of your fiancée?"

It was like Val had slapped him. The general stared at her, shock rippling across his face. "Who told you about Lena?" he breathed, but Val waved it off, too angry to think straight.

"Does it matter? This is why, right? Because I would get in the way of your plans? Is that it?"

"*Please,*" Aris whispered, taking a step towards her again, his hands reaching for her. "Please, Valeria, you must understand . . . The Legion comes first. It *has* to. To have you with *this* . . . I could not lead. I could not do my job." He took a deep, shaky breath, and Val heard pain in every syllable. "I cannot have something come between my duty to this cause . . . not again." His voice cracked, thick with emotion that Val could feel in her own body. She felt his heart breaking . . . and hers broke along with it.

She nodded, backing away from him, tears sliding down her face. "No, General. I *do* understand, I understand *completely.*"

And, just like that, she turned and walked away from him.

Leaving her mate standing in the snow, staring after her.

CHAPTER 31

Caelum transported all of them home to Nodaria that night. Including Deya. Aris had finally relented and agreed to allow Caelum to bring her home. As they were preparing to leave, Ulf appeared. Caelum watched as his grandfather said goodbye to Deya, before he turned to him.

They had spent the last hour in Ulf's study discussing what was next. Eventually, Aris joined them, and Caelum had watched the general with a sharp eye. Something was deeply troubling him, and Caelum couldn't help but notice a strange, faint shimmering of gold and red light around him that had not been there the last time he had seen him. No one else seemed to notice, and for a moment, Caelum thought he was going insane. Annoyed, he shoved it aside long enough to hear what Aris was saying.

"We know now what Praiton is after," he told Ulf and Kindra. "The Heart of the Mother must be something powerful and dangerous. We must keep it out of their hands at all times."

"But where is it?" Kindra demanded. "We may know what it is, Aris, but how in Flykra's name are you going to locate a bloody necklace when you have no idea where it was even last seen? It could be anywhere. Praiton, Ganiea, Laenimore . . ."

"I know," Aris said heavily. He shifted in his chair and Caelum could see the weight of something pressing down on him, something that was making it difficult for the general to focus on the conversation. "Which is why I think it's important that we make more active moves to secure the realm from Praiton control."

Caelum jerked around to look at him. "More *active* moves?" he echoed. "Are you out of your fucking mind?"

"Caelum—" Kindra cut in, but Caelum shook his head, silencing her.

"In case you haven't noticed, *General*, we are barely clinging to our position as it is," he hissed, leaning threateningly towards the general, who just looked tired and worn. "Nodaria is being torn apart from within, Bridah has just been set on fire, the Legion has been being picked apart by Praiton for *months* now, and yet you expect us to—"

"Take Ganiea and Laenimore back, yes," Aris cut in, a glimmer of his former calm cutting through. Caelum seethed, his mind still reeling, but he sank back into his chair. "Praiton is getting bold," the general said stiffly. "To attempt to take Nodaria and Bridah is an act of war. Now I'm not saying we storm Ganiea and Laenimore tomorrow. We play it smart. Gather reinforcements, seize the high ground where they are weakest. Only then will we be able to beat Praiton at their own game."

During this discussion, the High King of Bridah sat quietly on his large wooden chair, drinking it all in. Since he had stormed the battlefield on the large, crystalline elk, Ulf had been more subdued than usual. He was late to Caelum and Kindra's meeting and returned covered in blood, yet uninjured. Caelum realized he had helped carry the dead to the pyre and lit the match himself. As Ulf sat across from him, Caelum could see, for the first time, the heavy weight of Ulf's own crown.

"I agree," Ulf said finally, causing all of them to snap their necks to look at him in surprise. "Laenimore is their weakest territory, yet it offers a vantage into Ganiea. If we take Ganiea, Praiton cannot survive. The food and resources of the region are too important to them."

A flicker of pain crossed Aris's face, but it was gone in an instant. Nodding, he looked at Ulf gratefully. "My thoughts exactly. And if we corner Ganiea and Laenimore, that's two less places we have to worry about Praiton finding the amulet."

And so, they adjourned with the agreement that, come hells or high water, they would take back the fallen kingdoms. One by one.

It was absurd, maybe. Foolish, definitely. But Caelum found it difficult to argue with Ulf. And as the High King bent down to squeeze his shoulders gently, an irritating ember of affection for the large male burned in his chest.

"Thank you for coming to defend us, *Lostjarna,*" he said, smiling warmly down at him. "I am glad that we still have a friend in the Celestial Kingdom, even after all these years."

Caelum nodded curtly at him, but when he spoke, his voice was soft. "You will always have more than that in the Celestial Kingdom, Ulf."

The High King smiled at him, the corners of his ice blue eyes crinkling as he squeezed Caelum's shoulders again. And as Caelum pulled the air apart and sent the familiar purple portal spinning into the air, it was with a forlorn sense of finality as Deya, Luc, Rayner, and Aris ducked into the portal.

"Where's Val?" Caelum asked as Aris made to step past him. The general hesitated for a moment, his face stiffening.

"She opted to fly home on the dragon. She said she'd meet us there." He stepped through the portal quickly, leaving Caelum to stare curiously after him, the shimmering gold and red glow around him bleeding into the purple light of the portal.

With one last final goodbye to Ulf and Kindra, he followed after them.

After a few seconds of suffocating nothingness, Caelum stumbled out into the familiar council room, empty except for Saros, who was seated at the large table as they all tumbled into the room. But this time, when Caelum went through, he crashed into the table, sending papers flying and Saros leaping to his feet.

"Caelum!" Deya rushed to his side, and he felt a few pairs of hands attempt to right him.

"*I'm fine,*" he snarled, but even as he said it, a traitorous splattering of blood fell from his mouth, and his vision blurred as he sagged against the table.

"Easy, cousin." Saros had a firm hand on his elbow, and as his vision cleared, it was to see a concerned look clouding his older cousin's face. "You have been overdoing it for a while now," he said softly. "You cannot hide this anymore."

Caelum shook his head, gritting his teeth. He looked up to find Deya, Rayner, Luc, and Aris all staring at him with mixed looks of concern and fear, before he stood up. "I'm fine," he insisted again.

Saros looked at him closely for a moment, before sighing and letting the conversation drop, even though Caelum could already tell that the discussion about his powers was not over. Saros's purple eyes swept the room, and his face fell. "But . . . where is Val?"

"She'll be along shortly," Rayner replied, and Saros relaxed, looking relieved. With one last worried look at him, Rayner and Luc bid them all goodnight, and Deya made to follow, but Aris called her back.

"Hang on for a moment, Deya."

Deya stopped and turned. Ever since Caelum had noticed it, his eyes couldn't seem to stop looking at the black stain on her hands. The same feeling of anxious dread twisted around him at the sight of it. How had he not noticed it sooner? The same line was repeating in his head over and over in a sinister whisper, just like the one from his sword.

The downfall of all.

"Your hands," Aris said, and Deya hesitated, her shoulders stiffening. As if out of habit, her black fingers curled into themselves, as though to hide them.

"Yes, General?"

The general was watching her movement, those golden eyes tracking every twitch of muscle. "I know we haven't explored your powers fully, but I must say, this development makes me think we need to find the source of them sooner rather than later."

Deya's gray eyes darted to Caelum. When he did not come to her defense, she wilted.

"Yes, General," she whispered finally. "I agree."

Aris inclined his head, but Caelum didn't miss the way he looked at her. There was a wariness that was not there before. "Very well. We'll deal with it in the morning," he said, and he gave her a grim smile.

Deya nodded, looking relieved, before she turned to Caelum expectantly.

"I'll be up in a minute," he whispered to her. He squeezed her hand, and with a small smile, Deya left the room.

Caelum collapsed in the chair across from Saros, watching as Aris did the same. He leaned back, wiping blood from his chin, his gaze immediately going across the room towards the portrait of his father before he looked away hastily. He was too fucking tired for his judgmental gaze right now.

"Is everything taken care of?" he asked Saros, the weariness beginning to show in his voice. It felt like his body was undulating into the chair, unwinding ribbons of exhaustion and stress onto the floor.

Saros nodded, stacking a few sheaves of parchment neatly on the table. "The Silver Daggers' carnage has been cleaned, the courtyard restored, the others complicit have been captured, and both Deimos and Mah are on a ship to Havia as we speak. Well—what's *left* of Mah, anyway." he added, shrugging. "Helene did quite a number on him."

Caelum grunted, watching as Aris rubbed his eyes in the chair across from him, looking equally bone weary.

"I must say, Caelum, I was surprised at your restraint," Saros commented, casting a sideways glance at him. "A couple months ago, you would've ripped their heads off right there in front of everyone. That girl of yours must really be rubbing off on you."

Caelum opened his eyes, staring up at the ceiling. His immediate instinct was to bark out an instant denial, but instead he stopped himself.

"Yeah, maybe."

Finally, Aris sighed and rose from the table. "Well, I'm going to bed. We'll deal with all of this"—He gestured around the room— "tomorrow."

Saros mumbled an agreement, and the two males rose, leaving Caelum alone in the empty council room.

For a moment, Caelum just soaked in the silence, listening to the gentle cracks of the fireplace burning low in the grate. He knew Deya was waiting for him, but for a moment—just a moment—he needed to gather himself. To think.

If they were to take back the realm—to uncover the source of Deya's power—would there be a possibility that what he feared more than anything would come true?

The downfall of all.

Caelum sighed, and his eyes met his father's stare again.

"Oh, shut up," he muttered to it. "You're one to talk. Took every fucking secret to the grave, didn't you? Fat lot of help you are."

Angrily, he rose from his chair, glaring at the portrait. How he wished it could talk back. How he wished his father could tell him everything he wanted to know. But instead, the portrait remained irritatingly silent.

Swearing, Caelum moved to exit the room, his eyes coming to rest on his father one more time as he passed. He was a few steps out the door when he froze. Heart hammering in his chest, Caelum whirled around, sprinting back into the council room, disbelief rushing through him as he skidded to a stop in front of the portrait again.

Because there, hanging around his father's neck, was the Heart of the Mother.

ACKNOWLEDGEMENTS

As of December of 2024, as I finished the final edits on this book, I had planned on starting these acknowledgements very differently. But on December 6th, I lost my biggest fan and one of the most important people in my life.

To my dad, I begged you not to tell anyone about my books, but you did it anyway, much to my horror. But it was because you were so proud of me and my stories, of the things I accomplished. You told me you were proud, not because I finished a book, but because I put myself out there in a way that you knew was so difficult for me to do. You got to see me publish *A Crown of Star and Ash* and *The Lady of Fire and Light*. Got to listen to the audiobook and even endeavored to read the first hundred pages even though you were never a reader (and asked me repeatedly if I could put pictures in the next one for you), and I'm so glad you got to read your acknowledgement in *The Lady of Fire and Light*. Your pride for me and this dream were second only to the love you always gave me.

Thank you, Daddy, for always making my dreams come true. This dream would not be a reality if it wasn't for you. For many years, you not only fostered and nurtured all my random hobbies, but also my heart and soul. I believed in me because you always did. You are now with me in everything I do, and although finishing and releasing this book only weeks/months after I lost you has taken everything in me, I know nothing was more important to you than this dream of mine. Everything I do now, I do for you. For the rest of my life, you'll always be my biggest fan and I'll always be yours. I love you forever.

To Cody, who this book is dedicated to, thank you for . . . well, just about everything! This book, its plot, and its characters, would not be what it is without you. For the endless nights you sat and helped me work out plot issues, and brainstormed with me, for the many times I just wanted to kiss your brain, you have been an endless bastion of love and support for me—both in this career and out. Thank you so much for all that you do for me, especially during the difficult times around this book's release. I don't know what I'd do without you. I love you to the moon and back!

To Angie, this book is just about as much yours as it is mine at this point. Thank you for beta reading and loving this book with all your heart and supporting me in my (many) times of doubt over this manuscript. Meeting you and being able to call you my friend is one of the best gifts I've gotten on this journey. You are the best book buddy a girl could ask for.

To my favorite PA, Amelya, thank you for always rooting for me and this book series! It's been such a joy meeting you and being able to call you a friend is such a privilege. Thank you for all your hard work helping me on the VKT team!

To my mom, who was the first person to read this book as a freshly steaming hot mess, straight from my brain. Thank you for giving me your insight, and for loving these characters like they're real, and always skipping my sex scenes. Endlessly grateful for you in everything.

To my sister and stepmom, who cheer me on through this whole endeavor. For buying all my books, doing my taxes, and always being a shoulder to lean on. I love you both so much.

To Veronica, because you are this series' godmother, and I'll never not thank you!

To my amazing beta reader team: Isabella, Laura, Lucy, Keeya, Melissa, Angie, and Christin, thank you all! Compared to *A Crown of Star and Ash* this was a small but mighty beta reader group, but you were all instrumental in making this book what it is.

And finally, to my amazing editing team Noah Sky and Jennifer Murgia. Thank you for always blessing my stories with your diligent eyes. I'm forever grateful to you all.

ABOUT THE AUTHOR

Victoria mostly answers to Tori and has been writing books for most of her life. After specializing in Creative Writing throughout high school, she went on to study Communications, Journalism, and English Literature. . . and stopped writing completely during this time.

After a LONG break, she recently decided to delve into the world of Adult Fantasy with her debut novel A CROWN OF STAR & ASH.

She now resides in Florida and spends her day working her day job, reading, writing, playing the Sims 4 (I finally moved up!), and being a mother to a rotten Snowshoe Siamese cat named Sebastian.

If you want to know more about when Tori's future books come out, be sure to sign up for her newsletter and stay up to date with all *Fate of Ashes* related updates!

Visit Victoria's Website!
https://www.victoriaktaylor.com/
Connect with me on Social Media!
https://www.instagram.com/victoriaktaylorbooks
https://www.tiktok.com/@victoriaktaylorbooks

Made in the USA
Middletown, DE
16 September 2025

13446456R00283